The Swan Princess

A FIVE DIRECTIONS PRESS BOOK

The Swan Princess

A NOVEL

C. P. LESLEY

LEGENDS OF THE FIVE DIRECTIONS 3: NORTH

ISBN-13 978-0692645604
ISBN-10 0692645608

Published in the United States of America.

A Five Directions Press book

Cover photographs: Mute swan with reflection © David Benton/ Shutterstock; "Nature" (Karelia) © Liubov Trifonova/Thinkstock. Interior art: map based on Guillaume de l'Isle, "Carte de Moscovie," 1706, credit sergeyussr/Thinkstock; swan on half-title page © ejaquez/Thinkstock.

Book and cover design by Five Directions Press
Five Directions Press logo designed by Colleen Kelley

FIVE DIRECTIONS PRESS

CONTENTS

SITES IMPORTANT TO *THE SWAN PRINCESS*

Pechenga

Vologda

White Lake

Dmitrov

Vitebsk and Velizh

Moscow

Escape

SLEET STUNG HIS FACE. BROTHER STEFAN TUGGED THE rabbit-skin hat over his ears and turned up the collar of the worn fur coat—a gift to the monastery, no doubt, from some half-starved priest determined to secure prayers for his soul. Shivering, he squinted through ice-crusted eyelashes at an oval of red topped by a semicircle of bright blue. Against the white/ gray Arctic landscape, the patch of color sufficed to identify the Lapp herder guiding his rickety sleigh across the tundra.

"Can't that beast go faster?" Stefan kicked the front of the sleigh and chided himself for impatience—in vain. His demand for speed was irrational. He'd secured permission for his journey. No one would follow him in this blizzard. He had nothing to fear, yet his whole body urged him to press on, beat the reindeer—or the driver—if necessary. Whatever would increase the distance between himself and that godforsaken excuse for a monastery. He'd wasted months there already.

Getting out of the Arctic blast would be a blessing, but no hope of that for a few more weeks—unless this slug of a reindeer grew wings and took to the air. What a sight that would be!

Off to one side, through the driving sleet, he saw a small hut raised on logs, two of its chicken feet buried up to the ankles in snow, the front two swept bare by the circling winds. It looked like the home of the witch Baba Yaga, terror of his nursery days.

He shivered again—and not from the cold. How could one know, dashing past in a reindeer-drawn sleigh, whether a witch dwelled there?

The semicircle of bright blue swiveled toward him, then away. Stefan burrowed his nose in his collar. The Lapp riding the reindeer hadn't answered his question. He hadn't understood or, more likely, didn't care what his passenger wanted. One more insult added to the long list Stefan had composed over the last eighteen months.

A year and a half in Hell. People described it as hot, but Stefan knew better. Hell was Pechenga in winter—a place where the sun never rose and a crackbrained abbot ordered noblemen to wield axes like peasants in the silent, frigid dark. Even in summer, Pechenga brought a nightmare of hungry insects, eternal prayers, and demands to till the earth. But summer also brought light, not to mention berries and salmon and Arctic hare to fill a man's stomach as long as he stayed out of the abbot's sight long enough to cook and consume them. Once in a while, even a willing Lapp daughter or wife. In winter, none of those boons lightened his burden.

Stefan pushed his hands deeper into the sleeves of the fur coat. To either side, he heard the shushing made by the runners of the sleighs pulling his two monastic companions. His jailers. Another reason why his demand for increased speed would not be met.

But his fellow monks wouldn't confine him for long. Escape, and he would be free to pursue his real goal: vengeance against the relatives who had betrayed him. The thought had kept him alive these many months. They would pay, the lot of them—starting with that meddlesome Golden Lynx.

For a moment, Stefan allowed himself to dwell on the night of his capture. The Lynx's hair gleaming in the darkness, the worthless Tatar brat freed by the Lynx's arrow, the wound that collapsed Stefan and his plans in one searing moment. Oh, yes, the Lynx had much to answer for, and he would pay. He might think himself secure, but Stefan knew where to find him.

His cousin, Daniil Kolychev.

Shimmering water, paddling feet, the swift thrum of wings beating the air. The Sons and Daughters of Light circle, calling their grievances to the spirits of earth and sky. So many wrongs: treachery in high places; descendants at war; evil loose amid the snow and ice. Spouses yearning for time together; brothers fighting to stay apart; families robbing souls of life, by accident and design. And at the center, a young woman once chosen by the ancestors—trapped, as if sleeping, her past service forgotten.

The spirits decide. The swans, guardians of the north, take flight. Their mission is clear: awaken the young woman and recall her to her task.

Chapter 1

"IMPOSSIBLE." NATALYA KOLYCHEVA SWAYED, AS IF PUSHED off-balance by her daughter-in-law's request. Pearls quivered on her embroidered headdress; sunlight cast a glow on her layered silk robes. "Go riding in the city? After what happened last year?"

Nasan flinched. No one regretted the effects of last year's fall more than she. "I'm not with child now, Mama-in-law," she said. "How could I be, with my husband away these nine months?"

"There is too much work." Natalya gestured at the servants humming around them.

Too much work, indeed. Enough to keep a person busy from dawn to dusk. In winter, Nasan didn't mind. Better to occupy her thoughts than to sit by the stove worrying about Daniil, her warrior husband, last seen limned against a hazy July sky. Since his departure, Nasan had given her mother-in-law no reason to complain about insufficient diligence.

Not that good behavior sufficed. Natalya had a knack for identifying others' shortcomings, even ones Nasan didn't consider flaws. Like the urge to ride around Moscow on a fine spring morning.

For winter had passed into memory. Despite the snow that lay packed at the base of the fences, sunshine and crisp breezes called her forth.

"Just once around the outer walls?" she begged. How many times had she fallen during her days on the steppe? A dozen? A hundred? And every time she'd been told to haul herself up and get back on the horse. No excuses!

Natalya shook her head. "Your husband entrusted me with your safety. Would you risk another curse from an envious eye? It might prevent you from ever conceiving."

Nasan shivered and muttered a prayer—in Arabic, out of habit—provoking another rebuke for un-Christian behavior. "Lord Jesus Christ, protect me from the work of the Enemy," she added. Natalya responded with a curt nod. Nasan touched the amulet that hung from her neck, concealed under her robes beside her golden lynx pendant to keep Natalya from fussing about its "heathen" embroidery, and sent a silent plea for protection to her ancestral clan spirits, the grandmothers. "But Mama-in-law, I bear talismans against the evil eye."

"I won't permit it. Wives belong inside the house, not roaming the streets like loose women. Why do you think God punished you with that fall?"

So now God was responsible, and not the evil eye? "I did penance, Mama-in-law," Nasan reminded her. In truth, leaving church early for three months had disturbed her not a whit; her membership in this Christian community still felt artificial, even forced. Her reprieve should have lasted a year, but her mother-in-law had paid to reduce the term. Nasan had had no choice but to acquiesce. In the absence of her husband and son, Natalya ruled the Kolychev household, whether Nasan liked it or not.

Natalya grunted an acknowledgment. "Finish your tasks, then, and you may ride in the courtyard, among our own people."

The courtyard. Nasan glanced around the courtyard, which lacked enough free space to spin a top, let alone gallop a horse. Perhaps by evening she could *walk* her mare several times around the fences.

She thought of pointing out that more envious eyes existed within the household than without. But most likely, that would result in a complete ban on riding. *Natalya* had not learned to ride before she could walk; she didn't understand the need to maintain one's skills.

"Very well." Nasan tucked her hands in her long sleeves and bowed to the inevitable. A ride around the courtyard was better than nothing.

Natalya didn't answer.

Odd. Natalya placed great value on courtesy. Nasan raised her head and looked her mother-in-law in the eye.

And looked again. Lines of fatigue marked the older woman's face, and fine lines of red fanned out across her normally pale skin. As Nasan watched, a dry cough wracked Natalya's ample frame. What evil humor afflicted her?

"Mama-in-law, are you ill?" Nasan constructed a mental list, testing the results against the medical books she studied whenever the demands of household supervision and religious observance abated. Weakness, cough, a web of red across the skin—classic signs of a disordered temperament, but where did the imbalance lie?

"It's nothing," Natalya said. "I slept poorly." She touched Nasan's cheek. "When Daniil returns, he will ride with you. Until he does, you remain within these walls."

Nasan added sleeplessness to her list of symptoms. "When my husband returns," she said, avoiding his name as a respectful wife should. "Will that ever happen? This war drags on and on."

More important, did he want to return? They had parted on bad terms—she guilt-ridden, he cold and withdrawn. In his time away, he had not sent a single note addressed to her alone; only the rare message to the family confirmed that he still lived. He didn't read or write, of course, but even a Russian warrior could find a clerk once in a while and dictate, "I miss you," to his wife. Daniil had forgotten her, it seemed.

"Patience, my dear." Natalya produced a rueful smile. "One day, the envoys will run out of excuses and make peace. Then, perhaps, you will give me a grandchild."

"May God so ordain." Nasan winced again—she couldn't help it. How old had her son been when the *albasti* stole his soul from her womb? Four months? Five? Before birth, a woman couldn't be sure, especially her first time. But the sight of his tiny body haunted her dreams: covered in blood and hair soft as a cat's fur, fingers and toes perfect, no longer than her hand but clearly identifiable as the desired male heir. He had not drawn a single breath; she had not once felt him kick. And when she had pleaded with the women to send men to the duck pond with sticks to stir up the water and force the *albasti* to return the unwashed soul before it could be eaten, they had soothed her as one soothes a madwoman. Daniil had not spent the night with her since. This was God's will?

The priests preached submission. The imams and mullahs, too. Nasan tried, but submission didn't come easily to her.

Ana understood: even as she wrote of resignation, she had sent a wise woman with herbs to protect and heal her daughter. But Natalya had not allowed the shaman to cross her threshold, summoning Father Job to banish the woman with his cross. Nasan had slipped out the back and reached the healer in time to prevent her from cursing the household, had sneaked her into the stables overnight and paid for her journey home, but the ties that bound her to this Russian family had frayed under the strain. Trust no one here, the spirits whispered. Not even Daniil, in time of need.

Grim and distant memories better left for lonely evenings. She returned her attention to Natalya. "I'm sorry, Mama-in-law. What do you wish me to do?"

Natalya waved at a distant fence. "Supervise the preparation of the herb garden. See that the servants plant what we need for medicines and for cooking. Herbs do more good than those foreign books you love to study."

Books. Always books. What's wrong with books?

As if she'd spoken the question aloud, Natalya answered it. "I've told you before. Books are for priests. A wife should occupy her mind with household tasks and with pleasing God and her husband."

Advice that Nasan had heard many times since entering the Kolychev house as a bride. "The books tell me what to plant, Mama-in-law. Perhaps we can find something to help you sleep."

She fought an urge to run for the stables, leap on her mare's unsaddled back, and ride until she reached the steppe. Eighteen, a woman grown, a wife, a mother but for that fateful day—she couldn't run away like a petulant child. But with each day that passed, her yearning for freedom grew.

"Valerian will help me sleep," Natalya said. "You don't need a book to tell you that. We grow it by the bushel basket already."

"Yes, Mama-in-law. I'll prepare some for you." Using the recipe in her books, which prescribed valerian, too. And while she did, she could check for other cures. Doctors healed the sick, and so would she—whatever Natalya thought of books. Dismissed with a nod, Nasan took a few steps toward the herb garden.

A harsh cry brought her up short. She twisted her head right, then left. An injured child? A servant come to grief?

She saw no evidence of an accident. Work in the courtyard proceeded as before.

A second cry, a third—each timber slightly different—gave way to a flurry of calls, loud and raucous, as if designed to catch her attention.

And they had. She knew the sound. Where had she heard it before?

Of course! Nasan tipped her head back, searching the sky. Outlined against the pale blue of the April morning, a large flock of swans spread its wings. They flew in a ragged line, a leader followed by groups of two or three, feathered bellies barely clearing the church spires.

They had just taken off, then. She imagined them feeding in the Moscow River, tails raised as they upended themselves in search of a tasty sedge. Perhaps they had nested there overnight, and something had startled them into flight. If permitted her morning's ride, she might have seen them: webbed feet kicking the water, fat bodies ungainly until the magical moment when their powerful wings lifted them into the air and they soared among the clouds like spirits of air, blessing all who beheld them.

Awed by their beauty, she could not take her eyes off them—haloed by the morning sun, white against the clear blue sky, yellow beaks with their distinctive black rims the only indication that they were birds, not disembodied angels. As they flew higher, the leader slowed and the pairs and trios sped up, forming by some unwritten rule the familiar arc of an unstrung bow.

O, to fly with the swans and leave behind household duties, uncaring husbands, and sick mothers-in-law!

Someone prodded Nasan in the upper arm. "The garden," Natalya said—oblivious, it seemed, to the beauty of swans.

And why was that a surprise?

Nasan cast one last, long glance at the flock, then set off once more, only to jump aside as a manservant raced in from the kitchens. Eyes glued to the sky, bow in one hand and quiver slung over the opposite shoulder, he would have collided with her if she had not leaped away from him.

As a result, he had no defense when she hauled the weapon from his grasp. "Stop!"

Arrows spilled from his quiver and clattered against the edge of the duck pond—the same one where the *albasti* had completed its evil deed. The impromptu shower scattered the ducks and raised a storm of quacking. She quelled the man's instinctive protest with her best haughty stare. "To shoot a swan offends the spirits," she told him. "Will you bring bad fortune upon us all?"

"Spirits?" Natalya stepped forward, frowning. "Nonsense. Try again, Vanka. A pair of those birds would make a lovely dinner."

Dinner? Nasan choked down the bile that rose to her throat. Her hands twitched as Vanka raised his bow. Could she snatch it from him again? Trip him as he took aim?

Grandmothers, deflect his arrow. Save them!

She inched forward and extended a slippered foot, only to feel Natalya's hand close on her elbow.

Nasan tugged free, ignoring her mother-in-law's stagger. She couldn't let these fools curse themselves. For better or worse, they were her family. Their fates and hers were intertwined.

Vanka dodged her, repositioned himself, then lowered his bow before she reached him. Hearing him swear under his breath, she glanced at the sky and realized that her diversion had worked. The swans had flown out of range.

Thank you, Grandmothers. A soft breeze touched her cheek, a spiritual caress.

Alas, Natalya would be furious. What were the chances of heading for the herb garden and avoiding a confrontation?

Next to none, Nasan decided. Any attempt to avoid the expected apology would lead to yet another scolding.

With reluctance, she turned, ready to get it over with. But before she had a chance to speak, a third voice, high and clear, entered the conversation. "Spirits," it scoffed. "Who but a pagan thinks that killing a swan brings misfortune?"

"Exactly," Natalya said. Her toe tapped the packed earth of the courtyard, and her mouth was pinched. *"Quite* un-Christian."

No acceptable answer came to mind, so Nasan switched her attention to the newcomer: Maria—the widow of Daniil's brother, Boris. A year older than Nasan but not a day wiser, kinder, or more responsible. Such a creature *would* see a swan as nothing but food on the wing. And responding to Maria was easier. They were equals within the family, as Natalya was not.

"How am I more pagan than you?" Nasan asked. "You appease the *domovoi.* You fear it will curdle the milk and make mischief among the servants. Are house imps more worthy than swans? At least *my* ancestors had the sense to revere something beautiful."

"Your ancestors," Maria retorted, "were barbarians and killers."

"I come from the line of Genghis Khan!"

"The greatest barbarian of the lot!" Maria stamped an emphatic foot.

Unbelievable. Nasan clamped her hands on her hips and tried to stare her sister-in-law down. "As if your father wouldn't jump at the chance to marry you off to one of my cousins. Not that they'd have you!"

"Ugh! Who wants a Tatar husband? But when my father gives me to a good *Orthodox* Russian, I'll be sure to invite you to the wedding, so you can watch me serve swan." Maria plucked an imaginary piece of meat from the air and pretended to chew it. "Mmm. Delicious."

She must *want* to bring the wrath of Heaven down on their heads. Nasan, muttering a plea to the spirits to excuse her sister-in-law's stupidity, had no words left to explain to Maria the enormity of what she intended. Nasan's palm burned as it hit her sister-in-law's cheek, and Maria's howl of outrage drowned the cries of the distant flock. Nasan ducked as nails long as a hawk's talons reached for her face, but not before she felt her headdress drag at her hair. Maria grabbed it and pulled. Nasan let out a shriek of her own as the pins securing her braids dug into her skull.

"Girls, girls." Natalya caught the combatants by the arm and shoved them apart. "Behave yourselves, both of you. No insults, no slapping, no hair pulling. The Bible teaches us to turn the other cheek when we are provoked." She shook her finger in Nasan's face. "That applies especially to you, young lady. And Maria, what brings you here? I sent you to take charge of the laundry."

"I heard the noise and came to investigate," Maria said, simpering. "In case someone was hurt. Those cries—I thought a child must have fallen."

"Yes, of course," Natalya said. "Such a hubbub over a flock of birds." She frowned at Nasan. "Tearing weapons from the servants' hands, slapping your sister—I'm of a mind to send you off to confess your sins to Father Job. Fifty prostrations and no dinner should straighten you out. Especially fitting since you robbed the family of its feast."

Nasan lowered her eyes. Her cheeks burned. Every time she thought she had conquered her temper, something happened to prove her wrong. But really, Maria had asked for it. She should thank the stars that she didn't find itching powder in her sheets or a potion slipped in her food to rid her of that devil-spawn hair. And Maria had fought back. Why was Natalya not threatening to punish them both?

But how humiliating to be sent off to bed without her supper like a disobedient child, or even to fulfill whatever penance Natalya forced Father Job to impose. Nasan gritted her teeth and said, "I'm sorry, Mama-in-law. Please give me leave to tend to the herb garden as you ordered."

"Apologize to your sister," Natalya said, her voice steely.

Maria smirked and looked demure, like a person who wouldn't think of skipping her assigned tasks or ripping Nasan's headdress from her head.

The unfairness, when she had tried to save these reckless women from themselves!

But there was no mistaking the determination on Natalya's face. Nasan crossed her arms and bowed to Maria. "I apologize, sister, for my unruly temper."

"Very well," Natalya said. "I forgive you. Your turn, Maria. Irina's lack of control does not excuse yours."

Irina. Nasan gave an involuntary shudder at the sound of her Russian name, which Natalya insisted on using, as if bent on obliterating her unsatisfactory daughter-in-law's very self. Two years of marriage, and Nasan had yet to adjust to the loss of her past. To Daniil's credit, no matter how angry with her he became, he used her Russian name only with others, never when they were alone.

Maria couldn't contain her moue of distaste, but she straightened her face and stepped forward. "I am sorry, dear sister, for responding in kind to your unprovoked attack." She pressed her powdered cheek against Nasan's in a pseudo-embrace.

Nasan bit her tongue. *That* qualified as an apology? But Natalya was nodding in approbation, as if Maria had done what she asked.

I must go, before I say something unpardonable.

The herb garden beckoned, a refuge. Nasan bowed once more in farewell. But as she straightened, her mother-in-law hunched over. Another fit of coughing wracked Natalya's sturdy form. She pressed a hand to her mouth. For the second time that day, she swayed.

Nasan reacted on instinct. Her arm circled Natalya's waist, steadying her. "Mama-in-law, you are ill. Sit, please. Maria and I will tend to the household while you rest."

"Speak for yourself, *sister*," Maria snapped. "I have my hands full."

Nasan glared at her. "Standing there doing nothing? Don't be ridiculous."

"I'm overseeing the laundry—or was, until you caused a commotion." Maria looked so prim and proper that Nasan longed to slap her again.

Natalya patted Nasan's shoulder. "That's thoughtful of you, child. I'll stop if I must. But we have baking loaves to oversee, and I should tell the steward to order more hops before we run out of ale. I gave you a task. Supervise the planting."

"I can do those things, too," Nasan said, pitching her voice in the dulcet range Natalya preferred. "Unless you'd rather entrust them to Maria." Maria's smug expression evaporated in a snort, and Nasan suppressed a smile.

"I'd sooner rely on the butcher's dog," Natalya muttered.

Nasan stared at her. Had Mama-in-law *said* that? Natalya crossed herself and mumbled a prayer, her cheeks red despite the general pallor of her countenance.

Off to one side, Maria glowered. For a wild moment, Nasan wondered if Natalya saw through Maria after all.

Or does she mean me?

Probably. It was the last straw. "I'll get started then," she said.

Natalya waved her off, and Nasan went—as quickly as decorum allowed. She had had quite enough of the Kolychev women for one morning.

Nasan stalked across the courtyard, kicking her long skirts away from her boots. But as the hustle and bustle of her surroundings washed over her, her steps slowed and she drew a deep breath. Who could stay angry on such a glorious day? The air had the crisp sweetness of an apple, and the yard swarmed with chattering, laughing people. Artisans had set up tables in the open space. Cobblers bent over their lasts, seamstresses measured garments against willing bodies, potters threw clay for bowls and pots on foot-powered wheels. Kitchen maids sat on stools in one corner plucking chickens; another servant armed with a long leather strap honed a pile of utensils—knives, axes, awls. Boys in untucked shirts and linen trousers roped at the waist dashed hither and yon, dogs yapping at their heels and catching the sticks tossed to them. Girls in simple one-piece dresses defended crude wooden dolls from boys and dogs.

The scene was delightfully ordinary—different in kind from the world she had left behind for Moscow, but not different in spirit. Except for the constant pealing of bells and the absence of spices in the air, she could imagine herself back at the palace in Kasimov. How she missed her mother's swift, sure words, her hands clapping for attention, her laughing guidance, her ready sympathy.

Kasimov. Would it ever be home again?

Hah! I might as well yearn to fly with the swans.

She searched the sky, hoping for one more glimpse of the flock, but the last straggler had long since passed beyond her line of sight. Nasan followed them in her mind. They had a long way to travel through hostile territory filled with Russians bent on their destruction. Not all would reach their northern breeding grounds. Even fewer would return to the Tatar lands where they were safe. Beauty and grace couldn't protect them from the dangers posed by men. They were vulnerable, as she was, poised between worlds.

Daniil, too, was vulnerable in his theater of war. His face hung in her mind—tawny hair pushed back from his forehead, brown eyes with a hint of laughter, lips curved above his sparse young man's beard. If he were here, would the swans delight him as they did her? How could they not? They were symbols of fidelity, of married love.

Fidelity. Listen to her. She sounded like a child too young for school. Everyone knew that men at war took pleasure where they found it. And Daniil's silence confirmed how little he cared for her.

Unshed tears pricked her eyes, but she blinked them away, tired of yielding to despair. As it had once before, Daniil's indifference released her to follow her heart. The swans had not passed this way by chance. The sacred birds carried messages from above; their flight called her to freedom.

They would show her the path. And when they did, she must take it. In the meantime, she would care for Natalya to the best of her ability.

The swans saved his life. As cob and pen rose together, hooting their indignation at the horses' approach, Daniil saw the glint of steel in the woods and ducked, shouting a warning to his men. An arquebus blasted from the trees; another sounded behind him. With luck, the wretched thing would neither explode in his man's hands nor misfire, hitting his own side instead of the enemy.

Then the cacophony created by the swans as the entire flock took off from the nearby Dvina drowned even the roar of firearms. A feather drifted past his face, soft as a caress.

He pulled the recurve bow from its case and sent a volley of arrows into the smoke. One after another, rapid as a storm of angry bees. His troop followed his lead, and soon the air crackled with the snap of strings and the whine of arrows in flight. His eyes stung, and smoke and trees concealed the enemy, but screams told him that the arrows were having the desired effect. The racket set off by the arquebuses lessened. "Keep riding!" he called.

He urged his horse into a gallop, turning in the saddle to shoot. Pin the Lithuanians down long enough, and they could reach their destination.

Velizh lay just ahead.

Chapter 2

NASAN HAD ALMOST REACHED THE LOW GATE THAT separated the kitchen garden from the work area when a shadow crossed her path.

"Did you think to escape me, sister?" Maria had circled her prey like a hungry lioness and set up an ambush in front of the garden.

Shock propelled Nasan into action. She shoved Maria aside, but Maria cursed and held her ground. "Look after the laundry," Nasan said. "And leave me alone. Haven't you stirred up enough trouble for one day?" While Maria sneered, Nasan sidestepped her sister-in-law and entered the garden, where rows of freshly turned earth gave off tangy, lemony, green odors—the scent of earth, water, life. Just the atmosphere she needed, if she could rid herself of a certain redheaded snake.

Yet when she turned to close the gate, Maria still stood on the far side, arms crossed, watching. A lock of hair had freed itself from her headdress and curled, copper highlights glinting, against her flushed cheek.

Nasan stared, struck by the contrast between the joyful crowd in the courtyard and her sister-in-law's aggressive stance. What made Maria so angry? She had beauty, riches, intelligence, noble birth. Unlike Nasan, she belonged to this world; she twisted Natalya round her finger with ease. Yet every word that dripped from her lips was bitter as unripe fruit. As if Nasan's presence were a personal affront.

But Nasan had not asked to leave her home in Kasimov, to marry the relative of her brother's murderer, to convert to an alien faith or converse in an unfamiliar language, to master strange customs and adapt to a new household. She had far more cause for complaint than Maria.

They had both lost husbands, to death or emotional desertion. Maria insisted she had disliked Boris, but who knew the truth? Nasan didn't talk about how much she missed Daniil, either. No one wanted to become an object of pity.

"Don't be so mean, Maria," she said more calmly. "We both need to help. Mama-in-law is sick, although she won't admit it."

Maria's perfect rosebud mouth twisted. "And you think you can cure her? What a joke."

With that, she turned on her heel and stalked across the courtyard, threading her way by a circuitous path that kept a steady screen of servants between her and Natalya until she could slip into the house through a side door. The maids charged with the laundry would have to oversee themselves.

Nasan turned toward the garden. *So much for the olive branch.*

An afternoon under the sun restored Nasan's spirits. Within moments of entering the garden, she had settled in beside Anna, a junior cook recruited for garden duty, and overruled Anna's protest that ladies should stand and watch. Digging in the moist earth, inhaling the delicate scent of the seedlings, tamping the soil around them, reveling in the stillness of nature as the sounds of the courtyard faded to a soothing purr slowed the pulse and brought serenity to the soul. The aggravations of the morning melted in the rays of the warming sun, reminding her that Natalya could be kind as well as stern. Dust motes danced in the air, small birds sang in the trees, doves cooed and circled their cotes, and a pleasant fatigue tugged at Nasan's muscles as she bent and straightened. Physical exertion allayed the need to move that had driven her to plead for permission to leave the estate, although her determination to ride around the courtyard that evening remained.

And to visit the storehouses. As indicated, Nasan saw plenty of valerian growing in the moist reaches of the herb garden. The plants were small and far from flowering, but no doubt the servants had dried roots last autumn, and she would make the sleeping potion as promised. It couldn't hurt, and Natalya did need rest.

Suppose her illness proved serious? How would the household function without her? In teasing mood, Daniil called his mother "The General," and the nickname fit. Natalya directed the lives of more than two hundred souls, kept her estate running in good times and bad. If she sickened, that job would fall to Nasan, who could not hope to manage half as well even if Maria deigned to assist. And when had Maria ever offered to work?

How old was Natalya, anyway? Nasan counted. Daniil had turned twenty-one in December of last year, so his brother would have been twenty-six. Add a year to bear the child and fifteen or so before marriage: Natalya must have entered her forties. She didn't seem old, with her energy and commanding presence, but she had reached a point in life where her health might deteriorate.

But deteriorate in what way? Inability to sleep and coughing without phlegm indicated excessive dryness. Not a simple cold or consumption, unless at an early stage. And a patient who couldn't sleep *would* feel tired. But swaying on her feet pointed to a disorder of the internal organs—heart, perhaps lungs. The discolored skin had a meaning, too.

Heart and lungs were by temperament warm and moist. Most of the heat-producing remedies came from spices. Galingale and nutmeg, cinnamon and cloves—Nasan would check for those in the storehouse while preparing the valerian. But parsley mixed with wine and honey strengthened the heart, and sage cured many ills. Pulmonaria would help the lungs. Did they plant that here?

She asked Anna. It took a bit of explaining, but the answer was yes. They called it *medunitsa*—the honey plant. Good. She could use that if necessary.

The bell rang to summon the household to dinner. Nasan brushed dirt from her hands and surveyed a full plot of herbs planted with the aid of her ten assistants.

A good day's work. She congratulated the servants on their efforts and headed for the gate. A twinge of nerves tightened her stomach at the thought of yet another encounter with her sister-in-law.

Perhaps that red hair did indicate some kind of demonic possession. How else to explain such unremitting nastiness? Nasan touched her amulet, whispering another prayer for deliverance before pushing the fear away. She had survived her father's harem—and the far more malevolent atmosphere of Kazan. She could survive Maria.

The cheerful crowd of early afternoon had dissipated. Looking around, Nasan concluded that she would have enough space to ride by the evening, after all.

Only then did she notice the group of men and women who stood in a tight huddle at the center of the open space, chattering and wringing their hands. She halted as she reached the gate, searching for clues to what worried them. Natalya was nowhere to be seen.

But what conclave of servants would not feature Natalya at the center of it? Nasan pulled the gate aside, clutched her ankle-length skirts in both hands, and ran toward the huddle, Anna close behind.

"Where is Natalya Vasilyevna?" Nasan grabbed the arm of Pashka, the steward, who stood at the edge of the circle praying, hands raised to the heavens. "Stop that wailing and answer me this instant!"

Pashka groaned but extended his arm, indicating the circle of servants. "Our lady, she has died!"

"Died?" How was that possible? She was fine a few hours ago!

Well, not fine, but not at the brink of death. What did I miss?

Following the steward's finger with her gaze, she saw two embroidered shoes, toes pointing to the sky. "Mama-in-law!" She released Pashka and pushed through the befuddled servants, Anna still on her heels.

Nasan shook the nearest sobbing maid. "Fetch Father Job right away. And for the love of God, the rest of you stop howling and help us."

The maid ran to do her bidding. Nasan bent over her mother-in-law's prostrate form and pressed her palm against Natalya's cheek. "It's warm," she told Anna, crouched on Natalya's other side. "I don't think she's dead. She has fainted."

Anna touched Natalya's neck. "Her pulse is weak."

Nasan held a hand under Natalya's nose. "She breathes—just. It grows chill. We must get her to her room. Where is that useless steward?"

"Let me help, young mistress," Anna said. "What should I tell him?"

"To find his wits before I order him whipped," Nasan said. "Then fetch a blanket to wrap her in. We will have one of the men carry her inside."

Anna withdrew, and Father Job bustled up, his bearded face taut. "What happened? My lady!" He knelt beside Nasan.

"She lives, Father," she said. "We don't know any more."

He tapped the shin of the nearest manservant. "You, Vanka, tell us."

Vanka of the bow. Nasan edged away from him, noting that he also took several steps back, as if anxious not to attract her attention again. He shuffled his feet and twisted his cap in both hands. "She collapsed, Father. One moment she was standing there, giving orders as usual. One of the men upset her with his foolishness, and she waved her arms and shouted at him. Then she clutched her chest and fell. We thought she had died, so we were trying to decide what to do."

"Anna is fetching a coverlet," Nasan added. "Then we should move Mama-in-law indoors. It can't be good for her to lie around in this wind."

"Indeed not. You have done well, my daughter." Father Job stood and beckoned to the steward, still addressing the sky. "Pashka, aid us. I'm sure the Lord has heard your prayers by now—and if not, you can remind Him later."

Competent assistance, at last. Nasan sighed with relief and bent to touch her mother-in-law's neck, again feeling for a pulse. Natalya moaned. Her flailing hands pressed against her chest. "How do you feel, Mama-in-law?" Nasan asked.

Natalya moved her head from side to side and didn't answer. Anna arrived with the coverlet, and Pashka the steward assigned a sturdy manservant to wrap his mistress in it and carry her to her chamber. The group trailed mistress and manservant as they moved toward the house.

Hands tucked into her sleeves, head bowed, Nasan walked at the back. Father Job joined her. Lines of concern creased his normally placid face. "It speaks well that she has awoken," he said. "But I think her heart troubles her. See how she clutches at it, as if she could push the pain away."

"Yes." Nasan said. "I fear you are right."

An idea occurred to her. Once Natalya was settled upstairs, Nasan would check for swelling in her mother-in-law's legs. Dropsy was a clear indicator of a damaged heart.

The diagnosis fit, too. The heart was the seat of the emotions, and Natalya had suffered much in recent years. Her older son slain before her eyes, her husband and sole remaining son at war for month after endless month, one daughter-in-law lost in childbed with the infant she bore, a second grandchild dead before birth—what heart would not stutter under such powerful blows?

"We must pray for her," Father Job said. Nasan murmured assent and muttered a quick plea to the Almighty. But as she followed Father Job toward the stairs, she allowed him to handle communication with God and His angels and thought again about remedies.

Heart trouble. What did she need to balance the humors? Spices, to restore the lost heat. Purple nut sedge for moisture; blackberries and raspberries—no, wrong season for berries, unless Natalya had ordered them dried. Nut sedge bordered the kitchen garden, though. The roots had great power but equal bitterness. Honey to sweeten them, then.

"May the Good Lord have mercy on her soul," Father Job said.

"Have mercy on her soul," Nasan echoed.

"Should we not send a message to Nikolai Borisovich?" Nasan asked as she and Father Job mounted the stairs. Her father-in-law's chances of obtaining leave seemed slim, but one never knew. And he would want to hear about his wife's distress. Unlike many couples, he and Natalya had fallen in love at first sight, on their wedding day, and remained deeply attached.

"Yes, of course. When we know what to tell him, I will write." Father Job smiled. He had a charming smile; it lit his dark eyes with a boyish gleam that always reminded Nasan of her husband. Once a fearsomely pious presence—at least to Nasan—Father Job had over time revealed a tolerance of human frailty, a quick wit, and a sly sense of humor seldom recognized, let alone appreciated, by the other women in the household. In the months since she lost the baby, especially, Nasan had come to rely on his counsel. With a wife and a dozen children, Father Job had vast experience of family life. Although even he couldn't explain why Daniil remained silent.

She thanked him for his offer to contact her father-in-law. Although her command of spoken Russian improved each day, requests to learn the Cyrillic alphabet had foundered against the rock of Natalya's conviction that women had no need to read or write. So Father Job must send the letter to Natalya's husband while Nasan spread the news to her own relatives. Her brother Ogodai, her mother, her father.

No, not her brother or father. The army had stationed *Ata* only her mother knew where, and most likely, Ogodai's horde had already left its winter pastures for its summer grazing lands. A courier from Moscow had small chance of intercepting them, given the vastness of the steppe, but her mother in Kasimov maintained close contact with Ogodai, too. So one message to *Ana* in Kasimov would alert all three.

The air sang with the whistle of axes, shivered at each shaping blow, clanged as shovels hit dirt. The ground beneath Daniil's feet shuddered as a huge wagon bearing stripped oak logs overturned, sending its load rolling over the bare earth. Workmen moved soil from ditch to embankment, supporting and filling the initial line of massive wood-lined pits while leaving spaces for the cannon that would one day sit between them. A few hundred peasants recruited from the surrounding villages chopped logs, hollowing the ends and sides so that they would fit together in a seamless line.

Construction had begun ten days before, the sentry at the gate had told him, yet the workmen had already made remarkable progress. But then, progress was essential when building at the direct order of the grand prince's government in Moscow. The grand prince himself had yet to reach his sixth birthday, but neither his mother, Grand Princess Elena Glinskaya, nor her advisers had much patience with laggards. In twelve weeks, she had decreed in her son's name, the town of Velizh would have its fortress. The army had charged Daniil's father with overseeing the project and ordered Daniil to assist. A great honor—unless he and his father failed to complete the task on time.

Hence the hubbub—sufficient to drown the calls of the swans that, recovered from this morning's fright, glided in placid circles mid-river.

His own nerves still jangled. If the birds had not startled when they did ... But that was war. If God wanted you, He would take you. No point in worrying about it. Fear of death paralyzed a warrior.

Still, a man could rejoice that death had passed him by today.

What brought the Lithuanians here? Not in general— Russia had seized Velizh from the Grand Duchy of Lithuania a few months ago, and the enemy wanted it back—but this group, today. A small contingent, or the fire would have lasted longer. A foraging party, maybe. In which case, the swans owed their lives to Daniil, as he and his troop did to them. A gratifying thought.

Papa would know. Daniil scanned the crowd for a familiar burly form wearing a pointed helmet or a tall boyar hat. But he saw only the crowd and, beyond the walls, the swans—small groups and couples, dipping and feeding, graceful and serene.

Paired for life. Like him and Nasan.

If she still loved him. The accident had left her so injured, so sad. Each feeble attempt at comfort chased her farther into her protective cocoon. And when, to atone and to give her time to heal, he had moved to another room, he suspected Nasan didn't understand. The summons to muster had come as a relief to them both.

But that was months ago. It was time he went home. If the army would let him.

The church bells rang twice while Daniil dodged oak trunks, buckets of clay, carts, and workmen too distracted to watch where they were going half the time. He walked the entire boundary of the fortress-to-be, long lines marked with stones, bulging circles defining where the eight towers would soon rise. He stood at the edge of the embankment, looking into the emerging ditch that, when filled with water diverted from the river, would keep the enemy cannon at a safe distance from the fortress walls. Yet no amount of searching revealed the man he sought. Had Papa left the site altogether? But for where, and with what purpose?

Daniil scrutinized one face after another. Booted soldiers in calf-length coats gathered in clumps or spread around the perimeter of the embankment, ready in case of trouble. Peasants in loose shirts and homespun trousers, their feet wrapped in birchbark, chopped logs and carried baskets filled with soil and stones, while on the far side of the ditch others tilled the fields. Master craftsmen mingled with the throng, issuing orders, offering corrections, dispensing advice. At the edges of the crowd, groups of older women offered food and beer, thread to mend a ripped shirt, soap to wash a filthy one. Here and there, Daniil's eyes caught the dull gleam of mail or the occasional gray head among the ever-changing shades of blond and brown. But strain his eyes as he might, he could not see Papa's craggy visage amid the throng.

He had almost given up hope when a pair of strong arms wrapped around his chest from behind. His father roared, "There you are, my boy. I'd begun to think the Lithuanians got you!"

Daniil turned. Nikolai's cheeks, reddened by the wind, outshone his scarlet robe. His gray hair and neatly trimmed beard gave him an imposing air. The black fox fur that rimmed his hat rippled in the breeze. He looked like Grandfather Frost.

"They almost did. Instead, we got them." Daniil returned the bear hug with enthusiasm. No need to ask after his father's health. Nikolai seemed as hearty as ever. And with Papa in charge, life should settle down for a few months.

Good. It had been a rough winter campaign. He could relax for a bit and hope that the authorities saw fit to grant him leave before Nasan forgot his existence.

The sunset over Lake Borodava sparked thoughts in the former Brother Stefan worthy of a bard. The joys of freedom? Himself becoming soft? No. After Pechenga, any place with food and heat looked like Paradise.

Lord knew, the sight before him was pretty enough to justify a maudlin sentiment or two. Swans, settling for the evening on their journey north, circled in pairs atop the glimmering, pearl-pink water, entwined necks curved into heart shapes, wings reflecting every hue of the fading light. Behind him stood the ancient Russian forest; between him and the lake, ringed with masses of trees blackened by the descending sun, lay a rough collection of huts that had seen better days. A few clouts and a public flogging had convinced the villagers to accept him as their new master. Many of the huts lay empty—although that would change, for he had plans—but the fields were tilled. The peasants saw to that.

The hamlet lay far enough along the lake that the monks of Ferapontovo, who held the written charter to the lands, did not bother themselves with its affairs. Pay them off after the harvest, and they might not even notice that their property had changed hands. The prospect of keeping his distance from them suited him fine. He had had enough of monks to last him unto the Ages of Ages.

Although if his plans came to fruition, they would learn of his arrival soon enough. For in a flash of genius, he had seen his future in his former abbot's tale of woe. If the skinny, sainted Trifon could rule a bandit camp and terrorize the northern woods, Stefan could do the same.

But under his own name rather than the one forced on him by circumstance. His tonsure had grown in, and he went by Semyon again. Not Kolychev: best to keep his relatives ignorant of his escape until he held the knife at their throats. Until then, the world would know him as Semyon Severyanin. "Man of the North"—the name had an irony that appealed to him. If his family had spared him the frozen wastes, he would indeed be a different man. Less vengeful, less hard.

Instead, he intended to trouble them for as long as God gave him breath.

Starting tomorrow morning. His villagers included likely lads ready for adventure. Add some military deserters, an unemployed man-at-arms or two, and he'd have his band. A few practice raids, then wealth, fame, glory. Ahead lay the height of pilgrim season, and with two monasteries in the area rich travelers would swarm the place by August.

And he would find himself a woman. A real woman, not a chilly bitch like his divorced wife. A bandit queen of his own. He would be paired, like the swans.

Chapter 3

"I'M NOT DRINKING THAT." PROPPED FULLY DRESSED IN A corner of the women's quarters and surrounded by pillows, Natalya held out both hands, fending off the cup of purple nut sedge that Nasan had prepared with such care. "It is bitter as gall. You must have learned about it in one of your books, because no sensible person would offer such an abomination to one already suffering."

"I put more honey in it this time, Mama-in-law, and it will help you, I swear. The receipt comes from my mother, not from a book." A half-truth, that. Nasan had known about the plant from Dioscorides' herbal and remembered that her mother had used such a concoction, so she had written to ask for instructions. But two months of caring for a mother-in-law who insisted on prescribing her own treatments had taught Nasan not to waste time in defending the honor of dead doctors. Despite the incident with the wise woman, her mother's practical knowledge earned a grudging respect from this difficult patient.

Natalya acknowledged this statement with a grunt. "Blue yarrow works as well. Mix it with valerian and honey, and you have a medicine I can tolerate."

"I will remember that next time," Nasan promised. She would check, but she thought she remembered yarrow being useful for other things—fever and stomachache among them—not for heart trouble. She held out the bowl, coaxing her reluctant patient with a smile. Sunlight glinting through the window cast gold ripples on the thick, winy liquid and the elaborate embroidery that trimmed her sleeves. "Will you not try it? I tasted it. With the extra sweetening it is quite palatable."

Natalya was hesitating when Maria bustled in, bearing a bowl of her own. "Look, Mama-in-law. I have made you a garlic/onion stew, with saffron milk cap seeds to help your cough." She looked quite housewifely today, her coppery hair concealed under a white linen scarf tied at the back of her head. She glanced at Nasan's cup, emitting wisps of steam. "It will serve you better than that nasty stuff."

"That nasty stuff has been used for centuries to strengthen the heart," Nasan said. "Your garlic and onions will do nothing but make her breath stink."

"Garlic and onions have been used for centuries, too, and my mother swore by the power of saffron milk cap seeds for a cough. She always dosed us with it. Mama-in-law doesn't need your pagan brew."

"I'm sure your mother *did* dose you that way for a cough." Nasan waved her bowl—gently, to avoid spillage. "But Mama-in-law's cough comes from the dryness in her lungs. That mess of yours won't help her a bit. She's not a child with a cold."

"Don't you dare be rude about my sainted mother." Maria's mother had died last year—one reason she still lived with the Kolychevs.

Nasan gritted her teeth. "I'm not speaking against your mother. That remedy helps a cold, but Mama-in-law needs the nut sedge. It has both warmth and moisture, whereas onions and garlic lack heat."

"What do you know?" Maria retorted. "You're younger than I am."

"Girls, girls, must you squabble over everything?" Natalya extended a hand. "The first rule of the sickroom is not to aggravate the patient. I will drink the nut sedge, Irina, if you promise to bring me a cup of ginger-pomegranate tea to wash it down. It is nasty stuff, as Maria says, although I am grateful to your mother. And Maria, I appreciate your efforts, too. Can we agree that you will attempt the blue yarrow tomorrow? Now leave your potions here, and ask Father Job to visit me. His prayers do more good than any mortal cure."

"How are your ankles today, Mama-in-law?" Nasan asked as she placed the cup of nut sedge within reach, adding a murmured thank you. "Anna the Cook told me this morning that in her village they use cucumber baths for dropsy. It's early for fresh cucumbers, but we could try pickled ones."

Natalya shuddered. "Let us save that remedy for the end of our pilgrimage. Bathe in pickle juice? It will leave a smell worse than the garlic and onions."

"See?" Maria waved a triumphant hand as she placed her bowl on the same small table, pushing Nasan's to one side. It would have fallen if Nasan had not snatched the cup as it skidded toward the edge and nudged it back into place. She stood in front of the table to keep Maria from succeeding in her next attempt to knock it off. Maria edged past her one way, then the other, but Nasan, thanks to an active life, was faster and more agile. She blocked her opponent at every turn.

Only when Maria gave up and moved away did Nasan catch what Natalya had said. "Pilgrimage?" she asked. "Pilgrimage to where?"

Father Job spoke from the doorway. They had not even needed to summon him. "To Ferapontovo. My lady has decided to make her prayers before the altar of the Church of the Nativity in the monastery there—and in Dmitrov and at the White Lake as well."

Nasan gulped. Although her childhood schooling had not included Russian geography, she had a sense that the White Lake lay far to the northwest. "Ferapontovo, Mama-in-law?" Her voice came out as a squeak, and she steadied it. "Isn't that a long way from here?"

"Of course," Natalya said. "Six weeks' journey, if not more. But I wish to pray for my health and for a grandson. No earthly remedy can aid me in the absence of Divine Will."

It was madness. Not the sentiment, which Nasan had heard her entire life, but the reckless tempting of Providence. It would take all the protection the grandmothers could offer and a cartload of medicines to keep Natalya alive long enough to reach her destination, never mind find her way home.

But looking at her mother-in-law, Nasan saw from the set expression on the older woman's face that Natalya had made up her mind. Whether it made sense or not, they would be traveling to Ferapontovo.

Natalya drank the nut sedge, grimacing as she swallowed. "Better," she said, "although I still prefer the yarrow." She picked up a slab of rye bread Maria had upended on the side of her bowl, tore off a small piece, and dipped it in the garlic and onion stew, catching fluffy mushroom seeds with a lacquered spoon. "This tastes good."

Maria treated Nasan to a triumphant stare, and Nasan repressed a sigh. Right or wrong, try as she might, she came in second every time.

※

Father Job finished praying for Natalya's health. Nasan perched near her mother-in-law's feet and sought counsel of the priest, sitting with his hands folded, the picture of calm, on a bench near the window. "Is this journey wise, Father?"

"There is a wisdom of the body and a wisdom of the soul, my daughter. We must travel slowly, but we can go much of the way by water. If hope and faith sustain her, and we take good care of her throughout the voyage, it may serve better than you expect." He must have heard the fear in her voice, for the warmth of his smile contradicted the austerity of his words. She had the impression that, unlike the others, he saw her as an ally in support of Natalya's health.

Perhaps she read too much into an attempt to console. The belief comforted her, even so.

Maria, who had taken a seat at the far end of the bench, closed her eyes. She looked as if she might be plotting something, but Nasan couldn't imagine what.

"I grew up there," Natalya explained. "I met my husband there. He owns land nearby where we can stay. We need not rush. I hope to reach the monastery in time to celebrate the Feast of the Dormition in mid-August."

"But what of Nikolai Borisovich?" Nasan asked. "And my husband? They will be alarmed if they obtain leave, only to find us gone when they reach Moscow."

And there lay another source of trouble. The men should have responded but hadn't. For sure, they had had time to receive the messages Father Job had sent. The servant she had dispatched to Kasimov had returned in two weeks bearing *Ana*'s good wishes as well as the ginger and pomegranates that Natalya loved. The couriers to the west had taken four times as long to travel one and a half times as far and had yet to return.

She should have asked her own mother to contact Daniil and his father. Why hadn't she thought of that? If *Ana* had behaved true to form, fast Tatar ponies bearing skilled and inexhaustible riders had already tracked down her father and brother. Instead, fool that she was, she had placed her faith in the Kolychev couriers, and they had failed her.

She kept these worries to herself. Reminding her mother- and sister-in-law that she wrote letters would only start another fuss about stupid, submissive, illiterate women being closer to God.

"I will send word again before we depart," Father Job said.

At least one person understood her concern. "Thank you," she said.

But Natalya raised an admonishing finger. "Don't, Father. We must not worry them when they can do nothing to help. If they obtain leave, they will come here, and Pashka will tell them where to find us."

Nasan dug her thumbnail into the opposite palm, concentrating her attention on the sensation to keep her hasty words in check. Why on earth should Daniil and his father travel the entire distance from Lithuania to Moscow only to discover that they should have headed for the White Lake instead? And wouldn't they *want* to worry rather than be left in ignorance until word came that they had lost a wife or a mother?

While she sought a way to express these thoughts to Natalya, Father Job answered. "As you wish," he said, before turning again to Nasan. "Your concern for your husband and father- in-law does you credit, my daughter. You fear the distance and the danger, which shows you to be a young woman of good sense. Even so, such a journey is possible. Your husband could ride from here to Ferapontovo in a week and a half, if not less. We will go much more slowly. It is as yet early June, so we have ten weeks to reach our destination without taxing our lady's strength."

"You will accompany us, then?" Nasan's mind raced. Only she, it seemed, could imagine Daniil and Nikolai being furious when they learned that their women and their priest had acquiesced to this mad scheme. More evidence that she had no idea how Russians thought about the most basic things! "What of the household?"

"My eldest son does not yet have a parish of his own," Father Job said. "He will minister to the household. So yes, I will travel with you." He bowed his head toward Natalya, tracking the back-and-forth with watchful eyes. "If my lady permits."

She raised a languid hand. "It may be selfish of me, Father, but I would appreciate your spiritual guidance. Nikolai Borisovich, I feel certain, would expect no less."

Indeed, without Father Job the journey would be impossible. Three women—two young, one ill—could not travel so great a distance on their own. They would take an armed escort as befit a group of noblewomen, but they would need a man of stature to speak for them at the churches and monasteries along the way—even to help them hire a boat. And having Father Job close at hand would reassure Natalya.

"It is decided, then," the priest said.

Well, not quite. Nasan clarified her earlier question. "Should one of us stay, Mama-in-law, myself or Maria, to supervise things here?" Father Job's son could watch over the servants' spiritual needs, but their physical well-being lay outside his purview.

A fleeting memory of the swans—of the message she had thought they carried, her belief that they would show her the way to freedom—brushed at Nasan's mind. Did the ancestors want her to stay or to go?

But there was no way to tell. From where she stood today, both paths might yield only drudgery. Ten weeks on a boat with a sulky Maria and a reluctant patient hardly sounded like cause for joy, but bearing sole responsibility for running the household would be deadening. The last two months had brought an endless series of chores—most of them performed, despite Nasan's best efforts, in a way that did not meet Natalya's expectations. Maria had spent her hours at Natalya's side, avoiding all tasks but nursing while smirking at every criticism, every heartfelt sigh and grudging, "Well, it's the best you can do, I suppose." Even Natalya's thanks carried a sting in the tail. Yet Nasan felt she must ask.

"Pashka will manage," Natalya said after a while. "He doesn't react well to crises, but for day-to-day management I trust him. And I would prefer to keep both of you girls at my side."

No reprieve, then. No domestic drudgery, but ongoing battles over potions and pills. Weeks of being shut in a small space filled with tension and squabbles, perhaps without a room of her own. The very thought made Nasan want to jump into the river.

She must not despair. Perhaps the swans had chosen her direction after all. On a journey, anything could happen. Although if they traveled by water, her precious mare would be left behind. Again.

Poor Sorkhokhtani. How she would love two months on the road!

"You want to reenter my service?" Semyon glared at the stocky young man with light brown hair and gray eyes who stood before him, clutching a beat-up sword in his right hand and an ax in his left.

The glare was for effect. It wouldn't do to let his relief show. Stenka was the best henchman Semyon had ever employed: competent and reliable and solid as the proverbial rock. What brought him here today, Semyon didn't know. But Stenka's presence boded well for Semyon's plans.

Alas, Stenka had not come alone. His woman stood near the door, wringing her hands, her belly swollen with child. Pregnancy and poverty had stripped Grusha of her soft blonde prettiness. It disgusted Semyon to recall the one time he had lain with her—the silly cow. Stenka could have her.

"Yes, Lord," Stenka said. "I need the work. I'm not a farmer. The crops failed two years in a row, and I have to feed my family." He gestured at Grusha, who stared at the floor. "Man-at-arms, that's a job I can do."

Semyon nodded. "It's not like the old days, though. Not since those bastards in Moscow stripped me of everything I owned. I've decided to support myself through highway robbery. Death if you're caught, but rich pickings otherwise." Grusha whimpered, and he grinned. "Steal from the rich, give to the poor, just like the Scriptures say."

"The poor meaning us?" Stenka's hand gripped his sword hilt. He looked eager, expectant. Tilling the soil must really have worn him down. Remembering Pechenga, Semyon figured he understood. Except for Stenka's inexplicable attachment to Grusha, he and Semyon had always been kindred souls.

Semyon gave an expansive wave, indicating the entire village. "You, your whore, your brat, myself—and those out there. Plenty for all, if we do it right."

"I'm in, then?" Stenka asked.

"In? You're my second-in-command. Settle your woman with old Masha and start licking these brutes into shape. Most of them think a sword is a sickle; it's a miracle they don't chop off their own toes." Semyon strolled toward Grusha and raised her chin with one finger. He saw fear in her watery blue eyes. "No whining. Disobey me, and you'll feel the back of my hand. Behave yourself, and I'll leave you alone. Got it?"

He felt a flash of the old thrill when she mumbled acquiescence and scurried out the door, but he dismissed it.

She was too easy to intimidate, too easy a conquest—and besides, he needed Stenka more than a whey-faced bitch the size of a peasant cottage.

His bandit queen was out there, somewhere in the woods, and he would find her.

Fyodor Mikhailovich Koshkin tapped the scroll that his man had handed him an hour ago and smiled at the icon of the Holy Mother and Child placed at the center of the "beautiful corner" in his Vologda office. It was, he hoped, a smile as enigmatic as that of the Theotokos herself; he practiced the expression in his chamber, using a brass mirror purchased from the Tatars for verification. Brought into service at the right moment, the smile seldom failed to unsettle the person on whom he chose to inflict it.

The Holy Mother did not respond, of course, but when Koshkin turned to greet his subordinate, he kept the smile in place long enough to ensure its effect. "This document came from Moscow this morning," he said. "From Prince Vasily Vasilyevich Shuisky."

The subordinate appeared impressed, as he should. Prince Vasily Shuisky stood at the right hand of the young grand prince, on whose behalf Prince Vasily met with ambassadors and in general directed Russia's foreign policy.

"The grand princess has ordered the strengthening of our fortifications," Koshkin said. "Men will soon arrive to conduct the repairs, perhaps even an Italian architect. Prepare to receive them by the end of this month."

"Yes, General." The subordinate bowed. "Will there be anything else?"

"Send a scribe, with paper and ink. I would reply to Prince Vasily."

The subordinate bowed again and left. Within moments, the scribe appeared. Koshkin took the paper and ink and dismissed the man. He saw no reason to proclaim his ability to read and write to the uncomprehending world, which would only think the less of him as a result. But he had determined that no eyes but his would read this message before it reached its destination. Nothing must prevent him from attaining his goal: to leave this northern backwater and return to court, the source of all advancement.

Although everyone knew who gave the orders in Moscow, the pretense that the five-year-old grand prince ruled as an autocrat must be maintained. Koshkin, an old hand at the politics of the Moscow court, understood this. So his missive, although aimed at Prince Vasily Shuisky, required a different form of address. Koshkin sat, took up the pen, and listed the royal titles, in order, careful not to leave out the smallest principality or town. Men had been imprisoned for less. Once satisfied that he had omitted nothing, he switched to crafting the message itself.

To Ivan Vasilyevich, sovereign and grand prince of all Russia, and to your mother Elena, sovereign and grand princess of all Russia, he wrote. *I, your humble slave Fyodor do beseech that I may be permitted to perform the service requested of me by Prince Vasily Vasilyevich Shuisky in your name.*

A fine beginning, worthy of any scrivener. But what to write next, given that in response to Koshkin's own plea for clemency, Prince Vasily had responded with what appeared to be a test? For there was no obvious reason why the prince should yearn for yet another Tatar sultan to join Muscovite service, other than to prove that he could force Koshkin to dance to his piping as a traveling musician compelled a bear. Yet so Shuisky had ordered, and he, Koshkin, had no doubt that he should oblige. In short, Koshkin would agree to almost any request that required him to leave this benighted fortress.

Because he would have to leave, would he not? To woo this sultan, he would have to travel to Moscow. No Tatar sultan would deign to visit Vologda. Koshkin's head jerked up, and he tapped the feathered tip of the quill against the desk. Shuisky—cunning, as any man desirous of retaining royal favor had to be—had not conferred this mission on his humble supplicant Koshkin by chance. Shuisky wanted Koshkin at court, most likely because he needed an ally. Shuisky had presented the mission as a test only because even he could not afford the appearance of countermanding the ever-suspicious grand princess, who had ordered Koshkin to Vologda in the first place.

Yes, he understood now. He would get his wish, and the only cost was to perform this trivial task. And to remember who had offered help in his hour of need. Koshkin felt another smile, genuine this time, form on his face as he set down his request.

With luck, he'd be out of here by midsummer.

Nasan studied the expanding pile of baggage. Belted trunks packed tight as eggs in a basket threatened to tilt the sturdy wagon, yet Pashka the steward had beckoned for the next in the pile. "Send for another cart," she told him.

"There's room for one more row, Tsarevna," he said.

"Leave him, daughter. He knows his business, and you have many more tasks to oversee." The voice, Natalya's, sounded from behind. Nasan turned to greet her mother-in-law, who these days left her room for no more than an hour or two at a time before weakness forced her to rest once more.

"Could Maria not help?" Nasan asked. "There is much to do before we can leave."

The stern expression so familiar to her crossed Natalya's face. "Maria is brewing the yarrow potion and making blackberry leaf paste as well as sitting with me." Nasan's nut sedge had been banished, along with her other suggestions. Only the ginger-pomegranate tea still received a warm welcome. "She has to rest when she can. Besides, you will inherit these responsibilities. You must learn. Maria will have another mother-in-law someday who can teach her what she needs to know." Natalya crossed herself. "God willing, my son will live into old age, but I will not."

"May the Almighty grant both of you many years," Nasan said, imitating the gesture.

Natalya softened then, as she did whenever Nasan met her expectations of how a good Christian wife should behave. "It will surprise you, no doubt, but I remember how difficult this work was at first. I could not understand how my mother-in-law kept everything straight. And the servants! They ignored half of what I said and mixed up the other half, leaving me to take the blame for their mistakes. But I mastered it in time, and so will you, Irina." She touched Nasan's cheek. "But you, too, must rest. Daniil will not want to return to a pale, harried wife with dark circles under her eyes."

She spoke truth. If Daniil cared a bit, he would not. The Nasan who fell asleep before her head touched the pillow could not be the Nasan who two years ago had sneaked from the household at night and given rise to a legend. If the swans sought to free her, they had best act soon, before she collapsed under the weight of household tasks as the cart looked ready to collapse under too much baggage.

"Thank you, Mama-in-law. That does help me feel better."

"Come with me." Natalya patted Nasan's cheek once more and led the way to her private sitting room, where she spouted a list of questions she wanted answered as soon as Pashka finished loading their goods for the journey. As the list grew, Nasan wished for a piece of paper and a pen to jot everything down. Did the storerooms contain enough food, leather, materials, wood? How much money would Pashka need to purchase perishable supplies for the summer and early fall? Who would ensure that the servants appeared each day on time and fulfilled their assigned tasks? What of the animals? The newly planted garden? The orchards? If children grew out of their clothes, who would alter them or sew new ones? Did they have bast to make shoes?

Nasan responded when she could, promised to find answers where she had none, then helped Natalya return to her room upstairs and sat beside her until Maria arrived with another bowl of saffron milk caps in broth. With no books to read, no interesting conversation to share, and no skill in the embroidery that Natalya considered the only true pursuit (besides domestic management) for a noblewoman, watching Natalya drift into and out of fitful sleep left Nasan so bored that household duties seemed like a reprieve. When Maria at last appeared, Nasan greeted her with enough warmth to wring a startled "thank you" out of her prickly sister-in-law and dashed for the kitchen.

She was supervising the baking of bread when the clatter of hoofbeats in the street beyond caught her attention. A troop of horsemen, riding hard and traveling too fast for city streets—she would recognize that sound anywhere. She wiped her hands, flour-covered from correcting one young servant's errors, on a cloth and ran for the courtyard.

"Bar the gates, quick!" she shouted at the servants milling aimlessly in the yard. "Have you lost your minds? Suppose it's a raid?"

Too late.

A troop of Tatar ponies galloped through the open gates. Servants grabbed whatever would fit under their arms and scattered to the corners of the yard, overturning tables in their haste. The armored riders howled a greeting that only Nasan understood. A few of the warriors waved a bow or a sword, but despite the screams from the servants, no one was shooting.

The leader pulled off his helmet and called her name—her real name, her Tatar name. She saw a young man, black-haired and dark-eyed, clean-shaven except for a small beard in a line down the center of his chin. Her older brother, Ogodai Khan.

Only then did she recognize the riders as his personal bodyguard and the banner they carried as his: a stylized winged horse, gold embroidery on white silk. But what brought him here?

Her breath escaped in a long whoosh. Relief made her hands clumsy, and she dropped the cloth. Her long skirts felt heavy in her hands as she ran toward her brother. He slid off his horse and caught her in a hug, rubbing his nose against hers, inhaling the scent of her cheek. Nasan wrapped her arms around his neck, overwhelmed by his unexpected appearance and the blessed familiarity of his greeting.

"I'm so glad you're here," she exclaimed in her mother tongue when the lump in her throat cleared. "What brings you to Moscow? How is everyone?"

Her older brother released her. "Well. Firuza has recovered from childbirth, and the twins grow like the feather grass. And what of you?"

"I fare well enough," she said. "Did *Ana* write to you? I hoped she would."

"Yes. She says your mother-in-law is ill. How does she?"

"She would feel better if she took the medicines I prescribe. Since she won't, she is losing strength, but she will live for some time, I think. Only she wants to undertake the most ridiculous journey—to pray at some northern cathedral!" She caught his elbow, then released it. "In fact, it is good you reached us today. By the end of the week, you would have arrived to an empty house. But what brings you here? Not our news?"

His expression, attentive while they discussed Natalya's health, relaxed into a grin. "Alas, no. Our thrice-cursed half-brother—may the fleas of ten thousand camels infest his armpits—decided to try his luck with my horde again. Not the horde itself, but one of the tribes. You recall the circumstances of my father-in-law's death?"

Nasan nodded. Another event two years past, which had ended with Ogodai's elevation to khan. Only one tribe had not supported her brother's candidacy. "The sons of Shirin Bey?" she asked.

"Good for you." Ogodai patted her shoulder. "Exactly. Our dear Tulpar stirred up as much unrest as he could, then bolted. I chased him as far as Moscow, but he gave us the slip the moment we entered the citadel. We searched for most of yesterday without success, so I thought I might as well stop and see you. Tomorrow I head west. *Ata* will expect a personal report."

Nasan puzzled over this news, striving to recall her half-brother's face. The Tulpar in her mind looked like a handsome sixteen-year-old, although he must have reached his late twenties by now. "I don't understand," she said after a moment. "Has Tulpar abandoned Islam-Girei Sultan? Why leave Crimea again to stir up trouble for you?"

Ogodai shrugged. "I didn't catch up with him, so I don't know. But word has it that Islam-Girei is losing support. Perhaps Tulpar fears the wrath of the Crimean khan."

"Sahib-Girei would kill him?" She frowned. "I suppose he would. He must be getting sick of the constant rebellions."

"Most likely. Sahib wouldn't kill Islam-Girei himself, I think, however great a thorn he is in his uncle's side. But to punish him by killing his closest supporters—that's a vengeance that would appeal to Sahib." Ogodai ran a hand through his straight dark hair, as if he felt the pull of some long-ago allegiance. Tulpar had caused nothing but trouble in the last few years, yet Ogodai had looked up to him once—the capable, kindly older brother.

Nasan understood that reaction. Odd as it seemed to worry over the fate of a half-brother sent into exile when she turned five, even now she remembered Tulpar as a charming if distant presence. "I hate to think of him facing death. Silly, isn't it, given how little he cares for us?"

"So do I." Ogodai's brows drew together. "But no matter what, I must consult with *Ata*. If Crimea is about to descend into chaos once more, or even if our brother returns to make more mischief, I need reinforcements—especially if I can't count on the Shirins." He produced a rueful smile. "I would rather stay with Firuza and the twins. Damn Tulpar and his schemes! But I am glad to see you, *sengel*."

"And I you." She clasped his hand. "Welcome!"

Ogodai gripped her fingers in response before stepping back, hands on her shoulders, to examine her. "But tell me, what has this place done to you? You look very ... do-mes-ti-ca-ted." He grinned at her.

At last, someone who knew her well enough, loved her enough, to believe that the sight of her in a flour-covered, jam-stained apron was unnatural. She'd almost forgotten such people existed.

Nasan tucked a hand into the crook of her brother's arm. "I am healthy enough, as I said. Come, let me show you my hard-earned skills by finding you and your men something to eat and a place to stay."

Chapter 4

Velizh, June 1536

IT WAS A RELIEF TO GET OUT OF THE FORTRESS, EVEN FOR A short time. The earthen ramparts that supported the log walls and kept invaders at bay had acquired a covering of grass and wildflowers. The air was crisp and clear, not yet shimmering with heat, and a light breeze made Daniil's heavy armor tolerable. The swans had long since left the river to pursue their journey north, but geese and ducks had taken their place (and enlivened many a dinner table). Fortunately for the birds, work kept the peasants and soldiers occupied for much of the week, and the supply wagons had arrived with admirable and unusual regularity. Daniil was glad the swans had moved on; since that day in the woods, he could not imagine shooting one—still less eating one.

This morning he and his small company were hunting larger game. Scouts had returned last night with reports of enemy troop movements to the south, and Daniil had volunteered to find out what he could. Papa had hemmed and hawed, but not for long. He could not afford to show favoritism, even to his own son. He approved the mission, and Daniil thanked him sincerely. He could guess what agreement cost the old man, but he and his troop needed to keep in practice. The drill yard could provide only so much scope for their skills. And someone had to take the risk. Why not he?

So here they were, riding toward the same copse where the swans had intervened to save his life. This time, he would not relax his guard for a moment.

The unexpected arrival of so many visitors upended the cooks' plans for dinner, especially after Nasan ordered the removal of several dishes containing pork. Although the June sun remained in the sky for at least three-quarters of the day, the afternoon was far advanced when Nasan and Maria joined Ogodai and Rafik, his trusted second-in-command, in the Kolychevs' banquet hall. Natalya had promised to attend, but at the last moment, exhausted by the commotion, she withdrew to her sitting room. Not before scolding Nasan for her last-moment changes, however—and in front of Ogodai and Rafik, too! The khan's eyes flashed, and his hands clenched at the insult, but Natalya departed without a word of apology.

In an attempt to balance the demand that young noblewomen not display themselves in large gatherings of men against the need for someone in the Kolychev family to host a visiting khan, Nasan had arranged a small table in an alcove for Maria, herself, her brother, and Rafik. The sons of the two other beys who, with Rafik's father, formed Ogodai's council occupied the high table running the width of the room, together with Ogodai's hundredman and Karim, his third-in-command. From there, they could keep an eye on the assembled warriors and prevent potential disputes from escalating into open conflict. Not that such incidents were common among men who regularly fought as one, but the combined effects of koumiss and weaponry could undo the most careful planning.

From Nasan's perspective, the arrangement offered a real advantage. She and Maria sat on one side of the table, with their backs to the hall. Ogodai and Rafik faced them. Nasan could concentrate on her brother, addressing occasional remarks to the others for courtesy's sake. Ogodai's men could see what went on at the small table, but they could not hear.

Indeed, they seemed entirely satisfied with their own conversation. The dining hall had not rung with this much noise since Nikolai and Daniil departed. In pursuit of Tulpar, Ogodai had left the minimum number of men to guard his camp, and the better part of a hundred warriors filled the room, arranged according to their standing within the horde. Those farthest from the seat of honor wore the sheepskin coats and hats familiar from Nasan's days on the steppe, but she had noticed many silk tunics and fine linen shirts, jeweled hilts and elaborate turbans—raided, no doubt, from their previous owners. Her brother must be taking good care of his people.

As the highest-ranking male present, Ogodai called for silence, then blessed the food while the men raised their palms to the sky. The sonorous rhythm of Arabic rolled past Nasan's ears like water rippling across a stream. Words that spoke of home, words she had not heard since leaving Kazan almost two years ago. She took a deep breath, as if nostalgia had a scent.

Ogodai's "Amen" set off a renewed flurry as warriors raised goblets, speared pieces of mutton and beef with their eating knives, tore off chunks of bread.

And talked. How they talked. A cacophony of Tatar speech, filled with laughter and jokes. Nasan reveled in the noise. Except for the decor, she could have been back in her father's palace or the nomadic camp of her childhood. Not since her wedding had she felt so relaxed, so accepted, in Moscow—except when alone with Daniil, before the accident.

Between mouthfuls, Ogodai shared stories of his wife, Firuza, and their nine-month-old twins—a boy and a girl. For a while, he spoke in Russian for Maria's benefit, switching back and forth between languages to include Rafik as well. Nasan followed his lead. A year ago, she couldn't have kept up with him, but her constant immersion in Russian since her return from Kazan had borne fruit. If one did not count the occasional grammatical mistake—and Ogodai didn't care about such things—she had become as fluent as a native speaker. Nasan loved languages, and that thought gave her pride.

Maria didn't respond to their attempt to make her feel welcome. She greeted Ogodai and Rafik with a nod. Her body trembled when Ogodai blessed the food; she stared at the wooden plate before her as if the mere act of serving it amid Tatars had somehow tainted it. Her expression suggested that she saw her attendance as a kind of penance. Yet she had chosen to come here—insisted, even. Nasan wondered why. If their presence offended Maria, why subject herself to it?

As Maria maintained her silence, Nasan and Ogodai gradually abandoned Russian for Tatar. His twins had entered the world the month after Nasan lost her own baby, so she had yet to visit them. Suppressing an ignoble flash of jealousy at Firuza's good fortune, she demanded every detail about mother and children until her brother held up both hands in surrender. "I can't tell you, *sengel*. They spend their time in the harem. They seem like sturdy infants with good lungs and a fair set of teeth between them. And what of you? When can I expect a nephew or niece?"

She flinched. It still hurt. "There was an accident." Her voice shook, and she stopped to steady it. "I was riding, and a dog ran out in front of Sorkhokhtani. Before I knew what was happening, I was over her head and in a heap on the ground.

The *albasti* took the baby's soul that evening. Daniil left before I recovered."

Even to herself, she sounded woebegone. Ogodai caught her hands in his, and she clung to him, trying to control her tears. "You didn't have an iron talisman?" he asked.

"My mother-in-law doesn't like reminders of my past. I keep even my grandmother doll in the clothes chest since she threatened to have it burned. But I shouldn't have listened to her. I knew better." She spoke even more softly so that Rafik wouldn't hear. "It is all my fault. Everyone agrees about that. No wonder Daniil despises me."

Ogodai straightened, his dark eyes wide with astonishment. "I'm sure he does not."

Nasan blinked, hard, to drive the tears away and leaned forward to whisper once more. "He does. He won't admit it, but he does."

"You're supposed to speak Russian," Maria said from her right.

Nasan pulled away from her brother. "Forgive me," she said in Russian, wondering what Maria imagined she had missed.

"We can't discuss it here." Ogodai still spoke in their mother tongue. "Let's talk about it later. I'm sure you're wrong."

She nodded and sat straight. He responded with an encouraging smile and switched back to his Russian/Tatar mix. "Cheer up, *sengel*. I have a gift for you. For your mother-in-law, too, but I'll present that to her myself. Rafik, where's my package?"

Rafik handed over a leather bag, from which Ogodai pulled what looked like a tasseled pillow and handed it to Nasan. "The top one is from my wife; I thought you might prefer the second. But we deliver both with love."

A present: how exciting! Nasan cradled the wrapper in her hand. The rich gold brocade—smooth and soft, fragrant with rosewater and hints of sandalwood—was itself a thing of glory, but when she turned back the flap, her mouth dropped open. A decorated leather bridle and two small books lay within. She admired the bridle, soft brown with square and triangular insets in red and yellow, then picked up the top book and examined it. Geometric shapes and tiny flowers intertwined around the front cover as if in a garden, opening to reveal beds of flowing script; deer and rabbits romped among the greenery; rough-edged paper brushed her seeking fingers. She lifted the book and sniffed it. The smell carried her back to the library in Kasimov, in Kazan—and even before then, to her mother's cedar chest and the precious volumes it protected from the rigors of nomadic life. "*The Divan* of Hafiz," she said, reading the script on the cover. "Firuza sent me this? It's so beautiful!" Firuza, herself a poet, picked the verses she recommended with care. Nasan could hardly wait to explore her gift.

Ogodai plucked the book from her hands and opened it, flipping through the pages until he found a small slip of paper. "She asked me to read you this one, so you would know that she feels for you, so far from your home." He paused, then read the lines in Persian.

Nasan translated them in her head—not without effort. She had last read Persian before leaving Kasimov for her wedding, and the phrases kept tangling with Russian. But the verses had the exquisite simplicity that marks great poetry, and as Ogodai reached the essential middle, her memory revived. She had heard this poem before.

"Awake, my dear," he was saying, "Be kind to your sleeping heart. Take it out into the vast fields of Light / And let it breathe."

Nasan wanted to hug him again—and the absent Firuza. Her sleeping heart. That was just how she felt inside, as if her heart had followed her baby into death and lay waiting for the summer sun and gentle rains of love to revive it. She waited for him to finish before saying, in Russian, "Perfect. Thank you. Such gorgeous verses. I can't wait to read more."

On her far side, Maria harrumphed. Ogodai glanced her way, then closed the book and handed it to his sister. "Our pleasure. Now look at the other one."

The other one. The book he'd picked out for her. Nasan returned *The Divan* to its brocade holder and extracted its companion.

Here arabesques curled in lines of pale green etched into the leather against a rich blue background. She ran a finger over the bumps and hollows, extending the moment of discovery. Hands trembling, she turned back the cover and gasped. An exquisite miniature half the size of her palm glittered in the center of the page, brilliant reds and blues and greens portraying two young men—one a prince, the other a beggar—the first of whom clasped the hands of a moon-faced princess with round, dark eyes. "It's so lovely!"

She skimmed the pages, where one illustration after another lured her into the story. Delighted, she showed a page to Maria, who stared for a moment in what could have been awe before turning her face aside.

Nasan returned to the title page. The letters above the miniature used Arabic forms, but the words were Tatar. And she recognized the title—a favorite among the ladies of Kazan. *"The Tale of Sayf al-Muluk,"* she read. "Oh, Ogodai!"

"You like it?" Laughter lurked beneath his words. She saw that her reaction pleased him as much as his gift pleased her. "The heroine is not a warrior, alas, but she does save the hero. Naturally, I thought of you."

A lovely bridle for Sorkhokhtani, two new books—poetry and adventure—and the greatest gift of all: understanding. Her day gleamed with new promise.

To her right, Maria sniffed. "It's unwomanly to read books. Especially *pagan* books."

Nasan was still searching for the right response when Ogodai placed a restraining hand on her wrist, looked at Maria, and asked, "Why?"

"A wife should sew altar cloths, manage the household, and please her husband." Maria compressed her lips in a prim expression and folded her hands.

Nasan glanced at her brother, who winked at her. Maria, her gaze focused on the middle distance, missed the wink. Nasan waited. What would he say?

"Suppose her husband likes women who read?" Ogodai's voice conveyed casual curiosity, but Rafik's snort gave him away. Rafik didn't speak Russian fluently, but he could understand simple sentences.

"No man wants a wife who reads." Maria clenched her hands on the table, as if the question outraged her. "What good does it do?"

Ogodai regarded her steadily, his long body relaxed, a thoughtful expression on his face, as if he took this absurd question seriously. "Well," he said after a pause, "don't you want to find out what your Holy Scriptures say?"

"Our priests tell us that!"

Ogodai raised an eyebrow. "Suppose one gets it wrong? How would you know?"

"They are men of God." Maria's shock was audible. "Not heathen barbarians."

"Like me?" Ogodai's eyes narrowed. He didn't raise his voice, but it acquired a hard edge that Nasan knew from experience Maria would do well to heed.

"Let me tell you, Lady," he said, leaning forward so she could not avoid his gaze, "that every member of my family, male *and* female, learns in childhood to read, to write, to cipher, to appreciate literature and art and architecture and history. We recite the Koran in Arabic and treasure the heritage of the great Sufi poets. We master the arts of diplomacy so that we can trade with Cathay and Hindustan. We even learn your *barbarous* Russian tongue so that we can communicate with you on our own terms. To do less would shame us—and to expect less of yourself shames you."

Nasan bit her tongue. She wanted to cheer. Such a set-down made up for *weeks* of needling. Indeed, Maria looked ready to burst.

"I am not shamed," Maria choked out. Red stained her cheeks. "I don't care what you think of me."

Ogodai shrugged, the tight set leaving his mouth. "Then that makes two of us, doesn't it?"

As if the confrontation hadn't happened, he turned to Nasan. "Tell me about your mother-in-law. How does she? You said she lives, but her strength is failing. What does that mean, from day to day? She didn't feel well enough to preside at this gathering, I see."

Nasan followed his lead. "Maria has been tending to her," she said, to assuage Maria's temper. "But Mama-in-law does not thrive. And she has begun to talk of death as if she anticipates it cannot be long delayed. I fear she is right."

"Maria tends to her, not you? What about that library of yours?"

"Mama-in-law does not care for my medicines." She tried to keep the bitterness out of her voice, but Ogodai's quirked eyebrow suggested that she hadn't succeeded.

"Someone else who doesn't want women to read?" he asked.

"Just so," Nasan told him, ignoring Maria's muttering to her right. "Despite that, I have tried everything I can find. Wood sorrel, pulmonaria, valerian, hawthorn, ginger, purple nut sedge, pomegranates. Maria doses her, too. Not everything at once, of course."

"By the Prophet (may he rest in glory)," Ogodai said, "I hope not. The two of you will kill the poor woman through kindness." The twinkle in his eyes faded. "But she suffers, and that grieves me to hear. You can't dissuade her from this pilgrimage of hers?"

"Hah," Maria muttered.

One point on which she and Nasan agreed. "Alas, no," Nasan said. "Her heart is set on it, and Father Job thinks her faith will sustain her long enough to complete it. Even if he's wrong, it does no good to argue with her. She turns red and pants and catches her chest as if it pains her, which it probably does."

Ogodai drank from his goblet, then studied the swirling liquid, a contemplative frown creasing his brow.

"I don't look forward to it, though," Nasan told him. "The thought of ten weeks on a boat makes me cringe." She blushed and studied her hands. "That's small of me, I know."

"Ten weeks on a boat? Why? You could do it in half that time in a carriage. Less on horseback."

"She has to travel by water. We'll be lucky if we manage seven miles a day."

"But if she won't let you tend her, why insist that you twiddle your thumbs on a boat?" Maria yelped, but Ogodai paid no attention to her. He tapped his fingertip on the table, a sure sign that he was considering possibilities. "It makes much more sense for you to ride ahead and prepare the estate for her arrival. You still have Sorkhokhtani, don't you? I brought the bridle for her."

Nasan thought of Sorkhokhtani, her beautiful sorrel mare, and how wonderful it would be to ride, day after day—however out of practice she had become in recent months. A dozen rounds of the courtyard every evening did not prepare her for one full day in the saddle, never mind ten. "I do, although she gets so little exercise I might do better to let her travel west with you."

"Nonsense. Take her north."

"But Mama-in-law," Nasan sputtered.

Maria rested her elbows on the table, despite the danger posed by cups and food. "Yes, exactly. Mama-in-law will not approve of even a wild woman like this"—she waved a dismissive hand at Nasan—"riding off on her own."

Wild woman? I haven't left the house for months!

"You could ride with her," Rafik suggested. Nasan glared at him, and he flushed.

"I don't ride." Maria sprang to her feet, almost spitting the words. "Good women don't ride." Nasan jumped up, too, overturning their shared bench in her haste.

Ogodai clasped her wrist again. "You don't ride?" he asked Maria. "You don't read? Do you do *anything* useful?"

"Of course," Maria said with an angry sob. "How can you be so mean to me when the only reason I came here was for *her* sake?" She pointed at Nasan, then ran from the dining hall.

"Shrew," Ogodai said. "You don't need her assistance to dine with your brother. Why's she still here, anyway? Can't her father find her another husband?"

Rafik chortled. "Poor husband."

"Indeed," Ogodai said. "Who wants a bad-tempered wife who can't ride?" He gestured at the high table. "Leave us for a moment, Rafik. There are matters I must discuss with my sister." Rafik departed, leaving Nasan alone with her brother. Ogodai patted the bench, and she sat next to him.

"I couldn't tell you everything in the courtyard." Ogodai dipped a piece of bread into the mutton stew in front of him and held it, dripping gravy, over the bowl. "It's not an accident that we lost track of Tulpar in Moscow. He's up to something."

Nasan felt her own crust drop from her fingers. It disappeared into the thick brown liquid, leaving lazy ripples as evidence of its presence. "What?"

"We captured one of his men," Ogodai said. "If he told us the truth, our brother has opened negotiations with the Russians—and his contact is your so dear sister-in-law's father."

"Koshkin?" Nasan didn't know which news surprised her more, that Tulpar might switch sides or that Maria's father still had anything to do with the court. "How? He's not in Moscow. Grand Princess Elena sent him to Vologda, to get him out of the way. That's why Maria's still here, because no one wants to marry her while her father's in disgrace."

"She should keep him in chains. Elena, I mean. I would." Ogodai waved his goblet, as if emphasizing his point. "It's not safe to leave a man like that running around. She locks people up on the smallest excuse: her brother-in-law, her uncle, even her own mother and brothers. Why spare him?"

"Elena doesn't lock them up. The boyars do." Ogodai looked skeptical, and Nasan elaborated. "My husband explained it to me. The Moscow nobles arrested the brother-in-law, Yuri Ivanovich, because they feared his boyars would take their positions if he came to power. The grand princess's family worried them for the same reason. The gossips say Elena sacrificed her relatives to protect herself and her sons."

When Ogodai acknowledged this with a nod, she went on. "Koshkin has powerful supporters at court. We had no real proof of his wrongdoing, so they managed to persuade the others to appoint him to a prestigious but conveniently distant post. My husband says that's how the government always handles such things. If Koshkin is negotiating with Tulpar, though, maybe he sees it as a way to secure his return to Moscow."

"Tulpar will not travel to Vologda, for sure."

Nasan sipped cherry juice, savoring the tart sweetness flowing across her tongue. "But will Tulpar switch sides? I thought he despised the Russians."

Ogodai frowned at his cup. "So did I. But if Islam-Girei falls, he has few alternatives. I don't blame him for seeking a place among the Russians. Why he must first threaten me, though ..."

She tipped her head to one side, considering. "He would have preferred a place on the steppe, I suppose, but you stopped him. He took the only road left to him. If he had sense, he would apologize to *Ata*. Make peace. But from what you tell me of him, he would see that as a defeat."

"Yes." Ogodai ate soup in a contemplative manner. Nasan fished the sodden bread from her bowl with a spoon and chewed it, trying to recall what Father Job had told her of their destination. Her brother's unexpected arrival could not be an accident. Was this the sign she had waited for since she had watched the swans fly north?

"Maybe I can help you," she said after a while.

Ogodai jerked his head up. "You? How?"

He had not said impossible. He was listening. "We're going to the White Lake. The family owns an estate not far from St. Cyril's Monastery. Mama-in-law wants to pray there—and at a place called Ferapontovo. Father Job told me it is no more than a few days' journey from Vologda." Excitement rushed through her as she glimpsed the possibility of freedom, if only for a month or so. "If I rode there, while Mama-in-law went by boat—"

"You would have time to find out about Koshkin," Ogodai finished for her. "The men I would send with you, I mean. Since you will be in the area—yes, it might work."

He had agreed—not to everything but to enough. Who cared whether she or the men had the fun of spying on Koshkin? The absence of constant supervision would itself be a source of joy. "Can you convince Mama-in-law? She won't listen to me."

"Of course. How large is your escort?" He beckoned to Rafik, who was exchanging drinks and jokes with the hundredman and the other beys' sons at the high table.

"Fifteen men borrowed from next door." Nasan screwed up her nose in response to her brother's raised eyebrow. She didn't need him to point out that fifteen half-trained men-at-arms did not an escort make. "Ours mostly went west with Papa-in-law, and those that stayed must guard this house while we're gone."

Rafik arrived in response to his leader's signal, and Ogodai said, "Split our forces. Pick the fifty most reliable warriors we have and tell them they are responsible for the safety of the khan's sister. They are to escort her to her mother-in-law's estate in the north, then await my orders."

Rafik acknowledged the command with a dip of his head and went to fulfill his task. Ogodai turned back to his sister. "Most of the escort will go with you; the women will be safe enough on the boat with their fifteen guards; there are no pirates on those upper stretches of the Volga. From the estate, the warriors can scout the area, see what information they can gather in Vologda. Meanwhile, I will go west."

Nasan gripped her hands together under the table. Was that the thrum of swans' wings she heard, or the beat of her own heart?

Ogodai tapped her elbow when she didn't reply. "It's a good idea, and not only because it helps me discover what our half-brother is up to. It's time we reminded your mother-in-law who you are. A daughter of Genghis is neither a disobedient child nor a pincushion destined to suffer the jabs of an ill-mannered girl. Your marriage raised the prestige of this clan. Disrespect shown to you is disrespect for our whole lineage."

"I hope she will listen."

"She'll listen. Who dares gainsay a khan?" Ogodai burst out laughing, and she couldn't help but join in. He had read her mother-in-law right: if anything could convince Natalya, a demand from a man equal in rank to Russia's royal family would. Even if that man was no older than her beloved son.

"So," Ogodai said, "now that's settled, where do I look for my brother?"

Chapter 5

WHERE TO LOOK FOR DANIIL? IT WAS A SIMPLE ENOUGH question. Nasan saw no reason for her mouth to dry or her cheeks to burn. Yet she didn't want to confess that what seemed so obvious to her and to Ogodai—that a husband would send regular messages to his wife—did not strike Daniil as the least bit necessary.

Ogodai watched her, hawklike, eyes bright under his dark fringe of hair.

"I'm not sure," she stammered. "When he left here in July, he was heading for Borovsk to join Prince Andrei of Staritsa. From there, he traveled to Smolensk in September. We expected him in time for the Blessing of the Waters on Epiphany—and again for Easter, but the army refused to grant him leave. Instead, it transferred him to Sebezh. Wherever that is." Natalya had been upset, because the men had missed the celebration of the Resurrection and the vigil that preceded it. Nasan had simply hoped Daniil would return.

If he wanted to. If he'd remained as distant as when he left, seeing him would have been unbearable. And she couldn't shake the fear that he had *not* wanted to, with the failure to get leave being an acceptable excuse.

"Sebezh." Ogodai directed his frown at the footed cup he twirled with his right hand. "You mean Ivangorod, I think. The new one, on Lake Sebezh. The Russians built a fortress there last year."

"Probably," Nasan agreed. "That sounds right."

Ogodai continued to frown at his cup. "The Lithuanians tried to capture the fortress in February and failed miserably. Daniil had his hands full, I expect. But he survived?"

"He must have." Nasan shivered. Suppose she had lost her husband without even hearing of this specific danger? Was such a fate not what she feared their failure to communicate Natalya's illness would do to Daniil and his father? "A courier arrived before Lent, and another after that, with the news that he and Papa-in-law couldn't join us. He said nothing about any attack, though."

"Didn't want to frighten you, I suppose." Ogodai stared straight at her, as if reading her expression. "But you've heard nothing since Easter?"

She forgot, when separated from her brother, how quickly he picked up the hidden emotions of others. It was comforting and disconcerting at the same time. "Not since the Feast ..."

She stopped. Ogodai was Muslim, as she herself had been until her marriage. The Feast of the Annunciation would mean little to him. "Not since late March. Mama-in-law insists it's normal—and it's true, Nikolai Borisovich sends messengers, too, and those seldom—but it seems strange to me."

She stopped there. Even to a brother, she found it difficult to confess her fears that other women preoccupied Daniil's mind and kept him warm at night.

"From Daniil?" Ogodai said. "It's not strange. He wouldn't write if he stood at death's door."

Death's door? Nasan released a sobbing breath. She couldn't help herself.

"I'm a fool." Her brother clasped her fingers, then released them. "Trust me, *sengel.* He's not at death's door. Someone would have carried that news. I mean he doesn't think about letters. Nor does his father. They can't write, so most of the time, they forget others can."

She nodded, unable to talk. Tears traced a path along her cheeks, and she wiped them away with her palm. Daniil didn't think about letters. Daniil didn't think about *her*.

Ogodai patted her hand. "Be still, Nasan. The man adores you. I'm sure he's cursing every hard-nosed clerk who refuses to authorize his leave. It's the bane of military service, being at someone else's beck and call from dawn to dusk."

How did he *do* that—read her mind? It was uncanny.

"I know," Nasan said, and she did. Daniil had told her more than once how he envied Ogodai, who as khan answered to no one except his council.

Ogodai flicked her wrist with his finger and thumb. "What's really upsetting you—the child? Lady Diliara tells me it happens often. She lost several. We were lucky, my wife and I. You will have other chances. The *albasti* is vicious but not omnipotent."

There was no point in dissembling—even if she wanted to, which she did not. "He stayed away from me for weeks before he left. He said he did it for my sake, but his mother told me God confers children only on parents who have earned them through good deeds. She thinks the sun shines to light my husband's path, so who but I can have failed to perform enough good deeds? Of course, I don't believe her, but I did not keep the *albasti* away. And I fear that Daniil *does* believe her, or why has he become so cold?"

Ogodai's fingers tightened around hers, and he frowned. "A harsh view of God, indeed. But suppose Daniil told the truth, that he stayed away to let you heal?" The humorous spark lit his eyes once more. "From my long acquaintance with him, he must have regarded that as a considerable sacrifice. And he does have a few sins on his conscience, you know, whatever his mother believes."

A flicker of hope warmed Nasan's heart. Could he be right? Had she misjudged Daniil based on her own fears and his mother's clumsy explanations?

"You could send him a letter," Ogodai said.

"He can't read." But the flicker of hope strengthened into a flame. A letter. To remind him of her love. After almost a year, surely they could talk of that dreadful day that had unleashed a river of anguish between them. If she judged him for not sending her a message, should she not make the effort herself?

Except that she couldn't write in Russian.

Ogodai said nothing, just released her hand. And she saw the answer. "You would read it to him."

"If you permit," he said. "Once I speak with *Ata*, I hope to consult with Daniil before heading home. But even if I have no time for that, I can have the letter transcribed into Russian and ensure that it reaches him."

"Thank you," she said. "It's the perfect solution. I will write it this evening and give it to you before you leave. I will include news of his mother, but please tell him the whole if you can. The messenger we sent hasn't returned."

"I will." He drew small x's on the table with the tip of his knife, as if marking an invisible map. "So, he may be in Sebezh. His father will have heard, surely. Where is he?"

"Torzhok, most recently. I don't know where that is, either. And he may have left, too, because our message went unanswered, as I said." She broke a chunk of bread into small pieces and arranged them before her on the table. One soaked up Ogodai's droplets, and she watched it darken. "Both messages, to him and to my husband."

"And you sent them when?" Ogodai changed his x's to small circles, using a spill of dark-red juice as ink.

"Two months ago. The courier hasn't come back." Had the Lithuanians killed him—on the way there or during his return?

A possibility she should have considered sooner. Why assume that Daniil had made no effort to reach her, just because no message had arrived?

Despair had blinded her. It was good that she had decided to write the letter.

But if life there was so dangerous, what of Ogodai? "You needn't go," she blurted out.

Ogodai looked at her with astonishment. "Why not? I want to talk to *Ata*, and he can't leave Vyazma."

Still thinking of the courier, she said, "Your first responsibility is to Firuza and the babies. Suppose you die on the road?"

"I could die on a raid," he pointed out. "In battle. Of disease. Through the enmity of others. By accident. And if none of those, I will surely die in my bed, of old age."

But he must have understood, for he laid his knife tip on the back of her hand, leaving a cherry dot. "I won't die, dear one. Nor will Daniil. Not soon, anyway. Don't worry."

She patted his cheek, more touched than she could say.

"Our first task is to find him." Ogodai stroked his chin. "I'll start with the Military Service Chancellery. They keep lists of who's deployed where. Pray they don't hold it against me that Father sent me off to secure the horde a year ago and hasn't called me back into service. Which of the Moscow clerks owes me a favor, I wonder?"

Nasan had no answer, but he didn't wait for one.

"Meanwhile ..." He glanced across the hall, where his second-in-command and the hundredman remained in intense discussion. "Rafik, when you were with Bahadur Bey, did you ever raid in the west?"

"No, Khan." Rafik pressed his right hand over his heart to indicate his sincerity. "It's too far into enemy territory, and the Crimeans object to our poaching on lands they regard as their own."

"The hundredman knows the way to Vyazma. Get directions from him tonight, so that you can stay in contact with me. You will head my sister's escort, and when you reach the White Lake, she will tell you what to do next." Rafik signaled agreement, and Ogodai turned back to Nasan. "How soon can you leave?"

Tomorrow? Never? Next week? But Natalya faded more with each hour that passed. She had to conserve the strength she had, or she would not survive the journey. Best to get her on the road as soon as possible.

"Tomorrow," Nasan said. "If we can convince Mama-in-law of this plan."

"I'll have her eating out of my hand," Ogodai said. "I told you that already. Otherwise, fair enough. You heard that, men? We leave tomorrow." He smiled at his anxious sister. "Where can we pitch our tents for tonight?"

After dinner, Nasan escorted Ogodai to her mother-in-law's sitting room, at the edge of the women's quarters but still within the main section of the house. Maria sat at Natalya's side, embroidering a halo on the altar cloth she had been stitching since Nasan's marriage. Gold thread refracted the late afternoon sunlight in soft, shimmering hues; the heavy linen of the cloth fell across Maria's bronze skirts, but most of the images remained hidden.

Ogodai presented his promised gift: another brocade bag that opened to reveal an exquisite jewelry box patterned in inlaid wood and lined with scarlet silk. Natalya sighed with delight. Maria stared, her lips parted, then extended a finger to stroke the long brown tassel that closed the soft peach silk. When she noticed Nasan gazing at her, Maria flushed and pulled her hand back.

Natalya gestured toward the room's one chair, usually reserved for her husband. Ogodai bowed before accepting her invitation to sit, then proceeded to charm Natalya as if he wooed old ladies every day.

Nasan, watching, wondered at his self-assurance. He had grown up a lot since his marriage. Despite his joke about no one gainsaying a khan, he did not at first assume the mantle of authority with Natalya but instead coaxed her along the path he wanted her to take. Maria, perhaps reluctant to engage with him again after their earlier confrontation, sat silent in her corner. Her ivory needle flicked in and out through the cloth, her prim demeanor and her skill an implicit reproach to her sister-in-law, who regarded sewing as a craft invented specifically to torment her.

So the meeting went until Ogodai asked that Maria be excused. Cloth, thread, needle clattered to the floor, taking Maria's pious expression with them.

"Why me and not her?" She pointed at Nasan. Natalya uttered a sharp word of reproach.

Ogodai drew himself up and pinned her in her seat with a quelling stare. "Because what I have to say is not your business."

"Go, Maria," Natalya said, "and remember your manners. The khan is our guest." Maria, glowering, went.

"Lady," Ogodai said. "My sister tells me that, despite your illness, you plan to undertake a long journey without an adequate escort. My brother"—he meant Daniil—"wouldn't wish you to travel under such conditions. Since you prefer the care offered by Lady Maria, there is no reason for my sister to accompany you on the boat. For her sake and my brother's,

I will send fifty of my men to guard you, but I insist that my sister ride ahead and prepare your estate."

"Ride ahead?" Natalya sounded dazed. "With a troop of warriors? It would besmirch her husband's honor!"

"On the contrary," Ogodai said, "it is what your son would want for her. Rafik and his men will guard her with their lives. Unless you prefer to remain in Moscow?"

Natalya hesitated. Her eyes strayed to the icons in the corner, and her fingers traced the line of a cross against her skirt. "No." She raised her chin. "I must make this pilgrimage."

Ogodai's tone, so far smooth and coaxing, hardened. "Then do so under the terms I offer. They are more than generous. Our mother trained my sister well. She will have no difficulty fulfilling this task. You can send a woman with her if you fear for her honor, but I assure you, my men will protect her."

"Could she not ride alongside us?" Natalya asked. Her voice quavered, and Nasan allowed herself to hope.

Ogodai drew his brows together in a slight frown. "As far as Dmitrov, of course. But the roads don't follow the river. You would often be apart for days at a time. Safer to send her on ahead, with a proper escort, and she can return to meet you when you reach the debarkation point."

Natalya crossed herself and muttered prayers, as if seeking divine guidance. Nasan clasped her hands and said a few prayers of her own, mostly to the ancestors, that they might grant her this boon. A memory of the swans, flying high and free, called to her.

At last, Natalya spoke. "Her husband left her in my charge. Poor health does not excuse negligence, and I answer to God and to my son, not to you."

Ogodai leaned forward, elbows resting on his knees. "We all answer to God, Lady, but I swear to you: your son would tell you to accept my offer. I guarantee her safety—and yours. I will not break my word."

Natalya hesitated again, but the power of royal male authority triumphed, as Ogodai had predicted. "Very well, Khan," she said. "I will do as you wish."

Assured of victory, Ogodai allowed his rare smile to escape, and Nasan could see Natalya melting in the glint that lit the khan's dark eyes.

Her own anxiety dissolved in a flood of relief.

As evening approached, Daniil and his troop returned to the fortress—tired, hungry, exultant. He had lost no men, brought them back with only a flesh wound or two, and established that trouble was in fact brewing in the vicinity of Vitebsk, a day's journey to the southwest. Better yet, his warriors encircled three disgruntled Lithuanian mercenaries, bound and seated facing their horses' tails to discourage escape, reins held by members of his own force.

Papa would be pleased. Daniil and his men had had an excellent day.

Koshkin waved an expansive arm at his steward as the man ushered Prince Vasily's returning messenger into the hall. Surely the courier bore the summons Koshkin had known must come. "Prepare a room," he ordered. "See to his needs." He gestured at the messenger. "I will join you shortly for the midday meal. Leave the scroll here."

The messenger bowed himself out; the steward followed him. Koshkin shut the door to his office and raised both hands to the heavens. After two years of isolation in this contemptible northern fortress, his return to court life was—had to be!—on the horizon.

His hands trembled as he gazed at the paper he held. He hardly dared open it, lest its contents disappoint him. At the same time, he could not wait. He must learn the truth without delay.

He unfurled the scroll and studied the neat scribal script. The letters blurred before his eyes. He blinked until they cleared, then took a long, shaky breath.

His patience had been rewarded. In the name of Grand Prince Ivan and his mother, Grand Princess Elena, Prince Vasily Shuisky summoned his humble servant, Fyodor Mikhailovich Koshkin, to Moscow.

At last. Thanks to the machinations of those in power and the vagaries of a wandering Tatar sultan, Koshkin's long exile had ended. He was going home.

Between the village peasants and the men recruited by Stenka, Semyon's bandits numbered a solid thirty. He couldn't conceal a flush of pride as he surveyed them and their haul—the latest from a dozen or more successful attacks. The locals had begun to whisper his name. Word had it that mothers kept naughty children in line with threats that Semyon Severyanin would get them. By the time the authorities in Vologda woke up and paid attention, his men would have acquired a reputation for invincibility. And Semyon would have the gold he needed to pursue his real target—his relatives.

"Good work, Stenka," he said. "Divide the spoils and bring mine to my hut. And tell that slut Tanka to report here after supper."

Stenka signaled agreement, and Semyon strolled toward his home, admiring the sunset reflected in the rippling water of the lake. Although he had yet to find his bandit queen, Tanka—lusty, yielding, pretty, and possessed of an impressive imagination for things physical—was a candidate worth considering for the part.

Until his ideal woman came along.

With victory won, Nasan returned to overseeing the final preparations for the women's departure until the setting sun at last signaled the approach of night. By then, Natalya had long since retired to bed, with Maria in attendance. Nasan welcomed the opportunity to finish her chores in peace.

At last, she had a chance to escape to her own room. She pulled out her prayer rug and followed the chanting from the tents in the courtyard as best she could under the circumstances, glad to have a voice leading the sunset service for once. When the prayers ended, she retrieved her grandmother doll from the chest that protected it from prying eyes and arranged it on her dressing table. She needed inspiration from the spirits. Her desire to reach out to Daniil warred with fear that he wouldn't respond and a certain reluctance to reveal the extent of her pain, even to her beloved brother. It would take the wisdom of a divine ancestor to decide what to write.

From a separate compartment within the chest, she selected a piece of paper, a quill, and a small pot filled with thick black ink. The evening sun still gave enough light for her to see, and the dressing table made an acceptable writing surface. Nasan settled herself on the small padded bench before it and stared at the empty page.

What to write to Daniil, after so much time and in a way that would embarrass neither herself, her husband, nor her brother when Ogodai read it aloud? Worse, if Ogodai did decide to have the letter transcribed, what would convey her message without alerting the chattering clerks who would repeat her words to Daniil?

Forgive me—that came easily. *I never meant to cause you harm, still less to injure the life we made together. If I could, I would undo that day.*

What else? Simple things worked best in such moments, and in any event she felt tears pricking her eyes, ready to slip down her cheeks and splatter on the precious paper, turning the ink into flowing smudges that would defy the most skilled interpreter.

Nasan placed the quill on the paper and backed away, searching for a linen cloth to press against her cheeks. Once they were dry, she returned to her impromptu desk.

I love you, she wrote, forming the letters as fast as she could, desperate to outrace the tears circling in preparation for their next onslaught. *I miss you. I fear for your safety. And your mother is ill. Her heart troubles her, and she may not long endure. Please send me a message. Ogodai will ensure that it reaches me.*

She signed her name—her real name—and waited for the ink to dry. When she felt certain it would not stain, she rolled the paper into a scroll, tied it with a red silk ribbon, and laid it on the dressing table, ready to give to her brother in the morning.

Chapter 6

"THE WALLS RISE WELL," DANIIL SAID TO HIS FATHER, WHO stood beside him in the rightmost gate tower of the half-built Velizh fortress. The road opened behind them, crossing the artisans' and trading quarter, as yet unprotected by palisades. But the workmen had already completed the first layer of the fortress, together with its supportive ramparts and four of its eight towers. Stones lay piled against the riverbank, ready for use in diverting water to the moat. The air still rang with the whistle and thump of axes, but the bustle of carts and dirt-filled baskets had ceased to add to the din. Before long, the sounds of men at drill would replace the frenzy of the builders.

And none too soon. In the far distance, Daniil saw a small troop of horsemen riding hard for the fortress. Couriers from his own side? Scouts for the enemy? Too easy to forget, amid this loud but rewarding endeavor, that Russia remained a nation at war, facing powerful foes eager to burn the brand-new Velizh fortress to the ground.

"Yes, indeed," his father said. "We'll meet the schedule, I believe. Work on the wall walk and its roof will begin next week, and once that's done, we can flood the ditch and raise the fence around the trading quarter. At the moment, they're helpless out there."

Daniil acknowledged this point with a nod. "Who are they?" He indicated the onrushing soldiers with his chin.

The small troop had reached the river and was riding along the far side, as if searching for a ford or bridge. Steel helmets—pointed tips, chased decorations on the nose pieces—glittered as they passed. The men rode with short stirrups on good Arab horses, bow cases and quivers slung over their shoulders. Not Lithuanians or Poles, but the Russians had other enemies. The Crimean Tatars, most notably, who supported the Lithuanians whenever the Polish king outbid the Russian ruler, as he had for the last few years.

"Tatars?" Nikolai asked. He, too, must have noticed the helmets and the stirrups.

"No turbans," Daniil said. The troop's fur-trimmed coats, although differing in color, shared a style. "Ours, don't you think?"

The warriors found the ford and crossed it, bringing them within reach of the trading quarter.

"Yes, I agree. Let's find out who they are and what they want." Nikolai led the way from the tower, descending the wooden ladder with an agility Daniil could only admire. God send him such energy when he reached his father's age.

They hadn't long to wait. Less than half an hour later, the new arrivals had conveyed the gist of the messages carried from the court in Moscow. By the orders of the grand prince's government, the army in Velizh should prepare to attack. Expect instructions on where and when soon, but institute full drill tomorrow morning, in preparation for the arrival of Prince Ivan Barbashin and his fellow generals within the week.

Daniil didn't object to seeing his reprieve from active combat end. The new orders did not surprise him, and the recent raid had reminded him that action suited him better than inaction. But the change did mean that his hopes for leave must be postponed—again.

Despite the intense preparations, the moment of departure arrived before Nasan was ready for it. She had not closed her eyes, it seemed, before the clang of weaponry and horse tackle and the sounds of male voices woke her. Fearing attack, she jumped to her feet, so fast that dizziness forced her to grab the wall for support. She was halfway to the window before the call to morning prayer reminded her that, although her brother and the beys' sons slept in the house, Ogodai's men had pitched their tents in the courtyard. Weak with relief, she collapsed onto the window seat and rested her forehead on her knees. The sounds of prayer rose and fell around her.

By the time the service ended, she had recovered enough to dress. Normally, she would summon a maid to help, but today she wanted no prying eyes. A quick search of the clothes chest uncovered felt trousers and boots—old enough for comfort but new enough not to cause comment—and a fine linen tunic with embroidered wristlets. She put these on while considering what else to wear. Boys' clothes would be safer than her usual attire, allowing her to blend in among the escort rather than stand out. But the sight would send Natalya into an apoplexy. Rather than risk a demand to abandon riding altogether, Nasan stashed the boys' clothes in a saddlebag for later use and selected a calf-length robe of blue silk banded and trimmed with scarlet and a pointed hat with a white gauze veil attached to its tip. Gifts from her mother on the occasion of her wedding, the clothes would satisfy Natalya's sense of what was appropriate to their station, and the veil would protect Nasan from the dust and the many biting insects she could expect to encounter on her journey. An application of herbal cream before donning the veil would help too. She pushed the small jar of salve into a pouch attached to her sash for use on the road.

She added a jeweled dagger next to the pouch. A smaller, more serviceable knife went into her boot. Her bow and quiver she set aside, intending to slip them to Ogodai or Rafik on her way out. She stared with longing at her sword, but unlike the bow and quiver it was not easily replaced if lost, and it seemed unlikely that she would need it. Better to leave it here. No doubt one of the escort would lend her a sword if commanded.

She braided and secured her hair, arranged the hat and its veil, slipped Sorkhokhtani's new bridle and Daniil's letter into her sleeve, then picked up the bow and quiver and headed for the stables.

When she reached the courtyard, she found her brother organizing his men. It was a good day for traveling: overcast but no threat of rain, warm but not hot. Servants flitted back and forth, for the most part giving the Tatars a wide berth, but Natalya, Maria, and Father Job had not yet come down. Nasan handed over the letter, which Ogodai tucked into his sash, then the bow and quiver.

"Ask Rafik to hold them for me, will you?" she said. "I won't need them until we get beyond Dmitrov. But after that, they may prove useful, if only for hunting."

Ogodai accepted the weapons and passed them to the nearest warrior. "Take them to Rafik and tell him they belong to my sister." To Nasan he added, "What next?"

So many things. Too many to count, but one was paramount. "Sorkhokhtani," she said, "and something to eat. Have you broken your fast?"

Ogodai caught her arm as she turned, pulling her back to face him. "Stay. You're a khan's daughter, not a servant. One of my men will saddle your horse. Where's your new bridle?"

When Nasan pulled it from her sleeve and gave it to him, he tapped the nearest warrior on the shoulder. "The sorrel mare with the black mane in the Kolychev stables. Get her ready and bring her here."

"Yes, Khan." The man bowed, took the bridle from Ogodai's outstretched hand, and left.

"Come and break your fast with me," Ogodai said.

Nasan tucked her hand through his arm and let him lead her to the largest tent. It felt good to be treated, for once, as a person worthy of respect.

Sorkhokhtani sidled and shook her head, resplendent in its new bridle. Nasan held the horse firm while their escort assisted Natalya into the enclosed carriage she would share with Maria and the two female servants selected to accompany them on the first leg of their journey. Vanka, the servant whom Nasan still thought of as the man who tried to shoot the swans, stood ready to mount the sturdy horse already harnessed to their conveyance. Father Job would soon take his place in a smaller cart, a simple vehicle that he could drive himself, but for the moment he stood near Natalya, talking quietly. He said something that made her laugh, and for a moment her tense face relaxed and she looked like her old self. Nasan tucked the hand-sized icon of the Holy Martyr Natalya of Nicomedia that her mother-in-law had given her into the top of the closest saddlebag. If necessary, she could produce it as a token proving her right to occupy the family home. The baggage cart had already departed for the White Lake region, where its drivers would unpack the goods in preparation for the family's arrival.

The courtyard swarmed with servants bowing before their mistress, seeking a blessing, calling on the Almighty to grant the travelers a safe journey. They must wonder if they would ever see her again. And what of Natalya, leaving her home of thirty years for what might be the last time?

Nasan's attendant—Vera, one of the Christianized Tatars whom Bulat Khan had hired for his daughter six months after her wedding—rode up to join her mistress. "We are ready," she said. "The traveling bags are stowed, and we can leave as soon as Lady Natalya decrees."

Hearing an echo of her own impatience, Nasan smiled. Two glorious days of freedom beckoned—with luck, three—until their arrival in Dmitrov ushered in a period of prayer and supplication. After that, if all went well, she could enjoy eight weeks unburdened by supervision before normal life resumed. Even the thought of the domestic duties that awaited her at the estate near Ferapontovo could not undermine her joy.

Ogodai—stern and khan-like in full battle dress, only the tip of his helmet visible from the center of his white silk turban—moved his chestnut gelding into position at Nasan's side. Fifty of his warriors stood near the gates, next to the horses they had chosen, awaiting his signal to depart. Those assigned to escort Nasan and her relatives, already in the saddle, formed a tight pack near the latticework corral that held the replacement mounts. The fifteen Russian men-at-arms clustered near the carriages, as if the Tatars made them nervous.

Perhaps they did. A suitably warlike appearance could prevent trouble from ever rearing its head, and Ogodai's force looked formidable enough to frighten an army three times its size.

The assembled forces waited, and waited some more. After a while, Natalya poked her head out of her carriage, a two-wheeled cart not unlike those Nasan remembered from nomadic migrations on the steppe, and asked, "Where is Maria?"

Good question. "I don't see her, Mama-in-law," Nasan said.

"Send a woman to find her, Vanka," Natalya said.

Vanka bowed and departed in search of a female servant, and Natalya beckoned to Nasan. Ogodai at her side, Nasan kneed her mare into motion. Sorkhokhtani picked her way across the planks that lined the courtyard and dipped her head in salute as she reached the carriage.

As they approached, Nasan assessed her mother-in-law. Natalya's cheeks had flushed, and her breath came faster than seemed advisable. Maria's medications had failed to reduce the mottling of her skin, and her strength seemed questionable, even so early in the day. Nasan guessed that her mother-in-law still had trouble sleeping, valerian or no valerian.

She didn't ask. Space in the carriage would be tight enough to hold Natalya upright, making it likely that a long, dull day without responsibilities would lull her into rest.

"Come sit with me," Natalya said, "before we set off on our journey."

Nasan dismounted from Sorkhokhtani and passed the mare's reins to her brother. As he moved away, she took her mother-in-law's extended hand and climbed into the cart.

Natalya looked around the yard, her eyes soft and misty. "I will not see this place again. So many years gone. I was younger than you when my Kolya brought me here for the first time."

"Don't despair, Mama-in-law. Surely the Blessed Virgin will heal you when she hears your prayers. That's why we're making this journey, so that you may see your childhood home and return in better health." But Nasan did not believe her own words.

Natalya did not contradict her, instead staring at her with those misty brown eyes. Nasan saw grief there, and fear— of the unknown, of death? The moment of departure, so symbolic of that greater departure to come?

She didn't say that, either. They belonged to different generations and different peoples, and the prickly truce they sustained most of the time did not make them close. They sat quietly for a moment, each with her private thoughts, then Natalya touched her free hand to Nasan's felt cap and blessed her.

"Thank you," Nasan said. "May God"—and the grandmothers, she added silently—"keep you safe, Mama-in-law."

Her throat tightened. Suppose Natalya already saw what the rest of them did not? Those on the brink of death often sensed the approaching end before those who loved them could bear to admit the truth.

Yet it did not do to tempt the spirits by speaking of unwanted events before they came to pass.

"You're a good girl," Natalya said. As usual, she made it sound as if no higher praise existed. "Do you not think you should travel in the carriage with us?" Her brows drew together in a frown.

Again? "There is no room for me," Nasan reminded her. "I have spent most of my life on horseback, and Maria does not ride. Vera is with me, and Rafik will guard us. I will be fine."

After the first week, that is. In the last year, she had ridden less than at any other time in her life. But no amount of discomfort could make her agree to enter that carriage.

Natalya glanced at Ogodai, straight-backed and impassive on his chestnut horse. "Very well. See if Maria has arrived, please. If not, I may have to send you to look for her. I can't imagine what's keeping the girl. It will be midday before we leave!"

As Nasan slid from the cart, she saw that no further pursuit of Maria was needed. Her sister-in-law walked slowly toward the carriage. "She is here," Nasan told Natalya.

"Good," Natalya said. "Tell her to hurry."

Nasan delivered Natalya's message, feeling a certain sympathy for her sister-in-law. If Maria didn't look forward to hours spent in a jolting carriage with a sick old lady and two chattering maids for company, who could blame her?

The thought kept her from fussing as her sister-in-law crossed the courtyard and joined Natalya. The two servants clambered in behind her, and Vera came forward, leading Nasan's horse. Father Job moved to stand before the women. In his simple white cassock and plain wooden cross, his prayer rope tucked into the cloth strip that belted his waist, he exhibited the quiet dignity that never failed to impress Nasan. "Let us pray," he announced.

Nasan took her mare's reins from Vera, then bent her head. Father Job prayed for relief from danger and temptation, asking for a peaceful journey and a safe arrival. Nasan echoed the phrases as required and translated the sentiments into Arabic in her mind, but her heart called for more ancient rituals. Sprayed milk to guarantee prosperity and success; riders who set out and did not look back, lest the hearth spirits call them home before they could complete their mission.

Father Job blessed the travelers one by one, with a short prayer for each, then turned to say another prayer over the household. His "Amen" acted as a signal. Vanka mounted, and the priest climbed into his carriage. Nasan swung herself onto Sorkhokhtani's saddle, beckoned to Vera, and together they made their way past the Tatar warriors until they reached Ogodai. Nasan turned just in time to see Father Job set his horse in motion with a flick of the reins. The two carts rolled toward the open gates.

At a signal from Ogodai, Rafik crossed the courtyard. His men streamed by on either side of Nasan and her brother, catching up and surrounding the moving carts.

"See them settled, Rafik," Ogodai said. "Perform the tasks my sister will give you, and keep me informed of any difficulties you encounter. I'll send word as to where we should meet."

Rafik placed his hand over his heart. "Go with God, Khan."

"And you, my friend," Ogodai said as Rafik raised his arm, then galloped to the front of the escort.

Ogodai caught his sister's hand. "And you, *sengel*. May our ancestors watch over you."

"The grandmothers' blessing be upon you. You have the letter?" She couldn't help but ask, although she had barely left his side since she handed the scroll to him this morning.

"Of course." He patted his sash. "Right here."

Nasan embraced him. His cheek, warm against hers, belied his stern appearance, and his scent included the familiar blend of leather and horse. "Thank you, Ogodai. May our paths cross once more before you return to the steppe. Tell Daniil I miss him more than I can say."

"I will." Ogodai turned his chestnut gelding and trotted from the courtyard, his troops close behind him.

Nasan pressed her knees against Sorkhokhtani's flanks. The mare needed no other urging. She broke into a trot, Vera close behind, and they soon reached the center of Rafik's group of mounted men.

As Nasan set off, she was determined to enjoy every moment of the journey. And she did not look back.

Father Job and Vanka kept their carts rolling forward at a steady pace. As a result, the party made good progress, although the jolting caused by the rutted summer roads must have made the journey uncomfortable for the passengers. *Would* Natalya manage to sleep? Nasan felt more grateful than ever that her brother had secured permission for her to ride.

By noon, when they stopped to eat, Nasan's thighs and back and seat ached, and her stomach muscles—once taut as a tentpole—protested the demands placed on them. She did not *quite* groan as she slid from Sorkhokhtani's back and led the horse to a nearby stream, but the thought of riding on through the afternoon seemed far less appealing than it had this morning. At Rafik's suggestion, she released her mare from riding and allowed one of his men to transfer her gear to another horse. Vera's mount and the carthorses were also exchanged for fresher animals.

Things could have been worse, Nasan told herself as she rubbed her thighs. She had retreated into a thicket with Vera as sentry, away from the men's eyes. The last week had brought one sunny day after another; otherwise, carriages and horses would have had to battle their way through a sea of mud. The lack of moisture had reduced the number of gnats, flies, and other biting insects, although enough swirled buzzing around Nasan's head that she did not dare remove her veil. Relieving herself in the open was unpleasant enough.

When done, she returned to the stream to wash her hands and refresh her parched throat. The carriages came to a halt while Nasan, rolling her shoulders and flexing her hands to release tension, was walking toward the campfire tended by several of Rafik's warriors. When Maria emerged, Nasan stopped to ask, "How is Mama-in-law?"

"Sleeping," Maria said. "I will bring her food later."

"Good." Nasan said. So Natalya *had* nodded off. Tempted to imitate her, Nasan resumed her walk toward the campfire and propped herself against a tree.

A nap and a bowl of warm mutton broth restored her enough to get her onto the new horse's saddle by early afternoon. She would have blisters tomorrow, most likely, and the aches and pains would worsen before they improved, but she had made it this far. The less attention she paid to her discomfort, the sooner she would overcome it.

Or so her mother had told her. Until it happened, the salve in her saddlebags would get plenty of use. With luck, by the time she left Dmitrov, she would be hardened again to the trail. But first, she had to assess the pace and the nature of this new horse.

Rafik had chosen well, she decided after a while. The dapple gray mare he had selected had a mild temperament, an even gait, and an admirable serenity when facing the many unknowns of the forest road. Less spirited and playful than Sorkhokhtani, but also less inclined to take exception to waving branches and unfamiliar noises—the perfect mount for a lady whose mother-in-law had restricted her time in the saddle for far too many months. Nasan dubbed the new horse Mahal and praised Rafik for selecting such a worthy alternate for her own beautiful sorrel. He smiled his thanks before returning to lead the escort, leaving Nasan once more amid the warriors.

Moscow lay far behind them. The dirt track they followed wound among dense trees that reminded Nasan of the forest near Kasimov. Hamlets no doubt nestled in the woods, but Nasan could not see them as she rode past. The road, although obviously well traveled, appeared for the most part deserted. A herd of deer blocked their passage, until an arrow from one of the escort scattered all but the stag, who lowered his magnificent antlers before darting out of range. Wild pigs and beavers, weasels and squirrels, birds and fish—the forest contained more animals than people, it seemed. Nasan touched her lynx pendant, concealed beneath her robe, and wondered if the magical lynx watched over her even here. Was that a tufted ear in that birch tree? It was a comforting thought.

At last, the path to their right opened to reveal a clear, still lake surrounded by low shrubs and rushes of various sorts. A pair of swans glided at the far side, four fluffy cygnets in their wake. A wooden dome shaped like a sprouting onion cast its reflection on the water, and beyond it a one-story house stood amid a group of other buildings—some long and narrow like the house, others little more than huts.

They had reached their destination for the day, Nasan guessed. The estate of Olga Bulgakova, a friend of Natalya's who had moved from Moscow to Lake Kiovo after her husband died so that she could manage his property on behalf of their young sons. That had been years ago; the sons must be grown and in the army by now. Even so, Olga remained in the country.

According to Rafik, by the time they reached the estate, their group would have traversed about a third of the distance between Moscow and Dmitrov. A shorter day than usual, in consideration of Natalya's ill health. They would decide tomorrow whether to continue or to rest for a day or two before proceeding.

The lake was beautiful, the sight of swans reassuring, the estate well appointed, and the prospect of dismounting appealing. Yet as they drew closer to the cluster of buildings, Nasan's hands trembled on the reins. Would their hostess greet her warmly, or did she share Natalya's views on what noblewomen should and should not do? Would Natalya emerge from the cart refreshed or ready to carp and criticize? And what of Maria, confined for most of the day?

Their reception eased Nasan's fears. Olga exclaimed at her friend's pallor and ushered the family into her warm and welcoming home before dispatching a manservant to direct the Tatar escort where to confine the horses and pitch their tents. Remembering Ogodai's comment about being a khan's daughter and not a servant—had her brother said that only this morning?—Nasan left the mare in the capable hands of

Rafik's men and entered the house. In obedience to Russian custom, she bowed first to the icons in the "beautiful corner" next to the window, then to her hostess.

Natalya's excitement at her reunion with her old friend distracted her from worrying about her daughters-in-law, allowing Nasan to remove her veil and outer jacket, relax her cramped muscles, and assess her surroundings without interruption or demands.

Their hostess must be close to Natalya in age, but she clearly enjoyed better health. Rosy cheeks and an unwrinkled face made Olga look a good decade younger than her friend, and she appeared slimmer than most middle-aged Russian women Nasan had seen. With her hair covered by an embroidered cap and a stiff gold headdress that resembled the halos on the icons behind her, her neck hidden by ropes of pearls and a wide fabric collar over layers of brightly colored robes, she had a stately, almost queenly grace. One could imagine that she had once been a great beauty; she had the air of a woman accustomed to admiration. She had been spinning, it seemed, when they arrived: a distaff wrapped with wool rested on a sturdy table beside the window, and a fat ball of thread lay in a basket near her feet.

The building followed the basic plan that Nasan had come to recognize as Russian. Less elaborate than the Kolychevs' multistory Moscow home, this house consisted of a series of connected rooms, with benches along the sides and windows paned with small squares of mica to let in the light. A large clay stove in the main room would draw the entire family there in winter, but so close to midsummer it was neither needed nor lit. Rich fabrics and fancy utensils proclaimed the family's noble heritage, but otherwise the house looked like a larger version of a peasant cottage. The long building opposite probably held the kitchens, and the children running in and out of various huts suggested that these housed the servants and those who tilled the land. Lilacs and flowers the shape of blue bells clustered in one jar, and roses filled another on the table beside the window, next to a wooden box inlaid with gold curlicues that to Nasan invoked the elegant lines of Tatar decoration. The mingled scent of lilacs and roses gave the room a cheerful, domestic air.

Vera and the other two maids scurried off, under the direction of the steward, to unpack what their mistresses would need for the night. At Olga's invitation, Nasan sat on a bench where she could observe her mother-in-law. Natalya did seem more rested, and joy strengthened her voice. They might get her through this journey after all. If only she would accept medicines that had a chance of working!

Maria bustled about, pressing Natalya to sit here and not there, shading her from the sunlight that streamed with a soft breeze through the window, begging Olga for permission to make the mushroom broth that Natalya liked. As Maria's fussing continued, Nasan felt more and more awkward, as though she, too, should take part. But the slight frown between Olga's brows suggested she found Maria's attentions more bothersome than helpful, so Nasan folded her hands in her lap and tried not to add to their hostess's irritation.

"Enough," Natalya said after a while. "Your intentions are good, Maria, but we must not impose on Olga Pavlovna's hospitality more than necessary."

Olga clapped her hands, summoning a servant. "Juice and little bites," she said to the white-haired ancient who peered around the door in response. When he acknowledged her command and left, she turned back to Natalya. "My home is yours, darling Natasha. But are you well? Forgive me for mentioning that you seem paler and more worn than I remember you of old."

Natalya touched her chest. "My heart fails me, Olyenka."

"Your heart! Oh, Natasha, tell me that is not so!" Olga crossed herself before swooping down onto the bench next to her friend and clasping Natalya's hands. "Father, we must pray for her." She spoke to Father Job, who hovered near the doorway—as discomfited by this unfamiliar environment, Nasan guessed, as Nasan herself. He entered, slowly, and sat next to Nasan, but he didn't act on the invitation to pray.

Natalya crossed herself before answering. "Alas, it is so. Look at you, radiant as ever! But I grow old, I fear. It is the reason I undertake this long journey home, to pray for my sins while I still can."

"Your news grieves me," Olga said. "I can't tell you how much. But mushroom broth is not the right remedy for the heart." She released Natalya's hands long enough to beckon to Maria. "Come, let me teach you the medicine I learned from my grandmother. It is made from purple nut sedge, and she swore it never failed."

Nasan choked and clapped her hand over her mouth to hide her laughter. From Olga's far side, Maria was glowering at her as if Nasan had fed the words into their hostess's mouth. Father Job had a distinct twinkle in his dark eyes, but he too refrained from speech.

"That will not be necessary." Natalya extended her hand toward Nasan. "My other daughter-in-law, Irina, fancies herself skilled in the medical arts. She has been urging nut sedge on me for months. She can make it for me."

Olga glanced at Nasan, who was biting her tongue to suppress any retort she might make to this austere admission that her advice could have some value. Olga's red lips curved. "If she knows of nut sedge for the heart, then she is skilled indeed. This evening she will dose you. I will take her to the storeroom myself and ensure she has everything she needs."

"Thank you," Nasan said, keeping even a hint of triumph from her face and voice. Maria looked ready to explode, and Natalya, however amenable before her friend, had made her dislike of Nasan's remedies clear. She had nothing to gain from provoking them.

The white-haired servant returned with a small army of assistants bearing platters and jugs, and Nasan brightened. The mutton broth and bread from the noonday stop had long since vanished from memory, and hours of riding had left her famished as well as sore.

The ample platters of "little bites" drew her, but she waited her turn and let the older women go first. Rounds of bread and small yeast pancakes, delicate strips of whitefish and bowls of caviar, tiny turnovers filled with mushrooms and the ever-present cabbage soon filled Nasan's stomach and restored her spirits. Tart apple juice refreshed her even as its wispy scent added an additional note to the aroma of food and flowers. She felt sufficiently content to ignore Maria's occasional barbed comment. She had won a greater victory, at least for the moment.

Between mouthfuls, she listened to Natalya and Olga chatting. They began with Dmitrov, their destination—desolate, Olga said, since the incarceration of its prince in Moscow two and a half years ago.

"And the north?" Natalya asked when they had exhausted the subject of Dmitrov's woes. "What news of the lands where we grew up?"

"A great destination for pilgrims, as ever," Olga said. "The White Lake and Our Lady's Monastery—you will have plenty of company there. But it is good that you brought so large an escort—and Tatars, at that."

"Why?" Natalya clutched her throat as if anticipating trouble, and Nasan experienced a strange premonition, as if the ancestors had blown a breeze across her cheek. Her lynx pendant felt heavy around her neck—a hint of change to come, or just an illusion caused by the solemnity in Olga's face?

"But my dears," their hostess said, "have you not heard? A new bandit chieftain has arisen in the northern woods."

"A bandit?" Nasan, Maria, and Natalya spoke in chorus.

"A bandit," Olga affirmed. "A regular villain, my dears. Every merchant who comes through gossips about him and his men. Exaggeration, I'm sure—you know what merchants are—but if half of what they say is true, this chieftain and and his gang have a dozen thefts to their credit already."

"Oh, Blessed Mother." Natalya twisted the edge of her veil in trembling hands. "Should I continue? But I can't draw back. I have sworn before the Lord that I will make this pilgrimage. My entire hope of recovery rests on it."

Olga patted her visitor's hand. "Of course, Natasha. Have no fear. Your vow will protect you. You have a fearsome escort, too. These wicked men prey on lone travelers."

She clasped the gold cross that dangled from a chain around her neck, as if it were a talisman, and said, "These thieves will not trouble you, I swear."

Chapter 7

THE NEXT DAY, THE LONG DRY SPELL BROKE. NASAN AWOKE to the sounds of rain on the wooden tiles, and the storm did not let up until well into the evening. The Tatar troops moved into the barns and outbuildings that dotted the Bulgakov estate, but every time Nasan glanced out the window she could see the horses huddled together amid the downpour. Air and rain were warm, but she felt sorry for them, even though most were steppe ponies hardy enough to withstand the winter snows, never mind a summer storm.

Morning dawned fair, but Rafik appeared soon after the women had dressed to announce that the roads remained impassable: mud interspersed with puddles filled yesterday's ruts. A discreet examination of Natalya convinced Nasan that another day's rest could only improve her mother-in-law's health. Fortunately, their hostess begged them not to leave her alone again so soon, so they stayed a second day, then a third, while the mud dried. Nasan took the opportunity thus presented to spend as much time as possible in the saddle, restoring her own strength while Natalya rebuilt hers.

Olga was a huge help. She pressed the purple nut sedge on their reluctant patient several times a day, as well as the ginger-pomegranate tea and the paste of blackberry leaves, the only one of Maria's concoctions that met with their hostess's approval. She also insisted that Maria learn to prepare the sedge potion. By the end of the third day, Natalya did appear stronger—her skin less mottled, her color neither too high nor too ashen. But whether that had anything to do with the medicines or resulted from a few restful nights, Nasan could not tell.

As they set off again on their road north, she wondered whether, despite her offer to assist her brother, she should join the other women on the boat at Dmitrov. Olga had taught Maria to make the sedge potion and the tea, but would Maria prepare the needed doses without direct supervision? The answer must depend on Natalya, who could choose to continue the medicine or change it at any time.

Which answered the question, didn't it? For whatever pushed Natalya in one direction or the other, it did not depend on Nasan's presence. In fact, the other women might be more inclined to follow Olga's instructions if Nasan were not there to witness it. A lowering thought, that they had so little regard for her and her skills, but a freeing one, too. She could stick to the original plan with a clear conscience.

Thanks to her hours spent galloping Sorkhokhtani and Mahal across the open land surrounding the lake, the second leg of their journey to Dmitrov proved much less taxing to her as a rider. The storm had improved the ruts in the road a bit, although horseback still provided more comfortable and reliable transport. But the remaining puddles slowed the carriages, and in the late afternoon, Rafik suggested they camp overnight before proceeding.

Nasan was tempted to push on; the long summer days meant that a straight ride would bring them to the town before night fell. But she hadn't yet completely recovered her strength, and Natalya's wan face looked pinched. It wouldn't do to exhaust her further. "Let me ask Mama-in-law," she said. "You have tents for them?"

He nodded. "The priest can sleep in mine, and the one we set aside for you is large enough for six. With your permission, I'll send a few of the archers out. There is plenty of game in these woods."

"Do so," Nasan said, as she left to discuss the matter with Natalya. It didn't surprise her when her mother-in-law agreed to the overnight stay. Father Job praised the saints before remembering his place, and even Maria did not object.

Nasan felt sorry for them, although she still failed to understand what kept Maria and Father Job from learning to ride. Natalya was too ill, but did the others not see how much better off they would be on horseback?

But this, too, was not a problem that she could solve. She showed them where their tents would be, then went to ensure that someone had remembered to water and curry her horse.

It was good to be a khan's sister, Nasan concluded as she appraised the effort Rafik's men had exerted on her behalf. The rods and lattice frame snapped together quickly with enough willing hands, and the felt covering tossed over the top and secured by ropes provided essential protection from the elements. But the warriors had gone farther, rolling thick felt mats across the floor to prevent any remaining moisture from seeping from the grass below and sacrificing their own blankets to make beds for the three noble ladies and their attendants. The summer night would keep them warm; they would be both comfortable and private here.

"Well, isn't this cozy?" Maria swept past, her outstretched hand missing Nasan by a finger's length. Nasan had pulled off her boots as soon as she crossed the sacred threshold to avoid dirtying the cream-colored felt, but Maria didn't bother to do the same. Even her hem dragged a slim trail of dust in its wake.

Natalya did not imitate that piece of rudeness. She clung to Nasan's shoulder as she slipped one shoe, then the other, from her feet. "Remove your footwear, Maria," she said. "And be grateful that you need not sleep in the woods. Rafik is doing the best he can." She released Nasan. "Thank you, Irina."

The two Kolychev maids wrapped arms around their mistress's waist and, directed by Nasan, helped her across the mats and onto the pile of blankets opposite the door. Natalya might not realize that she occupied the seat of highest honor within the tent, but courtesy did not depend on the recipient's awareness of it.

Maria took off her shoes and her veil, then lowered herself to the nearest pile of blankets as if the very expectation that she might sit on the floor offended her. Nasan ignored her. Before removing her boots, she had extracted from her saddlebags the nut sedge potion that she'd made before leaving Olga's estate. She picked up a wooden bowl left for the purpose, poured a suitable dose into it, and carried the bowl to Natalya, who accepted it with a bleak but determined expression. Nasan wanted to laugh. Her mother-in-law looked like a child offered a sheep's eye, or some other delicacy that the child perceived as nothing of the sort.

But Natalya, unlike Maria, was complying with a good grace, so Nasan chose not to undermine her own purpose by laughing. Instead, she thanked her mother-in-law as she exchanged the empty bowl for a handful of berries.

"Ah, daughter," Natalya said when the berries were gone. "I think that horrible nut sedge is working, and the closeness of the Life-Giving Cross lifts my spirits."

Nasan squinted. *Life-Giving Cross?* Oh, the relic for which Dmitrov was famous. "May its divinely conferred power aid you, Mama-in-law," she said. "May Father Job's prayers be strong."

Maria muttered something under her breath. When no one responded, she raised her voice to a normal speaking level. "I said, do you really expect us to spend the night in a *tent?*" The two maids jerked their heads around at her tone, and Vera, standing right behind Nasan, gave an audible hiss.

"I told you, Maria." Natalya wagged an admonishing finger. "Be polite."

Respond to Maria's words? To her tone? To neither?

Soon they would take different paths. The patience so difficult to sustain when life extended, bleak and endless, into the distance came more easily when only days remained before a reprieve. "Perhaps you've never traveled before," Nasan said, "but this tent will keep you warm and dry. My brother's men will bring you food and guard you while you sleep. What do you expect from them: a royal palace?"

"She's right, Maria," Natalya said, her old sternness returning. "Your conduct is unbecoming. Remember your place."

Maria leaped to her feet and said, in a voice more cutting than Nasan had ever heard, even from her, "*My* place? What of hers? What does she contribute to the household? Why, she can't even sew!" She whirled to face Nasan. "Is it a wonder your husband can't abide you? You're useless. Barren and useless."

Maria could not have struck more deeply had she plunged a dagger into Nasan's heart and ripped her open. Her breath escaped with a sob. "How dare you!"

Maria's face twisted until she looked like an evil sorceress. "Wake up, sister! You think Daniil is not tumbling every peasant girl in the western borderlands? It's what he did at home. Why would he change?"

"Maria!" Natalya cried. Out of the corner of her eye, Nasan caught a glimpse of her mother-in-law trying to push herself to her feet. The attendants hurried to her side.

Nasan, hands clenched, advanced on her tormentor. "Leave my tent," she said, "and don't come back until you're ready to apologize. You can sleep on the ground for all I care."

"No, daughter," Natalya said. Nasan thought she heard regret in that level voice, but perhaps she imagined it. "She has behaved with abominable rudeness—and Maria, you *will* beg forgiveness—but you can't send her to sleep among the men. It's a question of honor. My honor." She extended a pleading hand. "Please, Irina. Let her stay, even though she has wronged you. For my sake."

Nasan glared at each of them in turn. To hear her Russian name invoked—Irina, the peacemaker—struck her as a low trick. And Maria deserved to sleep in the mud, since she had so little appreciation of the efforts made on her behalf.

But Natalya spoke the truth, and if Nasan had no use whatsoever for Maria, she couldn't say the same about her mother-in-law. Natalya might fail to understand the importance of education or the sophistication of (some) Tatar life, but she corrected both her daughters-in-law out of a sincere belief that her instructions would bring them greater happiness and the love of their husbands, present and future. She was often wrong, but she had good intentions. And she suffered from a fatal illness. Nasan couldn't bear to add to her distress.

"You may stay," she told Maria. "But don't insult me or my husband again. I agree to please Mama-in-law. I have nothing to say to you."

With that, she went to the door, put on her boots, and walked under a green canopy lit by beams of sunshine until the arrival of warriors carrying skewers of venison forced her to return to the women's tent. Vera trailed her, muttering, but the two women did not speak. Maria's behavior eclipsed every other topic, but Nasan saw no benefit in discussing it. Talking the situation over with Vera would not make Maria less hostile, and Nasan needed no confirmation of what she had seen.

The evening was, to put it mildly, awkward. Nasan made conversation with her mother-in-law—not an easy task, since Natalya tended to pontificate and her interests focused on domestic management, never Nasan's strength and quite pointless given their distance from home. After a while, Nasan asked a lucky question about Natalya's past friendship with Olga Bulgakova, unleashing a flood of memories about their childhood near Ferapontovo and their youth in Moscow that turned out to be quite fascinating.

Maria said nothing, ate a small amount of meat with a martyr's air, then lay down on the farthest pile of blankets and turned her back. Nasan finished her meal, gave the empty skewers to the warrior guarding the tent, watched the attendants help her mother-in-law get ready for bed, and lay down on the third pile of blankets opposite Maria. Vera arranged herself at her mistress's feet.

The long ride left Nasan eager to close her eyes, but as soon as she did, Maria's taunts plagued her. Old fears circled, awakened by Maria's spiteful voice. *Was* Daniil tumbling every peasant girl in the western borderlands? Was that why he didn't send a message? Had his wife's sorrow driven him back to the behaviors he had embraced before their marriage?

He had sworn fidelity, like the swans. And … the man adores you, Ogodai had said. Her brother had sounded sincere—surprised even, as if no sane person could think otherwise.

But Ogodai hadn't seen the stiff set of Daniil's shoulders as he left or heard the cool tone with which he bade her farewell. And love had little to do with fidelity. Her father loved her mother, yet he kept an entire harem of junior wives and concubines. Would tumbling a peasant girl mean anything to Daniil? Should it mean anything to her?

It did, though. It had from the beginning. She recalled telling *Ana* that it was the best part of marrying a Christian, that he could have only one wife. And her mother had laughed— gently, ruefully—and told her men were the same, whatever their religion.

Her mother didn't know that Nasan had resisted her husband with a drawn knife. But Daniil knew. He would not stray.

Would he?

Somewhere in that chaotic stream of thoughts, she must have fallen asleep. A cough woke her, followed by another and another. Nasan jerked to a sitting position and looked around, confused for a moment at finding herself once again amid the familiar lattice walls of a tent.

The coughs came from behind her head. By the dim light that shone through the open flap at the top of the tent, Nasan made her way to the north side and found Natalya doubled over, a hand shielding her mouth. She helped her mother-in-law sit up, then, in response to a whispered request, walked her to a place where she could relieve herself. The two Kolychev attendants woke with a start, and Nasan relinquished her position to them.

Maria did not wake—or did not reveal that she was awake— then. But when, sometime later, another bout of coughing interrupted restless sleep filled with nightmares of Daniil turning away in disgust as Nasan ran after him, Maria did rise from her blankets as the maids supported Natalya on each side.

"I apologize," Maria said stiffly after the two women had restored Natalya to her makeshift bed once more. "I spoke rudely and without justification."

Nasan looked at her, uncertain how to respond. Maria had never apologized before without being prompted.

It was late. The camp lay silent. Soon they would journey along separate paths for weeks. "Why do you dislike me so?" Nasan asked. "I didn't kill your husband. I bear you no ill will."

Maria's mouth twisted, as it had earlier. She curled her hands into claws, and Nasan braced for an attack. She had stopped expecting an answer by the time Maria's shoulders dropped, as if she'd decided fighting was not worth the effort.

"You think this is about Boris? It's not." She leaned forward and whispered in Nasan's ear. "Boris touched me just once, the night of the wedding. And that was nasty. I hated him."

Nasan rocked back on her heels. "Then why?"

"You don't know?" Maria made no attempt to whisper this answer. "Because you *have* a husband. A husband who loves you. Until you lost the baby, you were so happy together, the two of you, I couldn't bear to watch you. And even now, you have a place, a future here. I don't. And I never will. My mother is dead, and my father has abandoned me. He doesn't care what happens to me. No one does."

She turned away, leaving Nasan to stare as she stalked across the tent, rolled herself in a blanket, and closed her eyes.

Nasan, walking back to her pile of bedding, thought of her own first time—about how Daniil, although an enemy in those days, had gone out of his way to make her feel special and desirable and safe. If even Maria thought he loved her, perhaps he did.

No wonder her sister-in-law felt jealous. And how sad, to be left alone and forlorn, believing your own family had no use for you.

Incidents from the last two years twisted into unfamiliar forms: Maria's insistence that her parents loved her, revealed as bravado; her clinging to Natalya; her resentment of Nasan, who had unwittingly and unwillingly stepped into the place Maria viewed as her own.

Of course, pushing people away didn't help. But as Nasan measured her own sense of isolation and discomfort against the despair she had heard so briefly in Maria's voice, it seemed that they might have more in common than she would have believed yesterday.

2

"Have some more kvass." Semyon poured yeasty dark liquid from a clay jug into Stenka's waiting cup. The old peasant Masha, surly as a bear with a fresh-caught salmon most of the time, knew how to brew a rye beer that would stick to your palate—not like that horse piss the monks used to make!

"Don't mind if I do," Stenka said, "but it's me should be pouring for you, Lord, not the other way round."

Semyon slapped the man's shoulder. "See that you do, then. I'm in a mood to celebrate."

Stenka raised his cup in silent acknowledgment. "A good haul today. Gold and silks and that jeweled icon cover. And furs! I ask you, what maniac travels with furs in the middle of June?"

"Brass candlesticks, pearls." Semyon tossed a string of pearls at Stenka, who caught it in his left hand. "Give it to your Grusha if she delivers a son."

"I will, and thanks," Stenka said. "I'm glad there's no hard feelings there, Lord. I worried about bringing her here, it's the truth. But I couldn't leave her to starve in that miserable hut, and I hoped you'd lost interest in her."

"I had," Semyon said brusquely, which was true. Grusha had appealed to him for a day, at best. After that, he'd enjoyed watching her squirm as she tried and failed to get away from him. Stenka was too besotted to understand that. "She's not my kind of woman. I want a bandit queen. A warrior maid."

"A warrior maid? Where will you find one of those?" Stenka, as he'd promised, refilled Semyon's cup.

Semyon downed a large swig of kvass. Definitely, old Masha earned her keep. He wiped his mouth against his sleeve, no other cloth being to hand. "Don't know. My abbot had one, though, so they exist."

"Your abbot?" Stenka sounded more surprised than before. "When did you have an abbot, and what was your abbot doing with a warrior maid?"

"Ah, that's a story." Semyon, rendered expansive by victory and kvass, leaned his back against the wall of his hut. "Want to hear it?"

Stenka passed him a basket of bread and, when Semyon had taken a chunk, helped himself to another. Food kept a man from getting drunk too fast.

"I'd love to," Stenka said. "And why you decided to turn your hand to banditry. Last I saw you, you were one of the lords of the earth."

"Then listen," Semyon said. "It's quite a tale."

The disturbed night caused them to leave late the next morning. Nasan counted: six days to travel about one-tenth of the distance between home and their destination. At this pace, even the allotted two months might not be sufficient for them to complete their trip. But Natalya remained determined, so they pressed on. Nasan clasped her hidden amulet against the evil eye and asked the grandmothers to ensure that travel by boat proved restorative.

Maria had not spoken since her revelation of the night before, except to ask or answer the simplest, most practical questions. Nasan left her sister-in-law alone as much as possible, enjoying the freedom from verbal sparring while it lasted.

Last night's stopover meant that the final portion of this first stage required less than a full day's ride. As evening settled in, Nasan saw the road rise in a gentle slope. As they reached the top of a hill, the river that would carry Natalya and Maria to their destination near the White Lake became visible on their left. Shallow and banked by marsh on either side, the Yakhroma nonetheless had power enough to propel a barge, and it would widen and deepen as it approached the Volga.

Or so Natalya said. Nasan, studying the burbling brook to their left, wondered. She could see, though, that it did widen as it circled the town below.

A wooden fortress atop an earthen rampart, nine square towers and a gate bounding a cluster of buildings within, caught and held her attention. For an instant, she could have been looking at her own much-missed Kasimov. But the land lay too low, the river flowed too close and too sluggishly for the mighty Oka, and the grass-covered oval enclosed not tents and white stone and slender minarets but cathedrals and huts with peaked roofs. The town was small, smaller than Nasan had expected, even with the monastery in its separate palisade. Where would they stay? Natalya had told them not to worry, but she hadn't said why.

Nasan would welcome a return to the felt tent, but it seemed unlikely that her mother- and sister-in-law would agree. She would have to wait and see.

Black onion domes topped with gold crosses showed above the earthen rampart, tall as a man standing on another's shoulders, and the massive wooden gate and palisades that rose half-again as high. The domes, Nasan guessed from her mother-in-law's description, belonged to the Cathedral of the Dormition, which housed the Life-Giving Cross. As

Sorkhokhtani plodded steadily toward Dmitrov and the shadows lengthened on the ground, Nasan realized she was not looking forward to the next few days.

"After that business in Moscow, my family had me exiled to the monastery at Pechenga," Semyon said. He didn't mention the public flogging that had preceded his banishment; recalling that hour of agony and humiliation still made his insides burn. "My abbot was Trifon. The blessed Trifon, they called him, because the lunatic had spent a decade alone in the woods before deciding that his salvation demanded even greater spiritual feats. So he headed for the Frozen Sea, turned left, and went as far north as he could go. The most dreadful place I've ever seen: pretty in the summer, except for the man-eating insects, but the winters!"

"No light, lots of snow?" Stenka asked.

"Take a leak outside, and you'd be no more good to that woman of yours," Semyon told him. "Not to mention your chances of starving to death or turning into a pillar of ice fetching wood for the fire. I took one look at the place and decided to leave first chance I got. Only it wasn't so easy." He scowled at the corner, where Masha had again placed a crude icon despite his orders to the contrary. "The abbot turned me into a beast of burden. No excuses. And when I did get a moment to myself, I had nothing to do but dream of food and listen to the rest of them pray. I spent a whole year there before I managed to make friends with a younger monk. That's when I learned Trifon's story."

"And?" Stenka waved the bread basket before Semyon's nose again.

Semyon took a chunk and pulled it into fragments as he talked. "Well, it turns out the blessed Trifon wasn't always so blessed. They called him Mitrofan, and he was the scourge of these parts. Ever heard of him?"

"Mitrofan? *That* Mitrofan? The bandit chief who killed his woman in a jealous fit?" Stenka dropped the bread basket and leaned forward, elbows on the table. "You don't tell me he serves the Lord!"

"He does." Semyon, well pleased with the effect of his story, grinned. "If you can believe it. Worst bandit ever to ply his trade in the northern woods, besotted with the beauteous Vasilissa, a menace to travelers and his own men—and his monks lick his sandals and jostle for a chance to kiss his ring. Is life a joke, or what?"

"He can't still be besotted with Vasilissa." Stenka counted on his fingers. "He killed her twelve years ago, if not more. Stupid chit. What did she expect, pleading for mercy for some good-looking young man from a villain like that? As if he wouldn't suspect her of being sweet on the youngster and resent it." His cheeks reddened, as if he thought Semyon might take the comment personally.

Semyon grinned again. Keep Stenka guessing how far Semyon would go—a good principle for command. And Stenka would be even more impressed when he heard the rest of the tale. "He is still besotted," Semyon said. "More than ever, perhaps. Girl's dead, so he remembers only the good parts. That's how I got away." He laughed, thinking of the expression on Trifon's face. "I claimed to see visions of her, and when he didn't believe me, I showed him."

"How?" Stenka gulped kvass as if he needed the support.

Semyon gave another chuckle. The more he thought of the tricks he'd played, the better he felt. By the end, he'd evened the score with old Trifon, repaid every miserable task forced on him. "These places are cheats, you know—churches, monasteries. The weeping icons have holes beneath the eyes and priests dripping water through them."

Stenka gasped, as if he'd never heard of such a thing.

"You didn't know that?" Semyon asked. "Well, I didn't either till my friend showed me where to stand." He couldn't keep the pride out of his voice. This was the best part. His own cleverness still amazed him. "The young mutt should have guessed what I was doing after the miracles started coming, but they're all half-cracked up there. When no one was watching, I crept into the secret cupboard and waited for Trifon to start praying. Then I whispered through the eyeholes, sending him heavenly messages from his dear departed, how she forgave him and loved him still, how she regretted the sins they'd committed together and sought only to be reunited with him. Oh, I was inventive. In the end, he decided the archbishop in Novgorod had to hear the whole, and 'Vasilissa' convinced him to send me with the message."

"Alone, even though you were a prisoner there?" Stenka's voice held awe, perhaps mixed with a superstitious fear. But without question respect. Semyon loved respect.

"No," he admitted. "Not alone. I rid myself of my two traveling companions not far from Kandalaksha. Took their money and their furs, left the bodies in the snow. Two starved monks didn't stand a chance."

"Not against a fighting man," Stenka agreed. "Your young friend stayed in the monastery, I hope."

Just for a moment, Semyon flinched. His hands clenched, as they had around the young monk's soft neck. "He wanted to reach the next world," he said curtly. "Quicker that way than freezing to death in Pechenga."

Stenka's eyes widened, the mixture of awe and fear more obvious than before.

A short pause followed. Then Stenka said, "No doubt, Lord." His level voice and shuttered expression obscured his emotions, but Semyon's sense of being respected grew.

A week later, Nasan, again seated on her mare, watched with some trepidation as two dozen strong and cheerful bargemen lifted ropes over their shoulders and dragged the vessel bearing Natalya, Father Job, Maria, and their attendants—including the fifteen men-at-arms borrowed from the Kolychevs' next-door neighbor and an additional ten Tatars from Nasan's escort—away from shore. The boat had a sail and oars, but those would do it no good until the river traversed the marshes and widened.

In the end, Dmitrov had defied Nasan's gloomy expectations. The Kolychev clan had many friends in the town who recalled the days when one of Daniil's uncles had served Prince Yuri, the one now incarcerated in Moscow, and were happy to entertain Natalya and her daughters-in-law. The Life-Giving Cross—although from Nasan's point of view a strange and disturbing life-sized icon displaying the half-naked body of the crucified Christ—had cast its health-giving glow over Natalya to the point where she appeared to have acquired a new lease on life. At times, Nasan even believed they might meet again at journey's end.

Today, though, she had her doubts. The future looked cloudy, uncertain. If Natalya died en route …

Grandmothers, preserve them! The prayer rose unbidden, drowning the unwelcome thought that preceded it. Nasan clasped her hands, throwing the full force of her will behind the plea. Whether the ancestors responded to fervency, she didn't know, but it did no harm to try.

The bargemen found their rhythm, and the boat moved faster away from the quay. A mist wreathed the river in swirling clouds as the water spirits rose to greet those courageous or desperate enough to brave their realm, stretching their wraithlike fingers in greeting.

As the boat moved out of sight, Nasan lifted a hand in farewell. Natalya and Father Job waved in response, but Maria had already vanished inside the small enclosure that would house them and their two attendants on their journey.

Now she too would head north. No longer bound by the need to surround the carriages, she and her escort could ride straight to the White Lake—or as straight as forest and rivers permitted. With luck, the journey would not take more than two weeks. Then Rafik could leave a few men to guard her and scout out the situation in Vologda, as Ogodai wanted him to.

Nasan nudged Sorkhokhtani with her heels, and the mare followed Rafik's gelding onto the excuse for a track that wended its way between the slender birch trees. The sky shone clear; the birch maidens shook their bright-green locks in the breeze; sunlight gleamed against their silvery trunks. Sorkhokhtani stepped cautiously among the seedlings and brush, but Nasan smiled.

Chapter 8

INTERMITTENT RAIN, THICKLY GROWING BIRCHES, THE ever-twisting Volga and its tributaries, and winding forest paths turned the expected two weeks of riding into three, then three and a half. At last, Nasan and her escort reached the hazy serenity of the Sheksna River. It was mid-afternoon, and the sun cast a golden glow on the water, giving it the sheen of a black pearl. A soft mist, like a cloud pulled from the sky, clung to the shores, its tops ruffled in patterns that weirdly matched the branches of the trees that grew down to the edge, where the clear water reflected them in broken ripples. Fishing boats glided over the mirrored surface, and these became their transport, while the horses swam beside, coaxed and prodded by a half-dozen or so avid riders. Money and a large sterlet changed hands, and the escort stopped on the far bank to cook dinner before continuing.

Natalya's estate could not be more than a few hours away, based on the information she had given Rafik before they parted. If necessary, she had told Nasan, they could stop at St. Cyril's Monastery and receive directions there. But Rafik scorned the suggestion that he and his men could not find a location, even in unknown territory, based on spoken instructions alone. Nasan saw no reason to challenge him. If he could do what he promised, challenging him served no purpose; and if he could not, his failure would become obvious soon enough.

She herself both wanted and did not want the journey to end. She loved the return of her boys' dress, so much easier to handle than women's clothes and so much safer under the circumstances. She loved riding fast and hard, hunting with bow and arrow, speaking her own tongue. Her month of liberty had restored a way of being she had almost forgotten, one she must find a way to sustain as the demands of domestic responsibilities again swept her up.

Yet traveling was not all joy. Tents designed for life on the open grasslands leaked with the constant drip-drip of the Russian woods, bathing proved next to impossible, and the forest oppressed her spirits as the steppe never had. Endless clusters of thick-growing trees parted only occasionally, and each clearing held both the threat and the promise of adventure. Did it house a den of thieves? A peasant family? A holy man seeking salvation in the wilderness? Each of these possibilities was as likely as another.

But here in the clear air of late afternoon, with the sun casting its pale gleam across the water, the sounds of horses munching happily on the tall grass that lined the bank, and the scent of summer flowers borne on the light breeze that sent the clouds scudding across a sky the color of a dove's breast, Nasan felt at peace. The air was warm, and night would not fall for hours. Tonight she would sleep undisturbed by howling wolves or the strange snuffling sounds of the forest. It was enough, for the moment.

Or so she hoped. The condition of Natalya's estate had yet to be determined.

"Ready, *Khanim*?" Rafik's voice broke into her reverie.

Another thing she would miss when the Tatars left: her proper title—khan's daughter. "Yes," she said. "You know the way?"

He pointed with his whip, and she nudged her mare to follow him. The rest of the escort fell into line, the unsaddled horses trailing them—except for Mahal, who kept pace with Nasan and Sorkhokhtani. The two horses had become friends.

More woods. Nasan sighed. *We will be there by suppertime,* she reminded herself as their party moved onto yet another forest track—this one wider than most, as it led toward St. Cyril's Monastery, a great destination for pilgrims. When Natalya sent word, they would return to meet her there.

Let the estate be in good condition, Grandmothers. I have had enough of woods.

The black gelding, yielding to pressure from Daniil's knees, raced toward the straw target set up at the far end of the courtyard. Daniil rose in his stirrups as he approached the target. One arrow on the approach, a second as the horse veered left, a third from behind. In sequence, they thudded into the wooden disk that dangled over the target's "heart," so close together that the third split the first right down the shaft. He resumed his seat and drew on the reins. The gelding slowed.

"Not bad," an amused voice said over his shoulder. "I think we'll keep you."

Daniil turned his horse to face his commander. "Forgive me, Prince. I didn't realize you were watching."

Prince Ivan Barbashin, newly appointed to command the Velizh forces, acknowledged the apology with a nod. Black-haired, with strong hands and a vivid face, he didn't look his age, which Daniil guessed, from the details of the man's career and his elevated position, to be in the mid-forties. Not much younger than Daniil's own father, but lean where Nikolai was stout and dark where Nikolai had once been fair. In build and complexion, Barbashin looked like a man with a recent Tatar ancestor—not a rare occurrence among the Russian nobility. He had a good reputation as a general—unlike many of his fellows, who had attained their rank through lineage alone— and Daniil welcomed the chance to serve with him.

"You practice a lot, you and your men?" With his eyes, Barbashin followed the troops attacking the target, one by one, although Daniil assumed the question was directed at himself.

"Every day except Sundays and holy days," he said. "They complain, but I insist on it. The strength needed to pull those bows wanes fast. I tell them they don't want to be staring a Lithuanian in the face with no weapon but an arrow they no longer have the power to shoot."

Barbashin laughed. "*Molodets*," he said. "You will go far, young man."

Ah, Moscow. The very air smelled different. Ladies' perfumes left subtle traces of lilac and lavender, herbal concoctions a man had neither the skill nor the mastery to identify, mingling with the aromas of well-cooked food and baking bread. Rich carpets and tiled floors, gold ornaments and embroidered robes, red and gold, black and white—Koshkin had missed every dusty tapestry and velvet shoe in his two years confined amid the barren forests of the north.

The young man opposite showed no appreciation of his surroundings. He lounged sideways in a high-backed chair, one booted foot dangling from its arm, a scowl marring his handsome face. The white silk turban proclaimed his nationality no less than the layers of elaborate silk caftans, the tight sash, the jeweled hilt of what would no doubt reveal itself as a dagger of extraordinary workmanship and deadliness. Tulpar Sultan—the banished son of Bulat Khan and Koshkin's pass for a permanent return to court life—gave no evidence of being impressed with either the splendor of Kremlin appointments or the panoply of Russian power.

Koshkin repressed a sigh. For two kopecks, he would gladly abandon his efforts to attract Tulpar into service. He had no bone to pick with Bulat Khan, other than Bulat's inexplicable decision to ally himself with the Kolychevs, a clan that Koshkin regarded as his enemy. But the neat juxtaposition between the need to secure his own position and the opportunity to upset the Kolychevs left him in the uncomfortable position of putting up with this insufferable young man.

Gently, skillfully, Koshkin set out to convince his aggravating quarry of the advantages of switching sides.

The attack came without warning. One moment, Rafik was standing in his stirrups, saying sharply, "What is that?" The next, he was falling, an arrow sticking from his chest.

Nasan, too, stood, trying to see what had happened. Was he dead?

A voice cried, "Save the *khanim*!" A hand grasped Sorkhokhtani's bridle, and Nasan dropped onto her saddle with a thump as the hand hauled her mare sideways, dragging them among the trees. The impact caused her to loose the reins, and she clung to the pommel as she struggled to right herself.

Another whistling arrow, and the hand released her. She heard a sharp smack on her horse's flank, then Sorkhokhtani was galloping into the woods as if driven by demons.

No, not demons. By the unmistakable sounds of battle. Behind her, screams of rage mingled with clanging weapons. Nasan reached for the reins and tried to calm her mare, but the panicked horse did not respond. Branches slapped her face, and she bent low over the animal's neck—through packed trees, across streams. Tears of frustration blinded her. She should go back. She *must* go back. If her brother's men were prepared to risk their lives to defend her, the least she could do was find out what was happening to them.

But Sorkhokhtani disagreed. An immeasurable time passed before the horse slowed. Her flanks heaved with gasping breaths. Nasan patted the mare to soothe her and nudged her gently toward a nearby stream. While the horse drank, she sat straight in the saddle, brushed the tears from her face, and looked around. Mist curled around low bushes, spun tendrils across a small, uninhabited clearing. Birds sang in the trees; water rippled nearby. Otherwise, the forest was silent.

Nasan gulped. She had no idea where she was. She dismounted and turned in a circle, listening for her escort. Nothing. No men on horseback. Not so much as a neigh or a whicker.

Never mind. She would wait a moment for her horse to recover, then try to retrace her steps. Whoever had attacked could not have killed her entire escort. Those who remained would be searching for her. She need only head in the right direction.

If she could figure out what that was.

She had to move carefully, of course. The attackers could still pose a threat.

When Sorkhokhtani had drunk her fill, Nasan remounted and walked the horse across the clearing, searching for a place where they could rest before attempting to retrace their steps.

Could the horse find the river? The abilities of steppe ponies were almost uncanny at times. From there, they should be able to make their way to the monastery, where the monks would either allow them to stay for the night or direct them to their destination. But how would she communicate to a horse that the river was the destination of choice?

Crash! Nasan jerked in her saddle as a huge brown shape charged toward her, teeth and claws bared. She had no more than an instant to register the presence of two small furry bear cubs before Sorkhokhtani took off like the winged horse of legend.

They tore through copse after copse as if they were steppe. The mist rose in earnest, leaving damp trails across Nasan's cheeks, obscuring everything but the trees right in front and to either side. Nasan, as terrified as her horse of the pursuing bear, gave Sorkhokhtani her head.

A few feet from them, the ground dropped away. Frantic, Nasan hauled on the reins. Sorkhokhtani swerved right and dashed across a log bridge that shifted beneath her hooves. Nasan caught a glimpse of tumbling creek and hard, unforgiving stones. Then they were diving farther into the woods. Trees loomed out of the fog and vanished behind them.

One tree did not vanish. A massive branch whacked Nasan across the face, and she tumbled from the horse's back.

Nasan probed the left side of her head. A line of scratches marked her cheek, and the space above her ear hurt. A throbbing pain, unless she touched that spot—then sharp. No blood, but she could expect a fine collection of bruises tomorrow, and perhaps a lump at the source of the pain.

What happened? She'd been there on Sorkhokhtani's back, then ... not.

And she was lying on something uncomfortable. She pushed herself onto hands and knees and discovered a pine cone. With a curse, she threw it against a nearby tree.

Her head ached, and the leaves on the trees had odd fuzzy edges, but there was nothing to be done except try again to retrace her steps. She sat back on her heels and looked around.

And recognized the true horror of her predicament. There was no sign of Sorkhokhtani.

She rubbed her forehead. Listened, smelled, pressed her palms against the grass in front of her, as if she could conjure her horse from the soil beneath it. Nothing.

Nasan dragged herself to her feet, hoping the extra height would reveal a pair of ears above the bushes, a tuft of hair caught in a tree, any indication of which way the mare had run.

Nothing.

A sob escaped her. Forest surrounded her. Long-trunked birches mixed with other trees she could not name. Moss and grasses, saplings and shrubbery. Wildlife. Bears and wolves and boar, lynxes, foxes. Stags with massive antlers, trailed by does and fawns. Beavers near the streams, rabbits in the woods. Tiny prickly hedgehogs hidden in the leaves. Every sort of animal except the one she needed most.

Even the rickety bridge lay far behind her. In her mad flight Sorkhokhtani had brought them to a place Nasan did not recognize, then abandoned her. She was lost.

Confused, too. How had she fallen off her horse, and why didn't she remember? Why had she been riding alone in the first place? It didn't seem right that she should be wandering the woods with only a pony for company. Even if some of her men had ridden for help when she fell, someone would have remained to guard her. Vera would have stayed with her.

But she saw no one, heard no one. Turn and peer as she might, the forest stretched in every direction, its silence broken by the occasional complaints of bird and beast, the rustling amid branches hidden by the mists, but no sound attributable to people.

A wolf howled. A second answered it, then a third. Nasan shivered. She had to get out of here. She examined the soft ground again. After a while, she saw hoof prints. It was the only clue she had, so she set off in the direction in which the horse had been running, hoping it would lead her out of the forest—or if not, to her mare.

Her back hurt from having the breath knocked out of her when she fell; her head responded poorly to the demands of her legs; her memory of the accident remained hazy. But the need to find her way out of this fog-ridden, wolf-filled wilderness drove her onward. Her bruises could wait.

The trail of hoof prints soon petered out. Nasan kept moving in the same general direction. She had vague memories of a stream and a bridge, a clearing with bears. But she couldn't find them—and, in the case of the bears, did not want to.

The farther she traveled, the more she despaired. Huge pines and firs, so tall and straight that God Himself must have planted them at the dawn of time, cast an emerald glow on those below. Bushes, seedlings, the legacy of leaves from previous autumns, massive fallen trunks supporting entire colonies of fungi and insects, dangling vines, and reaching ferns fought for space and light. Black flies tormented her, and her feeble efforts to repel them failed, adding to her misery.

Worse, as time passed, she felt more and more dizzy. The emerald light set the edges of the leaves and branches aglow. Streams slaked her thirst, and the thought of food made her stomach churn, but she couldn't go much longer without rest. If she fell asleep in the open, what would become of her? The memory of those wolf howls haunted her.

As the northern twilight made its belated appearance, Nasan accepted that she would not find a path out of the forest before morning. She focused on locating somewhere, anywhere, she could spend the night in safety.

At last, she stumbled into a clearing that contained a crude shelter, little more than a lean-to with falling-down walls. She ducked behind a sturdy oak tree and examined it. Was it empty? If not, would the residents be friendly? Could they help her find her way in the morning?

Far overhead, she heard the whoop of swans calling their mates and their cygnets to settle for the evening. The twilight surrounding her shaded into purple. She had reached the clearing just in time.

She saw no people, no signs that anyone had visited the copse for some time. The fire ring before the hut showed not even a wisp of smoke, and the bones nearby could have been strewn by animals. The hut looked too small to support a family. Its logs, angled and tied in the center like a crude tent, listed in places, revealing gaps. It had no windows and no smoke hole. The whole area was quiet. As the sun settled behind the trees, no light showed from within. Even so, she approached cautiously. When she reached the deerskin that passed for a door, she took a deep breath before pushing it back.

The hut was deserted. It contained nothing. No furniture, however crude. No supplies. Not even a straw pallet to lie on, dirty and disgusting as that probably would have been. Nasan's headache returned with a vengeance. Could she stay here, even for one night?

She had to. The thought of walking farther made her want to curl into a ball and cry. Not to mention the wolves.

Where is Daniil? Where is my escort? Grandmothers, don't let the wolves eat Sorkhokhtani. Or me!

Nasan crammed herself into the least derelict corner of the miserable lean-to. The hut offered no comforts. She dragged off her coat to use as a mattress. Her hat made an unsatisfactory pillow, but she was too exhausted to care. It was August, and warm, so she curled up and closed her eyes.

She dreamed that her horse found her escort and led the men to her. Daniil was with them, but as they reached the clearing, wolves attacked. The warriors thrashed, bleeding, in heaps on the ground, and the wolves closed in for the kill. Only Daniil was untouched. He stood motionless in the middle of the clearing, but when she ran to him, he stared coldly at her, then turned into a swan and flew away.

She woke, sobbing for breath. It was still dark outside, pitch black and silent, not so much as a star visible through the listing poles. Outside, she heard the wind picking up and guessed that clouds covered the sky. It would storm before morning.

Where was Sorkhokhtani? Dreams were prophetic, sent by the grandmothers. Could the horse have gone for help—not with intention but through the instinct that connected her with her herd?

It seemed unlikely. The mare must be lost, too. Otherwise, she would have returned by now. But it was Nasan's only hope, so she clung to it.

Her throat felt dry. Too much time had passed since she last drank, but only a fool would push out into the dark forest in search of a stream. Her muscles ached from so much walking, and her head threatened to lift right off her shoulders if she moved too fast. She couldn't eat if she tried.

She closed her eyes again, but panicked thoughts pounded at her brain, robbing her of the sleep she needed to recover.

One thought led the pack. She had no way out of the woods, no horse, no friendly face to ask for directions. No food, although the forest would supply that. She could wander among these miserable trees for months without finding help.

Should she stay where she was, then? But suppose no one was looking for her? To her escort, it must seem as if she had ridden into the woods and disappeared.

If they lived, they would search for her. They had sworn to protect her. Ogodai would flay them alive if they let harm come to her.

But were they alive? The events of the morning were returning in pieces. She still didn't recall how she had fallen from her horse, but she remembered Rafik knocked sideways, an arrow jutting from his chest. The shout to save her, and the hand that dragged her into the woods and slapped her mare before falling back. If the attackers had killed them, she was lost indeed.

Daniil will never know what happened to me.

And perhaps, as the dream indicated, he wouldn't care. Her brother said otherwise. Maria, too, but suppose they were talking about the past? Daniil had loved his wife once. The question was whether he loved her still. Tears stung her cheeks.

The attackers! Who were they?

She bolted upright. Fear coursed through her veins, and she collapsed again as the blood rushed from her head.

Attackers. Bandits? Olga had spoken of bandits. A new bandit chief, she said, who preyed on pilgrims. The Tatars would be safe, she'd said, but they were not safe.

Whoever they were, they acted like enemies. They'd shot Rafik without so much as a word of warning. Villains to avoid, no matter what.

The distant howls faded to silence. Nasan willed herself to sleep. Time enough to worry in the morning. She could stay here another day, building the strength to go on.

Something wet dripped on her hand. She looked up.

Another drop hit her on the nose.

As if she had not suffered enough, the rain had started.

Animals jostling. Booted feet hitting the ground. Men's voices speaking rough, guttural Russian. The smell of horse manure and unwashed bodies. Sunlight on her face. Nasan jerked into wakefulness, eyes wide.

Angled logs, the gaps wider than before, thanks to the rain. She was still inside the miserable hut. Dawn had arrived while she slept—and had brought company.

Those outside had yet to approach the lean-to. If they did, they would find her, for she had nowhere to hide. She sat up, making as little noise as possible. Her head felt clearer this morning, but yesterday's bruises still ached, and her chafed heels and blistered toes offered brutal testimony of long and aimless walking.

On hands and knees, she crept toward the door, stopping as soon as she could see through a gap in the log walls. The men outside exhibited no concern about the amount of noise they made, no sense that the lean-to contained a living being. Nasan held herself as still as a quail on the steppe, hoping they didn't hear the breaths that came fast and hard despite her attempts to slow them. Through the chink, she saw two dozen or so unkempt ruffians in homespun peasant trousers and loose shirts, incongruously bright kerchiefs tied around their necks and scuffed boots on their feet. An assortment of well-kept weaponry—pikes, swords, bows, knives—stood in sharp contrast to the overall effect created by uncombed, uncut hair and the dirt that mired bodies and shirts. An equal number of horses wearing wooden saddles atop plain cloths and rope bridles nibbled grass on the far side of the clearing. Sorkhokhtani was not among them.

Nasan reached for the dagger in her belt, tried to ignore her bruises, and prepared to defend herself if necessary.

A man as big and burly as the mother bear who had chased her yesterday pushed through the ragged pack that surrounded him. He wore a shirt and trousers no cleaner or better made than the ruffians who, Nasan deduced from the way they cringed as he shoved them aside, served him.

Pure terror washed over her, and she clapped a hand over her mouth lest she attract his attention with a gasp or cry. She closed her eyes, then opened them, but the apparition did not vanish. His hair gleamed pale blond in the dawn light. His eyes, a peculiar shade of light blue, shone cold. A cruel twist distorted otherwise fine lips, and a scar ran from his cheek to the side of his mouth.

She must be dreaming. Another nightmare. She pinched her arm.

She was not dreaming.

What is he *doing here?*

"Semyon Severyanin," one of the men said.

The blond man turned in response to the call. Nasan breathed again, a silent exhalation. She felt her own hand tighten on her dagger.

She wanted to plunge the knife into his back, spit in his face, shout his lie to the world. She wanted to burrow into the earth like a rabbit, for the grandmothers to cast a glamour of invisibility over her, protecting her from his gaze. To keep him from learning of her presence.

But she knew one thing. The man was up to no good. In her experience, he never was. And besides, honest people don't change their names. He was Semyon, yes, but Severyanin?

No. She had recognized him at once. His last name was Kolychev. He was Daniil's cousin. The man who had slain her younger brother in front of her eyes and gone on, arrogant and heedless, to endanger his entire lineage with his schemes.

And who, last she heard, had been ordered to take monastic vows in distant Pechenga, on the shores of the Frozen Sea.

What brought him here, of all places on earth?

And perhaps more important, how could she get away without him noticing her?

Chapter 9

NASAN COULDN'T HAVE SAID HOW LONG SHE REMAINED motionless, listening to Semyon and his men, wondering if some ill chance would bring them into the hut and reveal her presence. It seemed as if she aged years watching forms cross back and forth through the gaps in the logs. Concentration blurred her vision—or was that fear?

At last, a curt order from Semyon sent his men scrambling for their horses. She crept closer to the gap to see them ride off. Before she left the hut, she wanted to be certain no ambush awaited her.

Silence fell, and she could breathe again. She stretched her cramped legs and rubbed sensation back into her toes, wishing she had the salve stored in Sorkhokhtani's saddlebags. It would soothe her blistered feet.

What should she do? The question loomed as large this morning as it had last night. Dawn had not brought the hoped-for clarity, and she remained as lost as when she staggered into the hut yesterday evening. She could stay here another day—or another century—but it would not help her find a path out of the woods. It would not reveal the fate of her warriors.

The thought slammed into her awareness as if a grand-mother had smacked the side of her head.

Semyon knows the way out.

His men had come from somewhere and were on a journey to somewhere else. They were not wandering aimlessly in the forest as she was. They had a destination. If they were bandits, they knew the paths.

And they had horses. Horses who also knew the paths. One pony—and she was set.

Nasan rested her aching head in her hands and sighed at the thought of more walking. But there was no help for it. She would keep as much distance as she could between herself and Semyon, but she could not let slip what might be her one chance of getting away from this forest.

The grandmothers did not forgive cowardice.

Last night's rain made the men's trail easy to follow, although difficult to walk. Soft squishy mud eased the chafing on Na-san's feet but slowed her pace. She stayed in the grass as much as possible to ease her passage and avoid leaving her own trail, which could eventually alert the men to her presence.

Here and there, she saw other battered lean-tos like the one where she had spent the night. Each time, she stopped to examine the hut, hoping to find a friendly person who could supply directions and make her frightening, difficult pursuit of Semyon and his men unnecessary. But every lean-to was deserted.

She walked and walked through eternal, unchanging forest. Roots reached out to trip her, but when they succeeded, she picked herself up and pressed on. Branches slapped her face, leaving welts. Gnats swarmed around her face; mosquitos settled on every exposed inch of skin. No matter how often she slapped at them, they remained undeterred, their buzzing whine a song of misery. Yesterday's bites itched; today's stung. Thoughts of food obsessed her, and handfuls of berries pulled from brambles as she passed did little to assuage her hunger. Rabbits darted past, squirrels chattered above her head; if she had her bow and arrow, she would have no trouble hunting dinner, although the thought of raw meat brought her nausea back full force.

As time went on, the weakness and blurred vision of last night returned. She lost the desire to eat—to do anything, in fact, except curl up in the woods and sleep. Her feet had become a burning mass. The urge to give up strengthened with every step, but she could still see the trail left by the horses, and to stop would sentence her to more nights in the forest, negating her hours of sacrifice.

Once in a while, the trees cleared enough for her to see that the sun had risen higher in the sky, but it was still morning. The thought gave her hope.

A pony. One pony that she could borrow. Surely that was not too much to ask. She would return it when she was done with it. She was not a thief.

Grandmothers, please! Send me a horse, if you love me.

No horse appeared. She had decided that the men would never stop long enough for her to catch up with them when she looked around and realized that the trees were spaced more widely than before, the saplings and bushes less thick, the light more visible. Ahead of her, a stream flowed, and she stopped to drink. Beyond it, the vista opened onto tilled fields. A group of eight, perhaps ten, rundown huts clustered between the fields and a flat expanse of water, so bright and clear that it mirrored the fluffy white clouds above and a stand of trees that lay on the far shore. In the distance, Nasan saw swans gliding across the cobalt surface, swimming in an upside-down sky.

Out of the forest at last. Grandmothers, thank you!

She raised both arms heavenward as relief flooded her. For the first time since the attack, it seemed possible that she might escape from her predicament. Surely *someone* here could help her find her way.

But where was she? Nasan hobbled as close as she dared to the edge of the woods, then hid behind the most substantial of the lean-tos that nestled among the trees so that she could assess the situation.

At first, she felt discouraged. The thatched roofs on the huts looked like extensions of the forest, and the wooden beams fit poorly, as if slapped together. Many of the houses needed repairs. The village must be abandoned, like every small settlement she had passed on her way here. But then she noticed that chickens scratched outside and the fields showed signs of tending.

Shrieks of laughter heralded a group of boys and girls— some young enough to run bare-bottomed, others fully clothed but shoeless and tousle-haired, chasing a big brown hen that rose, wings flapping, halfway off the ground, squawking loudly. A woman emerged from a rickety doorway. Solid and middle-aged, she wore a scarf around her head and bast shoes on her feet, a loose white blouse with full sleeves to her elbows, an ankle-length dress that fell from straps over her shoulders, and a homespun apron over the dress. She looked irritated.

"Leave that hen alone," she shouted at the children. "How are you not ashamed? The poor thing will never lay if you chase her like that!"

"Forgive us, Masha." The children stopped long enough to hang their heads, then raced to another house, leaving the hen behind. Clucking, it joined its fellows outside the door and began pecking at the soil.

"There's my biddy," the woman named Masha said. "Don't let those brats upset you." She went back into the house.

Nasan considered what she'd seen. Children meant families, and families might help her. That Masha would be a good person to ask. She had looked honest and kindly, despite her scolding of the children. They didn't fear her; that much was clear.

But was it safe to approach? She had followed the trail of Semyon's men and horses to get here, but she didn't know where they'd gone. She saw no evidence that they had come to this village—but no evidence that they hadn't, either. And desperate as she was for a place to eat and sleep, a horse to borrow, and directions to the Kolychev estate, she was much more desperate not to encounter Semyon again. The sight of him in that woodland clearing had reminded her of the last time they met. He had wanted to kill her then, and he would recognize her, just as she had him. She'd dressed in boys' clothes during that meeting, too. Even the Golden Lynx should avoid another encounter with a man vicious enough to murder a child.

She pulled off her boots and settled behind the lean-to, determined to rest while she waited. If Semyon and his men did not appear soon, she would approach the woman with the kindly face.

Daniil sat, sweating in his armor even so early in the day, on his fully caparisoned horse in the middle of the town square while a priest clad in cloth of gold said prayers over his bowed head and those of the warriors with whom he served. Icons on poles waved in the morning sun, which cast sparks on the jeweled casings of the holy images and polished the soldiers' steel helmets.

A short while later, the troops left the fortress, the cavalry in the lead. Daniil dropped his copper coin in the waiting basket as he passed and heard the clink of kopecks joining it. They would be retrieved, one by one, by those who returned, and those left in the baskets would indicate the number of casualties.

He passed through the gates, and the fortress walls rose behind him. It was the Feast of St. Olga, and he was heading into battle.

The sound of hoofbeats sent Nasan scurrying farther into the woods, her boots clutched in one hand. She crouched behind a large bush next to an oak tree and thanked every forest sprite in existence that the men on horseback did not spare her a glance.

Semyon led the pack, the same loud but disheveled bunch she had seen before, and they rode into the village without hesitation, obviously sure of their welcome. It was good that she had exercised caution.

Women and children spilled from the huts as the horsemen approached. They laughed and exclaimed, the women waving long pieces of cloth, the children hopping up and down and shrieking their joy. Nasan saw the kindly Masha with her chickens and fought off bitter despair as she said a silent farewell to the idea of seeking help from that source. The entire village, she had to assume, supported Semyon.

The men on horseback dismounted. The crowd of women and children clustered around them. Every man—except Semyon, who stood arms akimbo surveying the village— occupied the center of his own circle of hugging, chattering relatives, like raiders returning to a nomadic horde. If she had no prior experience with their leader, she would have thought it a pleasant family scene.

As Nasan watched, waiting for an opening that would allow her to grab a horse, another woman left the cottage nearest the lake and walked to join the welcoming villagers. Her swollen belly drew Nasan's eye first. In an otherwise slim frame, and with those waddling steps, it suggested that the woman would soon give birth.

As the woman approached, Nasan observed her more closely, drawn by a nagging sense of familiarity. It seemed likely that one of these ruffians had fathered her child. Semyon? Pregnancy had bloated a face that must once have been pretty, but she had long, light brown hair and watery blue eyes. A pleasing countenance, but under most circumstances unremarkable.

A bright beam of memory pierced Nasan's still-hazy sense of her surroundings. No wonder the woman looked familiar! Her name was Grusha, and she had once belonged to the Kolychevs. Still did, in fact, because she was a runaway slave, although for reasons of its own the family had not pursued her. The main reason being that before Daniil's marriage, Grusha had spent far too much time warming his bed, ensuring that both Daniil's mother and, especially, his new wife felt no inclination to push for Grusha's retrieval.

Yet here she was, in close proximity, pregnant. Sitting cross-legged under her bush, Nasan wondered what she'd stumbled onto.

Grusha, too burdened by her unborn child to rush, nevertheless covered the ground between her starting point and the happy group of families at a steady pace. She caught Masha's arm, punctuating what appeared to be a question with frantic gestures.

Masha shook her head and pointed to Semyon, still surveying the village with a lordly gaze. Grusha's face creased with distaste—did she dislike him then, and if so, why was she here?—then walked, more slowly, toward him. She stopped more than an arm's length away and spoke again, not loudly enough for Nasan to hear.

Semyon's boom, in contrast, reached the woods without difficulty. "Stenka? Your man's dead, woman. They killed him, the Tatar bastards!"

Grusha's anguished howl covered Nasan's sharp intake of breath. Grusha collapsed in a storm of weeping, and a group of motherly peasant women darted forward to comfort her.

But not Semyon. Nasan watched, stunned anew by his callousness, as he turned his back on the woman whose life he had destroyed with one sentence and entered the largest and most prosperous-looking hut.

The trading quarter of Vitebsk was burning. The smoke stung Daniil's eyes, and he blinked rapidly to clear them. Flames licked the sky, spreading wildly to either side, driven by wooden houses packed too close together and a summer that had so far withheld heavy rains. Thinking of the fence so recently raised around Velizh, Daniil could not avoid a flash of sympathy for the artisans and petty traders whose lives the battles of kings disrupted. The peasants in surrounding villages fared no better: their homes destroyed, their crops trampled, their animals driven off and slaughtered to feed the army.

He shook his head. He was getting soft. Marriage did that to a man. War was his business, just as raising food was the business of peasants and engaging in crafts the work of those who lived in trading quarters. In war, empathy was misplaced.

The Lithuanians would have to rebuild Vitebsk from the ground up. It served them right for trying to exploit Russia's minority rule, then dragging their feet during the negotiations.

And they would continue to drag their feet until they understood that he and his comrades-in-arms would hit back and hit back hard the longer they delayed. In that sense, the more damage the Russian forces inflicted, the better.

Ahead of him, the banner of St. George dipped three times. The red tails lifted in the breeze as the saint appeared to stab the bearer's horse with his embroidered spear. Prince Barbashin's aide, signaling the cavalry archers to advance.

Daniil looked right, then left, ensuring that his contingent was armed and ready, then pulled an arrow from his quiver and kneed his horse forward. He had a job to do.

Semyon glared at the wall of his hut. He heard Tanka squirming behind him. Trying to restore his good humor in the only way she knew—or so he guessed.

"Stop that," he told her without turning his head. "Didn't you hear me say Stenka's dead?"

"Didn't think you cared, Lord," she said. Hearing no hint that his brusqueness troubled her, he twisted to face her, giving her the full effect of a scowl that brought seasoned men-at-arms to their knees. Instead of cowering, she wriggled and tugged the neckline of her chemise lower. She wore nothing else. Her chestnut hair flowed over her left shoulder and pooled near her waist. She ran her tongue over her lips. Her eyes, round and hazel, regarded him with a bold gaze that seldom failed to arouse him.

It succeeded today, too, despite his glum mood. Determined to resist her wiles, he snarled. "I care. He was a good man, Stenka. Best captain-at-arms I ever employed. He'll be hard to replace. And now I have to avenge him before I can pursue my relatives, who have wronged me deeply. It's a damned nuisance."

"Yes, Lord." Tanka smiled and beckoned. "Come, relax with me. Life will look better in the morning."

Was the woman dense? "That's the only reason I came here," he said. "To make enough money, build up enough power, to go after my relatives. My uncle, my cousin. I just had one run-in with Tatars. I'd as soon avoid another one. But I can't. The men won't fight for a leader who looks weak."

Tanya beckoned again. "I know, Lord. Trouble, trouble, and more trouble. Let me ease your burden."

His desire to resist wavered. Her refusal to let him intimidate her excited him.

Yet responsibility tugged at him. His obligations didn't end with avenging Stenka. His men would expect him to take care of Stenka's woman and child—and their own, in time of need. One task after another, more than he'd anticipated. And here he'd expected to enjoy being a bandit chieftain. For the first time, he wished he'd never thought up this plan. With uncharacteristic reluctance, he joined Tanka on the bed.

But long after she slept, contented, at his side, Semyon stared at the wall, unable to join her in temporary oblivion. The raid and its aftermath had shaken him.

From the moment of his escape from Pechenga, life had been unalloyed bliss. Good fortune seemed to follow him. An accessible village, close to his ancestral lands but not so close as to attract the attention of anyone who might remember him from boyhood. The arrival of Stenka, who had recruited the likeliest lads from that same village and trained them into competent fighters—not yet warriors, but capable bandits. A series of raids that filled the coffers even as they heated the blood, his own and his men's.

Stenka's death changed that. How had they miscalculated so badly, selecting a group of Tatars for attack in place of the usual fat pilgrim with an escort more worried about its own survival than protecting its master's or mistress's worldly goods? Even a pack of monks would have made a better target. The monks themselves lived poor enough, for the most part, but the icons and vestments and paraphernalia fetched a good price.

But no, his men had to attack a contingent of Tatar warriors. As a result, Stenka's death was the least of his worries. Semyon knew Tatars. He talked about going after them, but his real problem was the certainty that they would come after him. This group had lost a few members, but enough had lived to give cause for concern.

In fact, who was he fooling, talking about avenging Stenka or caring for anyone's unborn brat? He hadn't time to worry about such things, or even to bury the man, second-in-command or not. He had to save himself—and his bandits, unless he planned to give up this enterprise altogether. The Tatars would hunt them down, just as they had tried to do when he killed that boy two years ago.

Unless he bought them off. He'd have to dig into his stores; his raid on the Tatars had yielded nothing but bodies.

Still, it was worth a try. August would bring more pilgrims, and he could recover his losses.

An annoyance, and one he couldn't afford. He was slipping back when he had expected steady forward movement. Better than more deaths, though.

God help him. How had he managed to get himself into this mess?

Semyon jerked as memory struck him, causing Tanka to moan and turn over. He eased out of the bed, willing her to stay asleep. He didn't need more distractions. A new problem raised its head.

What brought a group of Tatar warriors here? He would wager every kopeck of his ill-gotten gains that they didn't travel on pilgrimage. Most didn't practice the Christian faith, for one thing.

Raiding, then? Unlikely. Tatars rode up from the south along well-traveled paths, struck the first towns they encountered on the border, and retreated with their loot as fast as possible, to avoid interference from Russian defenders. Sometimes they besieged Moscow, but the White Lake? Semyon had not heard of any such incident.

He had seen only men, fully armed, which did suggest a raiding party. But something nagged at him, some half-remembered detail. He worried at it, teasing phrases from a clamor of weaponry and shouts. A sight? A sound?

At last, it came to him. He didn't speak their barbarous pagan tongue, but he recognized the Tatar words of status. Every Russian nobleman learned them in childhood. Early on, right after the first flight of arrows, he had heard the shouted word *khanim*. And seen a single horse plunge into the woods. It had not reappeared—or had it? He couldn't recall. Too much disturbance, too many plunging steeds and clanging weapons.

Khanim. Khan's daughter. He and his bandits had not caught sight of a woman, but that didn't mean no woman was present. The escort would place her safety above its own.

Semyon wanted to pound his head against the wall. A groan escaped him, causing Tanka to stir, and he patted her shoulder to prevent her waking.

If the Tatars blamed him for the loss or injury of their *khanim*, he and his bandits were dead meat. No amount of wealth would appease those warriors.

Forget responsibility. Forget vengeance, until he had a chance to assess his odds of survival. Forget decision, because his course for the next few days was set. At first light, he and his bandits must retreat into the forest and stay there, leaving the women and children to fend for themselves. Chances were, they'd do fine.

His life or the Tatars'—it came down to that.

After a while, the crowd of families dispersed to their individual homes. The peasant women helped Grusha to her feet and half-led, half-carried her into Masha's hut. The chickens trailed after them. Nasan could hear the women murmuring, "He was a good man, your Stenka," and "The child will be born without a father, but we'll take care of you. Don't worry."

It was reassuring, somehow, to think that kindness still existed in the world and that the villagers might have helped her, too, under other circumstances. Only a fool would approach them now, though, even to ask for a bite of food. And only a bigger fool would lie around waiting to be found by her worst enemy, whatever had brought him and Grusha here.

That simple speech of Semyon's had clarified one essential point, though. She vaguely remembered Stenka as the only one among Semyon's henchmen who had shown signs of a conscience. The first time Nasan had seen him, she had marked his interest in Grusha. The Kolychevs had suspected him of helping her run away, and it appeared that he had captured both her body and her heart. Then returned to Semyon's service—and brought Grusha with him?

She should stop speculating. How Grusha came here didn't matter, compared to what else Semyon had said. If Tatars had killed Stenka, then these men had been involved in the attack. And there was at least a chance that some of her escort still lived. Finding them must become her top priority.

A few boys emerged from the huts and led the horses to a paddock at the edge of the woods farthest from Nasan's hiding place. She marked the spot in her mind.

A good location. Reach it unnoticed, and she could grab a horse and lead it a short distance to the lakeside, then ride along the shore until she saw signs of habitation. Somewhere, even in this misbegotten land of abandoned villages and deserted lean-tos, there should be a cathedral, a wooden church, some small community where she could seek help.

But she must wait for the village to quiet before she dared try it. After so much walking, such effort to escape detection, the thought of capture had become intolerable.

Time slowed to a crawl. Nasan's legs cramped, and she moved to another part of the woods, closer to the paddock. The stream relieved her thirst, and a patch of blackberries restored her energy enough to get her to a copse that seemed isolated enough for safety.

She settled again into waiting. The sun stuck to its spot high in the sky, no matter how hard she stared at it, and she had dozed and awoken several times before it at last headed for the horizon.

She sat up and looked around. The huts lay dark and silent. No one stood watch that she could see. She would have no better opportunity. She slipped on her boots, wincing as her chafed heels touched leather once more.

The woods, so threatening before, provided enough cover to assure her that no casual observer would notice her passage. She reached the paddock without incident. By habit, she stayed upwind of the horses, assessing them for temperament, size, and strength. A beautiful chestnut with a white blaze on its forehead caught her eye; it resembled Ogodai's favorite gelding—too tall for her, but she would manage.

A touch on her shoulder made her jump. Nasan turned in mid-air and came down with her hands raised, flat as a knife to chop the throat of her assailant.

Her booted feet hit the forest floor with a small but audible thump. She froze, listening. But when she saw her assailant's long nose and gentle brown eyes, she had to struggle to contain her laughter.

Sorkhokhtani, still wearing her saddle and the new bridle, must have been hiding in the woods when she sensed others of her kind and, drawn by her herd instinct, decided to follow them. Somehow, the horse had escaped the bandits' notice.

Nasan embraced her mare, murmured blissful greetings into those beloved ears, and mounted without more ado.

Which way to head, east or west? Sorkhokhtani instinctively moved east, and Nasan supposed it made little difference: so long as they followed the shore, they must eventually circle the lake. Best to get as far from the village as possible before dawn, and heading east let them avoid the silent huts. She relaxed her hold on the reins and let Sorkhokhtani guide them, using knees and hands only as necessary to control the horse.

As the huts fell farther behind them, Nasan said a silent prayer of thanks to spirits large and small for bringing her and her mare through this latest trial.

She hadn't even needed to borrow a pony. With any luck, Semyon and Grusha would not know she had seen them until the Tatars returned in force.

If her men survived.

Chapter 10

NASAN WALKED HER HORSE AT FIRST, DETERMINED TO DO nothing to attract the attention of Semyon and his bandits. After a while, she reached a narrow strip of water—an inlet, she guessed, because more trees clustered on the far side. Sorkhokhtani turned right, and Nasan again let her lead, urging the horse into a trot as they put more space between them and the bandit camp. When the water ended, they continued more or less straight, keeping the lake on their left.

Nasan listened for sounds of pursuit but heard none. The silence reassured her. Even the wolves remained quiet in the forest. Sorkhokhtani maintained a steady trot, as if at home on the steppe. Nasan found that, too, encouraging. If her mare sensed no danger, surely none could be lurking.

As the sun sank in the sky, however, her fears revived. She couldn't drive the horse through the darkness, and although night would soon pass, they needed food and somewhere to rest until dawn. She saw occasional signs of cultivation, but after her experience with the last village she hesitated to approach strangers unless they carried some assurance of peaceful intent. She had even less desire to trust the safety of herself and her horse to the bears and wolves.

Another dip and curve, and the lake opened up before her. Nasan's jaw dropped. The setting sun, behind her left shoulder, turned the still water to flame. One swan's lifted wings glowed orange, as if the bird carried a candle on its back. Others glided in silent procession, dipping their heads from time to time as if in greeting. Almost directly opposite, a cross-tipped onion dome reflected the sun's glory. Other domes of black, tent roofs, and white stucco buildings clustered round that single brilliant center, and a long wall girded the whole, enclosing it.

A monastery. Most likely the one where Natalya intended to end her pilgrimage, but in any event a group of holy men whom she dared ask for shelter and who might, in the morning, direct her where she needed to go.

For the first time in her life, Nasan rejoiced at the sight of a Christian church.

The sun descended inexorably toward the horizon. Desperate to reach the monastery while she could still see it, Nasan pushed on through the deepening twilight. Her last turn to follow the course of the lake required an agony of concentration to keep Sorkhokhtani on the path and away from nesting swans or other denizens, animal or human, who might object to visitors. Days without adequate food, water, and sleep and the blurry vision that still troubled Nasan at moments when she least expected it combined to drag out this final stage of her journey, and the fading light added to her worries. She would have given anything for Daniil's beautiful smile, Ogodai's supportive strength, Natalya's once-sturdy frame, Vera's tender care, or Father Job's calm competence.

She pressed on, however, because she must. Pilgrims had worn the path smooth, and the water spirits took pity on her.

Even so, the sun had slid behind the distant trees by the time she approached the gate. Only the candles that lit the cathedral kept Sorkhokhtani moving in the right direction. But they had reached their destination.

Would the monks allow them entrance?

Nasan dismounted and rapped on the gate. The eye that peered through the peep hole in response did not at first appear friendly, but her fluent Russian and, she hoped, air of command soon convinced the holy father to let her in. At his request, she handed him Sorkhokhtani's reins.

With the horse went Nasan's bow and quiver. After her recent scare, she disliked having to surrender the weapon. But if a walled cloister couldn't protect her from Semyon and his men, then nowhere on earth would keep her safe, so she didn't reach for the bow. Only when the monk passed the reins to someone else with orders to stable the horse for the "young lord" did she realize that her boys' clothing had deceived him.

Should she correct him? Nasan knew little of monasteries. If she could believe Maria, monks didn't welcome females, human or animal; even agreeing to house Sorkhokhtani was a concession. Suppose they had admitted her *because* they thought her a man? In that case, if she told the truth, they might demand that she leave. She was so exhausted, and relief was so close. She *couldn't* tell them!

The man who had opened the gate for her gestured toward the courtyard. "This way, Lord. Have you eaten today?"

"I have not." Nasan lowered the pitch of her voice, as she used to do in her days as the Golden Lynx. Her stomach growled its agreement, and she felt her cheeks flush. "Nor yesterday. I would appreciate a bite."

"Come," he said. "I will show you to our room for guests." *Tell him? Don't?*

If he led her to a dormitory filled with men, she would have no choice. She must confess. But food, sleep, safety—the thought of doing without these things made her want to weep. She would take her chances with the guest room.

"Thank you," she said. He folded his hands in his sleeves and bowed, then picked up two candles and led her to a building close to the gate. The monk who held Sorkhokhtani's reins walked the horse in the other direction.

God and the ancestors still protected her. The room was empty. A tiny cell containing a straw pallet with pillows and coverlets, a small table holding a triptych, a stand with a glazed basin and jug, and a cross hanging on the far wall constituted its entire furnishings. Nasan's monk placed one of his candles on the stand with the basin and pointed to the pallet next to it, then the jug. "You may wash there and sleep here. I will send someone from the kitchen with food."

Nasan thanked him once more. When he left, she moved to the basin. What she must look like after three days wandering the forest, she couldn't imagine. But of course, the monks had no mirrors, which spared her a sight she assumed would horrify her.

She poured water from the jug, damped a linen cloth in the basin, and passed it over her face. The area in front of her left ear still hurt, although the sharp pain had dulled. Blood stained the cloth from the scratches that had begun to heal. Eyes closed, she reveled in the sensation of moisture against her skin. She dipped her hands in the clear water and rubbed them until they felt clean, then dried them on the other end of the cloth. A boy appeared with a bowl and bread, and Nasan sat cross-legged beside her pallet to eat.

Where are Maria and Natalya now? Where are my men and Vera?

Broth and rye bread, both kept ready at all times, Nasan guessed. Simple fare, but delicious to one as hungry as she. She ate slowly, savoring each bite, then set the bowl aside and lay down.

If the boy returned for the bowl, she didn't hear him. The next sound to assail her ears was the bells summoning the monks to Matins. The sun had risen.

The trading quarter had blazed into embers, but the fortress of Vitebsk stood firm upon its hill. The Russian army, borrowing a tactic learned on the steppe, pretended to withdraw, as if satisfied by its easy conquest. A day passed in retreat, and another at a distance just great enough to convince the Lithuanians that they had escaped lightly. Then Grigory Kolychev, deputy commander to Barbashin, dispatched his cousin Daniil with a small contingent of fifty warriors to scout out the effects of the apparent retreat.

Daniil welcomed the challenge. It felt good to pick up speed, to leave the dust of the army behind him. His troop raced across the short distance, and not long after sunrise, he waved his men into a copse that crowned a nearby hill and surveyed the terrain below.

Far to his right, he saw the straggling line of the Russian army, still hidden from the view of those inside the fortress and proceeding with caution while waiting for the intelligence he and his troop would provide.

Except for the smoldering remains of the trading quarter, the fortress looked much like Velizh: a solid construction of logs on an earthen rampart, with sloping roof, conical watchtowers, and holes for artillery and arrow fire. At first glance, it appeared silent, asleep, as if the Russian ruse had worked and those within no longer anticipated imminent trouble. But before long the gates opened and hundreds of armored soldiers marched out, descended the hill formed by the grass-covered rampart, and arranged themselves in the field. He heard the distant clang as the drawbridge shut.

"Go," Daniil told his fastest rider. "Tell Prince Ivan and my cousin that the Lithuanians are expecting them. They can't take the town by surprise."

The man left, but he had barely skirted the trees when an arrow pierced him, and he fell.

Daniil swore and started after the fallen warrior, but his second-in-command, Andrei, grasped his reins. "Daniil Nikolaevich, let me carry the word. You must stay and direct the others."

Daniil stopped, torn. "Not you," he said after a pause. "Pavel." He pointed to a slight young man with light-brown hair and eyes. "And keep your nose down. You don't want to end up like Yakov there."

Pavel nodded. Daniil frowned as Pavel threaded his way across the wooded hilltop.

"So far, so good," Andrei said, "but he has to cross open ground soon enough."

"Yes." Daniil waved in the direction of the fortress. "Can we create a diversion? The Lithuanians have guessed we're here. Or if they haven't, they will as soon as they catch sight of him. One Russian could be a coincidence, but not two."

"What kind of diversion?" Andrei was watching Pavel descending the hill. For the moment, it shielded him from the Lithuanians' eyes, but Andrei was right. To reach the army arriving from Velizh, Pavel had no choice but to cross the enemy's line of fire.

"A Tatar-style raid." Daniil enjoyed the raised eyebrows that suggestion provoked. Perhaps he'd spent too much time with his brother-in-law. Ogodai would love this idea. "We ride straight at their flank, shooting, then cut to the right before we get into artillery range and head for our own side. If we're lucky, we'll meet them halfway."

"And if we're not?" Andrei's voice held a note of anxiety, yet Daniil saw that the plan held a certain appeal. Better to fight than to wait on the hilltop for the Lithuanians to slaughter them.

"If we're not," he said, "we can probably save Pavel. And either way, our commanders will learn what awaits them. Tell the men."

In little more time than it took to say a prayer, they were ready. Daniil raised his bow and pointed the tip toward the field. Then they were off—forty-nine skilled archers howling as the Tatars did in battle, dashing madly toward the Lithuanians' right flank, and shooting one arrow after another, as fast as they could draw. Screams and shouts spoke to their accuracy. As they reached the limits of musket fire, Daniil swung his horse to the right, and the men followed. Pavel had seized his chance, Daniil saw: the scout's white gelding had crossed at least half the distance between Daniil's troop and the advancing Russian army.

Hoping his own side wouldn't shoot them by mistake, Daniil dug his heels into his mount's sides and rode as hard as he could to catch up.

They almost made it. Their surprise attack from the hilltop caught the Lithuanians off-guard, and the deluge of arrows combined with the speed of their horses and the sudden swing to the right created enough confusion to buy them some much-needed time. Then the whine of musket balls sounded over Daniil's head, and the deadlier zip of arrows mingled with agonized cries.

Something struck Daniil's shoulder from behind. He clung to the black gelding's mane and urged the beast forward. A good horse, it obeyed instantly—or perhaps it disliked the gunfire and the arrows as much as he did.

He reached his own lines before he collapsed. He heard Pavel explaining what had happened, his cousin's voice ordering men to carry him to the first Russian farmhouse they could find. Then the pain that he hadn't felt during the battle burned a hole through his shoulder, and the world turned to ashes.

Nasan, forgive me, he thought.

Negotiations had been going well—and then, the setback. The arrogant tilt of the sultan's head, the cool dismissal in his tone, should have warned Koshkin to anticipate disaster.

But it hadn't. He'd been thinking of his eldest daughter, how he had stopped by to visit her only to discover that she'd left for the Vologda region. The irony of that: what did it signify, if it signified anything? As a result, he'd taken his eye off his quarry for one crucial moment, forgotten where he was and to whom he spoke. Forgotten how important it was to win this difficult young man's confidence.

They had been talking of religious conversion. Surely Tulpar had heard of the Tatar sultan Kudai-Kul, whose adoption of Christianity as Tsarevich Peter had made him brother-in-law to Grand Prince Vasily III. An example to emulate, one would think.

"Even if it's true," Tulpar said, "that my advancement *here* will go faster if I convert, I would be giving up the chance to rule a Tatar horde."

"Why would you need one?" Koshkin tried to sound casual. "We can offer as much or more—your own lands, high military rank, honors at court. A bride of noble lineage, if you choose."

"I have a woman." Tulpar shrugged, as if the best Koshkin could offer weighed light in his hand. "And your court is not so grand compared to Crimea or Kazan. Perhaps I will serve the Ottomans. Istanbul—there's a city with much to offer."

"If you could rule in Crimea or Kazan, you wouldn't be here," Koshkin pointed out. His voice, although level, had a tart edge he couldn't control. "And the Ottoman sultan would turn you over to his vassal in Bakhchisarai as soon as he realized you support Sahib-Girei Khan's nephew. You must have calculated those odds before you approached us, so why pretend otherwise?"

Tulpar surged to his feet, hands clenched at his sides. "I will return to Crimea. A message reached me last night. My lord, Islam-Girei, demands my presence. I believe"—he bowed, mockery visible on his face—"he plans an embassy to Moscow. Until we meet again!" And with that he stalked out of Koshkin's study.

Koshkin slammed a hand against the tiled stove, then swore as a piece of mosaic cut his palm. Beads of blood traced a line across the center of his hand. He saw nothing that would absorb the blood except a scrap of paper, so he dabbed at it with that. When had he last let impatience get the better of him?

He must calm himself. Anger would not serve. He'd failed in the task that Prince Vasily Shuisky had set him, and if he could not find a good explanation, he would be back in Vologda before the Dormition Fast began. That wouldn't do, so he must conceal the truth from Prince Vasily and spin a tale that Tulpar had every intention of joining them as soon as he cleared up matters with his former master.

It should work. It might even be true. Tulpar had, after all, mentioned the possibility of them meeting again.

As Nasan had guessed, the monks of Ferapontovo were well acquainted with the location of the Kolychev estate. The novice who had brought her food the night before rode at her side, showing her the way.

The boy was a fount of information and gossip. He knew that a group of Tatars had established itself at the estate after falling foul of attackers whom everyone in the vicinity assumed to be Semyon Severyanin and his bandits. He told Nasan that the peasants who lived there had fled into the woods or to the monastery for shelter, to escape both the bandits and the Tatars. He assured her the local people would return as soon as the situation calmed down. They needed their homes and their lands as much as the Kolychev family needed them—more, perhaps, because it was the height of the growing season, and if they left the crops untended they would starve come winter.

The boy also told her that the peasants would leap for joy if the Tatars took it upon themselves to rid the neighborhood of Semyon and his men. Nasan promised him that they would do their best. It seemed a safe vow to make: if her brother's men were not already plotting vengeance for the injury inflicted on them by Semyon, she knew nothing of warriors.

The lad chattered without stopping, as if relieved for once to be rid of monastic vows of silence. Nasan let him talk—indeed, encouraged him with new questions whenever the flood of information and speculation threatened to abate. Soon she must think about Semyon: what had taken him away from his monastery, what brought him here, whether his choice had anything to do with Koshkin's presence in the area given that they had worked together before, how she should or could respond, and how best to deploy her escort, whose tasks for her brother took precedence. For the moment, though, she welcomed the distraction. Who knew what shape her warriors were in, how many survived, or whether the Kolychev estate was even habitable?

They reached the estate just before noon. Howls of joy greeted her. To get the novice out of the way while she took stock of the situation, she commended him to the care of Aziz, a young warrior confident enough in Russian to communicate with the boy.

"Feed him, Aziz, let him rest, then release him to return to the monastery," she commanded.

"Yes, *Khanim*." He touched his hand to his heart.

Reminded by his use of her title, she said in Tatar, "He thinks me a man. Let him think it. The monks were good to me, and I don't want to upset them by having them find out that they took in a woman unawares."

The boy was staring at her, bemused by her rapid switching between languages, but when she ordered him to go with her warrior, he bowed and thanked her. "Yes, Lord."

She nodded, glad that he continued to address her as male, then promptly forgot about him.

A few quick questions revealed both good news and bad. The baggage cart had arrived safely, so they had both supplies and a few servants. And contrary to her fears, Rafik lived. His armor had blocked the arrow to his chest, but his horse, lacking such protection, had rolled over him as it fell, and he lay sick unto death. Karim, Ogodai's third-in-command, showed her a bandaged right hand. She inspected the wound and heaved a sigh of relief to find it clean. It was fortunate that she'd arrived when she had.

"Good work," she told him. "I'll mix you a potion to help it heal. But first I must see to Rafik. And what of the other men? How many survive, and in what condition?"

Karim looked grave. "We lost five, and as many more suffered some wound to their bodies—not counting myself and Rafik. Bikbai will die, I think; he took what seemed like a mild blow near his stomach, but a belly ache torments him, and he worsens each day. The others have knife slashes or broken bones; they will recover, in time, so long as infection doesn't set in. And, *Khanim*, I am sorry, but your serving woman was killed."

"Vera? No! What happened?" In the rush of questions and the joy of reunion, she had not even noticed Vera's failure to greet her. The realization stung. She would miss her maid's quiet and constant presence. And although she had done nothing to cause Vera's death, she couldn't help believing that it was somehow her fault. If she had stayed in Moscow, if she had traveled with Natalya and Maria, Vera would still be alive.

"A stray arrow." Karim looked distressed. "They saw her as one of the men, no doubt."

"Yes," Nasan said. "I shouldn't have insisted we wear boys' clothes."

He shook his head. "I wouldn't put it above such ruffians to shoot a woman. And if they had captured her ..." He left the sentence unfinished, and Nasan shuddered. A swift death was not the worst thing that could befall a woman. Rape at the hands of Semyon and his men terrified her more.

"Where is Vera now?" she asked.

"We buried the dead at the edge of the clearing, *Khanim*. It seemed best. To wait in this heat would have been unwise."

He was right, and Tatar custom demanded burial on the day of death when possible. But Vera had been Christian. She would have wanted a church funeral, the chance to lie in sacred ground.

Nasan kept those thoughts to herself. Karim would hear a reproach that she didn't intend. The men had done what they thought was right, and it was too late now. She didn't yet know the area—or even where to find a priest, except at the monastery. When Father Job arrived, if he did, she would ask him for advice. He would pray for Vera's soul, if nothing else.

Karim had already moved on. He frowned at Rafik, who lay still and quiet on a pallet placed against the wall. "The khan would wish us to hunt these attackers down and punish them." He gulped, his Adam's apple rising and falling, making him look younger than his years. "We have notified him, *Khanim*. Your brother, that is. He will not be pleased that we lost you."

"You didn't lose me." Nasan tapped his elbow. "You saved me, you and the escort. Without your quick thinking and brave defense, I might be lying next to Vera. Then my brother would indeed be angry. And by the grace of the Prophet, may he rest in glory, my wanderings led me to your attackers. I can show you where to find them. You will have a chance to restore your honor."

"You, *Khanim*?" Karim regarded her with astonishment. He must be new to Ogodai's service, if he expected women to sit on their hands while the men did the work. Ogodai's Firuza handled a bow and a horse almost as well as Nasan herself.

"I stumbled on the village where they hide," she said. "The men who attacked us are bandits, preying on pilgrims. I heard their leader claim responsibility. I rode Sorkhokhtani from there to the monastery and from the monastery here. I can help you reach the village."

She hesitated, then decided to tell him the whole. "The leader is my husband's cousin. His behavior impugns not only your honor but that of his own family. And mine." She waved a hand at the walls, indicating the lineage of those who owned the estate that sheltered them. "We must avenge their wrongs as well as our own."

Karim worried his lip with his teeth. "We must. Yet our first responsibility is to you. By the mercy of God, you have been restored to us. We can face our khan with heads held high. Our desire for vengeance must not imperil you again."

"Agreed. Let us not act in haste." His dilemma mirrored her own. Attack meant splitting his forces to guard her or endangering her in battle; failure to strike back implied weakness. Neither option pleased her. "Stand aside, so that I may tend to Rafik. And bring me my medical books. You will find them in my saddlebags."

Karim bowed—silent, hand over his heart—then left to search for the books.

Daniil came to lying face down on a rough wooden bench. Pain radiated out from an area not far from his right shoulder blade. His head spun when he tried to lift it, and a fleeting attempt to move his arm set his teeth to chattering.

"Let that be a lesson to you, young lord," a dry voice said in the neighborhood of his left ear. "We removed most of the bullet, although we had to cut you up a bit. But if you behave yourself and avoid infection, you will do fine. Make him comfortable over there while we await the transport to Velizh, if you please."

Daniil was still puzzling out that last sentence when strong arms—two on either side of his torso and two more at his legs—lifted him off the bench. The pain in his shoulder became agony, and the room again faded from view.

Semyon, hands on hips, scowled at the collection of shaky lean-tos. He might as well be back in Pechenga, hauling logs and fishing for salmon to cook in clearings hidden from the monks. His damned relatives had a lot to answer for. Once he'd been a nobleman, with a grand house and a wife and servants ready to jump at his bidding. Even the leaky tents he'd endured before battles looked like luxury now. Hell, the peasant huts offered more protection from the elements than these makeshift cabins.

Never mind. A few days, a week at most, and the Tatars would have done their worst and moved on. They might not bother the village at all, since they had to find it before they could raid it, and he'd gone to some effort to keep the locals from learning where he and his bandits made camp. But just in case, a week in the woods at the height of summer would do his men no harm. Less than an encounter with a Tatar warrior bent on vengeance, for sure.

He said as much to a youngster he found blubbering near the fire. A good cuff to the head got the boy on his feet in a hurry. "What's your problem?" Semyon asked. "Haven't you ever spent a night in the forest before?"

The boy sniffed and wiped his cheeks. "It's my granny, Lord," he whimpered. "Ready to meet the angels, she is, and no one but me to care for her."

"Nonsense." Semyon raised his arm, and the boy flinched, anticipating another blow. "The women will look after her, and better than you can. You'll not be much use to her with a Tatar arrow through your chest. This way, you live to steal for her another day."

The boy nodded, although his scrunched face did not relax. Semyon dismissed him, and he ran into the trees. Semyon plucked a rye loaf from the stone where the lad had been sitting, broke off a piece, and carried it with him as he entered the least disreputable shack.

No point in wasting food.

Chapter 11

NASAN PERCHED ON A LOW STOOL NEXT TO RAFIK'S PALLET and considered her options. She had dismissed Karim to fetch her books and medical supplies, but she couldn't conduct a proper examination of Rafik while the two of them were alone. Every man in the force—including her absent brother and Rafik himself, if he recovered enough to learn about it—would be horrified if she, a woman, gazed at the body of a wounded warrior. And Nasan, despite her usual impatience with convention, understood the costs of disregarding this particular rule. She had no desire to dishonor herself, her husband, or her brother through inappropriate behavior.

But if she could not yet examine, she could observe and she could think—not only about the nature of Rafik's injuries but about the circumstances she faced in general. With her biggest concern—the condition of her men and the Kolychev estate—resolved for the moment, she could no longer dodge the big question. What to do about Semyon?

But really, she saw only one answer. Whatever had taken Semyon away from his monastery or caused him to establish himself in this area, armed banditry was a capital crime, among the Russians as among her own people. Semyon's arrest for such an offense would disgrace him personally, but his behavior two years ago had already placed him beyond hope of redemption by any normal standard. Although not the confidante of Grand Princess Elena, Nasan felt reasonably certain that the grand princess had spared him from execution only in response to Nikolai Kolychev's pleas—and then only because she owed his family a debt at the time. Elena was probably not the only one who had hoped that Semyon would die under the knout, but Semyon had not died. His escape from exile—if that explained his presence here—doomed him the moment Elena's government discovered him. His arrest for banditry would seal his fate.

And he deserved such an outcome. But his relatives did not, and his disgrace would drag them down, too. Nikolai, Natalya, *Daniil*—Nasan could not stand by and let them suffer because she lacked the stomach to intervene. Her men yearned for vengeance; Karim had already said so. Her brother would expect no less from them, whatever his concerns about Maria's father and their half-brother's schemes. Which meant that they must go after Semyon and kill him, and she must ensure that they did.

Although a few might set off for Vologda, as Ogodai had requested. She would discuss that option with Karim. He would have to plan and execute the raid. He knew better than she how many men he needed to complete it with minimal casualties.

She shuddered. Semyon was her one enemy, a brutal man who had sworn to kill her on sight. He was a dangerous and frightening ruffian who would attack her without a moment's remorse. She had barely escaped him the last time, yet she considered going after him again?

But there was no other course and no point in yielding to a cowardly impulse. No honor in that either.

And she must act soon. The bandits had attacked her party shortly before the Feast of St. Olga, and three days had passed while she found her way here. Natalya, if she still lived, and Maria would reach the shore near St. Cyril's early in August. At most, the Tatars had a month—more likely, two weeks—to launch a counterattack on Semyon and his men. Which raised another question: she had the skills to ride and fight with them and the right to insist on leading the raiding party. Should she enforce that right?

With Rafik, who remembered her from the steppe, insistence would work. Karim, though, viewed her primarily as a delicate harem flower who required his protection. A good look at her in action should change his mind, but she would have to find a way to convince him to trust her. She didn't want him worried or distracted. That would cause more harm than allowing him to reduce his force a bit to guard the estate.

Nasan sighed. Before the Tatars could attack, they had to recover their strength. And that, too, had to happen quickly. Once Natalya and Maria reached the end of their journey, any hope of a counterattack would be lost.

Strength, healing, Rafik. The rest could wait. Nasan focused on her patient.

Rafik had not moved since she entered the room. He lay on his back, eyes closed. Slow breaths raised the linen tunic that covered his chest and shoulders; she wondered if Karim and the others had drugged him to keep him quiet. When she pressed her fingers against his wrist, she found the pulse rapid, erratic, yet his forehead felt cool to the touch. She saw no obvious wounds other than the bandage that ran high across his chest, at the edge of the tunic—presumably covering a graze from the deflected arrow.

His horse, dying from multiple arrows to the chest, had rolled on Rafik as he fell. So Karim had told her. But where had the falling steed struck him? On the steppe, such incidents, if not common, occurred often enough to be familiar. Nasan had (thanks be to God and the grandmothers) so far escaped such a fate, but she had seen some men get to their feet with a bruise and a curse while others broke bones or suffered internal injury or even died from a kick to the head.

Rafik had not died, but he had not gotten to his feet either. Karim had reported no visible wound caused by Rafik's fall from the horse. There was no help for it. She needed to see for herself the evidence of his injuries.

Karim arrived with her books, and she ordered him to fetch a warrior with two working hands so that she could examine her patient without undermining either his dignity or hers.

Pallor, bruising down the left leg, rapid heartbeat, fainting—these were Rafik's symptoms. Nasan had already established that the warriors had given her patient no drugs—had done nothing, in fact, except clean and bandage the graze left by the arrow and check him for broken bones, then exert themselves to keep him quiet and undisturbed. She checked the books that Karim had brought her and frowned.

No broken bones, Karim had said. So what would disable a healthy young man? Not bruising, not an arrow that failed to pierce his armor. He should be awake and swearing at the pain that kept him from walking, promising to be back on his feet in no time, eager for revenge on the bandits. Not ashen and immobile as a corpse.

Something must be broken inside, where they couldn't see it. A bruised heart or lungs, a fracture the men had not detected, an abdominal injury. In that case, there was probably little she could do. And without certainty as to the cause of his injury, how could she heal him?

He had no fever. Which suggested that the pallor might result from loss of blood.

Bleeding would not help him, in that case. Indeed, in his present state it might kill him.

A broken bone, then? "Did you check his hips and his ribs?" she asked Karim. "As well as his arms and legs?"

"Everything we could touch, *Khanim*. Even his spine, in case the horse had damaged it. But when he is awake, he can move his hands and feet. It is his belly that hurts. Like Bikbai's." Fear tinged his voice.

"Hmm. I will examine Bikbai next, but the cases may not be the same." Nasan checked her books again. An injury to one of the internal organs, surely. She had expected as much from the beginning. But it made a big difference which one.

She recalled a technique Natalya had used on one of the grooms. "Raise his tunic," she said to Karim's chosen assistant. In the stress of the moment, she had forgotten his name and didn't want to ask. Her father always emphasized that a ruler must learn the name and condition of even the least important servitor.

She had no time for that now. She pointed to the area beneath her left rib cage. "Here is what I need to see. Cover the rest of him." When he nodded in comprehension, she turned her back until Karim assured her it was safe to look. Then she knelt beside Rafik and pressed the palm of her hand, as gently as possible, against the muscled flesh.

She felt ribs—apparently whole, as Karim had said, although something shifted beneath her probing fingers. That one, there. Nothing that would not heal on its own, but best to immobilize them, for safety's sake.

More important, she felt what Natalya had warned her to search for: a solid lump where she should feel nothing but soft flesh. With the pallor and rapid heartbeat, it was enough.

"It's his spleen, I think," she told Karim, kneeling beside her, concern on his face. "The horse must have ruptured it when it rolled on him. He's bleeding inside his body, which is why he faints and looks like death. We can't stop it, but he is young and strong. If we keep him warm and quiet, feed him broth when he can eat, he may well recover. See to it, and bandage his lower ribs." She indicated a band just above her waist. "The smallest one may be cracked. Set a man to watch him. He mustn't be left alone."

"At once, *Khanim*." Karim leaped to implement her orders.

With a nod of approval, she left him to his tasks. "I will await you in the other room," she said. "Attend me there when you've finished, and I will apply a healing salve to that wound of yours. Then take me to Bikbai."

He thanked her profusely, and she smiled. "Someone must direct the raid on those bandits, since Rafik can't. I will show you the way, but it will be your job to defeat them."

The army wagon that transported Daniil to Velizh might as well have been a gun carriage, given the level of discomfort it produced. Every bump in the road jolted the knot of raw agony that he had once called his shoulder, and he split his time between lying half-conscious on the pile of straw that masqueraded as a bed and sitting with gritted teeth and head in hands, trying to ignore the pain. It rained steadily throughout the journey, more or less straight northeast, so that a trip that might take two days on horseback lasted twice as long or more. Daniil soon lost count. He remembered being wounded, but everything since lay wrapped in dense and dirty fog, wheels dragged from sucking mud, damp, and suffering.

At last the fresh-hewn walls of the Velizh fortress rose above their earthen rampart. The skies cleared, showing the

Russian standard of St. George flying high and free atop the main gate. The wagon drew to a halt at the guardhouse, and Daniil looked into the eyes of a man he recognized from his sojourn here.

"Volodka," he said. His throat rasped, even to his own ears. "Is my father here?"

Volodka, a burly giant, lowered the back of the wagon and extended an arm. "He is indeed, Lord," he said, helping Daniil stand and supporting him up the stairs. "And most anxious to see you. I'm to bring you to him right away, though he's talking with a Tatar khan."

Daniil stopped on the sixth step. He had to cling to the wall to keep himself from falling. "Tatar khan? Which Tatar khan?"

"Don't know, Lord. All them names sound alike to me. Young man, about your age. Arrived two days ago. Asked after you. Nikolai Borisovich greeted him like he was family."

Ogodai? Surely not. He'd been fully occupied with his new horde last time they met. Daniil resumed his climb, balancing himself between Volodka and the wall. "Could be that he is family," he said. "I'll know in a moment. Think we can move a bit faster?"

But his knees refused to cooperate. Daniil barely made it up the stairs.

"Let's go back," Semyon told the assembled bandits. "You've seen no sign of the Tatars, Simka?"

Simka, a burly peasant with hands like slabs of beef, shook his head. A man of few words, like many of his kind. Nonetheless, the faces of those around him brightened. The boy with the sick grandmother smiled for the first time since the raid.

"Right," Semyon said. "Let's get a move on, then. Tonight we sleep in our huts."

The bandits produced a ragged cheer, grabbed their possessions—kept stowed for departure—and fell into line.

Semyon did not cheer, but he did spare a thought for Tanka, no doubt waiting at their destination. To his surprise, he missed the wench.

No matter. He'd eat well, then make up for lost time. After a week in the woods, he'd earned every kind of pleasure in existence. Food, ale, and warm and willing women were just a beginning. He still had to figure out how to wreak vengeance on his relatives. Then he'd restore his fortunes, even if it meant stealing for the rest of his life.

For the moment, getting out of that shack was enough.

A week after Nasan reached the estate, Karim's flesh wound had healed and Rafik, although still weak, had set out on the road to recovery. Bikbai, the warrior whose failure to rally had disturbed Karim on the day of her return, had died without Nasan ever identifying the nature of his injury. He lay buried in the woods next to his murdered comrades, but the rest of Nasan's escort declared itself ready to wreak havoc on any bandit who fell into its grasp. By then, she was inclined to believe them. She had never doubted their spirit, but their capacity, when she first arrived from Ferapontovo, had not struck her as up to the task at hand.

Karim had accepted her suggestion to dispatch two men to Vologda. He selected a pair who had recovered from their wounds but remained unfit to fight. More than that had to await the resolution of his plans for vengeance. To send fewer than twenty warriors against those bandits invited failure.

Besides, two men, working alone or together, had a better chance of gathering information without drawing attention to themselves than a troop, however well disciplined and small.

Nasan agreed. And in one sense, their departure made her own decision easier. With six dead, as many more in various stages of recovery, and two more away, every remaining man was needed for the forthcoming raid. Karim did not argue that she should remain at the estate because he could spare no warriors to guard her.

As expected, he had grumbled when she first suggested that she might show the troops the way to the village. A few demonstrations with bow and horse put paid to his objections, and by the day set for their departure he appeared resigned, if not happy, at the thought of a female commander. She reminded him of Queen Manduhai the Wise, who had led her troops into battle even while pregnant, and his face lightened.

"If she was such a warrior as you, *Khanim*, I can see why they followed her," he said. A small victory, and she treasured it.

As she greeted Sorkhokhtani, her conscience smote her. Two years ago, Daniil had exacted a promise from her that she would not undertake such missions alone.

But Daniil had left without a word. Her letter remained unanswered (although it might not have reached him yet), and she was not alone. Her conscience quieted.

For today's adventure, Nasan dressed in her traveling outfit, with the addition of a leather vest and steel skullcap confiscated from one of the fallen warriors and worn under her brocade coat and fur-trimmed hat to protect her from stray arrows. In July, the outfit was stifling enough to set her longing for cool streams and gauze draperies, but an impressive appearance took precedence over comfort, and only a child would ride into the vicinity of a battle unprepared. Her boys' clothes would not protect her here, especially if Semyon caught sight of her.

She might as well present herself as a leader, a descendant of Genghis, and trust her escort and her bow to keep her safe.

Nasan put her foot in Sorkhokhtani's stirrup and mounted.

Locating the village proved easier than Nasan had feared. They had only to ride due north and turn west when they reached the lake, then stop at the first settlement they found that contained more than three houses.

Karim seemed shocked by the absence of population, and Nasan herself found it difficult to believe. Although she had thought the land deserted during her twilight escape, she'd felt certain that cabins must line the shore. Now, with the advantage of daylight, she noticed that the individual homesteads clustered at the edge of the trees or along the lakeshore were, for the most part, unoccupied. No one tilled the land or drove animals across the scratchy fields. No one tended bees or gathered nuts in the forest nearby.

From the far shore, they heard voices drifting across the water as they passed an occasional village. But this side showed itself not only deserted but desolate. Unlike the lean-tos Nasan had seen in the woods, these huts stood strong and firm; she could not believe them abandoned for long. Could Semyon have wreaked such havoc in the region that the local people had fled? How long had he been here?

Long enough for Olga to have heard of him. But distant as Dmitrov seemed, that conversation had taken place less than six weeks ago.

Nasan shared these thoughts with Karim, riding to her right, between her and the deserted hamlets. But he had no answers either, so in the end they abandoned speculation for other topics.

Her already good opinion of Karim strengthened as she listened to him. He was quick of mind and speech, a good strategist, and competent—as she would expect of Ogodai's third-in-command. He had left two wives and five children to journey here, so he must have a few years' advantage over his leader, yet he seemed to hold Ogodai in great respect. "The khan orders," he said from time to time, as if he were speaking of her father instead of her charming, serious older brother, who had once made such a good lieutenant.

Although—thinking of Ogodai's brief visit to Moscow, the way he had chastised Maria and demanded that Natalya do what he wanted, his firm grip of authority over his men and the casual way in which he talked about wringing information out of reluctant Russian clerks—Nasan realized he had changed, just as her relationship with Daniil, once so close, had changed.

They were growing up, and in some senses apart. A dismal reality to consider on the way to an uncertain future.

By noon, the village where she had spent that endless day became visible. "That's it," she told Karim.

He looked grim, focused on the task at hand, their earlier ease with each other forgotten. She suspected him of wishing that she had stayed behind, but he didn't say so. Instead, he beckoned to two juniors among the thirty or so warriors who had accompanied them today. "Scout out the situation in the village," he ordered, "and return unheard and unseen. I want to know who's present, and how many. Watch especially for the leader: a big blond with pale blue eyes and a scar."

The remaining troops moved among the trees, where they could wait without attracting attention. Nasan, unasked, moved Sorkhokhtani to the back so that the warriors hid her from view. Karim's tense face relaxed.

Did he fear that she would force her way to the front, countermand his orders, insist on leading not just in name but in fact? "I place Karim in charge," she said to reassure him. "Do as he says. I will stay here unless I need to defend myself."

Karim grinned, and she returned his smile. He need not know—yet—that if she saw an opportunity to kill Semyon, she would take it.

The honor of her husband's clan demanded it.

The visitor was Ogodai. Daniil staggered into the room and hugged his father, then his brother-in-law, before falling onto a cushioned bench. "Dear God," Nikolai said. "What happened to you, son? The report said we took Vitebsk with no casualties."

Daniil touched his head, which demonstrated a disturbing tendency to spin. "Shot by a Lithuanian," he said. "The wound wasn't so bad. Someone dug the bullet out. My arm's stiff, and the shoulder burns like the fires of hell. But until they dumped me in the devil's wagon, I was holding my own."

"We'll get you cleaned up in no time," his father promised. "Volodka, on your way out find the healer you trust most from among the women and send her here."

"Yes, Lord." Volodka bowed and left.

"It's good to see you, Papa," Daniil said. "And you, brother. What brings you here?"

"My sister." Ogodai pulled a narrow cylinder made of paper from his sash and held it up. Daniil saw the red ribbon, so typical of his wife, and felt an ache in his throat. Nasan had written to him at last? Was she recovered then? Could his long nightmare be ending?

"Not only my sister, of course," Ogodai said. "I came from Vyazma. Matters to discuss with Father—my half-brother

Tulpar, mostly. I'll tell you that part later. You look like you're asleep on your feet."

"More or less." Daniil tried to concentrate. It wasn't easy. "But that is a letter, surely. From your father?"

Ogodai laughed—in sympathy for his friend's befuddlement, Daniil thought. "From your wife, brother. Once she heard that my journey would bring me within a few days' ride of you, she asked me to deliver it. If you don't object, I will read it aloud. Unless you'd rather wait until you can concentrate."

"Please." Daniil could hardly get the word out.

Ogodai handed him a goblet of mead. "Drink this. You sound like a frog."

Daniil sipped mead, which did help a bit. His fingers tingled with the urge to caress his wife's jasmine-scented cheek. Much good it did him. "Tell me what she says. We didn't part well, you know. Is she healthy?"

"Strong enough," Ogodai said, "but overworked. I'll explain why in a moment. But first, the letter."

Overworked? With three women to run the household and two hundred servants to perform the actual tasks?

He didn't ask. After so long without a word from Nasan, he wanted no more distractions. "Please," he said. "I long to hear what she has to say."

"Very well." Ogodai slipped the ribbon from the scroll and unrolled it. "She says, 'Forgive me. I never meant to cause you harm, still less to injure the life we made together'—"

Daniil couldn't let that pass unchallenged. "Forgive her? She did nothing wrong."

"I know that," Ogodai said. "But women often blame themselves, I believe. It doesn't help when your priests tell her she has sinned."

And his mother, Daniil added silently. "If anyone sinned, it is I."

Ogodai grinned. "No need to tell me that."

From the corner, Daniil heard his father chuckle. His own lips curved as he held out his hand. "What else does she say?"

"You could learn to read, you know." Ogodai dangled the unfurled scroll in front of his face. "It's not a sorcerer's art. We'd have to teach my sister the Cyrillic alphabet, but I'm sure she'd pick it up quickly. She loves anything to do with languages."

"She'll learn faster than I, no doubt." Daniil ran a finger over the dark, curling script with its incomprehensible message. Perhaps his friend was right. Imagine being able to speak with his wife in private, even when they were apart. Why had he never considered the possibility?

Stupid of him. Shortsighted, rather. But he could fix it.

"I will," he said. "But for now, read the rest, please."

"It's not long," Ogodai told him. "She writes, 'I love you. I miss you. I fear for your safety.'" For no reason Daniil could understand, Ogodai stopped and glanced to the side where Papa sat. Daniil heard his father clear his throat.

"She signs it, 'Your Nasan,'" Ogodai added.

The words swarmed in and out of Daniil's ears like so many buzzing bees. Nasan loved him? Missed him? How long he had waited to hear those words!

Yet Ogodai's hesitation suggested that he was withholding something. What? Amid the spinning of Daniil's head and the pain of his damaged shoulder, phrases whirled in a confusing dance, defying his efforts to make sense of them.

"If you'd like to reply," Ogodai said, "I can write it down and take it to her."

"I'd rather deliver it myself." Daniil twisted sideways, enough so that he could see both his father and Ogodai—not an easy move. The ache in his shoulder forced him to contort his entire body. "Is there any chance I could get leave, Papa? It will be a while before I can handle a bow again."

"We can ask." Nikolai didn't sound hopeful.

"I'll speak to Barbashin," Ogodai said. "He's a friend of my father's. I'll ask him to let Daniil ride with me. He's more likely to agree to that than to leave." He tapped Daniil's arm. "If you can ride, brother."

Daniil squinted. It did little to clear the fog in his head. "To Moscow?"

"No, north," Ogodai said. "You'll understand why when I explain it to you, but right now I'd be wasting my time. Yours, too."

That was probably true. "Nasan is in Moscow," he said, clinging to the certainty of basic fact. "You must have seen her there. How else did you get the letter? How would you know she's overworked?"

"She was in Moscow," Ogodai said. "But she isn't now. When I left, she was heading north with your mother and sister-in-law. I gave them an escort. Nasan should have reached the White Lake by now. She's on a pilgrimage."

"Nasan? Pilgrimage?" Daniil tapped the side of his head. He must have misheard. Nasan cared about her soul like everyone else, no doubt. She observed the household rituals and attended church when required, but she tended to murmur her prayers in Arabic whenever she thought no one was listening. He had seen the prayer rug and the grandmother doll concealed in her clothes chest. If Ogodai had announced her desire to visit the shrine of a Sufi saint, Daniil would have believed him. But the White Lake?

Ogodai was no longer smiling. Nikolai, too, had a worried frown. "You're sure she's well?" Daniil asked.

Ogodai again glanced at Nikolai, who folded his hands and looked at Daniil. "Your wife is well, son," he said. "It's your mother who needs the pilgrimage. Her heart is failing, and she has gone to pray at the monastery in Ferapontovo. She took Maria and Irina with her, and Father Job as well. They left Moscow at the beginning of June. God grant that my wife still lives."

His mother, his beloved General, was dying? He and his father were at war, but *she* was the one in danger. How could God be so cruel?

The shock was too much. Blinded by unshed tears, Daniil reached a hand toward his father, who clasped it. He heard the door open and rapid, light feet enter.

"Good," Nikolai said. "It's about time you got here. Khan, aid me, if you will be so kind. No point in talking about riding anywhere until my son can stay upright without help."

Chapter 12

THE SCOUTS RETURNED WITH REPORTS OF MEN HAYING IN the fields. Women and girls, too, trailing behind to tie the sheaves. More women near the huts, tending chickens and children. No sign of the big blond leader described by the *khanim*—this news delivered with a bow in Nasan's direction—and no more than half a dozen men overall. But many of the hut doors remained closed, as if their occupants had not yet risen, although the sun approached its zenith.

Karim glanced at Nasan, his eyebrow raised. "Attack, *Khanim*, or wait?"

"Attack," she said, after a moment's consideration. "If the leader is in a hut, you will surprise him. If not, you may have to return—or hunt him down. Begin with the largest hut, the one in the best condition. That's where I saw him last. And spare the women and children, if possible. We can use them on our own estate."

"Very well." He placed his hand over his heart in salute. "You will stay here?"

"I will stay in the back. That way, you need not leave men to guard me." She removed her bow from its case and strung it. "I promise I will take no unnecessary risks."

He shrugged. "I had to ask," he said, but he didn't look disappointed as he moved to the front of his small force. He tapped the scouts on the shoulder. "Look after the *khanim*."

Nasan's bow twitched in her fingers, as if ready for action. She might yet see Semyon.

Oh, his head. The celebration had gone well into the evening, and the need to satisfy Tanka had kept him awake and active long after that. The first rays of dawn stretched across the sky by the time Semyon collapsed in bliss on the feather-filled mattress that once upon a time would have seemed so poor and mean.

But every ale-filled night heralded a day of pounding skull, dull nausea, and regret, and today proved no exception. Semyon dragged himself onto an elbow.

He was alone. Tanka had plied him with drink but partaken little herself, so it made sense that she might have risen early—although she had participated with enough energy in those other activities that it wouldn't have surprised him to discover that she had exhausted herself as she had him.

Still, he saw neither her nor any evidence of her presence, so common sense indicated she had left the hut. He pushed with both hands against the mattress until he attained a sitting position, reached for the trousers left by the bed the night before, and pulled them on. He couldn't see his shirt, but his boots lay near the cooking fire. Using a flattened palm against the outside wall to keep himself upright, Semyon circled the hut and snatched his boots away from the banked embers. He shoved his feet into them and looked around, trying to remember at what point in the festivities he had removed his shirt.

The pounding in his head worsened until it felt as if clanging weapons sounded in his skull. The ground trembled under his feet, and he clutched his brow. He definitely should have drunk less ale. The queasy sensation in his stomach caused him to drop onto a bench.

That was when he heard the howls, the clatter of hooves. Shrieks from women and children worsened the clamor in his head, but none of that could overset instincts honed by years of experience on the battlefield. Semyon grabbed his sword and headed for the door. The moment he opened it, he understood what had happened.

He should have stayed away longer. Those thrice-cursed Tatars had tracked him down.

The scene outside the hut was enough to strike terror into the strongest heart, and Semyon prided himself on his physical courage. Women, children, and animals fled from armed horsemen. Bandits poured out of the closed huts, wielding pikes and swords with limited effect. Flaming arrows lodged in the thatch roofs, adding the crackle of flames and the curl of smoke to the nightmare of a Tatar raid.

Semyon hurried to join his men, urging them around the huts and into the woods. His plans had not changed: save himself and his men; assume the foe would spare most of the women and children; return to steal another day.

Some men refused to heed him, and he left them to their fate. The boy with the sick grandmother took an arrow to the throat and fell within moments. As Semyon had predicted, the boy's grandmother would need another protector now.

"*Bozhe moi!*" Simka stopped in his tracks as Semyon shoved him toward the woods. "A woman!"

In mid-stride, Semyon slewed his head around. By the saints, Simka was right. At the rear of the onrushing Tatar warriors, like one of the devil's own horsemen, rode a young woman in noble dress, her beautiful face taut, her dark hair tucked under a brocade hat trimmed in fur, a bow in her hand. In the split second that he stood transfixed, she rose in her stirrups and fired at him.

He stared, transfixed as a poleaxed sheep, before fear finally jolted his body into movement. The arrow flew too fast for thought to follow; instinct had betrayed him. He would not escape this time.

Simka hauled at his arm. Semyon, jerked off his feet, winced as the arrow grazed his left ear. Then he was tumbling amid leafy branches spiked with thorns. He heard the woman shout—or was that his own rage sounding?

Dragging himself free of the thorns, swearing at each rend and tear, he fled into the forest, his remaining men at his heels. But long after they stopped running, the image of the young woman stayed in his mind. She looked familiar, but he could not place her.

It seemed unlikely he would have met her before. She must remind him of someone else. But that realization paled next to the light that glowed in his heart.

He had found her. At last. His warrior maid. The missing *khanim*, he guessed from her dress. A pearl beyond price.

Too bad she wanted to kill him.

So close! Nasan smacked the pommel with the flat of her hand, then bent forward to pat Sorkhokhtani's neck. The horse had performed admirably, despite her inexperience with the sounds, sights, and smells of war. For this was war, however small the scale. And sure of her mount, Nasan had shot well. If that lout had not interfered, Semyon Kolychev would be writhing on the ground, if not already plaguing his unfortunate ancestors, and the Tatars could retire and take care of their business, this task complete.

Instead, their enemy had escaped, leaving havoc in his wake. Nasan studied the scene before her, wondering how to communicate with Karim. The huts would burn untended, the men lay dead or subdued; it remained only to determine what to do with the women and children—and to chase the fleeing bandits, if they could be caught.

Karim rode up with Grusha—a tie around her mouth, bound hand and foot, her gaze frozen with terror—sitting sideways in front of him. Another warrior carried the middle-aged woman Nasan had noticed before: Masha with the kindly face, who had scolded the children when they chased her chicken. She, too, was bound and gagged, but her flashing eyes and the reddened cheek of the man who scowled over her head suggested that she felt more fury than fear. When Grusha caught sight of Nasan, she emitted a pathetic whimper.

Triumph gave way almost immediately to empathy. Grusha looked so helpless, Nasan felt sorry for her. "Trust me," she said. "No one will harm you."

Grusha didn't respond. Her wide, tear-filled eyes made Nasan think of a puppy, beaten for some infraction it did not understand—or for no reason other than to satisfy the needs of a cruel master. She wanted to reassure Grusha, but she suspected it would take more than words.

Instead she turned to Karim. "You have captured them. Are there others?"

"Just these two so far, *Khanim*." His tone contained a hint of apology. "They were in the first hut we came to. No point in leaving them there; the roof is ablaze. You said we could take them back to the estate."

Indeed, she had. "You did well," Nasan said. "What happened to the rest?"

He turned his horse in a circle, provoking more whimpers from Grusha. "Most fled with the men. We caught this pair and perhaps a child or two. Should we bring the wounded? Although I don't think there are any. Our own men are uninjured, *mashallah*, and those on the ground beyond help."

Nasan stood in her stirrups to see past him. He was right. Other than a few corpses, the villagers had gone. Grusha, too, might have run had she been less burdened by her unborn child. "See if you can catch the leader. My arrow missed him by a hair's breadth. There." She pointed with her arm in the direction taken by Semyon. "If you leave me the scouts, they can carry these women to the house."

"The scouts and ten others, *Khanim*, I beg you. We can't predict what these men will do. Suppose they waylay you or attack the estate before we return?"

Who would dare—except Semyon, a madman if she had ever met one? "Very well," she said. "The scouts and ten others. But remember, these bandits know the woods better than you. Don't lose yourselves while you search for them. If you can't find their trail quickly, follow us to the estate."

Karim bowed his head. "Anything else?"

He had sense and experience; he didn't need detailed instructions from one less accustomed to war than himself. But a reminder of their true target might not go amiss. "Concentrate on the blond lord; kill him, and you avenge your dead comrades while making the road safe for travelers. A great deed to lighten your soul's burden."

When he nodded again, Nasan summoned the two scouts to her side with a lifted finger and gave them her orders. After the two women were transferred to their new mounts, she looked once more at her brother's third-in-command. "Go with God, Karim. You and your men. I hope to see you at the estate before evening."

"May your ancestors protect you, *Khanim*. We will join you as soon as possible."

She acknowledged his farewell, then turned her mare to the east. Karim knew his job, and he would fulfill her orders to his utmost ability. Her main concern now was to reach Natalya's estate without encountering Semyon and his men.

Although if the grandmothers allowed, she would not mind another shot at him. And this time, she would not miss.

Nasan's half-formed hope went unrealized. Her group of fifteen encountered no bandits as it traversed the lakeside path. Throughout the ride, she made no attempt to converse with her two reluctant guests. Gagged, they could not answer her, so talking to them struck her as pointless, even mean. Time enough to remove their restraints when she reached a place where they could sit still and listen. Although what she would say to them, she had no idea.

In short, she didn't know how she felt about Grusha, who still belonged, legally, to the Kolychev household. Nasan had rejoiced when Grusha ran away, and it seemed odd if not erratic to have changed her opinion.

Yet changed it she had. Grusha's agony during that brief scene in the camp had been painful to watch, as was her fear now. She was about to give birth. And Nasan would not condemn her worst enemy to live in Semyon's thrall. Daniil had left both of them, so Nasan had nothing to lose by extending a helping hand to Grusha. And if she did, Daniil might warm to her once more—or was that too much to hope for?

Such were Nasan's incoherent thoughts as she rode toward the Kolychev estate. But by the time they reached their destination, not long before supper, she had decided that the right thing to do was to offer their captives both sanctuary and freedom. If Natalya found out and objected (although neither seemed likely), Nasan could reimburse her mother-in-law later for the cost of the freed slave.

That, at least, was her plan. Reality proved somewhat different. At first, Nasan did the listening—or appeared to. Grusha, freed of her bonds but surrounded by twelve Tatar warriors, curled into an unhappy ball in one corner and refused either to speak or to eat. Masha made up for her silence. Nasan ignored the woman's tirade while she checked on Rafik, who lay conscious but weak on his pallet.

"Fetch him some broth," she ordered the scout who had ridden with Grusha, cutting off the old woman in mid-scold.

When he ducked out of the room, she patted Rafik's hand. "We will soon have you well," she said. "My brother will be pleased. As am I."

He groaned and pressed a hand to his forehead, then his ribs. "The khan will have my head, *Khanim*, and rightly so. I failed to keep you safe. But I thank you for healing me. At least I will die on my feet."

"Don't be silly," she told him. "You almost died as it was, and in defense of me. My brother is not such a monster. I shall tell him the whole, and he will forgive you."

"You are too kind," he muttered, as if unconvinced, but Nasan saw the tension drain from his face.

Behind her, Masha was still grumbling. Nasan drew herself up to her full height—a less effective move than it might have been, since Masha remained a head taller—and adopted the swift, cool, authoritative tone that she had learned worked best with the household servants. "My men captured you to ensure your safety," she said in Russian. "You may leave if you choose, but I suggest you stay. My warriors are chasing the bandit Semyon, and your village was burning when we left."

She gestured at Grusha. "That is no place for a woman so close to her time."

The sound of her native tongue stopped Masha's complaints. "Lady," she said. "I hope you catch him, that vile Severyanin. He took my village from the monks without a by-your-leave and turned our men into criminals. But the women and children have harmed no one."

"I didn't think they had," Nasan told her. "I have ordered my warriors to spare them. But in battle men make mistakes. So again I advise you to stay here."

"And what of her?" Masha in turn pointed at Grusha, still huddled in the corner.

Nasan sighed. Masha was a stranger. How would she interpret a truth so complex and unworked-out as Nasan's quixotic sense that she should help a pregnant woman to whom she owed little or nothing?

She settled for a simple explanation. "I mean her no harm. I recognized her when I saw her in your village a few weeks ago. She is a slave and belongs to this family. Her man was a bandit, was he not, and died in an attack on my men?"

Masha regarded her with superstitious awe. "And how do you know that?"

Nasan laughed. She couldn't help herself. The situation became more absurd by the moment, and she had no wish for Masha to think her a sorceress. "I overheard Lord Semyon tell her. When his men attacked mine, I became lost in the woods. I was about to ask you for help when Lord Semyon rode in. I know him, too, from before."

Grusha whimpered more loudly at the sound of Semyon's name. Nasan rounded on her, annoyed by her spinelessness. "Yes, you remember what he did. And your man, too. He nearly brought ruin on our whole clan, including you. What made you go back to him, you foolish girl?"

"I didn't. That is, I didn't want to, not one bit. When Stenka failed at farming, he heard Lord Semyon was in the area and looking for men. He saw it as a chance to undo his mistakes. What could I do but follow him? We had no food. And a babe on the way." Grusha patted her belly in illustration.

Arms akimbo, Masha strode into Nasan's line of sight. "Don't call her names, Lady. It was your men who killed hers, I bet. Shame on you!"

Nasan stared her down. "Shame on the bandits," she said, when Masha dropped her gaze at last. "They attacked us without warning or provocation." A wave of the hand called Masha's attention to Rafik. "You see how the commander of my guard still suffers."

Masha harrumphed.

"And my title is Tsarevna, not Lady," Nasan said. "I am the daughter of Bulat Khan."

Masha's eyes widened, and she bowed, hands clasped over her heart, but her pugnacious expression did not lessen.

"Grusha is near her term." Nasan kept her temper with difficulty. Indeed, the babe looked set to arrive any day. "I invite her to remain here, to have the child here. My men will protect her. Stay with us, Masha, and we will protect you, too. Grusha needs you, and so do I. I have books that tell me how to birth a child, but I have attended few women in labor, and never as midwife. I warrant you have brought more than one babe into the world."

Masha scowled—at Nasan, at Grusha, at Rafik, at the waiting men. Even those who couldn't follow the dialogue in Russian looked amused, as if the sounds of women's conflict entertained them.

"Well, I have that," she said after a long pause. "And no point fussing over what can't be mended, is there? I thank you for putting up with my crotchets, a great lady like you, and for offering to guard us from those ruffians—which they are, despite calling themselves Lord This and Lord That. I'll stay." She walked to Grusha and ran a comforting hand over the young woman's cheek. "Don't you worry, my pretty. We'll give that babe a good start! And when it's well and truly born, we can discuss what will happen to you both."

Masha, once committed to staying, proved a godsend. As the novice from the monastery had told Nasan the day he guided her to the estate, most of the peasants had fled to escape the bandits and the Tatars. Gossip, as always, traveled fast, and in the last ten days, the abbot's assurances had brought a trickle of families back to their huts, but Nasan had been too preoccupied with doctoring wounded warriors to pester peasants to cook and clean. The few Kolychev servants who had brought the cart from Moscow, together with the youngest Tatar warriors, had taken care of basic tasks like hunting and preparing food, and nothing else had seemed urgent enough to require active intervention—even if Nasan had enjoyed far more familiarity with the region than she did.

Masha's arrival changed that. Her conversation with Nasan had no sooner ended than she ensconced herself in the kitchen and ordered one of the scouts to build a fire. When he looked at her blankly, she indicated with gestures what she wanted, but Nasan had to intervene before communication was achieved. That done, she called for Aziz, by good fortune among the ten chosen to accompany her back to the estate.

"Remain with her, Aziz," Nasan said. "Tell the men to help her as much as possible, but keep an eye on her, too. She seems to have accepted my offer, but let's make sure." She left the three of them in the kitchen and returned to the main room and Grusha.

Masha appeared a short time later. "We'll need help, Tsarevna. Half a dozen more servants at least, to get this place cleaned up. I think we should send to the monks and ask if they can spare a few workers."

She hadn't asked what brought Nasan to this out-of-the-way property. Perhaps she thought the Tatars had seized it, as Semyon had seized her village. Nasan decided the time had come to clear up any misapprehensions.

"Indeed," she said. "Lady Natalya Kolycheva—my mother-in-law—will, if God so decrees, reach us by the Feast of the Dormition. She will be displeased to find her estate in such poor condition. She sent me to supervise its preparation, but the raid made that impossible."

Masha clapped her hands. "Lady Natalya! I knew her when I was a girl. How does she?"

"She has been ill," Nasan said. "In truth, I hope she still lives. Her heart troubles her. But she will be glad to see you, I'm sure, and happier still if we have her home in good repair by the time she arrives."

In truth, Natalya would expire of sheer fury if she saw the mess that fifty armed men had made of her house. "I think you'll find some women on the estate who can help," Nasan added. "And my warriors will bring any they encounter during their search for Lord Semyon."

Grusha again whimpered at the sound of these names, drawing Nasan's attention. "Lady Natalya and Lord Nikolai aren't looking for you," she said. "I brought you here because you're near your time, and I felt sorry for you after I heard Semyon say your man was dead. We weren't friends, but to leave you, with a baby, in Semyon's power—I bear you no such ill will as that. Once you have the child, you may go or stay, as you please. I will straighten things out with Lady Natalya, if necessary."

Grusha's mouth dropped open, as if kindness came her way so seldom that the possibility of it amazed her.

"We are your family," Nasan said. "My husband loved you." Her throat hurt with the admission. "He wouldn't want me to leave you in danger. Lady Natalya would not want it either." She turned away to hide the tears she refused to shed.

"He did not, Tsarevna." Grusha's voice shook. "He enjoyed me for a time, as he did the other girls. But from the moment he saw you, he had eyes for no one else. I didn't believe it at first, but he told me himself. That he was married and meant to stay true to you. That it was over between us. Why do you think I left with Stenka? And now Stenka's gone."

Nasan spun on her heel and stared at the woman hugging herself, sobbing, in the corner. Then, because she could think of no other response, she crossed the hall, sat on the floor, and put her arms around Grusha. They cried together.

When she could, Nasan patted Grusha's shoulder and said, "I'm sorry about Stenka. But we will see you safe, and you will have your baby, I promise you. And your freedom."

"That's good of you, Tsarevna," Grusha mumbled.

Nasan patted her shoulder once more, then rose to her feet. Only then did she remember Masha, still standing near the door waiting for orders and regarding her with approval. For a moment, Nasan imagined her as a peasant version of Natalya.

"She's right, Tsarevna," Masha said. "You have no reason to trouble yourself with the likes of us."

If they only knew. I do. Because I will have no child of my own. Daniil has left me, too.

She beckoned to Masha. "Help me get her to the kitchen. Your idea of contacting the monks is a good one, but for the moment we have no one to send. When the men return, we can decide what to do next."

Daniil woke and stretched. For the first time since his injury, his right shoulder felt better: still tight, still painful, but without the burning sensation. His time in the bathhouse yesterday, with its warm water and banked fires, had worked its magic. The compress applied by the healer probably helped too. Better yet, no one was trundling him over wretched roads in an unsprung cart. And his wife loved him, missed him.

Life was good. When would he see her?

He rolled sideways and used his left arm to push himself into a sitting position. The room his father had assigned him was spare, with a pallet on a frame, a bench near the window, and a chest to hold clothes. From a peg on the wall hung a simple robe, a linen tunic, and loose homespun trousers. He had a vague recollection of having seen them before. His boots sat flush against the wall.

He looked down, where nothing covered him but a linen sheet and wool blanket, half of which he had cast aside. Where were his own clothes? He'd worn them when he arrived, obviously. When he greeted his father and Ogodai— yes. The healer had helped him shed them before removing his bandages, applying her concoction, and leaving him to lie face down and sweat out any remaining toxins. Later she'd returned, with fresh bandages as well as the robe and tunic. After that, most of the rest was a blur. He had an image of Ogodai handing him food and a cup that turned out to contain apple juice, talking about his visit to Moscow while Nikolai tapped worried fingers on the table and alternated between questions about his wife's health and his son's. Daniil couldn't recall his own answers, or much of the information Ogodai had shared. He wasn't quite sure what brought Ogodai here, although he thought his brother-in-law had given an explanation. But he remembered Nasan's letter. Yes, he remembered that.

And he remembered that Mama was ill. Very ill, maybe already dead. Which seemed incredible, given how strong she had always been, how warm and loving and capable. Why, even the last time he'd seen her, she'd scolded him for not taking proper care of himself. And she had made an effort to welcome Nasan into her household, despite her outspoken wish for a bride closer to her in language, customs, religion, and personality. No matter that he had soon learned that Nasan was everything *he* needed. His wife still posed a challenge for his mother, just by breathing.

Daniil stood. His knees felt steadier today. He crossed the room and lifted the lid of the chest, but as he'd expected, it was empty. He put on the tunic and trousers, then the robe, which tightened uncomfortably across his bandaged shoulder. Boots in hand, he returned to the bed. No stockings that he could see, so he pushed one foot into its boot, then the other, and set off—steadying himself against the wall as he went—to find his father and his own clothes, not necessarily in that order.

Chapter 13

Estate near Lake Borodava, July 1536

KARIM APPEARED JUST BEFORE SUNSET, HIS SCOWL AS stormy as the gray clouds that scudded overhead. A line of warriors, more dour than Nasan ever remembered seeing, trailed him. He stood in the center of the large front room, dripping water until Masha bustled in with a mop and shamed him into stripping off his soaked outer garments. She carried them off to the kitchen, driving damp warriors before her as if they were kittens. Nasan bit her lip to keep from smiling, although Karim looked grim enough to cast fear into the heart of a saint.

"What happened?" she asked when the last chivvied warrior disappeared behind the door. "Did you lose more men?" Her quick count as they entered didn't reveal anyone missing, but the men had milled about so, trying to escape the lash of Masha's tongue, that their numbers remained uncertain.

"No." Karim, still glowering, scuffed the toe of his boot against the floor. "We hunted the bandits as you ordered. They were on foot, and we should have had no trouble. Caught sight of them once—a big blond leader and twenty or so nasty ruffians, more than I expected."

He looked embarrassed as well as angry, and he definitely knew something he was reluctant to share. "And?"

"Boys," he said, shocking the sinking feeling right out of her. "Boys with slingshots. Hiding in the trees. They pelted us until we couldn't see straight. Meanwhile, the blond lord got away, with his men." The words came rat-a-tat, like the sound of a kettle drum calling the troops into battle.

"Were any of ours injured?"

Karim shook his head. "Not seriously. The men will be black and blue by tomorrow, no doubt."

"And the village?" she asked, although she could guess the answer. "Did it burn?"

"To the ground, *Khanim*. We made sure of it. To teach them a lesson."

Of course. What Tatar commander would not have done the same? Ogodai included, gentle as he could be in other circumstances. Resistance could not be tolerated, especially if it led to the escape of dangerous criminals. Punishment must be swift and certain, as if stamping out a nest of vipers.

"You captured no more women and children, then?" It saddened but did not surprise her when he shook his head. The families had decided to stick with their men, then, even at the cost of homelessness. But one could hardly blame them for not seeing the Tatars as potential benefactors. They had started the fire, after all. In retrospect, they were lucky not to have burned half the forest.

She gave the response any *khanim* must give. "You did well, Karim. I will tell the khan. Rest now, and eat."

Semyon Kolychev had a great deal to answer for.

Semyon accepted a bowl of soup and a quarter-loaf from Tanka and watched appreciatively as she strolled to join the women, clustered with the children around a small campfire in a clear space not far from the main group of lean-tos. It impressed him to see how many families had joined his settlement in exile. Only that pain in the rear Grusha and her crabby self-appointed caretaker had remained in the village. Perhaps the flaming roof of their hut had collapsed on them. Either way, good riddance to them both.

"It's better to have the families here, I suppose," he said to Simka, sitting next to him. A poor replacement for Stenka in every way, but the only one available. "Keeps the men from sneaking off to see them. I just hope they don't cause trouble."

Simka grunted. "Women allus causes trouble, Lord. It's in their nature."

No argument there. Think how much trouble his warrior maid would cause, and he hadn't even won her yet.

"We need to get back on the road if we're to feed this lot." An image of the *khanim* as he'd last seen her filled Semyon's mind. No, this was not about catching another glimpse of her. That would come later.

"What of the Tatars, Lord?" Simka slurped soup, and Semyon gritted his teeth. One day, he'd be back in his rightful place, the *khanim* at his side …

He slapped Simka on the shoulder, and a small chunk of bread flew from the man's mouth, landing on the grass. "They won't be back, man. I know Tatars. They raided us, they burned the village—damn them—and they'll go on about their business now, thinking they made their point. So while they take care of their cursed affairs, we'll take care of ours. We're almost into August, by the Virgin's robe. The peak of pilgrim season. Every last one of them loaded with icons and jewels and gifts for the holy fathers. Wouldn't you rather see those valuables in our coffers than theirs?" He surveyed the clearing.

How many men had escaped the attack on the village? Not enough.

But the Tatars, in attacking, had played into his hands. Peasants had a deep-rooted hostility against those who invaded their fields. "Scout the forest," he told Simka. "Recruit more men. Tell them what happened to our village and urge them to join us, or prepare to surrender their wives and children, their own lives, to the Tatars. When we build a big enough force, we pick our moment and strike!"

"Yes, Lord. As you wish," Simka mumbled through a mouthful of bread.

The man's table manners were fit for a pig. And in a contest of wits, the pig would win every time.

If only Stenka had not died in the last raid. Then Semyon's bandit queen would be his for the taking.

Daniil found his brother-in-law in a large, airy room halfway up another tower, this one bordering the northern gate that marked the main entry to the Velizh fortress. Ogodai lifted a hand in greeting, but he did not divert his attention from the Tatar warrior, even younger than they, who stood next to him. Daniil didn't recall seeing the boy—it was impossible to think of him as anything else—before.

Ogodai was in full khan mode today—embroidered skullcap, light green figured-silk robe with elbow-length sleeves folded back to display a rich turquoise tunic, and darker green trousers tucked into his boots, which curled at the toes in the Tatar style. "I'm hoping to impress Prince Barbashin," he said in response to Daniil's raised eyebrow. "Convince him you can be more use to the state elsewhere."

"Where?" Daniil nodded at the young warrior, who hung his head as if accused of some crime. Unlike his khan, the boy wore the simple dress of a nomad: sheepskin coat and hat, felt trousers and boots. He carried a full array of weaponry, though—Ogodai and his father didn't skimp when it came to their servitors' safety. At least, Daniil assumed the boy served his brother-in-law from the deference he showed. "What's wrong with him?" he added, before Ogodai had a chance to answer the first question.

"You'd better sit down," Ogodai said. "You're not going to like this one bit."

Daniil sat. "Tell me."

"Ilgiz here came from your family's estate near Ferapontovo. He went to my father first, as ordered, and *Ata* sent him here." Ogodai held out a document covered with swirls and dots like the ones in Nasan's letter, then pulled it back. "Sorry. I forgot you can't read it."

"Mama?" A spectral hand squeezed Daniil's heart.

"No." Ogodai patted his good shoulder in sympathy.

Not Mama. Then what? Why does Ogodai look so grim?

Because he did look grim. His lips formed a straight line, and he had a look in his eyes Daniil hadn't seen since the final struggle between Ogodai and his half-brother, almost two years ago now.

"How much do you remember from the day you arrived?" Ogodai asked.

"Not much."

"I thought so. You were in a bad way. In short, your mother has gone on a pilgrimage to pray for her health. She and Maria planned to go by boat, and when I reached Moscow, Nasan was prepared to join them. But I could see she wanted to ride." Ogodai's hand clenched the paper. "She offered to help me with the mission that brought me here, and I agreed. The three of them had no real escort. So I sent her ahead with a group of armed warriors and dispatched a smaller force to watch over your mother and sister-in-law on the boat. You don't mind, I hope."

"I'd ride from here to Karakorum before I'd get on a boat with Maria," Daniil said with a grin. Ogodai's mouth quirked in response. "I'm sure Nasan feels the same. I thank you. But that can't be what makes you look like you want to punch someone."

All trace of Ogodai's smile vanished. "They were attacked. Nasan and her escort. Near the White Lake. Five men died, and Nasan's personal servant. And Rafik, most like. He was clinging to life when Ilgiz set out to find me."

"And Nasan?" The question came out as a croak.

Nasan whose letter had raised his spirits, who loved him and missed him and mourned their unborn child. She could not lie dead, her bright fire stilled.

Ogodai clasped his shoulder again. "The warrior closest to her slapped her horse, sent it into the woods. Someone else tried to do the same for Vera. Too late: she'd already been hit. But when Ilgiz left, Nasan had not returned. They don't know where she is." His voice had been soft, but now it hardened. "We must find her. And if these attackers have laid so much as a finger on her, I shall personally see them screaming in torment before I dispatch them to the demons they serve."

A sentiment with which Daniil heartily agreed. He said so. "But I can't just leave. The generals don't care about a missing wife."

"No," Ogodai admitted. "But I must go, no matter what. I didn't tell you this in our last conversation. You were having trouble staying awake as it was. My half-brother Tulpar made an alliance with the Shirins against me. I found out just in time and chased him the whole way to Moscow. He hid out there. But it seems he's negotiating with your old friend Koshkin, perhaps with the intent of changing sides."

"Koshkin?" Daniil shook his head. His ears must be deceiving him again. "Your half-brother is negotiating with that traitor whose shrew of a daughter married my brother? But how is that possible? Koshkin has been stationed in Vologda the last two years."

"Exactly. That was the part Nasan offered to help with. And it's why I'm going north. My men are investigating. I'd ordered them to send the information they collected to Vyazma, but with Nasan missing, it's best if I go to them instead. My father wants me to find out as much as I can about Tulpar's plans. So Vologda, then Moscow."

"Tulpar and Koshkin." Daniil turned the idea of such a pairing over in his mind. If Tulpar had decided to enter Russian service, he would start by looking for an ally—and the bad blood between him and his father meant that he would not seek support from Bulat.

But Koshkin seemed like an odd choice. The Moscow court had plenty of former Tatars in high positions, so Tulpar had no reason to seek out a disgraced Russian nobleman. No reason even to know where to look for Koshkin. Some as yet hidden factor must be in play.

But whatever brought them together, almost certainly the two men were using each other. Koshkin's weakness was arrogance: he manipulated others; he failed to anticipate that his tools might in turn manipulate him. And Tulpar was a master manipulator. "Koshkin's met his match in your brother," Daniil said.

Ogodai laughed. "True enough." Ilgiz looked puzzled. No doubt the name of Koshkin meant nothing to him.

"So," Ogodai repeated. "I'm heading to Vologda, and your estate is on my way."

"What of your own horde?" Daniil asked, still struggling to follow the rapid twists and turns of the conversation.

"*Ata*'s called in reinforcements from Kasimov. Tulpar makes him itchy. He makes me itchy, too." Ogodai extended a hand, palm open toward Daniil. "This news of Nasan is bad, but it should help us convince Barbashin to let you go."

Daniil nodded. "How?" He groped for his sword and did not find it. There seemed little point in repeating the unlikelihood of obtaining leave to search for a missing wife.

"Because of how it happened." Ogodai pointed at his unhappy courier. "According to the locals, the attack came from a new bandit chieftain who preys on pilgrims. With most of its troops at war, the state hasn't warriors to spare for maintaining law and order. I will argue that I'm doing your commander a favor by bringing these villains to justice—and that I need your assistance, since you know the area. You can help with Koshkin, too. He's a decent man, Barbashin, and it's not as though you can fight in your condition. I think he'll say yes."

Koshkin stood at attention, facing the burly nobleman who lounged at his ease in the room's one armchair. Prince Vasily Shuisky did not look pleased. His gray hair stood straight up, as if he had dragged his fingers through it, and the tall black-fox hat that marked him as a high-ranking courtier lay discarded at the far side of his desk.

The irony of the situation did not escape Koshkin. Normally he sat in the armchair, grilling an unfortunate subordinate forced to stand and await his pleasure.

He kept this observation to himself. Only the most subtle manipulation of the truth had kept the prince from sending Koshkin back to the northern fastness of Vologda. He said a silent prayer that none of the documents that littered Shuisky's desk contained intelligence that would expose

Koshkin's story for the tissue of lies he knew it to be. If averting punishment required standing at attention until he fell straight forward like a child's tin soldier, that was a price Koshkin was willing to pay.

"Islam-Girei is sending an embassy from Crimea," Shuisky announced after a pause long enough for Koshkin to worry that a future even worse than Vologda might await him.

"Is that so?" he asked. "And does our young friend take part in this diplomatic exercise?"

Prince Vasily stared at him, eyes narrowed under brows thick as fuzzy caterpillars. "He does. You have a second chance, Koshkin. Don't fail me again."

Koshkin dipped his head, a sharp down-up to indicate acquiescence without acknowledging the justice of Shuisky's dissatisfaction. "I told you he said we would meet again, Prince. I believe that clearing his obligation to Islam-Girei was always Tulpar's plan. This time, nothing will get in my way."

Shuisky dismissed him, and Koshkin wasted no time in leaving.

Nasan had gone to check on Rafik when a shriek from the kitchen sent her running for the door.

Grusha stood in the center of the kitchen, her dress wet and a puddle of water between her feet. Masha, busy shooing warriors away from the table and toward the main room, looked up as Nasan entered.

"Nowt to worry you, Tsarevna," Masha said. "Her water broke, is all. We'll have a babe with us before morning, God willing." She shoved Aziz in the back. "Take the food and your friends and be off. You'll not tell me that men attend a birth even among the Mussulmans, will you? Do something useful for once in your life and start a fire in the bathhouse. The child will make its entrance there, like a good Christian."

Aziz retreated with such haste that Nasan could not help but laugh. He looked like a hunting dog caught chasing the sheep.

She grabbed his arm before he could complete his escape. "Tell the men," she said in Tatar. "They can bang drums and sing, to scare away the *albasti*." She glanced around the kitchen. That carving knife would do excellently. "I have an iron knife to serve as a talisman," she said, "but keep sticks to hand, in case I call for them. The child's father is dead, so it is doubly vulnerable."

Aziz muttered agreement, and she let him go. He dashed from the room as if chased by an evil spirit. Masha's hearty chuckle sped him on his way. Nasan glanced at her and smiled.

Masha waved the wooden spoon she'd picked up while chiding Aziz. "Just the same, aren't they, Tsarevna, whoever they be? Men, I mean. Ever afeared of an approaching babe."

"Always," Nasan said. "Although to be sure, we keep them out."

"And better so," Masha told her. "A fair nuisance they are, most of the time. Pacing and wincing and worriting the mother as well as themselves." She wrapped a supportive arm around Grusha's waist as that young lady groaned and doubled over, clutching her extended stomach. "The pains are starting, are they? Well, let's get you to the bathhouse. And no fretting. With us to take care of you, that babe of yours will arrive strong and healthy."

They walked slowly to the outer door, and Nasan followed without waiting to be asked. A pile of linen cloths caught her eye, and she picked them up, wrapping the carving knife in one of them. No *albasti* would get the chance to steal this child's soul.

The bathhouse would be warm and dark, with hot water to hand and places for Grusha to sit, lie, and walk, as needed. What else should she bring? Her medical books, written by men, would be useless here. Midwifery was the art of women, and Masha appeared to be well versed in its mysteries.

Nasan would watch and learn and assist. It was enough, for the moment.

Walking. Sitting. Wiping Grusha's sweaty face with a linen cloth dipped in cool water. Encouraging her to breathe. Rubbing her belly. Walking some more. Reassuring her. Nasan cooed and patted and supported until her eyelids drooped. At Masha's suggestion she napped for a while, then took over the rubbing and walking and reassuring once more while Masha rested.

Despite Masha's prediction that the babe would appear without delay, night shaded into morning with no sign of a delivery. It was natural, Nasan supposed, for a first baby. She remembered her mother patting the head of a concubine younger than Nasan herself now was, reassuring the girl that she would survive the pain, that next time would be easier. The girl had gasped that there would be no next time if she could prevent it, but in fact she had survived, and forgotten the pain, and the next time had gone more smoothly and faster. That second time had been Nasan's third witnessed birth, just months before she left Kasimov for her wedding.

She bent forward, whispering the same reassurance into Grusha's ear. Grusha nodded, and her tense face relaxed. "No next time for me, Tsarevna," she said—just as the concubine had. Nasan didn't argue with her: Grusha might one day love again, but with her man dead such a short time, it seemed cruel to ignore a grief that must seem unending.

Fortunately, Grusha was strong. When not in the throes of a contraction, she relaxed into fitful sleep, only to jerk awake again when the next pain hit. As dawn broke, the pains came faster and harder and closer together. Sleep became impossible—not only for Grusha but for all of them.

Masha awoke and hustled to the bedside. Nasan handed her a bowl of warm water and, after an incredulous stare, she washed her hands before reaching inside Grusha's laboring body, shaking her head and grumbling about ladies' silly ideas. After a moment, Masha withdrew her arm and patted Grusha's thigh with her free hand. "The babe is pointed the right way and has its head near the entrance," she said. "Shouldn't be long now, dearie." She washed her arm in the bowl once more. When she was done, Nasan poured out the dirty water and replaced it, then brushed Grusha's hair back from her forehead with a damp cloth. An image of her maid Vera, lying dead in the woods, hovered for a moment in front of her eyes. If Vera had lived, she would be here now, performing these simple tasks. But such was the reality of childbirth: mistress cared for servant, just as those lower on the social ladder so often cared for those they served. Here in the bathhouse, they were women, working together. Equals.

Chanting prayers that Father Job, in all likelihood, would not recognize, Masha spread a paste made of reindeer lichen on Grusha's swollen belly and plied her with a drink made from wormwood. She murmured spells. Nasan listened, whipping her tired brain to remember the sounds and the potions, while Grusha clutched the acorn strung around her neck and begged the bath spirits for a safe delivery.

At last, Masha declared the babe ready to enter this sinful world. By then, a quick peek out the bathhouse door showed that the sun had cleared the horizon. Nasan would have sworn she was limp from exhaustion, but at this news she rallied.

Grusha, too, raised her drooping head, her face alight with renewed energy. At Masha's instruction, Nasan eased Grusha onto the wooden bench, spread with wool blankets, closest to the fire. Grusha was near-naked by now, only a loose linen robe tucked about her arms and shoulders.

"Push," Masha ordered. Grusha whimpered.

Masha urged her on. "Push. Harder."

Grusha pushed, then pushed again as Masha encouraged her with words and pats. Nasan offered her hands, then gave Grusha a cloth to hold instead. The strength of Grusha's clasp was a good sign, but Nasan's fingers ached from that crushing grip. Rubbing them, she went to stand beside Masha. Between Grusha's legs, a small dome appeared, covered in fuzz. Nasan gasped.

"Push, Grusha," she called. "It's almost here. Push hard!"

"Stand there, Tsarevna." Masha pointed to Grusha's side. "Press gently on her belly. Slow and steady, now. We want to help the babe on its way, not hurt it."

Nasan did as she was told, but she couldn't help craning her neck. She had never been so close to a birth before. Those times in the harem had been nothing to this. She'd fetched and carried, but her mother had sent her from the room before the child could appear, just in case something went wrong. Here no one could force her to miss the moment when the child emerged. And if she had anything to say about it, nothing would go wrong either.

"Good," Masha said. "Easy now, little one. We don't want you tearing your Mama. That's no way to say hello."

Grusha moaned, then pushed. Nasan murmured words of support. Under her hands, Grusha's skin tightened, held, then loosened. Not completely, but a bit.

"The head's out," Masha said. "Almost there, sweetness. One more big push. Come on, you can do it."

Grusha drew in a long, sobbing breath. "You can do it, Grusha," Nasan said. "One more." Her own stomach tightened in sympathy, but she didn't release the pressure of her hands.

And then it happened. With a rush almost like the breaking water of yesterday evening, the object tensing Grusha's womb slipped free. Masha gave a sharp cry of satisfaction as the baby slid into her hands. "Ah, good girl," she said. "Just the afterbirth now. That's nothing after this fine lad."

She handed the child to Nasan, who gazed in awe at the small crumpled face, red and wrinkled under its crown of fuzz. The cord still attached the baby to its mother. Tiny hands and feet waved aimlessly, and the pursed mouth made sucking motions. For an instant, she let herself imagine that the child she held was hers, hers and her husband's. What would it be like, to cradle her son in her arms?

The illusion would not hold. This child belonged to Grusha.

Yet still it seemed like a miraculous event, one that should not be diminished by a flash of sorrow. To distract herself, Nasan tickled the babe's feet. He drew in a sharp breath, then let out a wail of indignation that made her laugh. Masha was busy with the afterbirth, but Grusha had propped herself on her elbows and was looking at them. "Lad?" she asked. "It's a boy?"

Nasan stepped forward, the child in her arms, and turned him toward his mother. "A boy," she said. "As you see, a beautiful baby boy. Strong and healthy, too. Listen to that yell."

Grusha touched her son's cheek with one finger. "He's not beautiful yet. More squashed and red."

"Give the poor mite time," Masha said. "Think what he's been through, the darling."

"Let me wash him," Nasan said. "He'll look better then, I'm sure."

The child in her arms felt soft and warm. She bent her head over the tiny body and whispered a prayer in his ear to protect him from the power of Satan. Masha approached with string and knife, tied the baby's cord three fingers from his navel, and sliced it with the blade. Blood seeped from the cut. While Masha wrapped the afterbirth for burial, Nasan carried the baby to the basin set aside for him and gently washed him clean. Then she swaddled the child in the linen cloths set aside earlier and carried him to his mother. Before handing him over, she nuzzled his cheek, inhaling the fresh baby smell. "Welcome to this world, little one," she told him. "May you make your ancestors proud."

Grusha held out her arms. For the first time since her capture, she looked happy. Not just relieved at the cessation of pain but eager to make her son's acquaintance. What it must mean to her, to have this living reminder of the man she had lost. Something else Nasan understood too well.

But if Grusha could overcome her loss and find joy, so could she. There was no point in surrendering to self-pity. She would just have to work harder to regain Daniil's love. Or learn to forget him, if she could not.

Grusha waited, arms outstretched, but Nasan gazed at the baby, reluctant to surrender him to his mother. One day, if God took pity on her, released Daniil from the war, and allowed her again to conceive ... However small and wrinkled, red and squished, the little boy was beautiful. So might her own son look. One day.

Beautiful, but not hers. With a sigh, she placed the baby in Grusha's arms.

As she watched Grusha nuzzle the child, though, the sense of wonder flowed through her once more. She glanced at

Masha. Only then did the reality of what they had achieved hit her.

"We did it!" she said.

"Yes, Tsarevna, we did." A warm smile erased the weariness in the older woman's face. "A living mother and a healthy babe. A gift from Our Lady, indeed."

"I'll reward you well," Nasan promised. "Without you, we would not have succeeded. I learned so much from watching you."

Grusha, murmuring to her child, seemed not to hear. Her face soft, she traced the line of the baby's cheek. "It's a miracle," she said. "He's a miracle. Thank you for bringing him into the world."

"What will you call him?" Nasan asked. "Your Stenka cannot name him."

Grusha blushed. Her palm caressed the child's scalp, the silken fuzz, the squinched nose. "Stepan, Tsarevna, after his father."

"Very fitting." Nasan stroked the baby's cheek again. "Greetings, Stepan Stepanich. We will stand in place of your father and keep you safe."

Ogodai proved persuasive. A bandit who preyed on pilgrims, reckless enough to attack a troop of Tatar warriors, was indeed a source of great concern to the authorities. With the blessing of Prince Barbashin, therefore, he and Daniil—declaring that, of course, he could ride; nothing more plagued him than a stiff shoulder—set off as soon as they could pack. Ilgiz had left the day before to warn those at the Kolychev estate to prepare for the arrival of their khan.

By mid-afternoon of the first day, Daniil recognized that he had exaggerated the extent of his recovery, but stubbornness and anxiety drove him onward. And so it continued throughout the eight days required for their party to reach Tver and the three more days that brought them to tonight's destination, a field not far from the iron-production center of northwest Russia. Even the town's name—Ustyuzhna Zheleznaya, Iron Ustyuzhna—spoke of its dedication to military output. Watching the Tatars raise their round tents, Daniil could see in the background the thick dark smoke emanating from the manufactories, like wisps from Satan's realm.

But tough as the journey had been for him—and he wouldn't admit that to a soul, especially since he knew that, without him, Ogodai would have ridden farther each day— Daniil was glad that they had pressed ahead. July had turned to August somewhere around Tver, but another three days on the road would get them to their destination.

Or two. The long hours in the saddle, exhausting at first, had restored his strength as coddling did not, turning the lie he had fed Ogodai ten days ago into the truth. Except for a lack of flexibility in his right arm and shoulder that made handling a bow difficult, Daniil felt like his old self again.

And with luck, by the time they reached his father's estate, Nasan would have been found, alive and well.

Chapter 14

"PRINCE YURI IS DEAD." THE VOICE, FAMILIAR BUT unexpected in this setting, spoke from the doorway.

Koshkin hesitated for a moment, gathering his thoughts before facing his visitor. Prince Vasily Shuisky did not, as a rule, travel to meet those beneath him in the court hierarchy; he summoned them to his reception area in the Kremlin. Yet here he was, in the room assigned to Koshkin for his negotiations with Tulpar Sultan, currently on his way back from Crimea, according to Shuisky himself.

Moreover, Shuisky brought news—and dire news at that—of Prince Yuri Ivanovich, the former prince of Dmitrov. He must know that Koshkin had supported Yuri once upon a time. That was no secret. He might—or might not—believe that Koshkin had transferred his allegiance to Moscow long ago. That he had decided to deliver the news of Yuri's death in person, however, gave Koshkin pause. What reaction did Shuisky hope to pry loose with his surprise visit?

Koshkin took a deep breath to compose himself, then turned. Shuisky had much experience reading expressions; he would not miss a hint of grief or anger.

"Should that concern me?" He strove to keep his tone level.

"Doesn't it?" Shuisky moved, unasked, to a chair and lowered his considerable bulk onto it. "I thought you served Prince Yuri in Dmitrov before transferring your oath to his elder brother. Was I wrong?"

"Years ago," Koshkin said. "He was a good prince until his ambitions got the better of him."

Shuisky regarded him in the uncomfortable manner used by certain father-confessors, as if he could unearth Koshkin's soul. Koshkin stared back, daring the other man to probe further. To state his suspicions openly.

"The funeral is tonight," Shuisky said in a voice as cool and disinterested as Koshkin's own. "You will attend, of course. That's not why I came."

Koshkin, tired of playing the subordinate in his own office, settled himself behind his desk. "And why *did* you honor me with your presence, Prince?"

"To remind you of your assignment. Tulpar Sultan is due in less than a month. He has a fine record as a military leader, this young man, and we will benefit from the use of his skills— against his fellow Tatars, in particular. What have you offered him? What will you offer this time?"

"Land, honor, a position at court," Koshkin said. "He insists he can do better elsewhere, although I suspect he has fewer options than he pretends. Otherwise, why return to Moscow?"

"I agree." Shuisky tapped his fingers against the arm of his chair. "We must raise the price. He is unmarried. Perhaps a bride will tempt him."

"I will consider that," Koshkin said. As if he had not the wits to figure that out for himself. Oh, for the days when he had been the one giving orders! "He didn't leap at the opportunity when I offered it before. Insisted he had a woman already."

"Then persuade him to change his mind. A 'woman' will not give him legitimate sons."

In Koshkin's experience, Tatars regarded all their heirs as legitimate. How could they do otherwise, when most of the khans had at least four wives and dozens of concubines? But since Shuisky must know that as well, Koshkin saw no gain in pointing out the flaw in his superior's reasoning.

Shuisky placed both hands on the armrests, pushed himself out of the chair, and walked to the door. "It is not I who will return to Vologda if you fail," he said with chilly calm.

Koshkin ground his teeth. Some of his skepticism must have shown on his face, despite his attempts to remain impassive. "I won't fail," he promised. What else could he say?

Shuisky strode from the room without another glance. Not until he had left did Koshkin dare slump back into his chair. Even then, he wondered if the vaunted Kremlin spies were observing him through hidden peepholes. But if they were, they would see only a man depressed by the threat of failure, of exile. And they'd be right. Up to a point.

Prince Yuri was dead. Starved to death, according to the gossip that had circulated around the country for months, if not years. He'd been an honorable man, acting within his rights for the good of the Russian land. A friend, lost to the ambition and distrust and hatred of his sister-in-law. Koshkin spared a moment to mourn the Yuri he had known, whose funeral he must attend while taking care not to attract the attention of those same Kremlin spies.

He was sick of falling under suspicion, as if he were the only noble in Russia concerned about protecting his family and advancing the interests of his clan.

Too bad his beautiful Maria had traveled north just as he found a road south. She alone among his children had an inkling of how his mind worked. He could talk to her.

It was time he took thought for her future, in fact. He had left her with the Kolychevs too long. But he must first secure the cooperation of Tulpar Sultan. A difficult man with an exaggerated sense of his own importance.

Not like Prince Yuri, so soon to join his ancestors in the Cathedral of the Archangel Michael.

Or so Koshkin assumed. Shuisky hadn't said, had he? But surely even Grand Princess Elena wouldn't refuse to bury a prince of the blood in the royal mausoleum!

Koshkin reached for a small chest on the table at his right and hurled it to the floor. The clasps snapped, and the wooden lid spun across the polished planks, coming to rest against the stand of icons in the far corner.

The rage he had worked so hard to contain broke free, just as the contents of the small chest had spilled from their bounds and lay scattered on the floor.

Prince Yuri was dead. Because of that woman, Elena. Oh, some people tried to blame the boyars for the turmoil at court, but that was a poor attempt to shield Elena. Yuri was not the only highborn prince to suffer because of her single-minded drive to rid herself of those better qualified to rule than she. She would balk at nothing that might secure her power, her sons' power. Koshkin detested her.

She must be stopped. And he would be the one to stop her. But first he must fulfill his immediate task. Otherwise, he would be on his way back to Vologda, if not somewhere even more remote, his hopes of reinstatement dashed yet again.

Under Masha's skillful hands, the household purred into life. Peasants became servants, supplies appeared as if by magic, and before long the house gleamed, ready for Natalya's arrival. The two warriors returned from Vologda, reporting that

Koshkin had left more than a month ago. The strengthening of the fortifications had led to a huge influx of craftsmen from Moscow, and the town was filled to bursting. It was difficult to find anyone who could (or would) explain the military governor's unexpected departure. Karim dispatched another pair in search of more information, but he expressed little confidence that they would discover any evidence of contact between Koshkin and Tulpar.

The first of August came and went without word from their pilgrims. Nasan, caught up in helping Grusha tend her baby, missed the turning of the calendar. But when the crescent moon waxed into a half-moon and still no message appeared, she dispatched Aziz to St. Cyril's Monastery with instructions to discover whether any seriously ill lady with her daughter-in-law and priest had reached their gates.

Had Natalya died? Returned to Moscow with Maria? But either way, why no word?

The monks provided no information, but the full moon had yet to brighten the sky when a scrawny boy in a linen shirt too big for him, rough homespun trousers, and bast shoes stumbled panting into the foyer. When he walked in, Masha on his heels, Nasan was sitting in the middle of a large blanket, baby Stenka at her feet. She had removed his swaddling bands, fending off the Russian women's alarm with stories of the many harem babies who had somehow managed to grow straight arms and legs without being constantly bound in linen, and was watching him gurgle and kick in the summer heat. He wore nothing but a cloth tied around his lower body, and although too small even to roll over, he waved his fists with vigor and cooed. Nasan cooed back, touching the soles of his feet to see the tiny toes curl and singing softly in her native tongue. At the sight of the newcomer, she stood.

"A messenger," Masha said, unnecessarily. She gestured at the boy. "He has forgotten how to talk."

"He looks winded," Nasan said. "Did you run the whole way?"

The boy nodded.

"Sit over there, then, and catch your breath." Nasan pointed at the window seat. "Watch out for the baby. Masha, bring him some food. And something to drink."

Masha departed. Within moments, Grusha appeared, swept up baby Stenka and the blanket, and withdrew again. Nasan let them go. She could hear the tap-tap of Rafik's cane and the sound of shuffling feet that signaled the second-in-command's arrival.

When he appeared in the doorway, she pointed him, too, to a nearby bench. Although much recovered, Rafik remained weak, and it wouldn't do for him to suffer a setback.

"What brings you here?" she asked the boy when it seemed that he might have found his voice.

He regarded her with wide, terrified eyes. Although she and Rafik could hardly be considered threatening, the Tatar troops had displayed a belligerent air ever since their raid on the village—even off-duty, so to speak—and who could guess what rumors the boy might have heard? Be that as it may, he flinched every time a warrior entered or left the room. His eyes brightened, though, when Masha arrived with a tray on which sat plump turnovers, a simple clay cup, and a jug.

"No one will hurt you." Nasan gestured at Rafik, seated on his bench, and at Masha, who placed the tray at the boy's side and stepped back. "Did you bring a message for me?"

"Are you Tsarevna Irina?" The boy scrambled to his feet as if this possibility had not occurred to him before.

For once, the sound of her Russian name provoked no shudder of resistance. At the time, Nasan, caught up in concern for her mother-in-law, didn't even notice. "I am," she said. "Tell me the message."

The boy scrunched up his face, then said, "A Lady Natalya awaits you near the riverbank."

Nasan heaved a sigh of relief. "Good. Rest a while, then go home. We will follow." She glanced at Masha. "Tell Karim to summon the men. We leave as soon as he has them armed and ready."

A stick tapped against the floor, and she shifted her gaze to find Rafik standing, leaning on his cane. "Not Karim, *Khanim*. I will lead."

"You're not well." To put it mildly. The man staggered on his feet.

"Enough to ride," he said. His mouth thinned in a stubborn line.

She opened her mouth, but he intercepted her refusal. "Please, *Khanim*. I wish to atone for my previous failure. I can't face your brother else. And you won't stay here while Karim leads the warriors, will you?"

She would not. "My mother-in-law expects me," she said—which was true.

For a moment, she considered pointing out that Rafik's desire to cut short his recovery to prove his courage made no sense. But she refrained. A lifetime of experience with warriors had taught her that arguing would not deter him. Healed or not, he intended to fulfill his commitment to his khan, and fulfill it he would.

"Very well," she said. "You lead. Command the escort as needed, but ride at my side and remember that your primary responsibility is to defend me in case of trouble. That way, the others can deal with the bandits, if bandits appear."

"Surely they would not be so foolish as to challenge us a second time."

"Let's hope not," Nasan agreed. "But I have some knowledge of their leader. I wouldn't count on his common sense."

Rafik bowed, hand over his heart, then hobbled to the other room. Watching him go, Nasan hoped she had not just undone her doctoring of the last few weeks.

Screams and shouts alerted the Tatars to trouble long before they reached the riverbank. Nasan, armored under her clothes as she had been for her trip to the now-destroyed village, pulled her bow from its case and nudged Sorkhokhtani into a gallop. Rafik cursed as the sorrel mare leaped ahead, but within the space of a few breaths he was at her side once more. A wave of his arm brought the men into line, and the escort tore down the forest trail as if the Lord of the Underworld himself rode behind them, brandishing his mighty sword.

They soon broke through the last of the trees. Ahead Nasan saw riverbank and rushes, sunlight glinting off water, golden domes in the distance, and a familiar pale-blond head. Men dressed in the rough peasant clothes she had seen on Semyon's bandits milled around a single carriage pulled by three horses.

More men than she could count. Where had Semyon found so many?

The fifteen Russians borrowed from the Kolychevs' next-door neighbor, as well as the ten Tatars assigned to protect those traveling by boat, clustered around the carriage, slashing anyone who dared approach. The Tatars howled a greeting as they recognized their comrades-in-arms, setting off a ripple of alarm among the bandits.

A grizzled older man, leader of the fifteen Russians, was beating one of the attackers over the head with his whip, which accounted for some of the shouting. Vanka crouched next to the horse, but of Natalya, Maria, their attendants, and Father Job Nasan saw no sign. She guessed that they huddled under the cloth that covered the main part of the carriage.

And so it proved. As she and her escort galloped to the rescue, Natalya peered around the edge of the covering and stared at the scene before her with an open mouth.

She lived, then. Despite her illness, the journey, the attack—everything. The woman had a will of iron, and a body to match.

Nasan had hardly time to register the news, let alone rejoice, before she noticed Semyon's pale-blond head moving toward the carriage, heard him bellowing to his men. Natalya was his aunt, but he showed no sign of respect or affection. On the contrary, he snarled at the sight of her and strode toward her, drawing his sword as he went. Nasan shouted at him to stop, but he paid her no heed. Natalya shouted, too. Nasan couldn't hear what she said.

Seeing her opportunity, she rode closer, then stood in her stirrups to steady her aim as she had in the village. Oblivious to everything but his target, Semyon advanced on his aunt, swinging his sword. Nasan pulled an arrow from her quiver, nocked it, and let it fly. Semyon roared like a wounded bear, and a circle of red bloomed on his shirt, high on his left arm. *A hit!*

He spun toward her, gaped at the sight of her, jerked on his feet as her second arrow slammed into his left shoulder, just below the collar bone. Unwisely, he hauled it out and with a sneer tossed it aside. Another circle of red drenched the front of his shirt. While Nasan stared at him, stunned, he turned back toward Natalya, as if pulled by a string.

Nasan loosed a third arrow, which he deflected with his sword. Only then, as if finally sensing his danger, did he abandon his single-minded pursuit of Natalya and slash at the closest member of her escort. One of the neighbor's half-trained youth, a boy just past his fifteenth birthday—no match for an adult warrior.

The boy fought bravely, but Semyon dodged his blows with ease. Nasan nudged Sorkhokhtani with her knees, searching for a vantage point from which she could release another arrow without endangering her own men. But in the thrust and surge of so many horses, so many bodies, a clear line of sight was not easy to secure. It didn't help that warriors eager to protect her kept pushing her back from the front line.

She worked her way to the far right, away from the main press of Tatar troops. She positioned Sorkhokhtani next to a clump of bushes thick as a green wall, balanced herself in her stirrups, and took aim.

Too late. One mighty swing of Semyon's sword separated the boy's head from his shoulders. Her arrow hit the spot where Semyon had stood, but her enemy had already hauled the headless body from its saddle and mounted. Blood still spurted from the severed neck as Semyon, shouting for his men, galloped away. About half of the bandits raced after him; the Tatars had the rest pinned down.

Natalya ducked back beneath the cover as Nasan's escort unleashed volley after volley, fast and furious as a swarm of wasps, against the fleeing bandits. Men scattered in all directions, fell where they stood, crawled when they could no longer walk, collapsed when even crawling became too much. A few managed to commandeer mounts and escape, but the vast majority lay still on the ground.

Horses pressed forward in pursuit while Nasan stayed in the rear, out of the direct line of fire. Yet she kept her bow strung and ready. No more nights in the woods for her. Better to die in the saddle, with a weapon in her hand—although such a fate seemed less likely with every moment that passed. Her warriors, to judge from the ferocity with which they attacked the remaining bandits, had no more desire to repeat their prior experience than she did.

A glance at the carriage revealed that Natalya remained beneath the covering. Just as well, no doubt. The cloth would not deter a determined attack—or a stray arrow—but the bandits had long since forgotten the carriage.

Semyon had escaped, though. Her hands gripped the reins as she digested that outcome. Again she had wounded but not killed him. Loss of blood, infection, and rough-and-ready doctoring might yet take their toll, but for the moment he lived. He had lost many men, but he was not defeated.

The Tatars would have to pursue him once more.

As the noise died down, Nasan returned her bow to its case and walked Sorkhokhtani toward the carriage, urging the horse—made skittish by the smell of blood—in a wide circle away from the bodies that littered the ground. Rafik, who had verified her safety before leading his men into the fray despite their prior arrangement, approached. His grin made him look more like himself than at any time since the bandits' initial raid. Behind him, the two segments of the escort twirled hats and slapped shoulders in joyous reunion.

However horrendous the bloody scene before her, Nasan could not help returning Rafik's smile. He had made no secret of how he feared his khan's displeasure, and he must rejoice at this success. As he came closer, she observed that, despite her first impression, he had refrained from pushing himself into the thick of the fight. No blood stained his clothes, and his presence seemed to comfort Sorkhokhtani rather than increasing the horse's anxiety.

Nasan allowed him to resume his place at her side. "You did well." She gestured at the bodies. "You have reduced the bandit forces. They will have trouble replacing so many. But the leader got away. My fault, I fear. My aim was not true."

"You wounded him, *Khanim*," Rafik said. "Twice. He may die, and if he does not, we will find him."

"You must go after them, I agree. But let us first get my mother- and sister-in-law to the estate." She indicated the carriage with the point of her whip.

While she and Rafik talked, the five inside had scrambled to the ground. Father Job stood in the center, Vanka and the attendants clustered at his back. His right arm circled Natalya's shoulders and his left Maria's. The two women clung to him, their faces taut with shock. Maria opened and closed her mouth, as if words failed her, and Natalya took several steps back as the horses approached.

Only then did Nasan realize what Natalya and the others must see as they stared at her. In the weeks away from them, she had shed her façade of a Russian wife and become again the descendant of Genghis she had always remained inside. To the three new arrivals, she must appear foreign, exotic, even barbaric. Had Natalya not seen her shoot Semyon, just before the sky filled with a hail of arrows? Her ideal Russian daughter-in-law would never think of doing such a thing!

But in that moment of truth, Nasan understood in her soul that she could not go back to the way she had been before, whatever Natalya said. She could not be that flattened daughter-in-law, that perfect future mistress of the house. Even if she lost Daniil. Even if Natalya was right, and God refused ever to entrust Nasan with her husband's child. Nothing was worth that. She would die first.

Because hadn't she been dead already, in a sense?

Somewhere in the back of her mind, she heard the beat of swans' wings. As if she, too, flew free among the clouds.

Natalya clapped her hands to her cheeks as the carriage neared her estate. She had ordered the cover drawn back once they left the road, and Nasan, riding alongside, had a clear view of the five passengers. Rafik flanked her to the right, and the remaining escort surrounded them.

Although no one expected further trouble. Trouble had already presented itself and suffered defeat.

At first, the travelers didn't speak. Nasan didn't know where to start, and Natalya, Maria, and the priest seemed pulled into themselves, as if shocked by the nearness of their escape from death—and, perhaps, the realization that Semyon had led the attack. Nasan's own appearance, arrows flying, must have startled them, too. On the list of horrors, she thought the revelation of her skills belonged at the bottom, but past experience suggested that Natalya might disagree.

The attack had taken place about halfway between the river and the Kolychev estate, on a relatively deserted stretch of road. In a sense, Natalya and the others had brought it on themselves by setting out before the escort could reach them.

Of course, that was nonsense. The blame belonged to Semyon, not to the pilgrims. Nor had traveling in force prevented the earlier attack on her and her men: these bandits might simply be as mad as their leader. Or deluded enough to follow a leader who had long given evidence of extreme foolhardiness.

In any event, the distance, although not great, took time to cover, due to the slowness of the carriage along the rutted road, which then turned into an even more feeble excuse for a path. Nasan was yearning for her dinner by the time the outlines of the main house formed amid the trees. But the length of this last stage had one advantage: it gave the travelers a chance to calm themselves. From the expression on Natalya's face, Nasan guessed that one person, at least, rejoiced at reaching her destination.

Indeed, she must have wondered if she would live to see it. A triumph, indeed.

Watching Natalya glow from within as the carriage drew to a halt, Nasan saw in her mother-in-law vestiges of the young girl who had married Nikolai Kolychev so many years ago. Natalya looked almost pretty—her cheeks flushed, her eyes bright and clear. Perhaps her old friend's recommendation had done what Nasan could not, and Natalya had taken the nut sedge potion regularly throughout her journey. Or perhaps happiness itself strengthened her.

Masha opened the door, bowed low to the new arrivals, then rushed forward to help Natalya extricate herself from the carriage. "Come this way, Lady," she said, putting a hand under Natalya's elbow. "You'll not remember me, but I would recognize you anywhere. Saw you last as a girl, I did, not long after you married the young lord."

Natalya stopped and stared. "Masha. It's never you!"

Masha beamed. "You do remember. Well, saints be praised! Come inside then, Lady, and let's get you settled."

A child wailed, and Nasan turned her head to see Grusha standing in the doorway clutching her baby, restored to his swaddled state. When Natalya started, then sailed toward the sound like a boat across the river, Grusha turned the tightly wrapped bundle to face her. "My little Stenka, Natalya Vasilyevna. I hope you won't be angry. Tsarevna Irina told me to be brave and not hide from you, so I came to greet you."

Natalya staggered, despite Masha's supportive arm. "Grusha? My dear! Where have you been, and what brings you back to us?"

"What *have* you been doing here, sister?" Maria asked from behind her mother-in-law's back. "You deluge us with one surprise after another, and Mama-in-law's health won't stand it."

Her voice had the familiar scolding tone. Nasan flinched.

Flinched, then took a breath, straightened, and stared into Maria's pettish face, seeing it as if for the first time. It was the face of a spoiled brat, determined to make those around her as miserable as she was herself. Because she enjoyed hurting others, or because she had no idea how to achieve happiness?

And with that, Nasan realized that the answer didn't matter. What Maria thought of her didn't matter. Nasan had found her own source of contentment. She needed only Daniil to make it whole, and if he failed to return, she could overcome even that disappointment. Natalya had been right from the beginning: Maria couldn't upset her unless Nasan allowed it.

"There are no more surprises," she said, keeping her tone level. When Maria didn't reply, Nasan dismounted and handed Sorkhokhtani's reins to the nearest warrior. "You did the right thing, Grusha," she said to the woman cowering in the hall. "Lay your sweet Stenka in his cradle, and let us see what we can do to make everyone comfortable." She moved to Natalya's other side and spoke across her, "Masha, let's get her inside and settled, shall we? I feel certain that you have prepared a wonderful meal for us."

"That I have, Tsarevna," Masha said. "Why, it's not every day that the family comes home, is it?"

Natalya exclaimed over the state of her house until Nasan had to bite her lip to keep from laughing. If her mother-in-law tried, she couldn't make her expectations of Nasan's poor

performance clearer. What did she think Nasan had done during those weeks in Moscow while Natalya herself lay ill and
Maria nursed her? Had she noticed only the imperfections,
missing the reality that the household continued to run, if less
smoothly than under her own experienced hand?

True, the population of this estate was smaller, and Masha
had become an enormous help. Grusha, too, as she recovered
from childbirth and felt more comfortable with the idea that
she would not be punished or returned to slavery. Better still
had been the freedom from constant criticism and drudgery.
That freedom made the supervision of domestic tasks a
necessary but endurable part of daily life.

"I thought to find the house overrun with warriors,"
Natalya admitted as Father Job finished his blessing over the
food. The two of them—with Nasan, Maria, and Rafik as
the senior representative of the escort—had gathered around
a small table in the room closest to the kitchen.

"Some of your peasants fled to escape the bandits," Nasan
said. "Not all have returned. And since the first raid, we've
worried about bandits attacking the estate, so half the escort
remains on guard outside the house day and night, and those
not on duty sleep in the deserted cottages."

Masha arrived with a tureen of dark red soup, which she
placed before Natalya. A young peasant girl in white blouse
and bright blue sarafan embroidered in a long strip from
breast band to hem, her light brown braid dangling to one side,
followed with a basket of bread.

"Not Grusha?" Natalya asked, her eyebrows raised.

"She can't touch our food, Mama-in-law. She is not yet
churched." Nasan took a roll from the basket and passed it on,
then accepted a bowl of borsht. "Nor her babe, as we had no
one else to feed him. It upsets Grusha, I think, that Stenka is
two weeks old and cannot be baptized."

A ridiculous custom—that an infant must not nurse from its mother for forty days, lest it be declared unclean—but Nasan left that opinion, too, unspoken. Instead, she extended a hand to Father Job. "Now that you are here, Father, you will ease her mind."

"And who attended the birth?" the priest asked. "I must say the ritual over her, too."

"Masha and I," Nasan told him. "But the monks sent a priest on the eighth day to cleanse us." She pointed at the soup. "Otherwise we could not have fed you today. He would have returned to say the prayers over Grusha and the child if needed."

"I will take care of it," Father Job said.

Nasan nodded. She had expected no less. "And will you pray for Vera, Father? My men buried her in the woods, according to their own rite. But she was a good Christian, and I wouldn't like her to be cut off for eternity from a faith that meant much to her."

"Of course," he said. "You may also wish to leave some money with the monks. They will enter her name in the Synodicon and pray for her regularly."

Nasan agreed. She missed Vera—who, being a Christian convert and Tatar, had understood what it meant to live simultaneously in different worlds, as Nasan herself did. Sometimes her two identities merged into one; sometimes they remained separate. It was difficult to explain to those who had never left the land of their birth.

"I'm sorry for the loss of Vera," Natalya said. "She was a good servant, and I'm glad you will commemorate her." She frowned as that thought led her to another, less tractable problem. "But what are we to do with Grusha? She ran away from us, and we chose to let her go, lest she remain a distraction in our household." She meant a distraction for Daniil. "But here she is. Does she return with us to Moscow?"

It was good news that Natalya could imagine a return to Moscow, after so long a journey here. "I think she may prefer to stay," Nasan said. "If you wish, I will buy her from you and free her, but must we decide today? You won't want to take her anywhere until she is churched, and surely you would like to visit the monastery, having traveled so far to get here."

"My goodness," Maria said, "how you assume the air of command. As if a great lady deigned to speak to us."

Rafik drew in his breath, but Nasan laughed. Why had she ever taken such spite seriously? "I am a khan's daughter," she said lightly. "Authority is my birthright."

The spirit of her mother infused her, straightening her in her seat. She heard an echo of Ogodai's words, spoken that first evening after his arrival in Moscow. "Perhaps it's time you remembered that."

Maria sucked air through her teeth. Nasan ignored her and addressed Rafik. "Still no word from my brother?"

But it was Natalya who answered. "We do have word. I apologize, daughter. We met a courier at the monastery, but in the hubbub it slipped my mind. A young man. A very young man. I have forgotten his name."

"A courier? But what happened to him? Did Semyon's men kill him?" Nasan gripped her hands together under the table to still her fears. "Forgive me. It's no wonder you forgot. The boldness of the raid shocked us all."

Rafik limped toward the door. "I'll find him, *Khanim*, and demand to know why he didn't report as ordered." Nasan nodded at him, but before he could leave, Father Job pulled a scroll from his sleeve and held it out to her.

"He rode with our escort," the priest said. "You will find him with the other warriors, no doubt. He didn't report because he had already given me this, and I promised to deliver it. But I can't read it."

"Wait, Rafik." Nasan took the scroll, unwound it, and scanned the contents. Relief washed through her, and when she looked up again, she was smiling. "The khan is on his way here. He orders you not to leave, because he expects to reach us in a few days."

Rafik returned her smile. He touched his right hand to his heart and bowed. "If you will excuse me, *Khanim*, I will alert the men."

"You are excused," Nasan said. "You and your warriors have served me well, and I will tell him so."

"May he believe you, *Khanim*." He dipped his head once more and left the room.

Semyon threw his dagger at the nearest tree and swore every oath he had heard during a decade in the army. His shoulder ached, and his arm. Tanka had managed to extract one arrow, and he had hauled out the other in his first fit of rage. He hadn't felt pain then, but time and distance had turned numbness into agony. Loss of blood made his head spin. Only fury kept him on his feet and gave him the strength to toss that knife.

What saint had he offended that his men must needs make the same mistake twice?

Well, if it came to that, in the last two years he had probably offended every saint in the calendar. Even so, it had not always been normal practice for travelers along the Ferapontovo road to hire Tatar warriors as their escorts. Clearly, some bizarre spirit—good or evil—had taken as its goal the ruination of Semyon Kolychev and his plans. He would have to rebuild his force again!

And he had come so close to attaining his goal. That was the part that stung the sharpest. His Aunt Natalya, right there, where he'd never expected to see her. Revenge in the grip of his hand. And his warrior maid, damn her, getting in his way, shooting at him like a mad thing. He'd seen her exactly twice, yet she'd almost killed him both times. What a woman!

Well, he would show them both. She'd driven him mad, his Tatar *khanim*, and he would have her, whether she wanted him or not. As for his aunt, now that he knew Natalya was in the area, he could also guess where to find her.

And find her he would, just as soon as the demons in his head stopped pounding him with cannon balls.

Chapter 15

THE REST OF THE MEAL PASSED MORE OR LESS WITHOUT incident. Maria talked about how much she hoped to visit her father, just a few days away in Vologda. Nasan was pondering the most judicious and kindest way to tell her that Koshkin had left for Moscow, without revealing the concerns that had driven her brother Ogodai to order inquiries, when Rafik saved her the trouble. After that, Maria withdrew into a sulky silence that might hide true disappointment but could just as well express annoyance at being thwarted.

When dinner finally ended, Nasan expected her mother-in-law to rest. Instead, Maria and Father Job went off to inspect the rooms assigned to them, while Natalya summoned Nasan to sit with her in the main part of the house. Grusha rocked her child outside, crooning lullabies, and Masha summoned her assistant to help her clean up. For the first time in months, Nasan and her mother-in-law were alone.

Not entirely a comfortable sensation, that. Nasan and Natalya seldom had much to say to each other, and few of Nasan's adventures since leaving Moscow bore much chance of impressing her stern if pragmatic mother-in-law. Her domestic achievements had already received whatever praise they deserved, and besides, blathering about such unimportant details would soon set her to yawning.

"You look much better, Mama-in-law," she said. "Did your friend Olga's medicine work as promised?"

Natalya regarded her through narrowed eyes. "Your medicine, you mean."

Nasan shrugged. She couldn't deny it. "If it works, does it matter who prescribes it?"

"It has worked," Natalya said. "I do feel better, and I thank you. I will need more nut sedge, in fact. Father Job told me yesterday that we had used almost our whole supply."

"I'll search tomorrow," Nasan promised. "It must grow around here. It likes moist soils and shady places."

A brief silence ensued. Natalya broke it. "You have changed, daughter. You seem older, more sure of yourself. When Maria insulted you, you did not react. You order your men. And you—you!—rode to our rescue. I thought my heart would stop mid-beat when I saw you shoot my villain of a nephew."

There it was, out in the open. Well, better so, Nasan concluded. Her mother-in-law sounded calm, thoughtful, and she did not look angry. Maybe they could achieve some honesty between them after all.

"I surprised you," Nasan said. "It is my own fault, perhaps. I wanted to fit in, to win your approval so that you wouldn't turn Daniil against me. And I feared Maria's tongue, although I see now that she is a silly, spiteful girl. But I could never be the daughter-in-law you wanted. I grew up among the nomads. I love to ride and shoot, to swing a sword—but also to heal. I will learn to manage the household. I will love my husband, if he lets me. And if God gives me a child, I will do my best to be a good mother, but I can't be the same kind of woman you are."

It was a long speech, maybe the longest she had ever given in Natalya's presence, and Nasan saw that it provided food for thought.

"There's something more that you should know," she said when Natalya did not respond. Part of Nasan—the cowardly child part—urged her to hide behind the promise she had made to Daniil and his father to keep her secret from Natalya. But if she didn't tell the tale today, she might never tell it, and the unspoken truth would hang forever between her and her mother-in-law, poisoning their relationship as secrets do. Besides, had she not urged Grusha to take the courageous path?

"More?" Natalya sounded dazed. She rubbed her hands together, as if they felt cold. A symptom of her disease.

Nasan hesitated, then plunged into her long-delayed confession. "Two years ago, do you remember? There was a mystery hero in Moscow, the Golden Lynx. And Maria's father started a rumor that the Lynx was Daniil."

"I remember." Natalya's voice had steadied again. "He lied. Out of malice."

"He did lie," Nasan agreed. "He spread the rumor to cover his own guilt—and because he hates Papa-in-law, despite having married his daughter to your son. But he lied less than he meant to. The Golden Lynx did belong to your household."

"To us? But that's impossible. Daniil was away most of that summer!"

Nasan took a deep breath and touched her mother-in-law's arm. "Yes, Daniil was away until August. When he came back, he did help me stop Semyon, but Daniil was never the Golden Lynx. I was."

"You? Holy Mother of God!" Natalya swayed. Nasan grasped her above the elbows in time to keep her head from striking the window frame.

"I'm sorry," she said. "I didn't mean to give you another shock."

Natalya pulled free. Hunched over like an old woman, she touched her brow. Nasan bit her lip and clasped her hands in her lap. Had she destroyed everything? Had she undermined Natalya's fragile health?

For a long moment, they sat there, not speaking. Then Natalya straightened and looked her daughter-in-law in the eye. "I never knew you at all, did I?"

Unable to find words, Nasan shook her head.

It surprised her anew when Natalya patted her hand. "Then we'd better begin again, hadn't we?"

Nasan produced a tremulous smile. "I'd like that."

"Start by telling me the whole," Natalya said.

So Nasan did.

"Lord, have mercy!" Daniil jerked on the reins, and his black gelding reared back on its haunches. His right shoulder, scabbed over but still stiff and liable to odd twinges and aches, shot out a bolt of pain. He gritted his teeth and pressed his knees against the horse's heaving flanks, forcing it back into a normal riding position.

He didn't blame it for spooking. The sight ahead of them would terrify the most battle-hardened steed. Scavengers had already discovered the piles of raggedly dressed corpses that littered both sides of the path, and the combination of August heat and animal interest made for a grisly spectacle. A group of peasants moved among the stinking corpses, but they scattered at the horsemen's approach. A flatbed cart sat off to one side, arms and feet sticking out of it.

Ogodai's escort dismounted to examine the bodies. Ogodai himself had stopped at Daniil's shout, but as Daniil joined him, he kneed his favorite chestnut into motion, and the two of them walked their horses toward the gruesome sight. "Looks like all-out carnage," Ogodai said. "If this is the work of bandits, they are indeed a threat."

"They don't look like pilgrims." Daniil pointed at the frayed linen shirts and scuffed boots. "Not pilgrims a bandit would waste his time on, in any case." He drew his sword and leaned sideways, stabbing at the sheath that hung from the nearest belt. "They had weapons, but they don't now. Curious."

The head of Ogodai's escort returned and stood before the two mounted men. "Many arrow wounds, Khan." He held up a fletched shaft, its razor-sharp point un-dulled by the death blow it had delivered, then pulled another from his own quiver and held them up. They matched in every detail. "If I had to guess, this came from one of our own." Ogodai nodded, then turned his horse in a slow circle.

Daniil did the same. About a third of the way round, he saw something that had escaped him the first time, as he rode forward with his eyes fixed on the piles of corpses. "A carriage. See the ruts where the wheels dug into the mud? And the hoof prints? It stayed there for a while."

"And the carriage had a guard." Ogodai walked his horse toward the wheel ruts.

Daniil kept pace with him. They halted the length of an outstretched arm from the spot. Ogodai was right. At the side and front of where the carriage must have stood, hoof prints showed in the mud. Eight—no, ten—sets of four. More clustered at the back, blending into the grass that lined the road. And he noticed something else.

"No shoes," he said. "Tatar ponies. Are these your men?"

"Looks like it, doesn't it?" Ogodai asked. "But what happened to them? There are no Tatar corpses here."

"They must have fought like demons, to kill so many." Daniil waved at the pile to his right. "How many bodies do you see? Thirty? Forty? There can't be fewer." When Ogodai didn't answer, Daniil pointed to the wheel ruts. "As for where they went, if these were your men, then that carriage contained my mother, and we will find them—if they live—at our estate."

If they lived. They must. His mother—and he—could not travel so far and get so close, only to be separated in the end.

He thought of the bodies in the cart. Like the corpses that still littered the ground, they had been men in poor clothes, some with leather armor. No noblewomen. He must learn the truth, but he wouldn't learn it here.

He completed his turn and again faced north. Ogodai did the same. The head of the escort stood where they had left him, awaiting orders. "Mount," Ogodai said. "And follow me." The warriors rushed to their horses, and the party moved north, Ogodai and Daniil in the lead.

As they reached the far side of the small clearing, new sets of hoof prints brought about another halt. "More Tatar ponies," Daniil said. "Many more."

"Galloping." Ogodai leaned to his left and plucked a tuft of horsehair from a bush at the side of the road. "Look at the pattern of the hooves. The men guarding the carriage stood still, in defense, but these riders were attacking." He shook the tuft at Daniil, then angled it toward a separate set of four prints that stood alone beside the bush. "Except for one."

He held out the tuft again. Daniil took it and stared. Black horsehair, not unlike the mane of the animal he rode. "I don't understand," he said. "It's from a mane or a tail. Could be anyone's."

"Anyone who would ride with a group of warriors yet sit out the fight," Ogodai said. "And who rides a pony with a black mane and tail. A small one, from the placement of the hooves. Do we know a person like that?"

Daniil's stomach stooped like a hawk on the hunt. Nasan. Here, hence no longer missing—that was good. Observing a battle, if not a direct participant—not so good. He must get to his family's house as soon as possible.

For Ogodai's sake, he tried to sound lighthearted—not easy when his tongue felt glued to the roof of his mouth. "You think we could trust her to stay out of the fight?"

Ogodai grinned. "I wouldn't. Trust her, that is. If Rafik managed to keep her out of it, I'll have to devise a special commendation for him. But if we're right, at least she returned from the woods. Let's make some inquiries, shall we?"

Daniil returned the grin, but it felt like a pale imitation. His heels, as if self-propelled, were already digging into his horse's sides. "I thought you'd never ask."

Together, they kicked their horses into a canter and raced down the path, Ogodai's men close behind them.

The estate, when Daniil reached it, seemed too placid and bucolic to have any association with the carnage encountered on the road. They passed a pond, startling a mother swan leading her cygnets to water. The babies scuttled into the reeds while Mama ran—wings spread, trumpeting—at the horses. When they backed off, more unnerved by her ferocity than by a dozen bandits, she retreated, and after a while the feathered family reached its goal and paddled off, Mama in the lead, to join another magnificent swan gliding serenely in the distance.

Otherwise, the long wooden house and its associated cottages looked much as Daniil remembered them, with one exception. At the front of the house, a pair of Tatar warriors barred the door with crossed spears. Four more stood at the corners.

"Do you know them?" he asked Ogodai, but the men were already kneeling, right hands over their hearts. Whether Ogodai recognized them or not, they recognized him.

"Of course," Ogodai said. "They're standing guard. I wonder why."

"That appears to be the question." Daniil dismounted, ignoring the stab of pain in his right collar bone.

A Tatar warrior came forward and took the reins. "Don't stable him yet," Daniil said. "Walk him and let him feed, rub him down with a handful of grass, then tether him. I want to find out what's going on before I have him unsaddled."

Ogodai tossed his reins to another warrior. "Same here." When Daniil glanced his way, he shrugged one shoulder. "In case you need help."

Daniil clapped him on the back. "Thank you, brother."

"It's nothing." Ogodai clasped Daniil's arm above the elbow, then released it.

"Let's go inside." Daniil pushed the main door open and stood back to let the khan precede him, but a small voice in his head kept prodding, as if with a needle.

Why had none of the family come out to greet them—Nasan, especially?

Inside, too, nothing struck Daniil as unusual at first glance. He found his mother in the main room, Maria at her side, both bent over their embroidery. This time, Ogodai stood back while Daniil led the way. The crunch of his boots on the wood brought the women's heads up. Out of the corner of his eye, Daniil saw Maria push her chair back, an expression of intense displeasure on her face. He ignored her. His mother occupied his full attention.

Natalya jumped to her feet, dropping her embroidery and clutching her chest. He ran forward and caught her in his left arm, hugging her. She was alive!

He kissed one cheek, then the other, lowered her back to the bench where she had been when he walked in, and sat beside her. Maria bowed, her face taut. "Welcome, brother," she said.

He inclined his head. "Thank you, sister." He matched her chill tone. They had taken a dislike to each other at their first meeting, and nothing in the intervening years had altered it. "Where is my wife?"

"We don't know," Maria said with the honey-sweet malice that invariably made him want to throttle her. "She left the house this morning without a word. I suppose she didn't expect you. The khan's message did not mention you by name." She paused. "Then again, perhaps she did. Expect you, that is."

Daniil bit his tongue. Maria had seen his wife this morning. He and Ogodai had been right, and Nasan was no longer missing. Maria was being spiteful, as usual.

Before Daniil could do more than growl at his sister-in-law, Ogodai walked in. Natalya rose to her feet once more, more slowly and hence with greater steadiness, and bowed. "Welcome, Khan. We received your message. You arrived sooner than anticipated, but as you see, your men have protected us well." She glared at Maria. "You may be excused, daughter. Return when your tongue has less of the adder in it."

Maria drifted gracefully from the room, trailing a white gauze scarf. "I said no more than the truth," she announced as she reached the door.

"Those girls will be the death of me, I swear." Natalya sighed and gestured to Ogodai. "You have ridden far, Khan.

Please, take a seat and I will send for refreshments to welcome you properly."

But Ogodai had watched the recent byplay with narrowed eyes. "That's most kind of you, Lady," he said. "But if you will excuse me, I will settle my men, so that you may talk with your son alone. I trust my sister is in no danger?"

"Danger? Not at all," Natalya assured him. "She went out on an errand, no more. Maria wanted to cause trouble, I fear."

He dipped his head in acknowledgment and turned to go. "I'll leave our horses in the yard for now," he told Daniil before striding off.

Daniil called thanks after his brother-in-law's retreating back, then touched his mother's arm. "Sit, Mama, and tell me how you fare. Papa and I were fit to be tied when we heard of your ill health. He sends his love, and he's hoping to join us in Moscow, but Ogodai could secure permission for only one of us to accompany him."

Natalya had much indirect experience with the army. "And how is it, my son, that he managed to get leave for you?"

He should have expected that question. "I took a bullet to my shoulder," he said, trying to make the injury sound like nothing.

It didn't work. "Let me see," she exclaimed.

He fended off her reaching hand. "Later, Mama, I promise. It heals well enough. Tell me of yourself, rather."

"I do much better," she said. He must have looked as skeptical as she had in response to his assurances, for she smiled. "You hear how it sounds? But it is true, even so. When I left Moscow I thought my last hour had come. I could not stand for the length of one household task, and my breath caught every night and kept me from sleeping. But your Irina gave me a potion—a terrible thing, bitter as gall, however much honey she added—and my friend Olga persuaded me to take it. I protested like an infant, but in the end I agreed, and you see, it has almost cured me. That's where she went, your wife: to look for the ingredients. You will find her in the woods. Pay no heed to Maria's nonsense."

He laughed and hugged her again. "When have I ever? But it is good to see you as I remember you. I feared the worst."

Her face clouded then. "Well, I'm not quite the same, dearest. My heart still flutters and I tire easily. I've learned to rest more and to rely on my daughters for help."

Daniil grinned at her. "That goes against the grain, I'm sure. The General relying on her soldiers?"

She smacked his good shoulder, not hard. "Wicked boy. Will you never learn to respect your mother?"

Daniil kissed her hand. "Always," he said. "Right now, though, I must find my wife."

"Yes." She bent and picked up the sewing she had dropped when he walked in. "But Daniil, I must say something before you do. We were attacked on the way here—by your cousin Semyon—and Irina, with her escort, rescued us. She shot Semyon herself, my son. Twice, and from horseback! A third arrow missed him by inches, and only because he leaped out of the way. I had no idea she had such skill with the bow. And when I spoke to her about it, she told me the strangest story about running around Moscow dressed as a boy."

Daniil stared at her. He and his father had done everything possible to keep Nasan's adventures from his mother, yet Nasan had told her. Why? No one could imagine that Mama would approve of such a tale. And Semyon, who was supposed to be incarcerated in an Arctic monastery, had attacked his own aunt a few miles from here? Nasan had intervened to save them? Words fought for supremacy in his head, and he couldn't decide which question to ask first.

When he didn't respond, Mama continued. "I must apologize, Daniil. Your father and I did what we had to, and she is a lovely girl in many ways, but I can see she is not a suitable wife for you. Not like Anastasia. If you wish to send her to a convent, we will arrange it, even if her family objects."

"Send her to a convent?" Did his mother honestly believe even now that he yearned for wispy, fragile Anastasia, who had died five years ago? "Why would I want that?"

"Well, my dear," his mother said, as if the answer were obvious. "How will you ever have children with such a hoyden? God rewards the demure and the obedient."

She was his mother. He owed her courtesy, even if he wanted to roar at the stupidity of that remark. If Nasan had endured a steady diet of this, no wonder she feared she had lost him.

He stood, fighting to control his temper. "Listen to me, Mama. I love my wife. Nasan, Irina. I love her just as she is— beautiful and brave, passionate and responsive. I want no other. Certainly not Anastasia, whom I pitied but never desired. If you must blame someone for the death of our unborn child, blame me."

Her eyes widened in shock. He bowed, as if to a stranger. "I am going to search for Nasan," he said, stressing the Tatar name. "When I return, the khan and I will want to hear what you can tell us about Semyon."

Somewhere in these woods, purple nut sedge must grow, so why could Nasan not find it? It liked poor soils, of which the forest boasted an abundance. It liked damp places, and the intertwining vegetation held moisture in its roots, even in August. It did not care for sun, which the canopy of trees permitted to reach the leaf-strewn ground only through a soft green filter. She should fall over it at every turn, so how could she have searched for it for most of the morning without finding a single stalk?

Yet she continued the hunt. Natalya needed it, for one thing. She seemed so much livelier after her weeks on the boat—whether because the journey had forced her to rest or because of the potion, which did not heal but strengthened the heart. Her cheeks had a soft flush, and her voice had regained some of its former authority.

Her ideas, alas, remained as hidebound as ever—another reason Nasan felt no urge to return to the house. How silly it seemed in retrospect to hope that saving Natalya from robbery would convince her to change her mind. Surely hearing of Nasan's past adventures should have persuaded Natalya that confining her daughter-in-law to the kitchen would be, if nothing else, a waste of time and talent. But no.

So why did she search so diligently for the plant that Natalya needed? Other than to have an excuse to stay away from the countless domestic tasks of the estate?

But the answer cried out to her. *Because I am a healer, and I can't see her suffer when I have the means to cure it. And because I care for her, even if she doesn't understand me in the least.*

And because I love her son, although he has abandoned me. Pitiful, isn't it?

The woods beckoned. Should she go deeper into the trees? Clearly, perfect terrain or not, she would not find purple nut sedge here. But the memory of those three lost days haunted her, and she distrusted her ability to find her way home. She would circle the estate, straying just far enough from the house that she could retrace her steps. If she had still found nothing by the time she reached the huts where her warriors stayed, she would give up for today and go home. Hawthorn might make an acceptable substitute, and she saw plenty of that. She could ask Masha to send one of the girls out for it.

She had completed about half her circuit when she glimpsed the long thin stalks with their clusters of reddish flowers and grass-like blades. At last!

Several fistfuls of plants, their health-conferring tubers and intertwined roots still mud-covered, soon obscured the bottom of her straw basket. But as she again plunged both hands up to the wrist to tug at the rough, hardy stems, she heard the unmistakable sounds of hooves and horse tackle. The woods, heretofore so silent except for the rustling of leaves and the occasional bird song, in an instant became menacing. Nasan abandoned her basket, dashed behind the closest bush that seemed large enough to hide her, and peered out.

Had she misjudged, and Semyon and his bandits had returned? Could there be dangerous men loose in the forest, so dangerous that the presence of sixty armed warriors would not deter them? She'd been so certain that they had defeated the enemy yesterday. But that had been shortsighted. Reckless. She should have brought a weapon, or an escort. Didn't her father always say that?

The horse came closer, and she ducked. She hardly dared breathe. It seemed absurd, impossible, that she might suffer an attack so near the house.

Or was it one of her own men, looking for her? She grabbed the branches of the bush with both hands, so that she could lift her head to see who approached without giving away her position.

Seeing only the shape of a mounted man, she dropped behind the bush again.

No helmet, so most likely no armor. But would her men arm themselves just to fetch her from the woods? They had no reason to expect trouble, either.

No turban, though, which suggested a Russian. The rider might wear a skullcap; she couldn't tell from his outline. If not, he was definitely Russian, and she was in trouble. If he caught sight of her, which he must not.

She had reached this point in her deliberations when a voice called her name. Her real name, in a man's voice.

A familiar man's voice.

It can't be. Nasan pulled herself up and peered over her bush.

The voice called her name again. She walked toward it, her feet scuffling through the leaves, quickening as the thick growth cleared. The dim outline solidified into a young man with tawny hair and a well-trimmed beard, mounted on a black horse. He wore a fine linen shirt, open at the neck, an ornate sleeveless robe long enough to cover his trousers, and leather boots. As she reached the point where she could see him clearly, his face broke into a broad smile. At the sight, the pain and distance of the last year vanished as if it had never existed.

Astonishment knocked everything she had meant to say— the carefully planned phrases, the explanations, the apologies— out of her head. Her husband, inexplicably, was here; he was alive; and despite her fears, he looked glad to see her. The ancestors had taken pity on her at last.

"Beloved!" Nasan ran toward him, her arms outstretched. He came off the horse and, laughing, caught her in mid-flight. She felt him wince as she flung her arms around his neck, but then he was kissing her with the passion she had dreamed of and feared she had lost forever.

She stopped thinking about the wince. Stopped thinking about anything, except how good it felt to be in his arms again.

"I thought you'd left me," she said when she could talk. "That you no longer loved me. You never wrote."

He caressed her cheek. "I've been so worried about you. When the message came for Ogodai that you had gone missing, I thought I'd lost everything that mattered to me. I had to come and find you—and fortunately, I got leave. But no more. For you I will learn to read and write. Will that satisfy you, wife of mine?"

"Having you with me satisfies me," she said. "I'm so glad to see you. Please tell me you can stay for a while."

"Until we go back to Moscow, perhaps longer." He rubbed her nose with his, as her own people did. "I'm sorry for the misunderstanding, sweetheart. I missed you every day. Forgive me?"

"With a full heart. And you forgive me for doubting you, for losing the baby?"

"For doubting me, yes," he said. "For the baby, there is no need. You did nothing wrong, whatever Mama says." He kissed her again. "I love you. Remember that, even when I'm away."

She nestled into his arms. "And I love you, Daniil. Welcome home."

Chapter 16

SEMYON CAME TO WITH A GROAN. HE FELT WORSE THAN the night he drank three jugs of ale, celebrating a victory that had turned out to be hollow. His arm burned, his shoulder burned, his head ached, and he had the steadiness of a day-old foal. Other than that, he was doing just fine. Better than yesterday. A veritable king of the forest.

Something had woken him. A noise. Not Tanka, who sat quietly sewing in a corner. She'd proven unexpectedly capable last night when he staggered in, bleeding all over the earthen floor of the lean-to. Stitched him up—with that very needle, mayhap. And bandaged his wounds, clucking like one of the village chickens. It had hurt like the devil's pincers, but it had touched him, too. Seemed she might care for him a bit. He wouldn't have guessed it.

No, this noise came from a weapon. A sword hitting armor, something like that. Semyon turned his head and beheld Simka crouching in the corner, beefy hands dangling, a knife at his feet.

"Sorry, Lord," he said before Semyon could chastise him. "Didn't mean to wake you. I've news, though. Thought you'd want to hear it soon as possible."

Semyon bit back a sharp retort. Thought and Simka rarely occupied the same space, and unless the grand prince's army stood at the edge of the clearing—in which case he couldn't do much to stop them—any news would sink under the weight of his own inability to react to it.

"What?" he asked. "Keep it short. And help me sit." To show himself still the leader, he ignored Tanka's yelp of protest and let Simka prop him up.

Simka shuffled back to his corner. "I took some of the lads over where we ran into those Tatars yesterday. The women wanted the bodies for burial, and I thought we might reclaim a few."

"And did you?"

"Most. Peasants stuck them in a cart, so we took the cart. But that's not what I have to tell you." Simka pushed his hair back with one hand.

"What, then?" It would take a miracle to remain upright for as long as this rambling idiot took to tell his story. "Get on with it, man!"

"While we was watching, more Tatars came, Lord. From the river road, and no woman riding alongside, so probably not the same lot as before. And they had a Russian with them. Big blond, like you. Said something about that maybe being his mother you held up yesterday. Course, he couldn't know for sure, could he, Lord? Not unless he's a sorcerer." Simka, whom Semyon would have sworn didn't have a religious bone in his body, crossed himself and spat, warding off the evil eye.

Semyon forgot his injuries, forgot the weakness that dragged him toward the mattress, forgot the defeats that had plagued him since his warrior maid appeared. A big blond Russian, like him, Natalya's son—was his yearning for revenge to find an outlet at last? The saints hadn't been toying with him after all; instead, they'd given him a shot at everything he wanted in life.

His cousin Daniil, the thorn in his side, the Golden Lynx who had spoiled his plans might—just might!—have come to the north, unaware that Semyon lurked in the woods waiting for him. And as with his aunt, if Daniil had traveled here, Semyon knew where to find him—or at least where to look.

"One more raid," he told Simka. "Summon every man you can find. Drag them by the heels and arm them with scythes if you have to. Just don't give anyone a weapon unless you trust him to use it on the enemy, not on you. As soon as I get out of this bed, we're going hunting."

Simka stared, his mouth opening and closing. Tanka unleashed a flood of pleas and reproaches. Semyon ignored the searing pain in his arm and swung his legs to the side of the pallet. He *would* get out of this bed if it killed him, rather than see his chance for revenge slip by.

The morning after his arrival, Ogodai recalled his two warriors from Vologda. He wanted to concentrate on directing the hunt for the bandits. "Find them," he told his men, "and we can head for Moscow. We'll track Koshkin down there. Then we go home." Yowls of joy greeted that last statement.

Natalya visited the monastery every day to pray, but Daniil's unexpected arrival meant that Maria accompanied her, while Nasan spent most of the time with her husband. Three Tatar raids in search of Semyon and his bandits failed to yield much in the way of news until a saucy young peasant woman encountered near the burned village pronounced the lord dead and his henchmen gone. "She'd say anything, Khan, if she thought we'd leave her alone," Karim reported as he passed the news along.

Nasan silently agreed. The women of that village had already declared their loyalty to their bandit husbands, and it defied belief that they would aid the cause of the men who had burned their homes.

Even so, she couldn't shake the thought that the peasant woman might have spoken at least a partial truth. Untreated, Semyon's wounds could fester. Death came often enough under such circumstances, and bandits needed a leader. Without Semyon to bully them into compliance, his men might either disperse or succumb to the cutthroat rivalries of their kind. She shared these thoughts with Ogodai and Daniil, but without confirmation, they had no choice but to keep searching.

Rafik and Karim led groups of warriors into the forest every morning, but each evening they returned empty-handed. Sometimes they discovered traces of human habitation, but not the humans themselves. They took what satisfaction they could from pushing their enemy deeper into the forest, forcing them to keep moving, to remain constantly on watch.

Then even the traces disappeared. The troops continued to search, but the bandits had vanished into thin air, it seemed. Unless they had descended to join the Lord of the Underworld. That would set everyone's mind at rest.

In the midst of uncertainty, Nasan stayed close to the house during that first week after her husband's arrival, and when the need to procure more medicine for Natalya became impossible to ignore, she invited Daniil to walk with her as far as the nut sedge patch. She hadn't forgotten the look on Semyon's face when he stalked toward his aunt that day on the trail, and without proof that he had died or departed, it seemed unwise to brave the forest alone. Besides, after their long parting, every moment spent in her husband's presence gleamed like a precious gem.

It was a beautiful morning. The sun shone pale yellow in a clear August sky, and heat caused the air to shimmer despite the early hour. The woods beckoned with cool serenity, but even the area near the house lay quiet and still.

Unless the sense of calm came from inside her. The memory of Daniil's hands, his lips, his warmth still made her glow. He accepted her invitation with alacrity and strolled beside her toward the forest, a guiding hand on her waist. She resisted the urge to tug him back to the room they shared. Surely so delightful an exercise must result in the child they both wanted.

They found the nut sedge without difficulty, and within moments Nasan's basket lay filled on the ground. Daniil pulled her behind an entwined pair of birches, and soon they too were entwined. Nasan gave herself over to the pleasure of his touch.

Running feet. A bass roar—familiar, piercing. The metallic chorus of steel blades, shouts in Tatar, the hiss of arrows. Daniil and Nasan sprang apart as if sliced by an ax. She touched a finger to his mouth, and he nodded. He reached for his belt, but she knew he would find nothing there except the knife he had used on the nut sedge. A man doesn't carry a sword to walk in the woods with his wife.

They peered around the birches, then crept to the edge of the trees. An astonishing sight met their eyes. Semyon, thinner and paler than she remembered him, and a handful of bandits—no more than fifteen men altogether—ran in a wedge toward Ogodai's troops. Before Nasan and Daniil had a chance to react, the Tatars surrounded the invaders, who formed a circle, backs in, weapons out. The occasional swinging scythe kept the Tatars at a distance, but not for long. A volley of arrows, and the circle halved in size, although Semyon's blond head still towered over the warriors who surrounded him.

"He must be mad." Daniil caught his wife's hand and tugged her toward the house. "Leave the basket. We'll get it later. I have to find out what my cousin imagines he's doing."

As they walked onto the open ground, Nasan saw her brother, her mother-in-law, Maria, and every servant the estate possessed, including Grusha and her baby, arranged in front of the door. Ogodai came forward. Nasan and Daniil reached the circle at almost the same moment as the khan.

"We need to question him." Daniil pointed at Semyon. "Then we should turn him over to the military governor in Vologda."

"There is none," Ogodai said. "Your friend Koshkin left for Moscow two months ago. The government has yet to appoint a successor."

Daniil scowled. "Someone must be filling in. It's our duty to deliver him to the authorities."

"That's what I'm trying to tell you. *We're* the authorities." When Daniil accepted this statement with a curt nod, Ogodai signaled to Rafik. "Put that villain in the shed over there and keep watch over him."

"With pleasure, Khan." Rafik conveyed his orders, and soon six burly warriors were dragging Semyon, bound and raging, toward the small shed that under normal conditions housed gardening implements, axes, and saws.

Nasan assumed her brother's people would remove the tools before they left. And they did.

The door opened. Semyon gathered himself to spring, but one of the thrice-damned guards anticipated the move and slammed the base of his lance hard into Semyon's chest. The blow hit the rough bandage Tanka had bound around him with sufficient force to knock him off his feet, and the wound left in him by his warrior maid's second arrow did the rest. He collapsed, gasping.

"Was that necessary?" a woman said. The voice—familiar from childhood, yet unexpected within his prison—shocked him more than the blow from the Tatar's lance. He panted, trying to achieve some form of equilibrium. He'd known his Aunt Natalya was here, of course. Otherwise, he'd have stayed in his bed, with Tanka to fuss over him. The question was what brought Aunt Natalya to this shed. Here she was, though, without a doubt.

And, from the sound of it, not happy. But then, he couldn't recall a time when the sight of him had made her happy. Even when he had *not* been trying to kill her and the rest of her demon kin.

A swift exchange in Tatar followed, of which Semyon understood not one word. He grabbed the opportunity to catch his breath and pull himself back to the bench he had occupied when the opening door gave him false hopes of escape.

He had lots to mull over, even without the unexpected advent of Aunt Natalya. Why the raid hadn't worked, for starters. It should have, after Tanka spread false rumors of his death and the bandits' dispersal. He'd recovered enough to ride, despite being dragged from pillar to post to escape the marauding Tatars. The fifteen men who survived the last attack were his best fighters, and they had seen not a soul as they hid in the copse before deciding it was safe to move in. Not so much as a wisp of cooking fire clouded the sky. Yet the first scurry of feet brought warriors pouring out of cottages and tents like hornets from a nest, and before he even got a glimpse of his detestable relatives, Tatars had surrounded him.

Tatars. Curse the whole lot of them, from the beginning of time. Life never went his way when Tatars were involved.

You'd think he'd have learned that by now. Instead, what must he do but hanker after a *khanim* with a bodyguard the size of a division?

And growing by the moment, to boot. You'd think they were rabbits, not warriors. He'd have sworn she had less than half that many the day she slammed those arrows into his hide. What a bandit queen she would make!

She'd do his bidding one day, for sure. He just had to find a way out of here. For a man who could escape from Pechenga, a garden shed shouldn't pose much of an obstacle. Or even a miserable, canting old aunt.

As if conjured by the thought, his aunt spoke again. Semyon glanced her way, glaring at her. His men always said the scowl made him look a bear. *I'll eat you up, you nasty crone.*

His cousin Daniil joined her to the right; his hand gripped the hilt of a sword that from the state of its scabbard had seen much use. On Aunt Natalya's left pouted the redheaded bitch his dead cousin Boris had married. A regular family gathering. Semyon's insides churned with fury.

Let's go sneer at Semyon laid low. Charming relatives I have.

Two Tatars entered, a man and a woman. Like Daniil, both were armed, the man with sword and bow, the woman with only a bow. The man Semyon thought he'd seen before— although he couldn't be sure, and he didn't much care. The woman he couldn't mistake. His bandit queen, in the flesh, and more beautiful close up than he'd ever imagined from those glimpses of her in battle.

A woman of power. The one he'd waited for and never expected to find. He couldn't decide whether to kill her or kiss her, but whatever happened this day, he knew he would not forget her.

Then he saw Daniil place his hand on her waist. His cousin had married a Tatar. Two years ago, was it, or three? Semyon made an effort to attend the wedding—only to get thrown out, thanks to his uncle's unfairness, before the bride unveiled. He'd left Moscow a few months later, so he couldn't have seen her—although something about her face, the way she stood, struck him as familiar. But then, all Tatars looked alike.

He laughed silently at that. *All Tatars looked alike?* She and the rough guards? No, not one bit. Nor would anyone confuse her with the man who'd walked in with her—probably the leader, from his dress and his air of command.

Semyon's eyes narrowed. No, that wasn't true. His warrior maid and the leader did bear a certain similarity to each other. Her face was delicate, the young man's strong; her skin ivory, his bronzed; his frame a head taller than hers, if not more. Still, the resemblance was unmistakable. And now Semyon knew why the young man looked familiar. He'd been at the wedding too. He'd started the fight that ended with Semyon getting tossed out on his ear while the young man stayed. Yes, that's where Semyon had seen him: the boy was the bride's brother.

For the first time since his capture, he saw a way forward. Kill the men, steal the girl. Carry her off into the woods and find some isolated spot where no one would track him down. Let her fight him if she wanted. He wouldn't take his eyes off her for a moment. She'd get used to him soon enough, once she realized he loved her. A woman like that was worth an army.

But first he had to get out of these bonds and past the guards. He surveyed the assembled company—three women, eight warriors. It wouldn't be easy.

A hostage would help. One of these women would do just fine. His bandit queen would be best, but he could grab her later if necessary. Whoever came closest, that's the one he would choose.

The spurt of Tatar ended, and the bride's brother addressed Aunt Natalya in Russian. "It *was* necessary, Lady," he said with a firmness surprising in someone so young. "He lunged for the door. My man stopped him, as he should."

For a moment, Semyon couldn't figure out what the boy was talking about. What was necessary?

Oh yes, Aunt Natalya had protested his treatment by the guards. *Give it to him, Auntie!*

And Aunt Natalya, as usual, stuck to her guns. "I would examine his wounds, Khan," she said.

Semyon scowled. Khan? A boy like that? He looked no older than Daniil.

But the bride was Bulat Khan's daughter. He remembered that now. His uncle Nikolai had made peace when he should have waged war, then blamed Semyon for the trouble instead of recognizing who had defended the honor of their clan. Typical.

Better and better. He'd kill his cousin *and* Bulat's older son, then take Bulat's daughter for his own. He'd dispatch Aunt Natalya as well, repaying her for the many times she'd slapped his hand as a child. Then Uncle Nikolai, although absent, would suffer as well, with his house extinguished and his wife dead and gone.

"No," the khan said. "Leave his wounds alone. My men checked them earlier, and where he's going, he won't need a doctor."

Semyon snarled defiance at that, but the young khan didn't flinch. "Ask him your questions," the boy said. "Then we decide what to do with him."

Semyon heard the implicit threat. Decide what to do with him—it had a grim sound. More reason to attempt an escape. His enemies had had the better of him so far, but their luck couldn't last forever. He was worth a dozen Tatars—no, a hundred. The important thing was to distract them. Then he could make his move.

⁓

Natalya fixed him with that glare of hers, the one Semyon hated. "Attacking your own family! Have you run mad?" She spoke with the same snap in her voice that she had once used to chide him for stealing meat pies. "We sent you to Pechenga to save your life and protect our honor. I didn't expect to see you here, at the head of a band of ruffians. You should be ashamed of yourself!"

Ashamed of myself. Yes, Aunt Natalya, I'm ashamed of myself. I've been a bad boy. Box my ears, why don't you, witch?

Later, Semyon, later.

He twisted his hands in their bonds. He'd been working at the ropes since the Tatars dumped him here, but the warriors knew their job, and he'd made minimal progress. If he faked penitence, could he persuade his aunt that the beasts had tied him too tight? The thought of an apology stuck in his craw, but an escape with bound hands challenged even his skills.

"C'mon, Auntie," he said with what he hoped was a winning smile. "You don't believe I meant any harm, do you? I thought these men had stolen your property." He jerked his chin at the Tatars, some of whom hissed in response. The rest stared straight ahead, their eyes blank.

His bandit queen chimed in then, although she'd hung back while Natalya took the lead. "Liar. A week ago, I saw you stalking toward her with drawn sword. And a few moments watching the house would have revealed your cousin or your aunt. Don't waste our time."

Fiery little thing, sticking her chin out like that. Despite his wounds, the prospect of taming her heated his blood.

He produced a half-bow, tugging at the knotted rope as his shirt covered his hands. The twine burned his wrists, but he felt it release. Not much, but a start.

He was trying to keep the joy from his face when his cousin stalked forward, grabbed his collar, and yanked his head up. "Answer my mother," Daniil said in a hard tone, "and take your filthy eyes off my wife."

Semyon slapped Daniil's hand away with his bound fists. His bandit queen, he was sorry to note, had retreated behind her brother, who looked even more thunderous than Daniil. "Damn you," Semyon said. "What gives you the right to insult me? You ship me off to some godforsaken hole, then think I'll make your lives easy by staying there meekly until I expire of cold and hunger? Thank you. I prefer to chart my own course."

Daniil didn't so much as flick an eyelash in response, but his mother softened. Semyon had counted on that. "Of course, we didn't wish you to die of cold, you silly boy," she said. "Why should we?"

Daniil, unforgivably, snorted, and his Tatar friend muttered something that provoked a shout of laughter from the guards. Natalya turned her frown on them.

"So you left," Daniil said, not noticeably quelled by the frown. "And became a bandit. Are you trying to make us believe you're helping the family by roaming the woods preying on pilgrims?"

Semyon shrugged. Beneath the loose fold of his shirt, he tugged anew at the knot. He shoved three fingers under the rope, broke a fingernail, strove not to swear. It wasn't working. He held up his bound fists, showing Natalya the reddened wrists. "Can't you ask the khan to loosen them, Auntie, before my hands fall off?"

She leaned toward him, as if considering his request.

Come closer, Auntie—closer, closer.

The khan stepped forward. "As my sister said, he's wasting our time. Let's go."

Aunt Natalya drew back, and Semyon suppressed another curse. When he got hold of a weapon …

He sighed, assuming a hangdog expression for his aunt's benefit. Maybe his cleverness would impress them. Or his lurid tale lull them into a false sense of security. It was worth a try.

"Don't be in such a rush." He straightened, leaning back against the wall, his bound hands with their rope-burned wrists visible to everyone in the room. "You don't want to miss this. It's a story good enough for the campfire. You'll say I invented it, but I swear on my mother's grave, it's the honest truth." And he launched into the tale he had spun Stenka—was it really only a couple of months ago?

From Nasan's vantage point at the back of the room, half-hidden by her husband and brother, she watched the expressions flitting over the face of her enemy. Semyon was up to something. Another escape attempt, undoubtedly, but how could even a man as conceited as he imagine that he could break his bonds, elude nine trained warriors (including herself), and avoid drawing the attention of the eighty or so Tatars and fifteen Russians who stood between him and the forest?

He was talking now—an incredible tale, as he said, of a holy monk who had made his living as a thief, driven by his unconquerable passion for a boyar's daughter who had run away from home to join him rather than accept the man her father had chosen for her. Nasan did not let the story distract her. She touched the strung bow that hung from her right shoulder, the leather quiver that dangled from her left. Glancing at her brother, she saw him do the same. Daniil's injury prevented him from exercising his skill at archery for the moment, but his hand had not left his sword hilt since he entered the shed. He moved to one side, where he could prop himself against the wall without his wound touching the wood, but he did not sit. His gaze remained fixed on his cousin.

"He killed her." Semyon leaned forward. Nasan saw Natalya and Maria hanging on his every word. For herself, she thought he had stitched the story together from whole cloth, but she said nothing.

"He roamed the wilderness for a decade, seeking forgiveness," Semyon said. "And came at last to Pechenga, at the edge of the earth, where he decided to end his days praising the Lord."

Maria had so far remained uncharacteristically still. Now she took three steps toward Semyon, paused, then took three more. Her lips parted; she had the appearance of a rabbit transfixed by a hawk.

Nasan felt herself tense. Should she say something? Pull Maria back?

But Maria was no rabbit, and she would resent any interference. She might cause a scene that would attract the others' attention and give Semyon the opportunity he craved.

No one else moved. Nasan told herself not to overreact. For once, everything did not depend on her. Daniil, Ogodai, the warriors—they shared a common goal.

Semyon's unpleasant grin widened into self-congratulation. "He did, too. Praise the Lord, seek forgiveness, attain the reputation of a holy man. Mitrofan faded away, and the Blessed Trifon of Pechenga emerged in his place. A trusting sort, Trifon. Surprising in a former criminal. When the lovely Vasilissa returned to him in visions, it did not once occur to him that the visions might have originated with me."

And with that, Semyon lurched to his feet, snaked his bound arms around Maria's neck, and hauled her against his chest. One hand encircled her throat, and her brown eyes grew as round as those of the rabbit Nasan had just imagined.

"Lovers can be so foolish," Semyon said. He squeezed Maria's throat. "As can women. And now, you release me, or she dies."

Chapter 17

FOR AN INSTANT, EVERYONE FROZE. THEN NATALYA stepped forward. "Don't act foolishly, nephew," she chided, as if Semyon planned some childish prank. "You will not win your freedom by harming Maria." Maria emitted a gurgle—of outrage, Nasan assumed. Semyon sneered.

Daniil caught his mother's arm and pulled her behind him. "Stay there, Mama," he said when she protested. He drew his sword and edged sideways, positioning himself next to the guards who stood closest to his cousin.

Nasan glanced around the room. The six guards had fanned out along the side walls, ready to rush the prisoner at their khan's order. Ogodai raised his bow, nocked an arrow to the bowstring, and pointed it at Semyon, waiting for the moment when he could be sure of hitting his target while missing Maria. Nasan copied his movement. Daniil stood to her brother's left, so she moved right, stopping almost directly opposite her husband. The three of them—Daniil, Ogodai, and herself—formed the points of a triangle. Semyon, opposite Ogodai, turned the shape into a diamond.

Nasan's new vantage point revealed that however firm Semyon's grip on Maria's throat, his bound hands limited his ability to control her. His left forearm lay across her shoulders, but her own arms swung free. In the same situation, Nasan would have thrust her hands upward while kicking her assailant in the shins, taking a chance on dropping down enough to give Ogodai a clear shot, trusting Daniil, too, to grasp the first opportunity to help her.

But Maria did not have the advantage of Tatar training, and no one had encouraged her to take responsibility for her own safety. Semyon's grip on her throat would terrify her; she might imagine—not without reason—that he could break her neck at the first hint of escape. Her scared-rabbit eyes fixed on Ogodai suggested she saw him, too, as a threat. Did she really believe he would shoot her to get at Semyon?

Nasan checked for a clear target and didn't find one. An arrow aimed at Semyon's arm might immobilize him, but if he clutched Maria's throat in his first paroxysm, the result might exceed any damage he had planned to inflict. Anywhere else looked either too hazardous to the captive or likely to madden the captor rather than incapacitate him.

She spared a moment to appreciate the irony of again risking her life for Maria of the unkind tongue. Still, meanness of spirit should not condemn a person to death. And they needed to act fast. Semyon had miscalculated, as he must realize soon if he hadn't already. He could not release Maria without exposing himself to Ogodai's arrow, but he could not use her to escape either, because as soon as he stepped far enough away from the back wall, the guards would rush him from behind.

Nasan propped her bow against the window. Ogodai had the direct line of fire, and she relied on him not to miss, especially at this range.

She bent and drew the dagger from her boot. Compared to Daniil's sword or Ogodai's bow, the small knife wouldn't inflict much damage, but it would suffice to fend off an attack and to worry her opponent. She looked at Daniil, who took a step forward. His right thumb and forefinger clutched the sword, but at an angle hidden from Semyon he extended the three other fingers, then closed the third around the hilt. He was counting. Nasan nodded to show she understood, then glanced at her brother, who ducked his chin in acknowledgment.

Semyon swiveled his eyes back and forth like a snake wondering from which side the blow would come. Nasan looked again at Daniil. Only his little finger remained outstretched. She bounced lightly on her toes, preparing her muscles to move.

Daniil shifted the sword to his good hand. Nasan dashed in from one side as he attacked from the other. She slashed Semyon's left arm with her dagger, yanked Maria downward as his grip loosened, and rolled sideways toward the wall, dragging her sister-in-law with her. She heard the thrum of a bowstring, screams and shouts, then scarlet drops splattered over her, as if released by a late summer shower.

He'd come so close. The stupid girl hadn't tried to fight. No bandit queen, she. How he'd relished the thought of her windpipe snapping under his hands, savored the caress of his thumb against the smooth stem of her throat. He should have killed her while he had the chance; he'd be performing a service for humanity, ridding it of the snooty bitch. Even his relatives couldn't complain about that.

His bandit queen and that damned husband of hers, though—trust them to concoct some infernal scheme. The two of them, charging him at once from opposite directions—did they not care whom he killed? Then a slash of pain in his left arm, a mighty blow to his right shoulder, and a fireball exploded in his chest, slamming his head against the wood and collapsing him to the floor. As he fell, one thought tormented him.

I won't get to enjoy my bandit queen after all.

Daniil reached out a hand to help his wife to her feet, then kissed her soundly, heedless of the blood that covered her or the presence of others. He heard a bustle of skirts, a woman sobbing, his mother's voice exclaiming over Maria, and a blunt inquiry from Ogodai as to Semyon's fate.

"He's dead, Khan," one of the guards said. "You shot him through the heart."

He spoke with obvious admiration. Daniil lifted his head and saw the six warriors clustered around his fallen cousin. Ogodai stood in the center.

"What did they say?" Natalya asked. Only then did Daniil realize the Tatars had spoken in their own tongue. Despite his months of separation from Nasan, his language practice in Kazan remained with him. He passed the news along, softening it to spare his mother's feelings.

Ogodai bowed stiffly to her, his right hand over his heart. "I regret, Lady, that I caused the death of your relative." But his tone, pure formality, undercut the words.

Her mouth tightened in distress, and she pressed her hands together, the knuckles white. "His desire for vengeance maddened him," she said after a while. "He disgraced our clan; he sank into crime. His deeds merited death. Yet I grieve for him. I remember him as a child, you see. So long as his parents lived, he was high-spirited—an imp, a troublemaker, but not cruel."

Daniil, better acquainted with Semyon than his mother, chose not to contradict this rosy portrayal of a cousin whom he remembered as a bully ever ready to heap the blame for his own misdeeds on others. "We must bury him." He glanced at his mother. "He died by violence. I don't want to ask Father Job to betray his conscience by insisting we place Semyon in hallowed ground. The woods contain enough unclean spirits; one more will make no difference."

"I will ask Masha to prepare his body and the good father to pray for him." Natalya bent over Maria, sobbing in a heap on the floor, and tugged gently at the younger woman's brocade-covered elbow. "Cease your tears, daughter, and come with me. He scared you, but you will live many years, and he won't trouble us again."

Maria wiped her eyes and sniffed, rubbed her cheeks and stood. She looked at Nasan. "Thank you, sister," she said.

Nasan's lips parted, as if in shock, but she soon rallied. "It was nothing," she said with a slight inclination of her head. "It pleases me that you took no hurt."

Natalya and Maria departed. The door had not closed before Daniil heard his wife congratulating her brother on his archery. He went to join them.

Two days later, Nasan stood in the Cathedral of the Nativity at Ferapontovo, celebrating the Dormition of the Virgin, in whose honor both monastery and church were named. The service at the cathedral bore a disturbing similarity to the rites that Father Job had recently said over Semyon during his burial in the forest at the edge of the village the Tatars had razed.

The memory of that rite still left her reeling. Were she, her family, and the Kolychevs rid of that implacable enemy at last? She sent loving thoughts to her younger brother, at peace among the ancestors now that Ogodai had avenged his murder. The events of the last two days seemed hazy, unreal.

The others felt it, too. Maria wandered about the house, the bruises left by Semyon's fingers visible on her throat, her voice ragged when she chose to use it, which happened seldom and without her usual venom. She appeared more subdued than reformed, but Nasan hoped their temporary truce would hold.

Natalya had also spent the last two days in somber mood. Daniil and Ogodai occupied themselves during the day with the other men, attending meals and talking with the women in the evenings but, except when Daniil joined Nasan at night, somehow distant from the emotional turmoil around them.

Ogodai began to speak of returning to Moscow, where he might find an opportunity to tackle his half-brother directly. Nasan supposed the rest of them would accompany him. She didn't know whether she wanted that or not.

And now this new ceremony—stranger than anything she had encountered since her conversion. Nasan bent her head as necessary and produced the required responses on cue; otherwise she admired the exquisitely painted animals romping against their sky-blue background. From time to time, she thought of her maid, Vera, who had not received even the simple funeral said over Semyon. But Vera was better off, in spiritual terms, even so: Father Job had said a memorial service for her, and the monks would remember her here, in their church, every month for years to come. Nasan had taken care of that with a generous donation.

She made no attempt to distract the worshippers by sharing her reactions with them. That could wait until the service ended, and then she would talk mostly with Daniil. Her mourning for Vera anyone would understand, but her discomfort with the service itself would be more difficult to explain. Not only was the congregation worshipping a painted image of a human being, however virtuous and revered, but that image lay encased in a kind of coffin, atop a bier covered in black velvet embroidered in gold. The mother of the prophet Isa had fallen asleep in the Lord, and here they were conducting her funeral, a millennium and a half after the fact.

Perhaps if she thought of Mary as an ancestor—a grandmother spirit for the Christians? Yes, that lessened the strangeness. And it was more fitting. Muslims revered Mary too, calling her the Sainted Miriam, and even the Christians didn't regard Mary as divine. It still seemed odd to revere a grandmother formally, in a church, but a painting was not so different from a wooden statue or a stuffed doll. Nasan liked the idea of Mary, who took a special interest in the protection of women and children. Mary interceded for sinners and gazed tenderly into the face of her infant son, so in a sense she was a grandmother for the congregation, was she not?

On Nasan's right, Natalya prayed ceaselessly under her breath. She had attained her dearest wish, the goal of this entire pilgrimage, and her face glowed with fulfillment. Daniil stood at her far side, ready to support her in case of need or escort her from the building if she felt faint. Nasan, who had developed a healthy respect for her mother-in-law's strength of will, saw little likelihood of a quick exit, but she didn't interfere. It would happen or it would not, and meanwhile Natalya was happy. She had worked hard and risked much to reach the cathedral in time for the Feast of the Dormition, and she had succeeded despite the odds. Nasan would not, for a moment, diminish her mother-in-law's pleasure.

Moreover, the cathedral was beautiful, with stark lines and graceful proportions that gave it a lightness not often seen in the churches frequented by Natalya and her family. White stucco over brick without, its soaring towers covered in black, it counteracted any simplicity of form with a glorious profusion of images painted on every interior surface. Many showed the subject of today's celebration in various poses. The haloed head of the adult Isa stared at them from the central dome. But Nasan also saw Saint Nicholas with his book and angels of all descriptions: the Archangel Mikal, identifiable by his warrior garb; cherubim and seraphim; more disciples and princes than she could hope to recognize; and a pair of gorgeous winged lions—one pale and spotted, the other a rich orange brighter even than Maria's hair—next to something squat and brown that might be a bear or a dog. These last occupied much of her attention when the demands of the service did not intrude. She saw Daniil gazing at them, too. The lions' fierce energy reminded her of the lynx pendant Ogodai had given her before her wedding, which she wore, as ever, next to her skin.

Ogodai had remained outside the monastery. He would not enter a Christian church, because the monks would not welcome him if he did. Grusha had sobbed when told that she could not attend, but even after thirty days she and her child remained ineligible for purification and hence unchurched, although Father Job had taken it upon himself to baptize baby Stenka, just in case. Stenka flourished, but infant life could be snuffed out in an instant, and Grusha appeared comforted by the assurance that her baby would, if snatched from her care, live among the angels in Heaven.

Nasan sneezed as the censor swung before her, releasing a heavy cloud of scent. Two young men in brocade robes passed by, holding candles fastened to long brass poles. Two more, dressed in blue, took their place at either side of the entombed icon and held what looked to Nasan like suns made of overlapping gold petals at an angle over the representation of the Virgin Mother. To either side of the bier, tall stands held hundreds of tiny candles. With Natalya and the rest of their party, Nasan herself had lit one of them earlier today and placed it amid the rest, saying a silent prayer that God might, in His infinite wisdom, choose to bless her and Daniil with a child.

"You have passed to life," the priest intoned, "being the Mother of Life. Through your intercession, save our souls from death."

"Save our souls from death," Nasan murmured. She bent her head as the priest faced the altar and used his service book to form the sign of the cross several times. He turned to face them, launching into a story of miraculous journeys and equally miraculous discoveries as the mother of Isa passed into the celestial realm. Nasan listened and learned and admired the winged lions.

The service would end soon, but if she studied them well, she could keep those beasts in her mind forever.

"Let me examine your wound, husband." Nasan sat on the bench beside the window of the bedroom she had adopted as her own before Daniil's arrival, looking uncharacteristically serious.

"Yes, doctor." Daniil tapped her nose, then removed his outer tunic and pulled his shirt over his head. Nasan moved behind him, her delicate fingers smoothing the skin over his collar bone, caressing the spot where the bullet had entered.

He glanced over his shoulder, acutely aware of how short their time together might be. Her solemn face made him smile, but he'd learned not to tease her about her interest in medicine. Look what her potion had done for his mother! Of course, he had only the women's word for how weak Natalya had been, but he didn't doubt that she felt much improved. She seemed like the mother he remembered, except that she bustled less and tired more quickly.

"It heals well. No signs of infection." She traced a series of curving lines against his back. The sensation felt like a spider wandering at random. "You will have quite a scar, though. They dug into the flesh without mercy. Were they doctors or butchers?"

"You ask me that every time," he said. "They were neither, just fellow soldiers trying to help."

"I fear their attempt to help has left you with an injury that will never heal completely," Nasan grumbled. "Can you raise your arm today?"

Daniil experimented. With effort, he could shrug his shoulder and swing his arm forward and, if he ignored the shooting pain it caused, back. But try as he might, he could not lift his right elbow more than a foot to the side.

"Higher than yesterday," Nasan said in the same assessing tone. "Perhaps you can stretch it as the muscles heal. I would not have you stress it too soon, lest you tear the fibers more." She came to sit beside him, and he pulled her close with his good left arm.

She snuggled against him in a most satisfactory fashion. "Will we go south with Ogodai? It seems odd to travel so far, then leave after not much more than two weeks, but your mother has changed her mind about staying. And no wonder. The bandit attack, your cousin's death—and the funeral, so strange and sad. Who would want to stay without the escort, even if life should be safer with Semyon gone?"

He caressed her cheek. The abandoned village, the silent forest—his cousin's last resting place weirdly fitted that turbulent soul. The peasants had buried the dead bandits he and Ogodai discovered on the road; the Tatar warriors had dug graves for Semyon and the men who died during his raid on the estate, but the simple removal of corpses did not relieve the air of desolation. The place would give nightmares to the dead. Daniil wanted to lose no time getting his family as far from the scene as possible.

"Yes," he said. "I've already arranged with your brother to leave the day after tomorrow. Mama can attend one more service at the monastery, if she likes. But she received word from Papa this morning that he has orders to accompany Prince Barbashin to Moscow, and she's eager to meet him there. And since she feels strong enough to travel overland, we should accept your brother's escort."

"I wonder if we should insist that she return by boat," Nasan said. "Not that she listens to me, but she would to you. Surely three weeks in a horse-drawn litter will drain her."

Daniil shrugged the working left shoulder. "I doubt it. She has to rest the whole way, and it will jolt her less than a carriage. From what you say, she was too frail before, but now? At least I persuaded her not to ride alongside us."

Nasan laughed at that. "Can you imagine? And poor Father Job would have had to ride as well, because he couldn't spend the entire journey in a closed litter with Maria and the maids."

"I shudder at the thought. And so would he, I feel certain. The poor man would walk to Moscow before he let that happen, I'm sure." Daniil nuzzled his wife's cheek. "But, dearest, can't we leave these discussions for later? I have much better ideas about how to spend our time together."

Nasan kissed him. "Well, since you've already removed your shirt …"

Chapter 18

THE RETURN TO MOSCOW WENT ALMOST TOO FAST FOR Nasan, even though her months of constant exercise meant that she had little trouble keeping up with the men—a true accomplishment, as they were seasoned cavalry officers. In those long-ago days when she lived in the horde that her brother now ruled, she would have thought nothing of riding from dawn to dusk; it pleased her to have regained her old skills. Even the trip to Ferapontovo paled by comparison, since the company of Daniil and Ogodai added so much to the journey.

Father Job showed an unexpected tenacity by joining the riders, and Nasan sent him a silent apology for doubting his stamina. Grusha, when asked, had chosen to travel south with her baby, leaving Masha to handle the estate in their absence. What exactly the family would do with its former slave when the group reached Moscow remained an unanswered and undiscussed question. As the riders approached the halfway point of Uglich, Nasan raised the issue with her husband. Ogodai rode on her other side, with his men surrounding them.

"What can we do for Grusha?" she asked. "I had planned to purchase her from your family and free her, but that won't serve. With no means of support, she will have no choice but to sell herself and Stenka to someone else."

"She belongs to my parents," Daniil said. "They must decide."

Nasan blushed. "I know that, husband, but they won't object if we offer a solution, will they? Call me foolish, but I feel for her. She has lost her man." She caught his fingers in her own. "As I feared I had lost you. And I helped her birth her child. I can't wash my hands of them."

Daniil's smile warmed her. "You can't lose me," he said. "Still, I understand. And she ran away, so we can assume she would prefer not to remain a slave. Frankly, I expected her to stay with Masha. It surprised me when she didn't."

"No, that part makes sense to me," Nasan said. "Even more than for us, the place holds unpleasant memories for her. She told me as much. In Moscow, she felt safe—not happy but secure—until Semyon hurt her."

Ogodai had listened without speaking, but at this point he interjected, "We have women enough in the harem; why not one more? She could help Firuza with the twins, and Diliara would love another baby boy to dote on. Would Grusha agree?"

Nasan hesitated. To live in the horde wouldn't be easy for Grusha: a new language, new customs, new people—she would have to adapt, as Nasan had to the household in Moscow. Yet life in Ogodai's harem offered a kind of security. Her child would give her status, and Nasan could ensure that Grusha went as a free woman.

"It's a generous offer, *aby*," Nasan told her brother. "We will ask Mama-in-law. As my husband says, in the end, she and Papa-in-law must decide."

The Crimean envoys reached Moscow on 4 September. With the approval of Prince Vasily Shuisky, Koshkin wangled a place among those representatives of the grand prince charged with greeting the visitors on their arrival in Moscow. A week past his sixth birthday, the grand prince remained too young to perform the full range of diplomatic duties—he could not, for example, preside over ambassadorial dinners. But dressed in the full regalia of Muscovite royalty—Koshkin didn't envy the poor child, bundled into cloth-of-gold and furs and expected to sit still on a throne for hours—Grand Prince Ivan would receive the envoys in the Kremlin, after a suitable interval designed to demonstrate to the new arrivals that they were but supplicants and he a mighty ruler. Until that meeting happened, Koshkin could proceed, more or less unimpeded, in his quest to suborn Tulpar Sultan.

It took him a few moments to find the face he sought in the crowd. Although a descendant of Genghis, Tulpar did not stand with the more seasoned ambassadors but several rows back. He had not yet dismounted. Dressed in robes of the finest embroidered silks in shades from cream to a dark, rich blue, he sat atop a dark bay Arabian of such magnificence Koshkin yearned to rip the leather rein from Tulpar's hands and take the beast for his own. The sultan's jeweled cap competed in splendor with the strands of pearls wound around his waist and the gold chain dangling from his neck, but after a swift, impressed glance, Koshkin found his gaze riveted on the figure to the young man's left.

A woman. What was she doing here? Envoys were men. Their escorts were men. He had never heard of a woman accompanying a diplomatic mission—except that Kolychev girl, two years ago, and the gossips had had plenty to say about that. You'd have thought the Apocalypse could not be long delayed.

And the Kolychev girl, although pretty enough, paled into insignificance beside this woman. Even mounted, she swayed with a sensuous motion that had every man in the vicinity goggling at her. Koshkin couldn't take his eyes off her. And as he stared, the woman drew back her veil. He saw pale brown skin, a smile of promise, wide hazel eyes, rich brown hair, high cheekbones, and—most amazing of all, given her circumstances—a delicate gold cross at her neck.

She was exquisite. He desired her, with a blazing passion he had never experienced in reference to his dead wife. To any woman, slave or free, that he had ever encountered.

She placed a possessive hand on Tulpar's arm, and Koshkin felt his insides constrict. It could not be, but alas, that which could not be, apparently was. This Lilith belonged to the one man whose anger he could not afford to incur.

And to think it had occurred to him, as he prepared for this new round of negotiations, that he might woo Tulpar with the offer of his own oldest daughter, Maria. Tulpar had spurned the offer of a wife before, but he would need political allies if he intended to establish his place in Russian society. And heirs that Russians would consider legitimate, whether Tatars worried about that or not.

Looking at the siren, Koshkin wondered if he even dared propose the match. When Tulpar had announced that he had a woman, no one could have envisioned a woman like this one. However lovely, his gorgeous daughter, too, paled next to the siren who, without even acknowledging his existence, had captured and held his attention.

Perhaps he could organize a trade. One beauty for another less seductive but better connected in the world that Tulpar sought to enter, able to confer benefits an exile from Crimea could not even imagine. Surely Tulpar would understand the value of that.

Or would he? Koshkin needed him; he had yet to see much evidence that Tulpar needed the Russians.

For the first time in years, Koshkin didn't know what to do. But somehow, he must find a way. He had more to lose, now, than the threat of a return to the northern wastes of Vologda—and more to gain than reinstatement at the Russian court.

Pale orange brick, massive walls, river, hill had a comforting familiarity. Daniil directed his horse across the wooden bridge and glanced at his wife. "Home," he said. "Even the animals feel it." He patted the neck of the impatient gelding. "Or does your mare still think of Kasimov as her home?"

His question concerned his wife more than her horse. Their journey had provided much time for conversation—more than any period of their marriage except those few months in Kazan—and although Nasan had not complained of the treatment she'd received from his mother in Moscow, enough detail had slipped through to reveal her deep unhappiness with life in the Kolychev household.

For that, he suspected, Maria bore a considerable part of the blame. But Maria gave evidence of becoming a reformed character since he and Nasan had saved her from Semyon, whereas he worried that his mother might find it impossible to adjust her expectations to the reality of his wife's personality. Would she recall what he'd told her on the day of his return: that he didn't want his Nasan throttled by convention, constrained by obligation? He wanted her at his side because she couldn't bear to live apart from him—the way she behaved whenever he returned to act as a buffer between her and the unceasing demands of the household.

How to guarantee that happy result given the certainty that the army would soon draw him back into service, Daniil had yet to figure out.

She answered his question. "Sorkhokhtani is eager to reach her stable. Such a long trip. But I hope she won't find everything as it was before. The months without exercise were difficult for her."

For a moment, he thought he had fooled her into believing he asked only about the horse. Then a spark lit her dark eyes, her vivid face crinkled into a smile, and he knew he had not. "I will speak to Mama," he promised. "We can't have either you or Sorkhokhtani sitting idle for weeks at a time."

"Thank you." Her nose wrinkled. "I only hope she remembers when you are again called away." She did not look convinced, and Daniil did not blame her.

The road widened as they rode up the hill, and dirt paths gave way to streets paved with wood. The walls of the Kremlin rose ever higher, until they could pick out details on the towers and crenellations, the uniforms of the royal guards. It was market day, and as they approached the end of their journey, the sounds of trade resolved themselves from an undifferentiated clamor into moos and oinks, squawks and shouts, haggling and laughter, then conversations. At last, the unmistakable blue domes, studded with gold stars, of the cathedral where Nasan and Daniil had married appeared before them. One more street, and Nasan saw the ironwork that marked the defensive boundary of the Kolychev estate. She tried not to think of it as her prison.

Behind her, Natalya exclaimed, Stenka wailed, and Grusha murmured words of comfort or protest; Nasan couldn't tell which. Ahead, the great oak gates of the Kolychev townhouse stood open. At the far side of the courtyard a tall building made of neatly fitted logs rose, its topmost turret clearing the fence that separated it from the street. The very walls the Golden Lynx had climbed as she left on her nighttime adventures and returned not long before dawn.

If Daniil left her again, the Golden Lynx could return. The trip north had restored her skills, and the world never lacked downtrodden victims in need of a helping hand.

Yet she was older now, more responsible. The angry sixteen-year-old had found her place. And she suspected she might have another reason not to racket around town from dusk to dawn.

She had, after all, promised Daniil to take good care of their child.

The litter had no sooner stopped in the middle of the court-yard than a crowd of servants surrounded it, chattering like a mammoth flock of magpies. Daniil took a moment to ap-preciate the sight of the house he had at times wondered if he would ever see again, then dismounted. He had swung his leg over the saddle and still had a foot in the stirrup when he noticed the stalwart figure, dressed with a luxuriance that sug-gested he might have been summoned to attendance at court, standing at the top of the outside staircase.

He freed his foot, raised his arm, and shouted, "Papa!" Natalya—who, supported by the arm of Pashka the steward, had put one jeweled slipper onto the planks that edged the courtyard—gasped and clapped her free hand to her cheek. "Kolya?" he heard her ask, then more loudly, as her second shoe joined the first and she stood, "Kolya!"

Papa rushed down the stairs as fast as a portly middle-aged man dressed in ankle-length robes could rush, and his mother ran at least a dozen steps toward him before her damaged heart forced her to stop. Daniil caught his wife's hand as she slid off her mare's back, and together they watched his parents embrace.

"It's lovely to see them." He squeezed the fingers he held. "May you and I still love each other like that after three decades."

Nasan reached up to kiss his cheek, and he steadied her around the waist. "Yes," she said. "May God and the grandmothers grant us that wish."

The celebration of the family's reunion lasted well into the evening. Early the next morning, Ogodai departed in search of information on the movements of his half-brother Tulpar and Maria's father, Koshkin. Daniil accompanied him. Nasan supervised the unpacking, then went to check on the stores of purple nut sedge and her mother-in-law, in that order. She found Natalya in her sitting room with Maria in attendance. Father Job had gone to visit his family, catch up on domestic events during his absence, and relieve his son of responsibility for ministering to the household.

Nasan smiled at the sight of her mother-in-law. Natalya had weathered the journey remarkably well, and delight at her husband's presence gave her a kind of radiance. Nasan left them together, sewing, and went to supervise the kitchens.

She had finished her duties and rejoined them by the time her husband and Ogodai returned. Puzzled, she watched her brother stalk about the sitting room. Daniil kept pace with him, although, unlike Ogodai, he seemed more amused than irritated. Nikolai arrived before the women had received any answers to their questions.

"I don't understand," Natalya said. "What troubles you so, Khan?"

"Indeed, *aby*," Nasan added. "I have seldom seen you so agitated. Did you find Tulpar? Has he done something dreadful?"

"Tulpar?" Maria asked. She had trouble keeping Tatar names straight.

"My half-brother," Nasan said. "The one whose antics brought the khan here. Who caused so much trouble while my husband and I were in Kazan." She smiled at Ogodai, who glowered back. "You defeated him then, brother. If needs be, you will defeat him again. But do tell us what he has done now."

With a sigh, he dropped onto the chair he had refused twice before. "You're right. I'm fussing over nothing. It is not, thank the ancestors, my task to defeat him this time. I don't even know that he needs defeating. But he is here in the city, in negotiation with various boyars—including your father, Lady Maria. Not on his own behalf, as we were told. He's joined the embassy representing Islam-Girei Sultan, who has once again extended the hand of friendship to Moscow. And, not coincidentally, the offer of an alliance against Lithuania and Kazan."

"Islam-Girei plans to launch another rebellion against his uncle, and he wants Russian support," Nikolai said.

Ogodai nodded. "So it appears. I heard those rumors too, back in June. But why he must send Tulpar—"

Nasan interrupted him. "He trusts Tulpar. Why wouldn't he? But I don't."

"Neither do I." Ogodai scrunched up his face as if he smelled rotten meat. "Bad enough if he negotiates in good faith, because Islam-Girei will observe the agreement only as long as it suits him; a bribe from his uncle or the Polish king, and we'll be enemies again. But suppose our initial information was true, and Tulpar intends to enter Russian service?"

"*Ata* will split his boots out of rage," Nasan said.

Ogodai's strained face crinkled into a rueful smile. "Well, Sun Tzu did say, 'Keep your friends close and your enemies closer.' *Ata* will have time to consider the wisdom of that advice. Tulpar caused plenty of trouble on the steppe. Maybe it's your government's turn to deal with him. Good luck to you."

Daniil nodded. "Not a prospect that thrills me. What will you do now?"

"Send a courier to Vyazma, tell him to ride as fast as possible, and while I'm waiting for *Ata*'s response, look for an opportunity to confront my half-brother face-to-face and shake the truth out of him. Then I can go home." Without rising, he bowed in the direction of Nikolai and Natalya. "Don't misunderstand me, please. I much appreciate your hospitality. But I have urgent matters awaiting me at the camp."

"Especially Firuza and the twins," Nasan said, wrinkling her nose at him.

He laughed then, his lovable relaxed self once more. "Especially my family, yes. I haven't seen my wife for three months. And thanks to Tulpar, Islam-Girei Sultan, and their ambitions, I will be lucky to reach her before the fall migration begins." He slapped his thigh. "I almost forgot. You'll love this, Nasan—and you, too, Daniil. Tulpar brought Roxelana along. At least, I assume she must have traveled with him. I saw her roaming the marketplace this morning with a gaggle of veiled women in tow. She glided up to me as if we were old friends."

Nasan said, "Roxelana? Oh, no, you must be joking!" When he shook his head, she too burst out laughing. Daniil's guffaw drowned hers.

"I'm still confused," Maria put in. "Can you not explain things clearly?"

Her voice held an edge. Natalya said, "Maria," with a note of warning.

Maria blushed. "Forgive me, Khan. Help me understand, please." Nasan noted how tightly her sister-in-law clasped her embroidery. Not so apologetic as she pretended, Nasan guessed, but she gave Maria full credit for effort.

"Uncles, cousins, half-brothers," Natalya said in a chiding tone. "And I thought Russians had too many relatives." She patted Maria's hand. "I don't blame you, child, for becoming confused."

"I understand them," Nikolai said in his stately way. "Except for this mention of Roxelana. Who is she, and what makes news of her arrival so funny?"

Nasan cleared her throat. "My half-brother's concubine. I shouldn't laugh. She isn't funny, and why should she not travel to Moscow? But she *will* cause trouble. My sister-in-law tells me she has a devastating effect on men." She giggled again at the thought.

Daniil swallowed. "Not every man," he said, sober again.

"She is beautiful of face," Ogodai said, "but always seeking to better her position. It's impressive that my half-brother has succeeded in retaining her affection for three years, if not more. But I doubt he'll keep her for long."

The women pelted him with questions, but instead of answering he rose and bowed. "Excuse me. Daniil will tell you anything else you wish to know."

Chapter 19

BEFORE NASAN'S FATHER HAD TIME TO REPLY TO OGODAI'S message, events took an even stranger turn. The very next day, gray skies filled with ominous black clouds caused Ogodai, Daniil, and Nasan to abandon their early morning ride midway. They were racing for the courtyard gates when the first drops, big as the river pearls in Natalya's favorite necklace, fell. As they reached the stairs, Ogodai caught his sister's reins in one hand. "Upstairs with you. I'll order someone to take care of the horse." The drops turned to sheets as he spoke.

Nasan had no desire to argue. She kicked her feet free of the stirrups, slid from the saddle, and darted under the roof that covered the stairway. There she turned to watch her husband and brother ride for the stables, Sorkhokhtani galloping behind them. They would no doubt take refuge there until the first wave of the storm passed, then seek a change of clothing in one of the tents that dotted the courtyard. Then they would stay in the tents drinking beer and koumiss and trading stories with the warriors Ogodai had brought.

In short, they would have a lovely day.

She shrugged. Men. What could one do? At least, she was dry, thanks to her brother's consideration. She'd enjoyed an hour's ride. And Natalya's plans to wash clothes would have to wait for better weather. Life had looked worse.

Nasan climbed the stairs. When she reached Natalya's sitting room, she found her parents-in-law entertaining a visitor. Maria sat in one corner, the ever-present embroidery lying discarded on a small table, an unreadable expression on her face.

"Excuse me," Nasan said. "Should I leave you alone? We came home early, because of the rain."

Natalya held out a hand. "Irina. Please join us, daughter. This matter concerns you, too. Your brother and husband didn't return with you?"

"They took the horses to the stables," Nasan said. "I expect they will stay until the rain eases. Should I send a servant for them?"

Natalya glanced at the window, where rain fell in a river across the pane. "No. I would not risk their catching a chill. Come and greet our visitor." With extended hand, she indicated a small dapper man in the rich clothing of a boyar, his beard extending a finger's width or so from his chin. His black hair as yet showed no trace of gray, his narrowed brown eyes had a piercing intensity. Something about the tight set of his mouth convinced Nasan that he seldom spoke without deliberate purpose. The contrast between him and Papa-in-law, stolid and forthright, struck her, as did the hostility that hummed between them.

"Make your bow, Irina," Natalya said. "This is Maria's father, Fyodor Mikhailovich Koshkin. You met him at your wedding, but with so many strangers there, you may not remember." Nasan bowed as instructed, wondering what brought Maria's father here after so much time. And why Maria looked anything but happy.

Koshkin spoke. "Irina Bulatovna," he said. "My pleasure to make your acquaintance. Again."

"I too am pleased," she told him, determined to match him in courtesy.

The sound of his voice reminded her to say as little as possible, to step carefully. This man was not only Maria's father. Two years ago, he had tried to bring down the Kolychev clan, accusing Daniil of being the Golden Lynx. He had sought to bring down the throne. He had not seen her during her nighttime adventures, nor had she seen him, but she had heard him giving orders in the dark. Fyodor Koshkin was a dangerous man.

"Sit, my dear." Natalya handed Nasan a small brass cup filled with dark red liquid. "Fyodor Mikhailovich, you say you and your daughter have cause for celebration. May we assume that you have taken steps to secure her future?" She nodded at Maria, who lowered her eyes.

A new husband for Maria? Was it possible? Would Nasan be spared her sister-in-law's constant needling at last?

Although in truth, the needling has much abated since the incident with Semyon.

Koshkin raised his cup in reply. "Indeed I have, dear lady. But first let me thank you for showing such kindness to her while I settled my affairs. If my wife had not passed away last year, I would have reclaimed Maria sooner. But God moves in mysterious ways, as they say, and He has rewarded us for our patience by providing her with a stepmother and a husband in one package."

Maria, her eyes still lowered, compressed her lips in a tight line.

Curious. From the day Maria entered this house, she had wanted to leave it (or so she said). Yet there she sat, her face as sour as if Nasan had poured unsweetened nut sedge down her throat. Why?

Because she knew whom her father had picked and didn't like the idea. Her father suffered from overweening ambition.

To advance his lineage, he would not scruple to barter his beautiful daughter. Had he not done so twice already? He might have selected an old man or a child, an ugly drunkard, a creature incompetent in body or mind. Only the future husband's bloodlines would count. Nasan felt a flash of pity for her prickly sister-in-law.

Natalya leaned forward—her cup still in her hand, her face showing polite attention. "I congratulate you, daughter," she said. "Who is your new husband?"

Maria bit her lip and did not answer.

"She is overwhelmed with joy," Koshkin said after a pause.

He didn't see? Or did he not want to admit that his daughter disliked the match he had contracted for her? Nasan compressed her brows in a small frown, puzzled by Koshkin's reticence to reveal the promised husband's name. He was playing a game, obviously, but with what object?

"Will you not share the source of her joy, Fyodor Mikhailovich?" Nikolai asked when it became clear that Koshkin would not continue.

Maria's father bared his teeth. Nasan recoiled, then relaxed when she recognized the odd expression as an attempt at a smile.

"Like you, my dear friend," Koshkin said, "I have secured a descendant of Genghis in marriage for my darling child. I sponsored his conversion to Christianity this very morning, after he accepted the hand of my dear Maria. We shall celebrate their wedding on the first auspicious date." He raised his cup. "To Tsarevich Alexei Bulatovich."

"Bulatovich?" Nasan forgot to drink. The name, "son of Bulat," came out more like a squeak. Of course, her father was not the only Bulat in Moscow. But it seemed too much of a coincidence that Koshkin would withhold the name of the son of a different Bulat, especially with Tulpar newly arrived from

Crimea and reported as negotiating with Koshkin, among others.

That would confirm the rumors that he planned to switch sides. But why, of all the noblemen in Russia, must her disreputable half-brother choose Koshkin for his ally?

Because Koshkin hated the Kolychevs, who through Nasan were allied with Tulpar's father. Bulat stood high in the Russian hierarchy, and Tulpar wanted a counterweight to advance his own career. Koshkin would have no trouble making *that* sale, even if the price was marriage to Maria. What was a woman, after all? If Tulpar disliked her, he would ignore her once he had sons by her. Nasan didn't need a codebreaker to decipher how her half-brother thought.

Nasan glanced at Nikolai, then Natalya, but saw no evidence that the name Alexei Bulatovich held any special meaning for them. "Formerly called Tulpar?" she asked.

Koshkin again produced his catlike smile. "Why, my dear, do you know him?"

Nasan placed her cup on a nearby table, balancing it to prevent a spill. Although she tried to control her face, enough of her reaction showed to delight Koshkin. Like a magician, she guessed, he loved to unsettle others with his tricks.

"My half-brother," she said in the steadiest voice she could muster. "I know *of* him. He left the family when I was a child, but my husband and brother encountered him not long ago. I congratulate you, sister. The women in Kazan sighed at the sound of his name."

She added that last to reassure Maria, but glancing at her sister-in-law again, she saw Maria's eyes still downcast, her lips taut. Only then did Nasan recall that day in the courtyard when she had saved the swans from Vanka's bow. "When I marry a good *Orthodox* Russian," Maria had said, emphasizing her low regard for Tatars. Nasan had countered that Maria's father would leap at the chance to wed her to a descendant of Genghis. And they had both been right: Maria would wed an Orthodox descendant of Genghis in Russian service.

Nasan's sympathy evaporated. If Maria had no cause for complaint other than marriage to a young and handsome Tatar, she needed to grow up. The ancestors loved to challenge their descendants by granting wishes in ways that defied expectations. Look at Nasan's own marriage to Daniil—how much she had dreaded it, and how foolish that seemed in retrospect. This match bore every sign of having been crafted by the grandmothers to educate both bride and groom.

When Maria didn't respond, Natalya raised her cup to Koshkin. "We should toast your good fortune, too, Fyodor Mikhailovich. You mentioned a stepmother. What is the name of your new bride?"

Nasan reached for her cup once more. The heavy red wine was not to her taste, but courtesy required her to join the toast. Then Koshkin said, "Roxelana."

Her brass cup hit the floor and bounced, soaking wine into the carpet. Nasan grabbed it, but it was too late to conceal her shock.

"Why, my dear girl," Koshkin said, "do you know her too? How well connected you are, to be sure."

"I know of her," Nasan said. She saw no need to elaborate. Daniil and Ogodai would choke when they heard this.

Fortunately, Koshkin had left by the time Daniil returned from the stable with Ogodai. Maria had retreated to her room—for a good cry, Natalya said, although Daniil couldn't imagine what Maria had to cry about. The prospect of a husband who could woo and win the exquisitely sensuous Roxelana ought to gladden a young woman's heart. In fact, Tulpar should be the one weeping. But he had no exposure yet to Maria's shrewish tongue.

Daniil shared neither thought with his mother.

"Honestly," she scolded. "The pair of you, howling like jackals on the steppe. You should be ashamed to have such bad manners!"

Daniil, still laughing, didn't protest, but his wife stepped in to defend him. "They wouldn't laugh if our guest were still here, Mama-in-law. Or if Maria had minded her tongue. And Roxelana as the stepmother of grown children—from what I have heard, that is indeed a joke." She turned on Ogodai. "You knew! That's what you meant when you said Tulpar wouldn't keep her for long."

Ogodai straightened in his chair. "I guessed. I saw how the Russian noblemen snapped at her heels like dogs spying a juicy bone. But marriage? Your Koshkin must be besotted. She will lead him a merry dance; your Maria, too, may find herself glad to escape to Tulpar's section of the house."

"Why? Will this Roxelana mistreat her?" Natalya asked.

Daniil stopped laughing long enough to shrug his good shoulder. "I doubt it. Unlike Maria, she seemed good-natured to me, but I didn't spend much time with her. Why do you say that, Ogodai?"

"She taunted my wife often enough." Ogodai rested his cheek on the spread fingers of his right hand, as if conjuring an image of Roxelana in his mind. "But your Maria will respond in kind. No, the problem is that Roxelana has no morals to speak of. That Koshkin desires her doesn't surprise me; to learn that she desires him would surprise me a great deal. She wants the security of marriage, I would guess, and she'll seek to discredit any rival, including Maria, whom she perceives as standing in her way. Roxelana is not vicious, but I doubt she cares for anyone besides herself."

"Maria has been good to me since I fell ill," Natalya said. "And she has quite reformed that malicious tendency of hers. I don't like to think of her being unhappy."

"I wouldn't worry, Mama," Daniil said. "Maria can hold her own. So can Tulpar. The two of them *and* Roxelana—it will be a contest of giants."

"Still, I will miss her," Natalya said. A sentiment so outrageous that neither her son nor the other two could come up with a response.

It was his greatest triumph yet. Alone in his favorite room in his Moscow house, Koshkin raised a goblet of red wine to the visage he saw dimly reflected in the highly polished cabinet opposite him. Who would have thought that the situation in Crimea could deteriorate so badly in just a few months that Tulpar Sultan would not only abandon his pretense of indifference and enter into an alliance but even accept Maria's hand in exchange for his own voluptuous Roxelana?

Koshkin frowned at the swirling wine. And why had Tulpar, after some initial reluctance, agreed to surrender a woman any man must desire? Did the sultan know something he had chosen not to communicate to Koshkin? Tulpar had said, offhandedly and unexpectedly, that he was tired of her, but Koshkin didn't believe him. No one could tire of such beauty. No, the sultan must be in worse trouble than he wanted anyone to discover. Why, he'd even converted, with Koshkin as sponsor! Two months ago, Koshkin would have sworn he'd die of old age before he saw that happen.

He took a deep draught from his goblet and let the complex, fruity flavors roll over his tongue. The taste evoked the memory of that Kolychev girl, the sultan's half-sister—the shock on her face, the clatter of metal against the floor, her inadequate attempts to appear calm and collected. He'd invite the whole lot of them to Maria's wedding. The Tatars, too. Just watching them pretend they liked what was happening would give the event the spice it needed. He'd wed Roxelana first, so she could act as mother of the bride.

It had been a good day. An excellent day. And this was only the beginning. Once he had his oldest daughter safely disposed of, he would enlist Tulpar—Alexei, now—in his plans to settle scores with that meddlesome Lithuanian sorceress who saw herself as the ruler of Russia.

Yes, Elena Glinskaya was not long for this world.

Ogodai's second courier galloped out of Moscow that afternoon, headed for Bulat's headquarters in Vyazma. Several days passed before the two messengers rode in together, bearing terse messages of approval and release. Ogodai grumbled to Daniil and Nasan about his father's lack of appreciation, but they could see from the distracted expression on his face that he was already planning his departure.

Daniil was watching Nasan shoot arrows in the courtyard when his brother-in-law came to say farewell. His own efforts to test his injured right shoulder against the straw target had fallen by the wayside after his first attempt revealed that he still lacked the flexibility to pull his arm more than halfway back. He would have to start practicing with his left if this went on.

"Time for me to go home," Ogodai said. "Nothing more to do here."

Nasan sent one more arrow into the target's hand-drawn paper heart, then dropped her bow and quiver to hug him. "We will miss you, *aby*. But it's been wonderful to see you. Will you bring Firuza to the wedding?"

"It depends when they hold it. I have to reach the horde, settle any problems that arose while I was away, supervise the migration. Unless Tulpar plans to wait six months—and why should he?—he can marry without my help. It's too long a trip to make twice in so short a time."

Daniil assumed Nasan understood her brother's reasoning, because she didn't argue. Instead she asked, "You will give Firuza our love then? Perhaps we can meet in Kasimov, after the migration ends."

"I will, and I would like that." He rubbed his nose against her forehead. An odd gesture, Daniil always thought, but it was the Tatar way; only husbands and wives kissed. Nasan had told him more than once how the familiarity of the gesture comforted her.

He slapped Ogodai's shoulder, and Ogodai responded in kind. "Try to stay out of the war, so you can escort her, brother."

"And you," Daniil said. "You leave today?"

"At once." Ogodai shaded his eyes with one hand and scanned the courtyard, where his warriors were already dismantling their tents. "The men, too, are eager to see their families. Tell that slave of yours to ready herself and her child. We ride this afternoon."

And sure enough, the midday meal had just ended when Nasan and Daniil stood with his parents at the bottom of the stairs—Maria, as usual, had chosen to absent herself—and watched Ogodai and his men ride out through the gates. Grusha, with baby Stenka wrapped tightly in a shawl that tied him to his mother's back, clung to Rafik's waist with both arms. She looked apprehensive, Daniil thought, but she hadn't complained. On the contrary, she had resisted any suggestion that she stay in Moscow. In the face of her determination, his parents had agreed readily enough to release her. They had refused Nasan's offer of payment. He would have been surprised if they hadn't.

Daniil didn't understand Grusha's motives for traveling south, although as the solution to a problem, her departure with his brother-in-law struck him as more than adequate. Nasan also had no explanation to offer other than her belief that Grusha wanted to start anew.

But then, Grusha's reasons didn't concern him. Besides, she could always change her mind. And with that, he dismissed her from his thoughts.

"How can you grasp this writing business so quickly?"

Nasan smiled at her husband, who held up a piece of paper that looked, to be kind, as if an ant in the last stages of inebriation had staggered into the ink pot and wandered at will over the page. He pointed to her own neat line of printed characters, complete with curlicues marking the omitted letters that characterized sacred words. "Russian isn't even your native tongue," he complained.

It was the morning after Ogodai's departure, and they were in Nikolai's study, where Father Job had agreed to teach them to read and write the Cyrillic alphabet. Husband and wife sat opposite each other at a square wooden table, with Father Job supervising their efforts. They'd been working almost since first light, and Nasan had made her way through the alphabet. Each letter had a sound associated with it, and the sounds seldom varied. Soon she would have them memorized; then she would be able to read just by sounding out the words. As languages went, she found this one blessedly simple—to read and write, that is. It had other complexities.

Daniil, however, struggled with the concept of replicating spoken words in printed shapes on a piece of paper. It didn't help that his wife had mastered that concept so long ago that she couldn't recall a time before it informed her understanding of the world.

He would grasp it, in time, but not between dawn and midday.

"I have years of experience in using a pen to form shapes," she told him. "I sometimes mix up the endings of words, and I have trouble with numbers—why should 'z' be 7 and 'r' 100? It makes no sense. Still, the letters are easy to learn, even the strange ones—easier than patterns of curves and dots."

He shook his head. "They all look like squiggles to me."

"You must apply yourself, my son," Father Job said. "You asked me to teach you. As a skill, it is not more difficult than riding a horse or shooting a bow."

"I'm trying." Daniil picked up the pen again and traced one long stroke, another intersecting it at the tip, and a third criss-crossing the first two. A recognizable, even creditable A.

"See? I have faith in you, husband." To encourage him, Nasan drew a line across her paper and printed a new line of text at the bottom. She handed it to him. "When you can read that, you may do it."

Father Job glanced at the paper. He frowned, but the twinkle in his eyes gave him away. "Most ingenious, my daughter," he said. "If not strictly canonical."

Nasan giggled, and Daniil snatched the paper from the table and perused it. "Devil take you, wife of mine. What have you done now?"

She stood and bowed to the priest, then to the icons behind him. "You will enjoy finding out, husband, and when you do, you will enjoy yourself even more. Meanwhile, I should go and see if Mama-in-law has work for me to do. Lucky for you, it is a Thursday." And with that, she glided from the room.

A Thursday. And what, pray, did she mean by that? Daniil, left in Papa's study with the priest, who was chuckling in the wake of Nasan's departure, pondered the incomprehensible message left by his wife.

"You're not going to tell me, are you?" he demanded what seemed like hours later. He waved the paper for emphasis. He'd stared at it until his eyes crossed, but so far he had deciphered only his own name.

"I wouldn't dream of interfering, my son." The priest still looked amused, damn him. "Although I will note that if you can't unlock the message today, you should wait until Saturday."

Thursday, now Saturday. An inkling dawned. Wednesday, Friday, and Sunday were holy days on which even married couples were supposed to practice abstinence. Nasan, in his experience, had little regard for that canonical requirement, not having grown up with it, but she would hardly admit as much in front of the family chaplain. So she had sent him a loving message, which the priest could read and he could not. It was too irritating for words.

Father Job was amused, not shocked, so she couldn't have said anything *too* provocative. Daniil studied the line of print again. His name came second, and the first word began with the same letter. She must have written his name to help him, because normally she never spoke it aloud, except once in a while when they were alone: some Tatar custom that he accepted as implying respect without fully grasping why it should be so. It was a long word, the first, and included the "d," "a," and "i" but no other letters from Daniil. He took a stab at it. "Dear?"

"Dearest." The priest ran his finger under the end of the word, emphasizing the ending.

"Dearest Daniil?"

The priest nodded, and Daniil turned back to the message. "What letter is this?" He pointed to a shape with two upright lines joined by a straight one at the bottom and a small tail on the right side.

"Ts," Father Job told him.

Daniil squinted at the letters, matching the lines and curves against the sounds in his head, looking for repeated instances of the same shape, asking for help as needed. Nasan had the whole alphabet at her fingertips already, whereas he struggled after five or six letters. So many of them looked alike, with only a small tail or the angle of a crossbar to distinguish one from another.

But he *would* learn. If, God forbid, those in power demanded he return to the war—and what could be more likely once his arm healed?—he wanted no more silences filled with misunderstandings between him and his wife.

Father Job sat next to him, sounding out the letters once more. "It's difficult," he said, without being asked. "But I have faith in you, my son. Compared to shooting an arrow into a moving target or imagining the design of a fortress, let alone repeating strings of orders verbatim, reading and writing are tasks for children."

Daniil laughed, a rueful sound even in his own ears. "Perhaps they should be left to children, Father. It doesn't console me to hear that I can't match the achievements of a six-year-old."

"Nonsense. You need only apply yourself." The priest's eyes twinkled once more. "And I assure you, I would not allow a six-year-old to read that line from your wife."

That did it. Daniil bent over the paper, tracing each shape with his fingers. He had a good memory for sounds, as Father Job had pointed out, and he had already deciphered half of the words in the message. But what was this long one?

He looked at Father Job's list. "Ts"—yes, he had that. And not many words began with that sound.

But one of his favorites did. Daniil traced out the third word again, and his mouth dropped open. "Dearest Daniil," the message said, "I want you to kiss me from head to feet."

Warmth rushed through him. Imagine reading *that* on a cold, lonely night on campaign.

A bit embarrassed at his own eagerness, Daniil stood to thank Father Job. He looked at the priest, expecting censure. The Church took a dim view of physical pleasure, even between husband and wife.

But Father Job was smiling. "You worked it out. Good for you. We'll have you reading in no time."

"You're not offended, Father? I'm glad."

"I, too, was young once." He touched the end of the message, crumpled in Daniil's fist. "It is not, perhaps, the tactic I would have chosen, but your wife knows you well. Go with God, my son, and try to remember the rules."

Daniil laughed. "I will, Father. And if I forget, I promise to confess my sins."

Chapter 20

SIX WEEKS PASSED. DANIIL'S SHOULDER CEASED TO ACHE, except on the cold, soggy days that grew in number as the light faded and the first snows fell—just once in a while, then more often. By the end of the month, the sleighs would be out in earnest, although the rivers would not freeze for some weeks more.

What did not return was the full use of his arm. Nasan tut-tutted about the damage done by ignorant soldiers who shouldn't be trusted with knives. Daniil forbore from pointing out that he might have died without their intervention. She was probably right about the scars they had left and the impossibility of full restoration.

Still, he hoped not. He had prided himself on his skill as an archer. The thought that he might never again pick up a bow loomed, vague but threatening, on the horizon. If not a warrior, what was he? The injury affected even the power of his sword. He had assisted in disabling his cousin by using his left arm, but that tactic wouldn't save him in battle. An opponent could dispatch him with one powerful double-handed blow while he fumbled to raise his own weapon to shoulder height.

The prospect disturbed him, and he avoided dwelling on it. Yet it would not be still, gnawing at him at odd moments as he fell into or woke from sleep, jarring him awake amid the silent household, tormenting him with dreams until Nasan wrapped her arms around his restless body and murmured consoling words into his ears. Her loving touch comforted him, but in the morning, when he saw the dark circles under her eyes and the listlessness that had replaced her normal vibrant energy, he berated himself for disturbing her.

The previous night had brought an especially troubling vision of himself as a large toad battening on his parents' household, unable to fulfill his purpose. In the dream, his wife had drawn away from him, horror on her face, while he flicked a long and sticky tongue aimlessly into the air. Even after he woke, the dream clung to him, refusing to dissolve into the usual wispy incoherence.

He had not confided in Nasan, who saw great significance in dreams. His reluctance to share his experience with anyone else in the household he attributed to a fear of ridicule. The dream embarrassed him. When had he become fanciful?

So it was with some trepidation that he responded to his father's invitation to join him in the study. His fears took flight at the sight of the grin on his father's face.

"We're in luck, my boy." Papa handed him a cup of ale. "I had a meeting with Barbashin this morning. He asked after you." He raised the cup. "To friendship!"

Daniil savored the dense, somewhat bitter taste. "To friendship," he repeated. "And Barbashin honors me with his interest. What did you tell him?"

Papa motioned him to a seat, and Daniil took it. The slight ache in his fingers and the sight of his quill and Nasan's, side by side behind the inkwell, reminded him of the hours spent here every day with Father Job. Without thinking, he had taken the seat he normally occupied during his lessons. He glanced at his fingers, where dark stains marked his progress.

He showed them to his father. "I can read and write whole sentences. If they do send me back, I will at least know what my wife does with her days."

"Good for you, son." Papa sounded amused. "But Barbashin has arranged something better. I told him you had recovered, but not completely. I asked him for help. An assignment off the battlefield. He remembered your wound; he was impressed by your bravery—and your persistence in riding fourteen days straight to find your wife."

An assignment off the battlefield? Was it possible? "That was nothing," Daniil said. "Any husband would do the same."

Smiling, Papa shook his head. "Unlikely, but no matter. He wishes us well. So he has secured positions for us in Moscow— you as an adjutant, myself assisting my cousin as tutor to the young princes. I can look after your mother, and you can do the same for your wife."

Adjutant—charged with attending the grand prince on a hunt, at various court functions, or during journeys, with occasional missions outside the capital to keep life interesting. It seemed too good to be true, but Papa's happy face confirmed it. Daniil couldn't wait to share the news with Nasan. "To Prince Barbashin," he said before draining the cup.

"To Barbashin," Papa echoed, "and to health."

With each sunrise, it seemed incredible that Maria still lived among them. True, her father's announcement of his plans for her wedding had, so far as Nasan could tell, completed the transformation begun at the estate near Lake Borodava. Maria no longer lurked in corners, ready to pounce. With her departure imminent, Natalya made few demands on Maria, and the family saw the future bride only at meals. The rest of the time she spent in her room. For the first week or so, she oversaw the servants charged with packing up her belongings, but after ten days that task had progressed as far as it could. Two carts loaded with chests had conveyed everything but a few necessities to the Koshkin household. Nasan caught the occasional glimpse as she passed of a room stripped almost bare, a sad sight that must oppress the spirits of the room's occupant even more, especially as Koshkin's failure to set a specific departure date dragged on.

She half-expected Maria to pelt her with questions about her half-brother Tulpar, now Alexei. This habit that Russians had of changing their names made life very confusing.

Not that Nasan could have produced ready answers if asked, but Ogodai and Daniil—and even more Firuza, who being a woman spoke about things that *mattered*—had shared their impressions. So she could have given Maria a sense of what to expect, as well as ideas about what Tulpar might look for in a wife. But Maria didn't ask, and Nasan felt awkward about either meddling or reawakening her sister-in-law's mockery, so that opening for conversation, like its predecessors, died stillborn.

But a fortnight or so after Daniil's conversation with his father, the promised day arrived. Koshkin—magnificent in crimson velvet, a black fox hat, and a gold chain that fell to his waist—exchanged the necessary minimum of false pleasantries with the family before ushering a rather stiff-faced Maria toward the waiting litter. His horse, a white palfrey of Arabian or Turkmen descent, stood nearby, fully caparisoned in shades matching its master's clothes. They must make quite a spectacle parading through the streets.

"When is the wedding?" Nikolai asked as Koshkin and Maria reached the bottom of the stairs.

"In a few months," Koshkin said. "Early February, most like. You will attend." He waved an expansive arm, indicating that he meant the entire family, then stopped with his hand extended to Nasan. "The groom's sister, especially. And the rest of your family, I trust."

An awkward invitation, since Nasan had no right to accept on behalf of the Kolychevs and some doubts that her parents and brother would agree to celebrate Tulpar's wedding. "I will let my parents know of your kind invitation," she said. "And if my in-laws permit, I will join them."

"Yes, yes," Nikolai said, as though the answer were obvious. "We should be delighted, of course. Such an occasion. Our dear Maria, settled at last."

Nasan gulped. Beside her, Daniil gave a small cough, hastily suppressed. Sometimes it was good to be a daughter-in-law, condemned to silence. She clasped her hands in front of her and hoped she looked meek.

Maria bowed before Daniil's parents. Nikolai bestowed an austere kiss on both her cheeks; Natalya hugged her and sniffled; Daniil copied his father's gesture and wished his sister-in-law well in the cool tone that they always used to each other when not actively spatting. Then it was Nasan's turn.

She had spent some time wondering what to say. Even reformed, Maria had extended no offer of friendship; before that, she had gone out of her way to torment her sister-in-law at every turn. Yet Nasan couldn't forget that passionate voice in the darkness insisting that Daniil loved his wife, how it had comforted her more than any assurance from a friend, setting the stage for the healing that followed.

She stepped forward, placed her hands on Maria's shoulders, and kissed her sister-in-law's right cheek, then her left. "Now you have a place," she said quietly into Maria's ear. "Whatever happens with my half-brother, you will be the mistress of your own home." She stepped back, releasing Maria. "May God and the ancestors bring you happiness, sister."

For a moment, Maria stared at her, her rigid expression lost in wide eyes and parted lips. Her father touched her elbow, and she mumbled, "And you." Then she turned away. He helped her into the litter, and with a final bow he mounted his horse and led the way from the courtyard.

"They're gone," Nasan said. "I thought it would never happen." Beyond Daniil, she heard his mother sobbing. Someone, at least, would miss Maria.

"Are you sad?" he asked, keeping his voice low. "You were so gentle with her, there at the end. More than I could manage, and she never sharpened her claws on me as she did on you."

"I remembered something she told me." Nasan decided not to share exactly what. "I think she was unhappy here even before Boris died. Right then, I felt sorry for her. She makes life so hard for herself. But I feel only relief that she has left—which may be sadder still."

"I understand." Daniil pulled her against his left side and kissed her ear. "You have a lovely soul. And I'm so glad, my sweet, that the next departure is not mine."

Balanced by his arm, she stood on tiptoe, and he bent his head toward her. Her voice dropped to a whisper. "Especially now. I want you by my side when our child is born. Although we may have to delay the trip to Kasimov."

Taken by surprise, he let out a shout of laughter and lifted Nasan off her feet. "Are you sure, wife of mine?"

"Well, I think so," Nasan said. "It's been almost three months, and while I haven't been sick, *Ana* told me that she never was—just rather tired, and that only in the beginning."

"And I thought that was my fault, waking you up every night with my ravings!"

His exclamation broke through Natalya's absorption. "What is this? Daniil, are you ill?" His parents clustered round, their faces taut with anxiety.

He pushed Nasan in front of him. "No one is ill, Mama. Prepare to welcome your grandchild. Next May, if I can count."

Any trace of sorrow vanished. Natalya clapped her hands and performed a small jump, quite incongruous in a lady of her age and bulk, before embracing Nasan. "Oh, my dear child, such wonderful news!" She drew back. "No riding this time, right?"

Nasan glanced over her shoulder at her husband, who was still laughing. "She may ride if she likes," he said. "I'll keep an eye on her."

Nasan kissed his hand. "I love you, dear heart." Then she turned to face his parents. "I promise you, Mama-in-law. You will see your grandchild, even if it means I have to stay off a horse. So long as you understand that I will ride again after the baby arrives."

The household had settled into its normal evening quiet. Most of the servants had finished their chores and retreated to their own huts to eat and rest with their families. Nikolai and Natalya had retreated to her sitting room to talk over the day, as they did whenever he spent time at home. Daniil and Nasan walked hand in hand around the silent courtyard.

"Maria has gone." Nasan squeezed her husband's fingers. "And you will stay. How unhappy I was in the spring, and how blessed I feel today!"

He stroked her cheek with his free hand. "And soon we will have a child. Be prepared for cosseting, beloved. I haven't forgotten Anastasia."

His first wife, who had died in childbed. "I am not fifteen and frail," she said.

"But you are small. And slender as a boy. It does make me anxious, wife of mine."

"My mother bore three who lived, and others who did not," Nasan reminded him. "And she's no taller than I. What happens in childbirth is the will of God, just as much as when I have to send you into battle."

"Nonetheless, I plan to watch over you like a hawk. And give you a hundred iron knives, if they will protect our baby." He kissed her nose, and Nasan laughed softly.

A raucous cry, like the shriek of a child in pain, interrupted what she might have said. One cry, then another, and a third. Nasan tipped her head back. "Daniil, look. The swans. They are returning!"

The great birds—calling to one another, wings spread— swept across the sky. As Nasan and Daniil watched, the lead swan fell back, and a new one took its place at the front of the arc. They were heading south, to their winter nesting grounds—where, exactly, Nasan did not know. But somewhere in the Tatar lands, where they would be safe until the spring.

The setting sun cast its rich light on them, illuminating their glowing feathers from within, like phoenixes rising from the flames.

"How beautiful they are," Daniil said, his voice filled with awe. "How can men hunt them?"

"Yes, it's like killing hope." She touched his good shoulder, and he bent and pulled her close. "Hope and happiness. But the Daughters of Air have blessed us, husband. They have brought us together again, like the swans."

Above their heads, the brilliant birds flew on, into the sunset—bearing good fortune on their wings.

The Sons and Daughters of Air settle onto their ancestral rivers and streams, their mission accomplished. The grandmothers welcome them home.

In the south, a new bird awakens—an eternal creature of feathers and flame, often extinguished, forever reborn.

Historical Note

THE POWER OF THE FOLK TALE LIES IN ITS ABILITY TO capture and express the emotions of ages past and present. For much of history, many women lived constrained by the demands of domesticity, often bound to men not of their choosing under circumstances where they enjoyed little respect among people unconcerned with their needs, feelings, or desires. Marriage and motherhood defined the identities and the worth even of elite, wealthy women under circumstances that few sought to avoid, and even fewer succeeded. Is it any wonder that almost every culture includes some variation of the legend in which an animal wife escapes to her wild homeland (earth, sea, sky) after many trials or a selkie or fairy king lures a woman into a world promising enchantment and freedom from toil?

This is the dilemma that faces Nasan in the third book of her series. The tomboy of *The Golden Lynx* has not vanished, but she is growing up. The world—in the persons of her mother-in-law, Natalya, and her sister-in-law, Maria—imposes relentless demands for conformity, and Nasan's husband, who sympathizes and if present could relieve some of the pressure, has been sent far away. Nasan, desperate to lessen her domestic responsibilities, faces the same stark choice as any animal or bird wife.

Among the Turkic peoples, this legend typically involves swan maidens and swan wives—as expressed in the related twin poems *Altyn Pyrkan* and *Ai Mergän and Altyn Kus*. For more on these legends, see Nora K. Chadwick and Victor Zhirmunsky, *Oral Epics of Central Asia* (New York: Cambridge University Press, 1969), 202–4. Kira van Deusen presents and discusses another version of the swan maiden myth in *Singing Story, Healing Drum: Shamans and Storytellers of Turkic Siberia* (Montreal: McGill-Queen's University Press, 2004), 62–74. And for a thorough exploration of the swan maiden/wife theme in world folklore, take a look at Barbara Fass Leavy, *In Search of the Swan Maiden: A Narrative on Folklore and Gender* (New York: New York University Press, 1994).

Even historians make mistakes while writing historical fiction, and I managed one howler in the first edition of *The Golden Lynx* (corrected in the second). According to the Russian chronicles, Prince Yuri Ivanovich was arrested when he came to Moscow to attend his older brother on his deathbed in December 1533 and imprisoned in one of the Kremlin palaces, where he died—allegedly of starvation—on 3 August 1536. I'm not sure how I managed to misread or misremember this detail, but I am indebted to Ann Kleimola for pointing it out. Here the unfortunate Prince Yuri has been restored to his Moscow prison.

As one might expect, given the cutthroat politics of the day, by June 1537 Prince Yuri's younger brother, Andrei, found himself in custody in the same prison, where he died in December 1537. But that is a story for *The Vermilion Bird* (Legends of the Five Directions 4: South).

Amazing as it may seem, the tale about Abbot Trifon of Pechenga and his bandit past, complete with the murder of the beautiful Elena (renamed Vasilissa here to avoid confusion with Grand Princess Elena Glinskaya, the mother of Ivan the Terrible), is part of his saint's life. It may not be true, but it is attested, and it was far too good a story to exclude from my novel.

For those encountering Nasan, Daniil, and their extended family for the first time, a note on the Tatar words sprinkled throughout the book. Here they mostly express relationships, which Tatars even today often use in preference to names (the custom, now mostly confined to older women, of showing respect by avoiding a husband's name is an extension of this practice). The terms given here—*ata* (father), *ana* (mother), *aby* (older brother), and *sengel* (younger sister, with the "ng" as in song)—may not be exactly those common in the sixteenth century, but they are close. *Khanim*—khan's daughter—is, as Nasan notes, properly translated into Russian (even in the 1530s) as *tsarevna*, just as *khan* was translated as *tsar*, *khatun* as *tsaritsa*, and *sultan* as *tsarevich* (son of a tsar).

Russian has separate words for mother, husband's mother, and wife's mother—hence Nasan's use of "Mama-in-law" and "Papa-in-law." Traditionally it also used different words for brother, wife's brother, and husband's brother and the equivalents for sister, although that usage is fading. Because Ogodai and Daniil are sworn brothers (*qarïndashlar*) as well as brothers-in-law, they don't bother with that distinction.

Last, a note on language in general: some historical novelists refuse to use any word not in circulation at the time in which their story is set. Although I approve of such diligence in principle, in practice I find it somewhat cumbersome—not least because language often changes faster than the sources recording it. If my characters were real and present, they would be speaking sixteenth-century Russian and Tatar, and sixteenth-century Russian, in particular, was both quite different in grammatical structure from its modern form and in flux. But the conceit of this series is that these stories are legends passed down and recorded after the fact. So while I strive to avoid post-Enlightenment concepts of the world and vocabulary or phrasing that obviously derives from twentieth- or twenty-first-century Western life, I occasionally employ a word or a metaphor that may not be attested in 1530s English but nonetheless conveys precisely what I want to say.

For images of Ferapontovo, including the frescoes that Nasan admires, painted in 1502; St. Cyril's Monastery; the White Lake region; and the Kola Peninsula, through which Semyon journeys during his escape from Pechenga, see William Craft Brumfield's gorgeous *Architecture at the End of the Earth: Photographing the Russian North* (Durham, NC: Duke University Press, 2015). Many of these photographs first appeared online in his "Discovering Russia" series and are stored at his photo archive "Architecture of the Russian North," http://cultinfo.ru/brumfield/photoarchive/index_e.htm. A complete archive of the photographs Brumfield has taken during his decades of travel is at the National Gallery of Art in Washington, DC.

The quotation from Hafiz (ca. 1320–89) comes from "Awake Awhile," as translated by Daniel Ladinsky for *I Heard God Laughing: Poems of Hope and Joy* (New York: Penguin Books, 2006), 38. The term "adjutant" as a translation of the Russian *striapchii* and the names of the chancelleries (*prikazy*) come from Grigorii Karpovich Kotoshikhin, *Russia in the Reign of Aleksei Mikhailovich*, trans. Benjamin Phillip Uroff, ed. Marshall Poe (Warsaw: DeGruyter Open, 2014). And thanks to David W. Page, *Body Trauma: A Writer's Guide to Wounds and Injuries* (Lake Forest, CA: Behler, 2006), for suggestions on internal and impalement injuries, as might occur if a horse rolls on its rider or a young man is shot.

For the details of Elena Glinskaya's court—including the reasons for Prince Yuri Ivanovich's imprisonment, the arrest of Elena's relatives, and the role played by Prince Vasily Vasilyevich Shuisky in her government—I am indebted to Mikhail Krom, whose *"Vdovstvuiushchee tsarstvo": Politicheskii krizis v Rossii 30– 40-kh godov XVI veka* ("The Widowed Kingdom": The Political Crisis in Russia in the 1530s–40s [Moscow: Novoe literaturnoe obozrenie, 2010]) is a rich and precious source of information. Neither he nor any of the other scholars mentioned here bears any responsibility for my fictional adaptation of their work.

Cast of Characters

(in alphabetical order by first name)

FICTIONAL CHARACTERS

Bulat Khan: Tatar khan in Russian service; occasional ruler of Kasimov, a Russian town traditionally assigned to Tatars; fictional older half-brother of the historical Shah-Ali (actual ruler of Kasimov in this period) and Jan-Ali (khan of Kasimov, then Kazan, assassinated September 1535); father of Nasan, Ogodai, and Tulpar.

Daniil Kolychev: Bulat's son-in-law, a Russian nobleman; husband of Nasan; hero of *The Golden Lynx* and *The Swan Princess.*

Diliara: Stepmother to Jahangir and Firuza; their father's widow and hence the senior woman in Ogodai's harem.

Firuza: Ogodai's wife and Nasan's sister-in-law; mother of twins.

Fyodor Koshkin: Maria Kolycheva's father; an enemy of the Kolychev clan (circumstances described in *The Golden Lynx*).

Grusha: Slave who escaped from the Kolychev household (circumstances described in *The Golden Lynx*).

Jahangir: Twin brother to Firuza, hence brother-in-law to Ogodai and bey of his horde (events leading up to this arrangement described in *The Winged Horse*).

Father Job: The Kolychevs' chaplain. Married, like all Orthodox priests (except monastic priests), and father of a large family.

Karim: Ogodai's third-in-command.

Maria Kolycheva: Widow of Daniil's older brother, Boris.

Masha: Peasant woman from a village commandeered by Semyon Severyanin and his men.

Nasan (Irina) Kolycheva: Daughter of Bulat Khan, sister of Ogodai and Tulpar, and wife of Daniil Kolychev; heroine of *The Golden Lynx* and *The Swan Princess.*

Natalya Kolycheva: Daniil's mother and Nasan's mother-in-law.

Nikolai Kolychev: Daniil's father, a high-ranking Russian nobleman (boyar).

Ogodai Khan: Son of Bulat Khan, older brother of Nasan, half-brother of Tulpar; married to Firuza under circumstances described in *The Winged Horse* and leader of her deceased father's horde; father of Firuza's twins.

Olga Bulgakova: Natalya Kolycheva's childhood friend.

Rafik Argyn: Ogodai's friend and second-in-command.

Roxelana: Tulpar's concubine, originally a Christian slave from the area that is now northwest Afghanistan, intent on using her considerable female charms to secure the best deal possible in this male-dominated world.

Semyon Kolychev (Severyanin): Cousin to Daniil Kolychev; tonsured as Brother Stefan (circumstances described in *The Golden Lynx*).

Stenka: Former henchman of Semyon Kolychev/Severyanin, member of his gang of bandits, lover of Grusha and father of her child, whom Grusha names after him.

Sumbeka: Bulat's chief wife, mother of Nasan and Ogodai, stepmother of Tulpar.

Tulpar Sultan: Bulat's eldest son and Ogodai's older half-brother, cast out by Bulat after a disagreement when Tulpar was sixteen; convert to Christianity under the name Alexei Bulatovich. (In Tatar usage, sultan means "son of a khan," not "supreme ruler," as among the Ottomans.)

HISTORICAL CHARACTERS

As often happens with medieval and early modern people, we have limited information about Russians and Tatars, even royalty, who lived in the sixteenth century. To the extent possible, I have ensured that details about real people included in the Legends novels match the historical record, but their appearance, their personalities, their words, and their motivations are just as much my invention as those of the fictional characters.

Grand Princess Elena Glinskaya: Mother of Ivan IV, known to posterity as Ivan the Terrible; widow of Grand Prince Vasily III, whose death in 1533 led to much uncertainty and aggression at home and abroad.

Islam-Girei Sultan of Crimea: Nephew, rival, and heir of Sahib-Girei Khan and his predecessor; Tulpar's chosen overlord since his exile in 1524. After years of strife followed by a period of reconciliation, Islam-Girei again rebelled against his uncle in the late summer of 1536. The Girei dynasty ruled Crimea for centuries; the name is often spelled Giray.

Prince Ivan Barbashin: Commander assigned to Velizh in the summer of 1536.

Grand Prince Ivan IV Vasilyevich: Ruler of Russia (1530–1584, r. 1533–1584); crowned tsar 1547.

Safa-Girei Khan: Ruler of Kazan, nephew of Sahib-Girei Khan of Crimea; an enemy of Bulat's family.

Sahib-Girei Khan: Ruler of Crimea, 1532–1551, despite the periodic attempts of his nephew Islam-Girei to unseat him.

Trifon of Pechenga: A hermit who, according to his vita, had lived as a bandit chief before killing his sweetheart and finding religion during his search for divine forgiveness; in 1533, he established the world's northernmost monastery at Pechenga, along a river that flows into the Barents Sea.

Grand Prince Vasily III Ivanovich: Ruler of Russia (r. 1505–1533), father of Ivan IV and Yuri Vasilyevich.

Prince Vasily Vasilyevich Shuisky: Head of one of the most important princely clans in 1530s Russia and a major figure, especially in diplomatic affairs, in Elena Glinskaya's government.

Prince Yuri Ivanovich: Younger brother of Vasily III, uncle to Ivan IV; died in captivity 3 August 1536.

Prince Yuri Vasilyevich: Younger brother of Ivan IV.

Family Trees

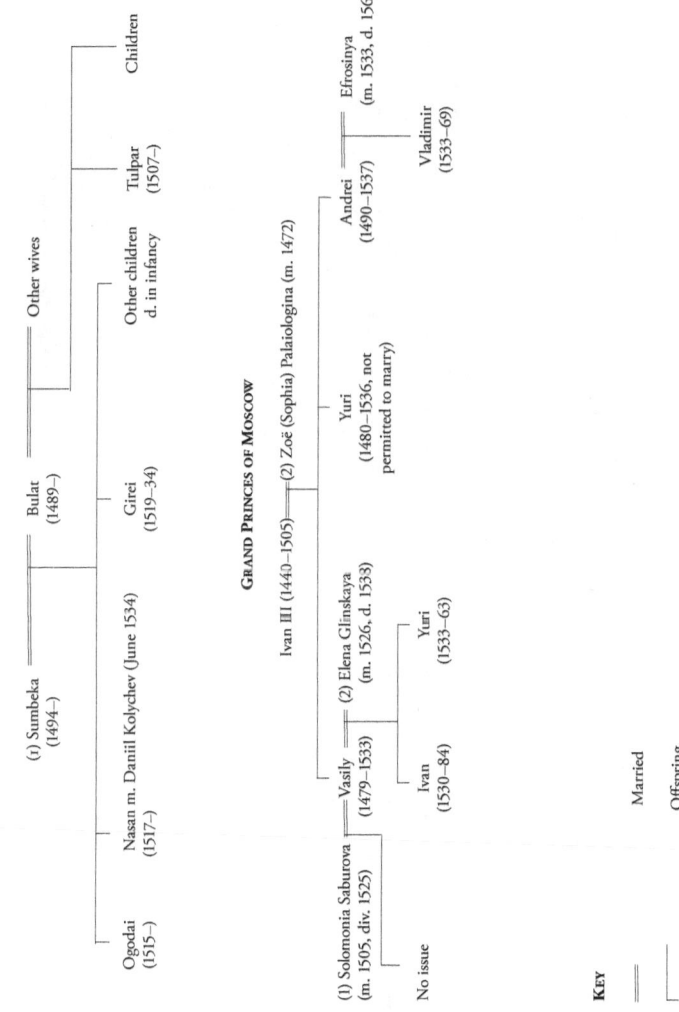

NASAN'S FAMILY

Ogodai (1515–)

Nasan m. Daniil Kolychev (June 1534) (1517–)

(1) Sumbeka (1494–)

Bulat (1489–)

Other wives

Girei (1519–34)

Other children d. in infancy

Tulpar (1507–)

Children

GRAND PRINCES OF MOSCOW

(1) Solomonia Saburova (m. 1505, div. 1525)

Vasily (1479–1533)

(2) Elena Glinskaya (m. 1526, d. 1533)

Ivan III (1440–1505)

(2) Zoë (Sophia) Palaiologina (m. 1472)

Yuri (1480–1536, not permitted to marry)

Andrei (1490–1537)

Efrosinya (m. 1533, d. 1569)

No issue

Ivan (1530–84)

Yuri (1533–63)

Vladimir (1533–69)

KEY

Married

Offspring

KOLYCHEV CLAN

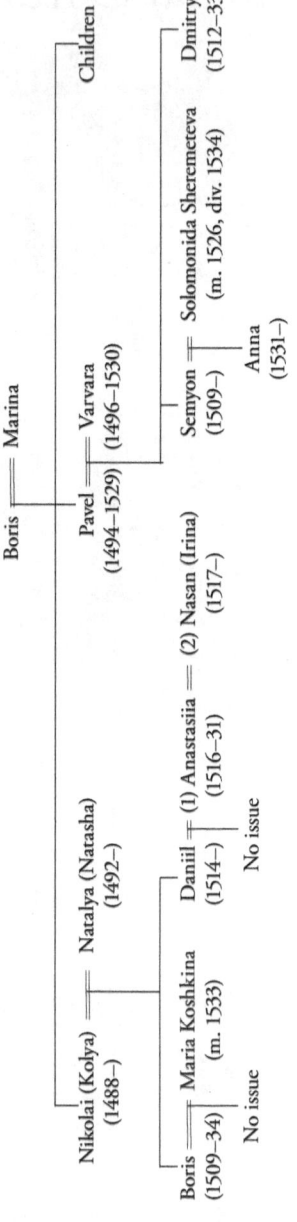

Except for Boris/Maria and Daniil/Anastasia, all married couples also had children who died before birth or in infancy.

Acknowledgments

IN ADDITION TO THE SCHOLARS MENTIONED IN THE Historical Note, I tip my hat here to my invaluable writers' group, now in its eighth year: Ariadne Apostolou, Courtney J. Hall, and Gloria Rabinowitz, all of them members of Five Directions Press. *The Swan Princess* would be a far more muddled and poorer book without their input. I also thank Irina and Catherine, who read the novel in draft form; Anna Altyn, Andrea Apter, and Susanne Chetkowski for information on the symptoms of heart disease and concussion; Clare Griffin, for suggestions of which medical books Nasan might own; Liza Perrat, Ann Swinfen, and Joan Schweighardt for their helpful comments and wonderful endorsements; Ann Kleimola for research PDFs and suggestions, pictures of the frozen north and its turbulent rock-filled rivers, Semyon's *nom de guerre*, and a fun discussion of whether he would suffer more if he escaped from Pechenga in the summer or the winter; and Diana Holquist for friendship, emotional support, and advice delivered regularly over lunch at our favorite deli.

To my husband and son—and, of course, the cats, who purred encouragingly at all the right moments—words cannot express my gratitude. And to those who read the earlier books, my thanks. I hope you consider *The Swan Princess* a worthy addition to the series.

The Author

AS A CHILD, C. P. LESLEY THOUGHT EVERYONE MADE UP stories while falling asleep. It never occurred to her that anyone would pay her for them, and for a long time, she was right—no one would. But after years of producing horrible prose, reading books about novel writing, and pestering hapless fellow-writers and friends to read her drafts, some of the advice stuck, and she finished *The Not Exactly Scarlet Pimpernel*, then *The Golden Lynx* and its sequels, *The Winged Horse*, *The Swan Princess*, *The Vermilion Bird*, and *The Shattered Drum*.

She is currently working on a new series, Songs of Steppe and Forest, featuring secondary characters from the Legends novels who never had space to tell their stories.

When not thinking up new ways to torture her characters, she edits other people's manuscripts, reads voraciously, maintains her website, and practices classical ballet—an interest reflected in *Desert Flower* and *Kingdom of the Shades* (Tarkei Chronicles 1 and 2). You can find out more about her and her books at www.cplesley.com.

ALSO FROM FIVE DIRECTIONS PRESS

The Vermilion Bird

LEGENDS OF THE FIVE DIRECTIONS 4

Moscow, February 1537

"IT'S A SCANDAL, I TELL YOU. FYODOR HAS GONE MAD."
Over the plink-plink of psalteries, the chatter of fifty women,
the murmurs of servants in corners, and the noise from the
courtyard below, Aunt Theodosia's voice soared like a song.
"Marrying a hussy two years older than his own daughter?
Then wedding his own girl to his new wife's former lover?
Abominable! Where is his honor?"

"Auntie! How can you?" Maria, tempted to shrink into
herself like a tortoise into its shell, instead gripped the hand of
the hated Roxelana, whose fingers returned the favor with equal
strength. "Stop squeezing me," she hissed at her stepmother,
who narrowed her eyes and hissed wordlessly back.

But Roxelana, although a general irritant, bore no
responsibility for Maria's present agony. On the contrary,
she shared it. *Must* Auntie announce their predicament to
the world? Thanks to her, every woman here knew—now,
if she hadn't before—that Roxelana had lived for years with
the man destined to become Maria's husband tomorrow, only

to abandon him for Maria's father and the respectability he offered.

A hint of sandalwood and cinnamon released into the air as Roxelana shifted in her seat. Among the many perfumes wafting around the room, hers stood out: seductive, elusive, foreign.

Respectability? Roxelana? As if that's not a contradiction in terms!

Aunt Theodosia was still talking—bellowing, rather, with the blissful unconcern of the hard of hearing. "Twenty-two years old, and him a ripe thirty-seven. What does he want with a lovely nincompoop to warm his bed? After wearing my dearest sister to the bone, bearing and raising his children. Thirteen she gave him. Thirteen. And seven who lived!"

"We know, Auntie. We can count." This voice, young and sweet, belonged to Maria's sister Varvara, second of the seven living offspring. She spoke in softer tones than Theodosia.

"Don't mumble like that, girl," Theodosia snapped. "Speak up."

"Hush now." Varvara raised her voice as commanded. "The whole room can hear you." She gestured with her right hand. "Including our stepmother."

"Don't be absurd. I'm whispering, just as you are," Theodosia said at top volume. "Stepmother, indeed. Harlot, more like."

Roxelana hissed again, louder this time, and Varvara pressed her lips together, as if trying not to giggle. In response Theodosia fixed Roxelana with her basilisk glare. "Ridiculous. Just ridiculous."

http://www.fivedirectionspress.com/vermilion-bird

MORE BY C. P. LESLEY

The Not Exactly Scarlet Pimpernel

Legends of the Five Directions
The Golden Lynx (1: West)
The Winged Horse (2: East)
The Swan Princess (3: North)
The Vermilion Bird (4: South)
The Shattered Drum (5: Center)

Tarkei Chronicles
Desert Flower
Kingdom of the Shades

PRAISE FOR THE LEGENDS OF THE FIVE DIRECTIONS SERIES

"An action and suspense-infused historical adventure that kept me turning the pages right to the end. The characters are so well-drawn, the historical facts so cleverly woven into the narrative, time and place so brilliantly evoked, I felt I was experiencing sixteenth-century Russia firsthand."

—Liza Perrat, author of the Bone Angel Trilogy

"A richly depicted, exciting adventure set amongst the Tatars of 16th-century Central Russia. Fans of historical romance will find [*The Winged Horse*] a delight."

—Yangsze Choo, author of the acclaimed novel *The Ghost Bride*

"Lyrical and compelling, *The Swan Princess* draws the reader into the world of sixteenth-century Russia, a world unfamiliar to many readers, which becomes vividly real in the hands of this master storyteller. The characters of Nasan, Daniil, and the others leap off the page. Perhaps most intriguing is the portrayal of the clash between the two vibrant but alien cultures of the Russians and the Tatars—frequently at war, occasionally bound by an uneasy and watchful peace."

—Ann Swinfen, author of *Voyage to Muscovy*

"*The Vermilion Bird* vividly envisions the culture clash between Russians and Tatars in the sixteenth century. Fans of historical fiction will enjoy this glimpse into a seldom explored corner of history, while fans of romance will delight in the unlikely love that blooms between a bluff Tatar prince and his scheming Russian bride—who is also the stepdaughter of his former lover."

—Linnea Hartsuyker, author of *The Half-Drowned King*

If you enjoyed this book, please consider leaving a review at the place where you purchased it or your favorite online review site.

Five Directions Press publishes fiction, often but not exclusively devoted to exploring the rich tapestry of women's lives in many times and places—some real, some fantastical.

http://www.fivedirectionspress.com/books

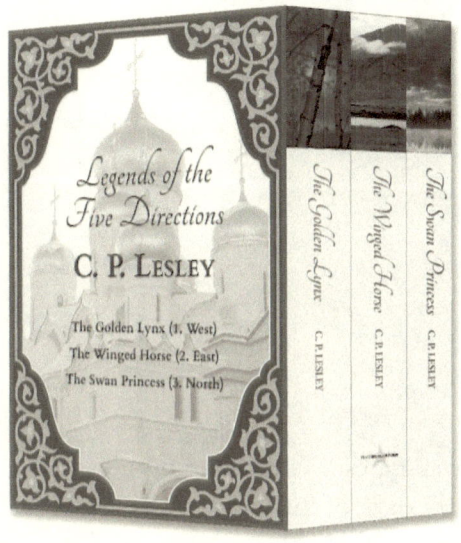

WHO IS THE GOLDEN LYNX?

This question drives the first book in Legends of the Five Directions, a series that will sweep you to the distant world of sixteenth-century Russia, amid the descendants of Genghis Khan and courts that could teach the Borgias a thing or two about political ambition, assassination, and chicanery. Follow Nasan and her kinsfolk as they struggle for power, honor, identity, and love across the steppe and through the vast forests of the Russian North.

"A richly depicted, exciting adventure set amongst the Tatars of 16th-century Central Russia. Fans of historical romance will find this a delight."
— Yangsze Choo, author of the acclaimed novel *The Ghost Bride*

http://www.fivedirectionspress.com/boxsets

This book was typeset using Garamond, a body font dating from the early days of printing, with headings in Tangerine, chosen for its Arabic lines, evocative of Tatar script. The ornaments come from Kfon (swans) and Type Embellishments One LET.